TROLL QUEEN

TROLL QUEEN

ELVEN ALLIANCE BOOK FOUR

TARA GRAYCE

Published by Sword & Cross Publishing

Grand Rapids, MI

Sword & Cross Publishing and the Sword & Cross Publishing logo are trademarks. Absence of ™ in connection with Sword & Cross Publishing does not indicate an absence of trademark protection of those marks.

Cover Illustration by Sara Morello

www.deviantart.com/samo-art

Typography by Deranged Doctor Designs

Derangeddoctordesign.com

Map by Savannah Jezowski of Dragonpen Designs

Dragonpenpress.com

To God, my King and Father. Soli Deo Gloria

LCCN: 2021904797

ISBN: 978-1-943442-14-0

THE **WORLD** OF
ELVEN ALLIANCE

CHAPTER
ONE

Essie wasn't sure what to wear to the wedding of a former enemy troll prince and her elf sister-in-law turned traitor.

As the icy breeze whipped through the canvas doorway of the tent, threatening to steal away the heat thrown by the wood-burning stove, Essie knelt and dug into the bottom of her pack and pulled out the one dress she'd brought along. She had debated long and hard about it, but a princess should never be without a fancy dress. Just in case she had to attend a state function.

Essie held up the midnight-blue dress, the silk wrinkled beyond all hope, and faced Farrendel where he sat on the cot. "What do you think? Should I wear the dress or my battle-stained tunic and trousers?"

Farrendel gripped the edge of the cot, as if he needed the help to stay upright. The light green tunic he wore bagged around his torso and around the straps of his swords strapped across his back. He'd had to cinch the straps as tight as they would go.

Still, Essie wasn't about to suggest he skip wearing his swords to this wedding.

The firelight cast dark smudges beneath his eyes and shadows in the hollows of his face. He gave a small shrug. "I do not believe it will matter."

Essie gritted her teeth and tried to keep her smile in place. Yesterday, Farrendel had seemed to be more himself, but that morning, he had gone back to staring listlessly.

"Perhaps you're right. These are the trolls with their whole obsession with honor and battle and all that. My war-torn clothes are probably considered standard wedding attire." She glanced at the dress and its flowing, thin silk. "Besides, this dress probably wouldn't be warm enough, unless I wore my boots and warm, fur-lined trousers underneath and coat over it, and that would defeat the purpose of wearing the dress in the first place."

Thanks to the trolls slinging around so much ice and snow during the war, they had brought on an early winter here in the cold reaches of the northern mountains.

But…this was a royal wedding. She had the reputation of Escarland to uphold. It seemed wrong not to wear a dress.

Farrendel just stared at her, not even the slightest twitch to his mouth at her rambling.

What was she supposed to do? She didn't know how to bring the smile back.

After setting the dress on her pack, she sat next to Farrendel on the cot and gripped one of his hands. "Is it the wedding? Do you actually want to go?"

Farrendel stared at the floor, his hand remaining limp in Essie's grip rather than holding her hand in return.

She rubbed her thumb over the back of his hand. "It is all

right if you don't want to go. You don't have to. I'll stay here with you or go with you, whichever you decide."

For several long moments, Farrendel remained unmoving and silent. Then, the taut muscles of his back relaxed. He huffed out a long breath. "I would like to go. I need to protect Weylind and your brothers."

Right now, Essie suspected that Farrendel's brother Weylind and her brothers Averett, Julien, and Edmund would do more of the protecting.

"And I need to be there for Melantha." Farrendel straightened and gripped one of the straps across his chest.

Essie wasn't sure how she felt. Farrendel seemed determined to forgive, but she wasn't sure it was a good idea. His sister Melantha had plotted to kill him. Perhaps she had changed, after spending two weeks in the trolls' dungeon. But Essie wasn't ready to fully trust her yet.

But she would stand by Farrendel if he wished to go. A hundred years from now, he would likely regret it if he didn't attend. Melantha was still his sister, even after everything.

"All right, but let's not stay long. We have a morning train to catch to go home." Essie trailed her fingers up and down Farrendel's back, avoiding his sheathed swords.

Home. It was such a beautiful word. Essie couldn't wait to hop on that train and go home. Probably to Estyra. With Farrendel like he was, it would be best to stick to the place where he felt most comfortable.

A knock rattled against the post of the tent a moment before Julien's voice called from outside. "Are the two of you ready? May I come in?"

"Come on in." Essie shook her head and leaned her elbows on her knees. "Though, isn't it a little early for the wedding? I haven't even started to get ready. Unless I'm going in what I'm wearing. Then, I am actually ready, though I probably should see if I can do something with my hair."

Julien strode inside, then wrestled the tent flap back into place. "We have about an hour yet. Averett sent me to check on you."

Her brothers were hovering. Almost as much as Farrendel's siblings. If Weylind hadn't been so busy arranging the peaceful transfer of power back to the troll prince and Jalissa hadn't been helping Melantha get ready, Farrendel's brother and sister would probably have been breathing down Essie's and Farrendel's necks as well.

"I am fine." Farrendel's voice had a growl to it. It was the most emotion he'd shown all morning.

Essie wasn't sure she preferred anger over listlessness, but at least it was something.

Julien studied Farrendel and nodded, though his frown indicated that he wasn't sure Farrendel was as fine as he claimed. Sinking onto the one chair in the tent, Julien propped his feet on the cot next to Essie. "Considering I'm going to this wedding like this, you're ready to go, Essie."

Good point. Essie leaned down and stuffed the midnight-blue dress into her pack, mentally apologizing to the silk and whichever elf servant would spend hours getting the dress presentable once again.

Instead, Essie reached for her rifle where Julien had stashed it under the cot when he'd returned it. She slung the rifle across her back, trying not to elbow Farrendel. "In that case, I might as well accessorize to complete the look."

That earned her the slightest twitch to Farrendel's mouth. Even though Julien was still there, Essie reached for

Farrendel's hand again. This time, he squeezed her fingers back.

They had survived being strangers in an arranged marriage. They had survived capture and a war. Surely, together, they could face whatever the future held.

SIX DAYS EARLIER...

Prince Rharreth of the trolls didn't resist as his brother King Charvod shoved him down the passageways of the dungeons of Gror Grar. Charvod's shield band followed, menacing and glaring as if Rharreth had done something wrong.

Had Charvod discovered that Rharreth had allowed Princess Melantha to stay in Laesornysh's dungeon cell, a mercy Rharreth should not have extended to that enemy of his people? Even if it had seemed the right thing to do, at the time.

If Charvod didn't already know, he would find out when he stepped into that dungeon cell. Rharreth hadn't had a chance to fetch Princess Melantha and return her to her cell.

Perhaps Rharreth could delay him? Rharreth reached for Charvod's arm. "What is this about, brother? What has happened on the front?"

It could not have been good. Kostaria's warriors were in

retreat, much of the army returning to Gror Grar. Why would Charvod order such a retreat instead of fighting for every inch of ground?

Charvod glared at him and didn't answer, as he hadn't answered the last several times Rharreth had questioned him on their march from the main gates to the dungeons.

As Charvod opened the locked door at the end of Laesornysh's passageway, the door to Laesornysh's dungeon flew open. Princess Melantha raced out, making it halfway to her own cell before she glanced up and skidded to a halt, wide eyes focused on Charvod and Rharreth standing there.

"All of you stay here." Charvod barked at his shield band before he stalked down the corridor in Princess Melantha's direction. She gave a short cry and tried to both hit and kick Charvod as he gripped her arm.

Rharreth strode after his brother, his stomach sinking into his toes. How had Princess Melantha escaped the stone shackle Rharreth had secured around her ankle? It had not been tight, but it should have been impossible for her to slip free.

Charvod shoved Princess Melantha back into Laesornysh's cell, and she tumbled to the floor, looking piti-fully small at Charvod's feet as her black hair straggled around her.

Rharreth stepped into the cell and caught his breath at the faint crackle of elven magic filling the space.

Still pinned to the floor, thin and haggard, Laesornysh's eyes blazed, his jaw hard as he focused on Charvod.

"Why have you allowed her to stay here?" Charvod glared, his fists clenching as if he intended to turn his violent anger onto Rharreth next.

"A small compassion for a captive, nothing more."

Rharreth glanced from Princess Melantha to Laesornysh. It had seemed like a tiny gesture, a way to ease the guilt gnawing in Rharreth's chest. It was not honorable to torture even the despicable Laesornysh the way he had been tortured by Charvod.

Yet, in trying to right one dishonor, had he dishonored himself more by aiding an enemy of his people?

Charvod's eyes flared, and he lifted his hand.

Rharreth braced himself. Would Charvod strike him? Charvod had always promised he would never lash out at Rharreth the way their father had.

And yet, the more Charvod had tortured Laesornysh, the more Rharreth had seen their father in him.

At the last moment, Charvod changed the direction of his strike so that he jabbed Rharreth in the chest with a finger instead. Cold dripped from his words as he met Rharreth's gaze, tilting his head up since Rharreth stood a few inches taller. "Thanks to your *compassion*, some of his magic was used during the fighting on the front lines."

What? Rharreth glanced to Laesornysh, but Laesornysh's hard eyes gave nothing away. "How is that possible? No one can use their magic in a place without being there in person. Are you sure it was his magic? Magic like his is rare, only appearing every few generations, but perhaps the elves discovered another who can wield a similar magic."

Yet, Rharreth's gaze dropped to the broken shackle around Princess Melantha's ankle. The taste of crackling magic still filled the air. It had not been Princess Melantha with her healing magic who broke the shackle.

But even if Laesornysh had figured out a way to use his magic here, no one knew how to wield magic over such a distance. Otherwise, Rharreth would have done so to aid his people in holding back the elf and human invaders who had stormed their way into Kostaria's borders while he had been stuck here in Gror Grar guarding Laesornysh.

"It was his. I recognized the taint of it." Charvod sneered, shoving Rharreth away as if he found him too unintelligent to discuss such matters. "If there is a way to launch such an attack from a distance, I'm sure this murdering elf could discover it."

"Then I have failed you." Rharreth braced himself against the stone wall, bowing his head in submission to his brother. Could Laesornysh have attacked from a distance? What if Rharreth's compassion for an enemy had led to the deaths of his own people?

It would be to his shame. His dishonor.

Yet, a part of him wasn't entirely sure he regretted it. And that tore straight through his chest. Honor was supposed to be a clear path to follow. Something was either dishonorable or it was not. There should not be a muddy area in between.

With a growl deep in his chest, Charvod grabbed Princess Melantha by her hair, his mouth twisting almost in pleasure as she cried out. Her hands scrabbled to tug Charvod's fingers free. Charvod shook her. "What did you do? It must have been something you did. He would have done something before now if he could have."

Rharreth clenched his fists, his chest aching. He must not react. He must not step in between his brother and justice to an enemy.

"What did you do?" Charvod shook Melantha harder by her hair, her slim body looking frail and breakable compared to his looming presence. "I shall have you punished for this."

Why didn't this feel like justice? Why were Rharreth's

knees shaking, his head pounding with memories of his mother's cries of pain, his father's accusations of weakness?

Rharreth could not stand by. If this was what justice to an enemy looked like, then he wanted no part of it.

As he pushed off the wall and reached for Charvod, the sizzle of magic choked the air a moment before blazing bolts of power surrounded Laesornysh on the floor. With a crack, all of the restraints on his hands and arms snapped as easily as thin, late spring ice.

Silver-blue eyes glinting nearly as much as his magic, Laesornysh lifted a hand. Magic shot toward Charvod.

Charvod's magic flared around him, though not quickly enough. Laesornysh's magic blasted his hand, and he dropped Princess Melantha with a growl.

"Do not touch my sister." Laesornysh's voice was hard, his muscles tensed as if he was about to push off the floor that had held him captive for so long.

Rharreth remained frozen where he was. He should call on his magic to defend his brother. But he had been about to fight his own brother over his treatment of the elf princess if Laesornysh had not intervened first.

The members of Charvod's shield band piled into the corridor outside, but with Rharreth and Charvod in the doorway, they could not rush into the room to help.

Charvod's mouth twisted in a snarl as he blasted more of his magic at Laesornysh. Rharreth had to brace himself against the wall as the ground shook with the force of Charvod's magic clashing against Laesornysh's. Fingers of the stone floor tried to reach for Laesornysh, but blue magic held them back.

Rharreth should aid his brother. It was dishonorable to

do otherwise, and he could not allow Laesornysh to take this fortress down around their heads.

As Rharreth pressed his hand to the wall next to him and called on his magic, his gaze caught on Princess Melantha. That was the only reason he saw the slight shake to her head.

Laesornysh's magic ceased of its own accord a heartbeat before Charvod's magic-filled stone swarmed over him, restraining him once again.

When Charvod turned back to Rharreth and Princess Melantha, he smirked, as if he thought he had bested Laesornysh and wrestled him into submission.

But Rharreth knew the truth. Laesornysh was still biding his time for the right moment.

He should tell Charvod. They should kill Laesornysh here and now because he was not as contained as they had thought. They had a feral wolf locked in their dungeon, and he would kill them all the moment he believed the time was right.

Would Charvod even listen if he said anything? He had not listened when Rharreth had counseled against the plan to capture Laesornysh. Nor had he listened when Rharreth had protested Laesornysh's torture or Princess Melantha's treatment.

More than that, Rharreth had come to respect this elven warrior Laesornysh. He hadn't wanted to. He had wanted to continue to hate the elf assassin who had murdered his father and killed so many of his people.

But, it was hard to see this Laesornysh—the one who had endured so much torture with a strength that would have brought honor to any troll warrior in similar circumstances —as a dishonorable enemy.

Charvod gripped Princess Melantha's upper arm again, jerking her to her feet and giving her another shake. "You will regret turning on us and helping him."

Princess Melantha's face whitened, but she straightened her shoulders with the look of a warrior preparing to face certain death in battle.

Pinned to the floor once again, Laesornysh glared at Charvod, his fists clenching. After a moment, he glanced to Rharreth and held his gaze, seeming to ask something of him.

Rharreth heard the echo of Laesornysh's accusation the first day he'd been brought to Gror Grar, *You are just like your father. He enjoyed torturing helpless victims as well.*

Laesornysh was a warrior. He could be expected to endure pain and torture, even if Rharreth was torn over the honor of inflicting it.

But Princess Melantha was not a warrior. She was a healer. Could she truly be faulted for trying to heal her brother, perhaps as an attempt to assuage her own guilt over the dishonorable things she had done to her brother and kingdom? After all, Charvod had been the first to push her to heal Laesornysh after torture. Could she be blamed if she continued to do so?

As Charvod dragged Princess Melantha from Laesornysh's cell, Rharreth found himself clenching his fists to stop himself from saving her from his brother's grip. "Don't punish her. He is her brother, after all. The failing was mine. I will accept your punishment."

If what Charvod claimed had happened at the front was true, then Rharreth had failed his brother. He had failed his king. And, most of all, he had failed his kingdom. It was a dishonor that shamed him to his core. He deserved punishment. Princess Melantha did not.

Charvod's mouth curled as his grip tightened on Princess Melantha's arm until she winced. His blazing eyes focused on Rharreth. "Oh, you will face my punishment as well. You have betrayed your brother and your king in aiding Laesornysh."

Rharreth glanced from him to Princess Melantha, her head held high as if she intended to take this pain as bravely as her brother had taken Charvod's torture.

But, Rharreth could not continue this argument in front of Laesornysh, no matter his inner turmoil over what was honorable when it came to the elf warrior. His confrontation with his brother should not happen before their greatest enemy.

Instead of protesting further, Rharreth marched from the dungeon cell, his shoulders braced as he stepped into the center of Charvod's waiting shield band.

After Charvod stepped out of Laesornysh's cell and shut the door behind him, still dragging Princess Melantha, he gestured from his warriors to Rharreth. "Seize the prince."

This was Charvod's shield band, the group of warriors with whom he had trained for years. Their loyalty to him was utterly unshakable.

Rharreth didn't resist as several of them grabbed his arms and wrenched his hands behind his back. Hopefully he could convince Charvod to exhaust his anger and spare Princess Melantha.

Charvod led the way down another passageway, this one ending in a dark room complete with stone chains hanging from the walls and a table with several implements of torture laid out in the center. Such torture was not necessary to use on Laesornysh since troll magic and stone were the most agony they could inflict on him.

But for fellow trolls? This was the place where the dishonored proved their worth through pain and suffering.

Rharreth halted in the grip of his captors and faced Charvod. "I have failed you in allowing the elf princess to tend to her brother. While she was merely doing what the honor of her people would demand, I sacrificed my own with the weakness of mercy for an enemy. The punishment belongs to me, not her."

Charvod shook Melantha hard enough that her teeth clacked together. "And yet, you defend her. She is your enemy, just as much as he is."

Was she? All Rharreth saw was a woman caught in a web of her own making. But, while she betrayed her kingdom, she had helped Kostaria. She had handed them Laesornysh, after all. She should have been their honored guest, not their prisoner.

But he could not tell that to Charvod. Instead, he faced his brother as boldly as he could, willing him to remember the pain of their childhood. "She is not a warrior and should not be punished according to the warrior's code. It is not honorable to so torture a woman."

Charvod snorted, sneering first at Princess Melantha, then at Rharreth. "She is an elven vixen. She might be able to betray the elves, soft and pampered as they are, but she won't get away with betraying us."

In Charvod's grip, Princess Melantha had regained her feet. She raised her chin, her pale face smoothing even she glared at Charvod as if she intended to rip out his hair the moment she had the chance.

Rharreth struggled against the warriors restraining him. "Do not harm her. It isn't honorable."

"She's the enemy. Everything is honorable when done to the enemy." Charvod snarled and pointed at him. "Shackle him to the wall."

Rharreth shoved away from those holding him, calling on his magic as he faced Charvod's shield band. Was he willing to fight his own people for Princess Melantha?

Honor demanded loyalty to his king, kingdom, and people. Honor also demanded he protect the innocent and helpless. How could honor demand such conflicting things of him? What was wrong, that the right thing to do was so unclear?

Magic surrounded Charvod's free hand. "So this is what it has come to, Rharreth? You would fight your king for an elf? You show by your actions the depth of your dishonor and disloyalty."

"I don't want to fight you, Charvod. I will willingly take any punishment you deem fitting for my actions. But I cannot allow you to harm her." Rharreth focused on Charvod, even as he kept the prowling members of his brother's shield band in the corners of his vision. "You promised years ago that you would not become like our father. This is something he would have done."

Something flickered in Charvod's gaze before he looked away from Rharreth. "Fine, then. The punishment is yours."

Beside Charvod, Princess Melantha's shoulders relaxed just a fraction, even as her gaze locked on Rharreth, her brows knit as if she wasn't entirely sure why he was doing this for her.

Rharreth released his magic and held out his hands. He did not resist as the warriors dragged him to the wall, shackled his hands above his head, and tore open the back of his shirt to bare his back. He did not so much as whimper as the whip cracked through the air and tore across his back, wielded by his own brother's hand. He did not ask for mercy as blood trickled down his back and pain weakened his knees while Charvod raised the whip again and again.

Finally, the whip fell silent, leaving only ragged breathing filling the room. Rharreth leaned his forehead against the cool stone, trying to hide the weakness and pain shaking through him. His stomach heaved, his back burned. All he wanted to do was collapse, but he had agreed to take this punishment. He would bear it with all the bravery and honor of a warrior.

Charvod's voice rang through the room. "Tie her to the next set of chains."

Princess Melantha gasped, jerking in the grasp of the two troll warriors.

"No." Rharreth twisted, grunting at the pain. Charvod still gripped the bloody whip, a wild light dancing in his eyes even as sweat beaded on his forehead. Surely, he wouldn't do this. He had given his word to Rharreth. No matter how much they disagreed, this was an old pact between them. Honor demanded that their word was binding, but especially to each other. Rharreth tried to hold Charvod's gaze. "We agreed...I would take...the punishment."

"I agreed you would be punished. I never promised I wouldn't punish her as well." Charvod sneered at Princess Melantha.

Her shoulders shuddered with a deep breath, then the panic disappeared from her face, replaced with a firm serenity. Her eyes flashed as she lifted her chin and faced

Charvod. "Very well. I deserve this. Not for helping my brother but for the harm I caused him. I will bear this and more without regret."

Something stirred inside Rharreth's chest. Princess Melantha had just witnessed Charvod whip Rharreth's back to a bloody pulp, yet she faced him with steel in her spine and dignity in her voice.

Charvod spat a slur in her direction and motioned to his warriors. They yanked her to the wall, clamping shackles around her slim wrists.

"Charvod." Rharreth tried to put as much strength into his voice as possible. He was not sure he understood the raw dread twisting his stomach.

When Charvod finally looked at Rharreth, it was as though Rharreth had gone back in time, huddling on the ground at his father's feet. Even Charvod's words were an echo of their father's. "You are weak, Rharreth. Father knew it, and now I see it, too. You were never worthy to stand by my side. You are weak, just like Mother."

No. No. Surely, Charvod did not mean that. Could not mean that. Rharreth reached deep inside him and, despite the pain tearing across his back, he called on his magic and wrapped it around the stone shackles. They cracked, and it took all of Rharreth's willpower to remain standing without their support.

Rharreth clenched his fists around his magic, facing his brother. "You promised you would not turn into him."

Charvod growled, his own magic flaring. "It seems I should have made you promise that you would not become like her."

Falling into a crouch, Charvod flicked his hand.

Rharreth tried to get his hands up. He attempted to

shield himself from the power his brother sent in his direction.

But with the dizziness in his head, he was not fast enough. He slipped and fell into a puddle of something warm and sticky and dark red spreading beneath him. Before he could call on his magic again, something smashed into the back of his head, and darkness snatched him away.

RHARRETH WOKE to damp warmth dabbing at the burning pain of his back. His shoulders ached, his feet numb. He tried to move into a more comfortable position, but his wrists seemed to be caught by something.

He blinked up at his hands until his blurry vision cleared. Leather bindings covered his hands and arms up to his elbows, pinning his fingers into fists, while stone shackles around his wrists prevented him from tearing the leather free. Chains ran from the shackles to the ceiling, and Rharreth dangled with his weight from his hands, crouched on his knees on the floor.

At least this was his room in Gror Grar. His bed had been shoved to a corner, and his clothes hung in their nook, though he could not see his sword anywhere. Rharreth had half-expected to wake up in the dungeon like Laesornysh.

Water dripped as someone wrung out a rag behind him. Rharreth tried to twist to see the person helping him, but pain shot up each of the gashes across his back.

"Hold still. You'll only make things worse." Zavni's voice came from behind Rharreth.

Rharreth relaxed at the sound of his shield brother's voice. Zavni had been his best friend and more of a brother than Charvod had been for years. "How did you convince Charvod to allow you to tend me?"

"The shield band tried to find out what had happened, but only Drurvas had any luck. He was able to convince King Charvod to allow me in, but I only have a few minutes. Drurvas is outside with the guards the king has placed at your door."

Rharreth should have known. Drurvas was Rharreth's and Charvod's cousin, the son of their father's younger brother. Since he was Rharreth's age, he had ended up in Rharreth's shield band. Only family would have enough sway with Charvod right now, and Drurvas always had known the right thing to say to Charvod, even when Rharreth didn't.

"Is it true what King Charvod is saying? That you defended the enemy warrior and his sister?" Zavni's voice, normally so cheery, was flat and serious. "King Charvod intends to try you for treason, just as soon as the human and elf armies are turned back."

Treason. How had things gone so far? When had doing the right thing been considered treason? Rharreth hung his head, letting his body sag from his arms. "Yes, I tried to keep Charvod from torturing the elf princess as he has been torturing her brother Laesornysh."

Had Charvod gone through with hurting her as soon as Rharreth was unconscious?

Of course, he had.

Was she even now in pain? Who would help her? Would she be able to heal herself?

Rharreth didn't dare ask Zavni to check on her. His shield band had pushed Charvod to allow them to tend Rharreth, but would they stand by Rharreth when he was accused of treason? Or would they disown him to preserve their own honor and standing?

"Charvod is taking Kostaria down a dangerous road that will lead to our destruction." Rharreth flexed his fingers as much as he could inside the leather restraints that bound him so that he couldn't use his magic.

"I know." Zavni spoke in a lowered tone, perhaps to keep the guards outside the door from hearing. "The king plans to keep you restrained even during the final battle. I fear without your help, we might not be able to turn back the elf and human armies. They are strong."

Bracing himself, Rharreth twisted as much as he could to look at Zavni. Zavni's eyes were a lighter blue than his, his gray skin a shade darker. He wore his white hair long enough to braid bits of leather into it to hang around the points of his ears. "Zavni, I know I cannot ask this of any of you, not when my loyalty to Kostaria is in question. But if the battle turns against us, could you see to it that I am freed? I will fight for Kostaria."

Zavni met his gaze, then bowed his head. "I vow that when the time comes, I will free you."

THREE DAYS EARLIER...

Rharreth tugged on the shackles and restraints. Even standing, he couldn't get enough leverage to do more than bruise his wrists, though he could peer out of the arrow slit window at the main gates of Gror Grar.

The whole fortress shook as a blast, both magical and mundane, blew apart the main gate, the dust and stone fragments shot through with blue bolts of Laesornysh's magic.

With elves holding shields above them, human soldiers hustled forward with a makeshift wooden bridge to span the gap in the stone bridge caused by the blast. Troll warriors rushed to the gate to hold them back, but without Rharreth's strong magic to provide a shield, many of them fell beneath the sustained firepower of the humans' repeater guns trained on them.

Rharreth had to get out there. His people were fighting and dying and about to be overrun in their own fortress. What had Charvod been thinking, confining his best warrior on the eve of this battle? Even after what Rharreth had done, surely his brother still understood where his loyalties lay. He had to know Rharreth would fight for Kostaria in this battle.

Voices roared from outside Rharreth's door. The clash of steel, then a crash.

The door flung open, and Zavni rushed inside. Through the opening, Rharreth could see the other members of his shield band holding off Charvod's guards. There were Drurvas and Nirveeth wielding their battle-axes. Vriska, the only remaining female warrior in their band, swung her sword at Eyvindur's side with Darvek and Brynjar flanking them.

Zavni gripped first one shackle, then the other, flooding them with his magic until they fell free. He yanked the leather restraints from Rharreth's arms.

"My sword?" Rharreth glanced around, but he didn't see it anywhere.

Zavni shook his head. "Couldn't find it. I think Charvod has it."

No matter. Rharreth's magic was probably more useful than his sword at this point.

His back aching, his legs still shaky, Rharreth charged

from the room, his shield band gathering around him. He raced through the passageways and staircases of Gror Grar, even as the fortress shook with more of Laesornysh's power.

Rharreth rammed into a door to the courtyard with a shoulder, bursting through and skidding to a halt, even as black spots danced at the corners of his vision from the lingering dizziness and pain from his still healing back.

Laesornysh stood only a few yards away. Magic crackled from him in waves, the building power so strong that Rharreth's hair prickled along his scalp and he could barely draw in a breath.

Behind Laesornysh, more people poured from the door that led into the dungeons from the courtyard, including an elf warrior who carried Princess Melantha's limp form over his shoulder.

Elves and humans filled the courtyard, pushing back the defending trolls step by step. If Laesornysh added his magic to the mix, this battle would be lost. Kostaria would be lost.

Rharreth blasted Laesornysh with as much magic as he could gather.

Laesornysh staggered a step, then steadied. His magic overwhelmed Rharreth's in a surge of power so strong it burned all the way back to Rharreth's hands.

When Laesornysh snapped his head toward Rharreth, his gaze was white-hot blue in its depths.

Rharreth only had a moment to attempt to gather more magic, a heartbeat for his stomach to drop with the knowledge that it would not be enough, before an inferno of Laesornysh's magic roared at him.

Fiery magic stabbed through his wrists and hurled him backward, pinning him against the stone wall with such force that Rharreth struggled to draw in a whisper of breath.

He fought against the blinding power, but it only tightened, searing like fire into his skin until he couldn't help but cry out.

Behind him, he could sense his shield band as they were tossed back from the doorway. They huddled against the wall behind him, unable to take another step under the force of Laesornysh's magic.

What had Charvod unleashed? They had tweaked a captured tornado, and now its fury was about to descend upon them.

What fools they had been, to think they could contain Laesornysh forever.

With one hand, Laesornysh kept Rharreth pinned, helpless as a snowflake against the rays of the sun. Eyes glowing, Laesornysh turned his head, his gaze fixing on Charvod where he fought King Weylind of the elves.

With a mere flick of his hand, the movement almost contemptuous, Laesornysh sliced a bolt of power toward Charvod.

It was over in an instant. One moment Charvod was fighting King Weylind. The next, he was dead, blasted through the chest by Laesornysh's power. His lifeless body was hurled through the outer wall of Gror Grar, the stones crumbling like dust in the seething fury of power poured upon them.

More magic filled the courtyard, scouring Rharreth's skin with more pain even than Charvod's whip. He tried to call on his magic, tried to fight.

But he was outmatched. He had always been outmatched, though he hadn't known it.

When Laesornysh turned that feral, magic-seared gaze to him again, Rharreth knew.

He was going to die. His people were going to die, his kingdom would be destroyed, and there was not a thing he could do about it.

In torturing Laesornysh, Charvod had doomed them all.

Now...

Rharreth braced himself against the wall in his bedchamber in Khagniorth Stronghold, the royal residence inside the walls of Osmana. At least, it was supposed to be the royal palace. His grandfather, father, and brother had spent very little of their time there, preferring the more war-like setting of the fortress of Gror Grar instead.

Once he had been released from the custody of the conquering elf and human armies, Rharreth had pulled his warriors back into Osmana, leaving the ruins of Gror Grar and the nearby plateau to the invaders.

A knock came from his door a moment before Zavni stepped inside, giving a brief glimpse of the rest of Rharreth's shield band waiting in the passageway, before he closed the door behind him. "The elf king has given the signal that they are almost ready for the wedding to begin."

"I am ready." Ignoring the flare of pain from his still-healing back, Rharreth pushed away from the wall, his hand dropping to the sword he had once again buckled at his side now that it had been retrieved from his brother's body.

Zavni stayed where he was, a pace inside the room. He met Rharreth's gaze with the boldness of a longtime friend rather than as a warrior facing his king. "Are you sure about this, Rharreth? There have already been enough rumors about you. Marrying an elf will only make the warriors more suspicious."

"I know." Rharreth glanced around the room, from its large bed piled with furs and wool blankets, to the clothing nook that he had partially cleared of his clothes to make way for his soon-to-be wife to claim instead.

Only the members of Rharreth's and Charvod's shield bands had known Rharreth had been accused of treason. Charvod's entire shield band had been killed in the battle at Gror Grar, and Rharreth's shield brothers and sister were loyal to him. They would not talk.

Still, there were vague rumors. Something like that could not be fully hidden. Already, many among the most powerful warrior families questioned Rharreth's motives in signing a peace treaty with the elves and humans. They argued that they should have kept fighting. That, once winter came in truth, they would be strong enough to repel the invaders. They cast aspersions on Rharreth's honor and courage.

At least Rharreth was the only one who knew that he—and not the elves—had been the one to include this marriage as part of the treaty. Perhaps it was the coward's way out, but Rharreth had allowed everyone, including his own shield band, to believe that this marriage was being forced upon him as the cost of peace.

Zavni still stood there, waiting for Rharreth's answer.

Rharreth straightened his shoulders, meeting Zavni's gaze. "You saw Laesornysh's power when he destroyed Gror Grar. He would have destroyed Osmana and who knows what else if I had not surrendered. I know we trolls do not like to admit to strength other than our own, but he is capable of wiping Kostaria off the face of the mountains should he choose to do so. To ensure that he never feels the need to continue what he started at Gror Grar, I must make a permanent, lasting peace with Tarenhiel."

"By marrying a Tarenhieli traitor?" Zavni raised his eyebrows, his gaze studying Rharreth.

Zavni was too good of a friend not to see past all the official reasons Rharreth could give.

Rharreth glanced away, not willing to show Zavni a part of himself he still did not understand yet.

He claimed he was doing this to save Kostaria. But, was it possible that he hoped to save Princess Melantha as well?

"I know what it looks like, Zavni. I know how difficult this is going to make the start of my reign. But I have to do this." Rharreth filled his heart and gaze with stone, bracing himself for the war with his own people that he would start the moment he married Princess Melantha. "I am not sure how or where, but Kostaria has gone wrong, and I will do whatever it takes to set it right once again."

That could be the only explanation for why Rharreth felt such a tearing inside his own sense of honor over his actions in the last week.

Under his grandfather's, father's, and brother's reigns, something had gone terribly wrong inside Kostaria and corrupted the honor that it claimed to hold to.

Rharreth had to fix it. No matter what it took. He never wanted to look into an enemy's eyes and see more honor there than he saw in his own people.

THREE

Melantha brushed at the dark green dress she wore, trying to pretend her fingers were not shaking. She was about to marry a troll, an enemy. Would she ever return to her homeland and people again?

Not that her homeland or people wanted her any longer. Nor was it likely that her new people would like her any better.

Melantha swallowed and leaned against the wall of her wooden shelter—her prison, really. Elven guards stood outside the door.

From this prison to marriage, a marriage that could turn out to be just as much of a prison.

Her breathing hitched, and Melantha gripped the wall harder as her knees threatened to buckle. She squeezed her eyes shut and concentrated on breathing steadily as her stomach churned.

Surely it would not be like that. Prince Rharreth would

not hurt her. He had tried to prevent King Charvod from harming her. Surely that meant he would not harm her himself.

This was not how she had always envisioned her wedding. She had thought she would be dressed in white silk, getting ready in one of the side rooms of Ellonahshinel with her sisters Jalissa and Rheva, Weylind's wife, at her side. That was the wedding she had been planning to have with her betrothed Hatharal, before he had ended things.

Concentrate on the good things. Marrying Prince Rharreth was better than banishment. Better than execution in the forsaken grove. Better than marrying an elf like Hatharal.

Melantha dragged herself upright and forced her breathing to calm. She could do this. She was a princess of the elves and soon to be the queen of the trolls. An elf princess did not break under pressure. She remained calm and composed at all times.

She could still see Hatharal with that slight curl to his lip when she did something that betrayed the emotions boiling inside her. *You are too much, Melantha.*

Outside, the muted sound of the guards' voices came a moment before someone threw back the canvas door and ducked inside. Her face set into hard lines, Jalissa straightened and faced Melantha, her eyes colder than the breeze that accompanied her.

Melantha swallowed. Jalissa had not yet spoken to her since the rescue. What could Melantha say? How did she even begin to repair the damage she had done? "I did not think you would be coming."

"I would not have, but Elspetha and Farrendel seemed to

think I should." Jalissa's fingers tightened into fists at her sides. "They are far too forgiving. More forgiving than I am. How could you, Melantha? How could you do this to our brother? Our new sister?"

Melantha stared at the floor and did not try to answer. What could she say? She had told Farrendel about her anger, her horrible choices. But he, of all people, had deserved an answer from her.

And, for some reason, he had found Melantha's explanations to be enough. Jalissa would not.

Because, truthfully, no explanation was enough for why a sister would plot to murder her own brother. Sure, Melantha had not tried to do it with her own hands. But turning Farrendel over to the trolls to be tortured and killed was even worse than if she had attempted to kill him herself.

Finally, as the silence stretched, Melantha sighed and risked a glance at Jalissa. "It was wrong. And I am sorry."

"That hardly makes up for what you have done." Jalissa glared, her dark brown eyes glinting even in the poorly lit shelter. "Now, do you want help with your hair? If not, then I am leaving."

"Please, if you would." Weddings were one of the few times elves wore their hair in a style other than down. Without a mirror, it would be difficult to do anything with her hair herself.

Melantha sat on the floor, since she had been given no chairs, tables, or even a bed besides a blanket to spread out on the wooden floor. After what she had done, the fact that she had even been given a blanket was an unexpected kindness.

Jalissa's hands in Melantha's hair were rough, yanking

instead of gentle. But Melantha did not protest. Did not let herself flinch. Did not so much as let tears pool in her eyes.

After a few minutes, Melantha drew in a deep breath. She was not sure how to approach this topic with Jalissa.

But, this was likely to be her only chance, and Jalissa needed to be prepared. Even if she was not going to like this conversation.

"Jalissa, I am also sorry for what my actions and my marriage will mean for you." Melantha swallowed and stared at the wall in front of her as Jalissa's hands stilled in her hair.

"What do you mean?" After a moment, Jalissa went back to roughly tugging Melantha's hair into what felt like a braid.

"Until now, I have been dangling possible marriage to me to the sons of several of the influential nobles whenever Weylind needed to calm the court. Even if the elven nobility was in no hurry to marry into our tainted family, they still want the power of the possibility." Melantha tried to hide her wince as Jalissa gave an even stronger tug. "With Farrendel's marriage to a human and my marriage to a troll, one of us needs to be scandal-free. I am sorry that will have to be you. It would be best if you married into the nobility, though I am sure the court would appreciate it if you at least marry an elf."

"I see." Jalissa twisted a section of Melantha's hair so roughly that Melantha felt several hairs rip from her scalp.

When Jalissa was finished, she marched out of the shelter without another word or a glance back, her face even harder than it had been when she entered.

With shaking fingers, Melantha explored the intricate weave of the braids Jalissa had done through her hair, all coming together at the base of her skull before the rest flowed free down her back. It must look stunning, though Melantha did not have a mirror to view it herself.

She would look like a bride, even if nothing about this wedding was as she had hoped.

Melantha sank to the ground and hugged her knees. She blinked at the burning of tears in her eyes. She would not cry. She deserved this.

But it hurt. How it hurt. She wanted her family. Her home, in the beautiful tree palace Ellonahshinel. Everything about the life she had thrown away.

Was she about to cry or scream? She was not sure. Heat built inside her chest until Melantha dug her fingernails into her palms, concentrating on those pinpricks of pain rather than the roiling inside her.

Another knock, and this time it was Weylind who stepped inside. His dark brown eyes swept over her before he stated in a flat voice, "I see you are ready."

As ready as she would ever be for this. Melantha pushed to her feet and forced her own face to go as hard and blank as his. "Yes."

Weylind stared at her, opened his mouth, then closed it and gave a sharp nod. He spun on his heel. "Come."

That was all the warmth she was going to get. Melantha ducked through the door, blinking at the morning sunlight.

The camp seemed to be less busy than it had been the day before, the last time—only time—Melantha had been allowed out of her prison.

Weylind waited for her, but he did not hold out an arm. When she fell into step beside him, he did not so much as glance at her.

The elven guards fell into step behind her. Were they really going to guard her all the way to her wedding?

As they strode between the shelters and tents, the few elves and humans bustling about stopped what they were doing and stared.

Melantha tipped her chin higher and tried to ignore them. So what if they stared? After today, she would never see any of them ever again, most likely. Who cared if they gossiped about the traitor elven princess? They did not matter to her anymore.

Weylind led the way down a winding trail from the plateau into the valley that stretched between the ruins of the mountain that had once been the fortress of Gror Grar and the distant town of Osmana at the far end.

On their side of the valley, at the base of the mountain, rows of hard-faced elven warriors and solemn human soldiers, all festooned with weapons, sat ramrod straight on wooden benches. Troll warriors, likewise bristling with weapons, perched on stone benches facing them.

Were they going to have a wedding or another war? Melantha fisted her fingers and tried to pretend she did not want to lean on Weylind's strength.

She was so alone. Even as she passed the first row where Jalissa and Farrendel, with his human wife beside him, sat in the middle of the Escarlish royal family, she was still alone.

Weylind halted in the space between the two gathered armies.

Before them, stood Prince Rharreth, dressed in a dark green shirt, black pants, and a black leather vest.

Melantha swallowed and tried to hide the way her legs were trembling. Even with Jalissa's help braiding her hair, she did not feel much like a bride in the plain, dark green dress she had been given to wear since her other dress had been in tatters.

When Weylind turned to her, the hard edge to his dark brown eyes softened. "You do not have to do this. I will not force you."

Yet if she did not, he would be forced to choose a different punishment for her. She had betrayed her kingdom and her family. A pardon was not an option for her.

Banishment or death or marriage to the troll prince. Those were Melantha's options.

Surely marriage had to be the best option. It was the only one that gave her the chance to redeem herself by making sure the trolls of Kostaria kept the peace treaty with Tarenhiel and Escarland that Prince Rharreth had signed.

"I know, shashon. But I have to do this." Melantha straightened her shoulders and faced Prince Rharreth and her future people. She was a princess of the elves. If that bubbly, annoying human princess could find the courage to marry Farrendel, then surely Melantha could do this.

"Then you will need this." Weylind drew the dagger he wore strapped to his waist.

Melantha took it and turned it over in her hands. "To use on Prince Rharreth if he tries to hurt me?"

"No, I am told you will need to give your intended a dagger as part of the troll wedding ceremony." Weylind shot a glare across the way toward Prince Rharreth. "In return, he will give one of his daggers to you. That is the one you will keep on hand for self-defense."

Not that she had ever been trained in anything remotely like self-defense. She was a healer, under oath to heal rather than harm. In the peaceful forests of Tarenhiel, there had never been a need to train her, nor had anyone believed a healer should go around armed.

Not that she had done a very good job of honoring her oath when it came to Farrendel.

She tucked the dagger into the sash of her dress and squared her shoulders. She would show these trolls just how much courage and dignity an elf princess possessed.

She strode forward and joined Prince Rharreth. An older troll, his face lined with wrinkles, stood before them. He must be some kind of official, though Melantha was not going to ask who he was.

The official started the ceremony. Thankfully, it was a short speech that compared marriage to a battle. Or life to a battle. Melantha was too nervous to listen very closely.

The troll official finished his speech, then gestured to Prince Rharreth.

Prince Rharreth drew the dagger from his belt, held out his right hand, and sliced his palm. His mouth did not so much as twitch at whatever pain he was in. He held out the dagger to her, its edge glistening red with his blood. "With blood and blade, I pledge to you my life and my honor until death overtakes us."

Melantha reached a shaky hand but stopped short of the dagger. "I am supposed to take this, right?"

The official stared down his nose at her. "By accepting the dagger, you accept his pledge."

That was what she thought. With a deep breath, Melantha took the dagger. Assuming she would need her hands free, she slipped it into her belt.

"Now your turn. Slice your left hand." The official's tone turned even colder as he told her to slice the opposite hand from the one Rharreth had sliced.

Why did even the trolls' marriage ceremony have to involve blood and knives? Gritting her teeth, Melantha drew the dagger Weylind had given her. Not letting herself think about it, she swiped the blade across the soft skin of her palm.

Blood welled a moment before pain throbbed across her hand. After the whipping she had endured in Gror Grar's dungeon, this pain was not something to scream at. But it still brought the heat of more tears that Melantha refused to shed. If the trolls valued strength, then giving any sign of pain at this small slice would not help them respect her as their queen.

She held out the dagger and forced her voice to remain steady. "With blood and blade, I pledge to you my life and my honor until death overtakes us."

Prince Rharreth took the dagger from her and slid it into the sheath where his dagger had been. It did not fit, since it had a longer and slimmer blade than his thick, slightly curving knife.

"Now clasp hands." The official's face might as well have been carved from stone.

Prince Rharreth held out his bloody palm.

They were supposed to clasp the hands they had sliced. That did not seem sanitary. Though, Melantha could heal herself if she got an infection. Depending on how nice Prince Rharreth was to her the rest of the day, she might consider healing him too.

She clasped his hand and met his gaze. She would not back down.

The officiant pulled out a black sash and tied it around Prince Rharreth's and Melantha's clasped hands. "Blood and blood, bone and bone, I declare you one and bound together from this moment until death takes you."

And, just like that, Melantha was married to a troll. Perhaps, by trading herself to this troll, she could buy her kingdom peace.

E ssie gripped Farrendel's hand and braced herself as he leaned against her. As the benches didn't have backs, he seemed to be struggling to sit upright through the ceremony, even as short as it was.

On Farrendel's other side, Julien kept glancing over at them, as if checking to make sure Farrendel wasn't about to pass out.

Beside Julien, Edmund was sneaking glances past all of them to Jalissa, who had taken the seat next to Essie instead of sitting next to Edmund as she had been doing for the past few days. By the way she sat stiff-backed and hard-eyed, something had happened, though Essie wasn't sure what it was and wasn't about to start whispering during a wedding ceremony to find out.

Averett and Weylind sat at the end of their row, both wearing their crowns and looking every inch the regal kings they were.

The troll ceremony itself was fascinating. It definitely

made Essie thankful that elven wedding customs involved a lot less bloodshed and fewer knives.

When the ceremony ended, Weylind stood, approached Prince Rharreth and Melantha, and gave what Essie assumed were congratulations. Though, it was hard to tell past Weylind's hard mask, complete with a glare for Prince Rharreth.

Essie leaned closer to Farrendel. "It's nice to see Weylind giving that distrustful glare to someone else for a change. I don't think I'm his least favorite in-law anymore."

That earned her a small twitch to Farrendel's mouth. But the spark didn't return to his eyes. Nor did he lift the iron wall he'd placed between them in the heart bond.

Averett joined Weylind in giving congratulations to Prince Rharreth and Melantha. As the king of Escarland, it was his duty in a situation like this.

Essie squeezed Farrendel's hand. "Do you want to talk to Melantha? Or we can leave now and head for the train?"

Julien, Edmund, and Jalissa were watching them, as if waiting to take their cue from Farrendel.

Farrendel pushed to his feet, swaying a moment before he steadied himself. He strode forward, as if forgetting all about answering her or that she was still gripping his hand.

Essie sprang to her feet and trotted for a few paces before she fell into step with him. Edmund and Julien quickly caught up to them, and Edmund nudged Farrendel with an elbow. "If you need any pointers on threatening your sister's new husband, just ask."

"You know how good we are at it." Julien smirked as he strolled on the other side of Edmund.

Farrendel didn't respond to either of them. He seemed too focused on Melantha and Prince Rharreth to even notice the rest of them. He halted in front of Melantha and let go of Essie's hand to grip Melantha's shoulders instead. "Remember my promise, isciena."

"Thank you, shashon." Melantha squeezed Farrendel's shoulder with one hand. Her other hand was still tied to Prince Rharreth's.

It would have been a sweet moment, in other circumstances. Right now, Essie just wanted to drag Farrendel out of there as fast as she could, bundle him onto the train, and get him home.

When Farrendel turned to Prince Rharreth, his gaze went ice cold. A hint of magic played around his fingers. "Treat my sister well. I have killed two troll kings. Do not make me kill a third."

Before Prince Rharreth could so much as glare back, Farrendel spun on his heels and marched away.

Julien shook his head. "I see he didn't need any tips on making threats."

Edmund shrugged. "I think we should have been the ones taking notes from him."

Essie didn't feel compelled to talk to Melantha or Prince Rharreth. She wasn't up to offering insincere congratulations right then. Instead, she hurried after Farrendel.

Most of the Escarlish and Tarenhieli soldiers who had attended the wedding were also lining up and marching toward camp. There wouldn't be a large wedding feast. Or, at least, not one that any of the elves or humans were invited to. The trolls might have one planned.

As Essie caught up with Farrendel and clasped his hand again, Averett and Weylind joined them.

Essie's bag was already packed and had been loaded on

the train along with the wounded. All they had to do was climb the path up to the plateau and walk to the train.

By the time they walked that far, Farrendel was panting and leaning on Julien and Essie. Weylind kept glancing at him, as if he was about to sling Farrendel over a shoulder if he looked ready to collapse.

As the train came into view, they joined a bustle of humans and elves carrying some of the injured on stretchers and helping the more mobile of the wounded onto the train. The train belonged to the trolls, since trying to get an elven train across the Gulmorth River and retrofit it to work on the Kostarian tracks was a lot more work than simply commandeering the trolls' train.

Jalissa touched Edmund's arm and pulled him to the side. Perhaps for a goodbye of her own. The two of them had seemed to be growing close, though Jalissa's expression just then seemed too hard and tense for a romantic farewell.

Essie squeezed Farrendel's hand and nudged him. "We're almost there. We'll be sleeping on the Tarenhieli royal train tonight."

Farrendel glanced up, and, as his gaze focused on the train, his eyes widened. He halted so abruptly that Essie was yanked backwards by her grip on his hand. A tremble coursed down his back and into the hand Essie gripped. "No. No. I cannot...no."

"What's wrong?" Essie glanced from Farrendel to the train and the bustle. She couldn't see anything wrong. Maybe it was all the bustle? "I know there are a lot of people around right now, but once we're on the train, things will calm down. I'm sure we can find a quiet corner in one of the cars."

Farrendel's gaze focused on the train, and he shook

harder. He yanked free of her grip on his hand and backed up a few steps. Blue bolts of his magic crackled at his fingertips. "No. No. I cannot...not that train..."

What had the trolls done to him? Essie eased closer to Farrendel. "It's all right. I'll be there the whole way."

Farrendel was still shaking his head, holding out his magic-laced hands as if prepared to fight off anyone who came too close.

Julien grasped Essie's arm, holding her back when she would have stepped closer still. "Give him space."

"But..." Essie would have pulled away from Julien, but Averett stepped in front of her, as if to protect her.

Instead, it was Weylind who eased closer to Farrendel. "Shashon. You need to remain calm."

Farrendel didn't resist as Weylind gripped his arms.

Weylind gave a nod to someone over Farrendel's shoulder, and one of the elven healers crept up behind Farrendel.

A weight sank into Essie's stomach. Weylind wasn't just trying to keep Farrendel calm. He was restraining him.

The healer pressed a glowing green hand to Farrendel's temple. Farrendel stiffened, but then he sagged in Weylind's grip.

"Farrendel?" Essie lurched forward, but both Julien and Averett held her back.

Averett turned her away as two human soldiers hurried to Weylind with a cot. "Essie, will you be all right? I can send Julien with you."

"We'll be fine." Maybe. Essie had seen Farrendel caught in nightmares for a week straight. She'd seen him listless and struggling before. But never like this.

She'd thought him broken when she'd married him, but she hadn't taken into consideration how much coping and healing he'd done in the fifteen years since the first time the trolls had tortured him.

The orderlies had loaded Farrendel on the stretcher and were using leather straps to hold him to the cot. Essie pulled away from her brothers. "Not his hands."

The orderly who had been about to tighten a leather strap across Farrendel's chest and over his upper arms paused, glancing at Essie. "He will fall off if he isn't strapped down."

"I know. Just leave his hands and arms free, all right?" Essie couldn't find the words to explain past the pressure in her chest. But it seemed important to make sure Farrendel wasn't fully trapped the way he had been in that dungeon. Even if the elf healer had sent him into a deep sleep and he would never know if he was pinned or not.

Averett studied Essie for a long moment before he sighed. "All right. I won't send Julien to hover. But Julien and I will return through Tarenhiel in a few days. We'll see you then." Averett pulled her in for a hug.

Julien drew her into a bear hug, then patted her back. As he released her, Edmund strode up, his face strangely tight. Jalissa brushed past all of them and strode straight onto the train without a glance over her shoulder.

Essie hugged Edmund, feeling something like a shudder in him. "Are you all right?"

"I'm fine. Don't worry about me." Edmund gave her a smile, but it was so strained it hardly held any warmth.

Essie would have questioned him more, but the soldiers were carrying Farrendel's stretcher onto the train. As much as she wanted to figure out what was going on with Edmund, Farrendel needed her more.

Only when Essie was halfway up the ramp to the train

did she realize that Averett had said that only he and Julien would be returning. He hadn't mentioned Edmund.

Essie glanced over her shoulder, but her brothers and Weylind were already strolling away, their heads bent together in some conversation. Shaking her head, she hurried the rest of the way into the train car.

Inside, metal brackets held the stretchers with the wounded against the walls, stacked three high. An elven healer was walking up and down the car, checking on each of the patients, while the Escarlish soldiers carrying Farrendel attached his stretcher to the brackets on the bottom bunk near the front of the car.

Jalissa slumped against the wall, her knees drawn to her chest, her eyes staring off into space.

The female elven healer smiled and bobbed her head to Jalissa and Essie. "Amirah. You will wish to brace yourself and hang on tightly."

Essie sat on the cold floor of the train beside the head of Farrendel's cot. His eyes were closed, his breathing deep and even as he slept. Leather straps ran over his chest and legs, holding him in place. Even though he was deeply asleep, thanks to the elven magic he'd been dosed with, Essie rested a hand on his shoulder. With the other, she gripped the pole of his stretcher.

With a start, Jalissa gripped the metal support holding Farrendel's stretcher, still not looking at Essie.

Within a few more minutes, the train car's door was shut and locked, plunging them into a darkness lit only by two elven lanterns swinging from the center bar running the length of the train car.

With a squeal of the metal wheels on the tracks, the train

shuddered into motion. The elven healer gripped one of the metal supports, her knuckles turning white.

Essie tightened her own grip. The tight look on the healer's face wasn't a good sign.

As the train gathered speed, it leaned precariously, still shuddering. Was this thing about to fly off the mountain? Or fall apart?

The train screeched into a turn. The whole car tipped so dangerously that Essie slid on the floor and only her death-grip on Farrendel's cot kept her from smashing into the opposite wall. Cries filled the car, and Essie wasn't sure if she had shrieked or if the scream had gotten stuck in her head.

Behind her, Jalissa gave a soft shriek, her soft slippers scraping against the floor as she tried to keep herself from sliding.

Essie had to let go of Farrendel's shoulder to hold on with both hands. "I understand why Farrendel freaked out about getting back on this train. I would have too, if I'd realized how terrifying this would be."

Jalissa grimaced and hugged the metal support. "I think I would have preferred to sleep like Farrendel. At least then I would not have known when the train goes flying off the tracks."

"I want to wake up in Tarenhiel, not wake up dead." Essie gave a squeal as the train lurched around another severe turn, lifting her fully from the floor.

Jalissa just stared at her. At least she had been willing to talk to Essie, and some of the shattered look left her eyes.

Essie winced. She was probably less funny than she thought she was. Risking letting go with one hand, Essie patted Farrendel's shoulder. "You would have laughed, wouldn't you?"

Farrendel, of course, remained asleep.

IT WAS A LONG, arduous day, but finally the train rumbled to a stop at the end of the line near the Gulmorth River. It was fully dark, the stars shining clear overhead, as Essie and Jalissa staggered across one of the wooden bridges spanning the river.

As they set foot on the other side, Essie breathed a sigh of relief. They were back in Tarenhiel. Back in the safety of the peaceful forests and the sprawling camp at the border where Leyleira, Farrendel's grandmother, oversaw the transfer of wounded back to Tarenhiel and Escarland and the shipment of supplies into Kostaria.

Within moments of their arrival, Leyleira had mobilized an army of both elven and human stretcher-bearers from the support personnel at the camp. With a nod to Essie, Leyleira saw to it that Farrendel, who was still unconscious, was transported to the royal train. Only the tight line of Leyleira's mouth betrayed how affected she was by seeing the state that Farrendel was in.

Jalissa also disappeared into the royal train after exchanging only a quick greeting with Leyleira, as if she was just as eager to leave Kostaria behind.

"Essie?"

Essie turned from watching as the stretcher-bearers disappeared into the royal train to find Illyna, one of her and Farrendel's elf friends, hurrying out of a tent. Illyna gripped Essie's shoulder with her one hand, the stump of her left arm resting against Essie's other shoulder. "Are you all right? Did you rescue Farrendel? Where is he?"

"Yes, he is..." Essie glanced over her shoulder at the royal train. How much should she tell Illyna? She wasn't sure she could bring herself to say, *he looks mostly dead.* "He's resting."

Illyna's eyes saddened, her mouth pressing into a taut line. Perhaps Essie didn't have to explain more than that. Illyna released Essie and stepped back. "Now that the war is over, this camp is being dismantled. I believe I will be sent home to Estyra tomorrow or the next day, whenever the next train has room. If you need anything, do not hesitate to ask."

"I will." Essie ducked her head and hurried away before Illyna saw too much of the truth in her eyes.

When Essie entered Farrendel's private train car, her muscles relaxed at the familiar, comfortable space encircling her. For the first time in over two weeks, she could relax. Farrendel was safe. She was safe. And they were going home.

Farrendel lay on his side of the bed, and Essie took the time to spread the blanket over him. How long would he remain asleep? At least it was a restful sleep. He needed it.

As tired as she was, a hot shower called more than the soft bed. While Essie washed away the dirt of a week of fighting across the frozen mountains of Kostaria, the train eased into a gentle rocking motion as it headed for Estyra.

When she had finished her shower, dressed in a clean shirt and trousers, and stepped from the train car's small water closet, she found Farrendel awake and sitting cross-legged on the bed, staring out the window. Essie climbed onto the bed and rubbed his back. "You're awake."

Farrendel didn't turn to look at her, and when he spoke,

his voice was flat. "Last time, they did not allow me to wake up until I was in Estyra."

Essie wasn't sure what to say to that. "Um, well, I made sure there's enough hot water left if you'd like to wash."

Farrendel nodded, eased to his feet, and disappeared into the water closet.

Essie curled beneath the blankets. She tried to stay awake. She really did. But as the water ran and ran and ran, she eventually drifted off to sleep.

BY THE TIME Farrendel finished his shower, the train's water heating system was only spitting out lukewarm water and his skin was red and throbbing because he had scrubbed so hard.

Still, even after over an hour of scrubbing under water as hot as he could stand, his skin still crawled with the feeling of filth and stone and blood. How many showers would it take before he felt truly clean?

He dressed, but he avoided looking at the mirror or any of the shining surfaces, even though he had left the light off so that it would not keep Essie awake.

But he had no wish to see the state of his hair. As he had washed it, he had been able to feel how short and ragged it was, thanks to the now dead troll king chopping it off as part of his torture.

He stepped from the water closet, swaying to the gentle rhythm of the train as it glided down the tracks. Outside the windows, a faint hint of moonlight filtered through the broad leaves of the forest, outlining the silhouettes of the broad tree trunks.

Essie was a lump under the blankets on her side of the bed, her red hair spreading across her pillow, the blankets, and her face. Her face was soft in the moonlight, a hint of a smile playing around her mouth even in sleep.

He should slip under the covers beside her.

But, for some reason, he could not bring himself to do that. She was too soft and vulnerable while he was sharp-edged and broken.

Instead, Farrendel strode around the bed and crept out the door at the end of the train car, stepping onto the small platform beside the walk that led to the next car. He sank onto the floor of the platform with his back to the cold metal of the train car's wall.

He closed his eyes and leaned his head against the wall behind him. Cold wind blasted his face, whipping through his short hair and tugging at his clothes. At least this cold wind smelled of the deep forest and damp earth, not ice and frigid mountains.

He was safe. He was on his way home.

And yet, his chest hurt with the pressure of all the shattered pieces inside him. All day, he had let himself go numb. It was either that or feel, and if he gave in to the emotions, he would break into even smaller, sharper pieces.

He could not let himself break. Back there in Kostaria during the final battle, he had let himself unleash his pain and anger. In the end, he had lost control of his magic and had nearly destroyed a large swath of Kostaria.

If he gave in to the pressure here, it would be this train and a portion of Tarenhiel's forest that his magic would incinerate. He would not risk the lives surrounding him.

Instead he slowly, silently, let the pain shred him inside until he was not sure what would be left come morning.

CHAPTER
FIVE

Melantha refused to glance over her shoulder as her new husband led her away from her family toward the pack of trolls who had witnessed the wedding. She could not show any weakness or these trolls would eat her alive.

The fire in her chest built until she barely stopped a scream from pouring out. How was she going to survive this constant fire burning her up inside?

She was all alone now. Her family hated her, all except Farrendel, the one who had the most reason to despise her. Her new husband was only marrying her to secure peace between their two kingdoms. She could not trust him. And her new people? They would as soon kill her as look at her.

Would her family even care if she were stabbed or strangled some night? Or would it be a relief that the worst scandal of their family was now eliminated without Weylind having to order her execution?

The heat in her chest strengthened her spine even as it shredded her inside. Who cared what her family thought?

Or what these trolls thought? She would not be cowed. She would not bend. She would wear her regal mask even as she burned away from the inside out.

As they neared, the gathered trolls remained silent and staring. Were they sizing her up to figure out how best to off her?

Prince Rharreth let out a piercing whistle that made Melantha flinch. "To Osmana for the wedding feasting!"

That earned a roar from the gathered warriors, including a stomping, hooting kind of cheer.

Melantha eased closer to Prince Rharreth. At least she was currently tied to him. She did not have to worry about getting separated in this crowd.

Three trolls closed around her and Prince Rharreth. After nodding at them, Prince Rharreth started in the direction of Osmana, the trolls' capital city. Even with her own long legs, Melantha still had to trot to keep up with him as he was still several inches taller than she was.

Melantha sneaked a glance up at him. His tousled white hair brushed his forehead and the collar of his shirt. His gray skin was the same color as the stone around them. His shoulders were bulkier than the sinewy build of the elves while his square jaw and chiseled cheekbones were broader than the slim features she was used to seeing.

About the only thing familiar to her was the tapered point of his ear, which showed the shared ancestry the trolls and elves had. Thousands of years ago, they had all been one people, the forest elves and the mountain elves, until war tore them into two.

Prince Rharreth glanced at her and raised an eyebrow.

Melantha quickly looked away. She had been staring.

But, she was stuck with him now. Was it too out of the ordinary that she would stare?

She stumbled over a rock, catching herself by her hand still tied to Prince Rharreth's. Perhaps she should spend more time watching her feet and less time studying the troll she had married. The trail at the bottom of the valley was littered with rubble from all the nearby mountains that Farrendel had blasted apart less than a week ago. Her soft slippers were not suitable footwear for hiking in these northern mountains.

When she glanced up, they still had over a mile to hike to reach the wall of Osmana, rising across the far end of the valley. Melantha tried to pretend she was not breathing hard. How far would she be expected to walk every day?

Prince Rharreth cleared his throat. "Princess Melantha, I would like to introduce you to my shield brothers, Zavni, Eyvindur, and Nirveeth." As he spoke, he gestured to each of the three trolls surrounding them in turn.

Zavni grinned and gave her a small wave. His front teeth had a large gap between them, and his light blue eyes had a twinkle to them.

Eyvindur crossed his arms and studied her intently. When he huffed and looked away, Melantha felt as if she had failed his inspection.

Nirveeth just grunted, and that was all.

"Shield brothers?" Melantha glanced between them. If Kostaria was going to be her home for the rest of her life, she would need to figure out their customs.

"When a troll becomes of age, they form a shield band of thirty to forty shield brothers and sisters to train. As long as they maintain their honor, they remain a part of this band for life, even when age or injury force them to retire from fighting." Prince Rharreth kept his gaze focused ahead. "I have only eight members left in my band, counting me. The war took the rest."

By the war, he probably meant Farrendel had killed a large portion of them. "Were those your shield brothers with you when you…" Melantha was not quite sure how to ask about that battle at the Escarlish border. "On the mission to Escarland?"

"No. Our task was to capture the elf monster Laesornysh. It was considered a suicide mission." Prince Rharreth's tone was flat. He might as well have been talking about the weather. "I was sent with a band of those who had dishonored themselves in some way. For going on that assignment, their honor was restored, whether they lived or died, as long as they fought bravely at my side."

As only one of the trolls who had gone with Prince Rharreth had survived, it had truly been a suicide mission.

Melantha raised her chin. She was not sure if this would be an inappropriate question to ask, but she needed to understand the trolls' mindset about honor if she was going to survive as their queen. "What would have happened if they had not fought bravely?"

"If someone dishonors themselves once, they wear that shame but are allowed to live and are given the chance to redeem their honor." Prince Rharreth's deep blue eyes flicked to her before focusing back on Osmana ahead of them. "But if they throw away their honor a second time, they would be doubly dishonored. If they lived, they would be hunted down and executed. Their whole family would wear the shame and dishonor until someone in the family did something especially great to redeem them."

Melantha stared down at the path for several moments, navigating around the pieces of rock rubble.

By the trolls' standards, she was dishonored. Perhaps even doubly dishonored, considering the severity of her crimes. She had turned traitor to her own kingdom and had attempted to kill her own brother. Was death and being blotted out of her family the only thing left for her now?

Or was there a way she could redeem herself? What could she do to earn redemption?

She had tried, there in the dungeon as she and Farrendel waited for rescue. She had healed Farrendel over and over again, giving him all the strength she could. She had even broken her own feet in an attempt to rescue him.

But, somehow, even that did not seem like enough. It did not undo the pain and the consequences of what she had done.

Prince Rharreth gave a tug on their clasped hands. "We are here. Welcome to Osmana."

Melantha glanced up and barely stifled her gasp.

The sheer stone wall of Osmana rose far above them, spanning the valley between the massive towers built into the mountains on either side. The gates were made of large blocks of stone, and only the seam where the doors met the wall and the fact that the trail ended at their base showed that they even were a gateway.

Prince Rharreth raised his hand and pressed his palm to one of the large stone doors. It swung open with a groan of shifting rock against rock, revealing a tunnel through the fifty-foot wide wall.

Melantha strode at his side through the tunnel and resisted the urge to gape as they stepped back into the sunlight.

Stone houses sprawled up the mountainsides, built into the mountain themselves. The houses were arranged in neat rows, and trolls bustled along the main road in the center of the valley and along the side streets. As Prince Rharreth and Melantha strode by, they paused to stare or glare. A few even spat on the ground and muttered, and Melantha guessed it was probably something derogatory about her.

At the far end of the valley, a large residence rose out of the mountainside. It was not quite a castle, though mansion seemed too tame a word for it. It was a well-fortified palace, the type that seemed to fit these warrior trolls. The front walls were grown out of the mountainside, with the rest of it melded into the mountain itself so that it was hard to tell what was a mountain peak and what was a troll-created spire.

Prince Rharreth gestured to the palace. "That is Khagniorth Stronghold, the official residence of the royal family in Osmana."

"If this is your palace, then what was Gror Grar?" Melantha gestured back the way they had come, toward the ruins of what had once been a fortress on the far mountain. Only a small portion of a single wall remained standing. Farrendel had demolished the rest.

"That was a stronghold for the military, though over the past hundred years, my grandfather, father, and brother lived there more than here in Osmana." Prince Rharreth's jaw tightened, and something about his clipped tone told Melantha that there was more to it, but the troll prince was not about to tell her now.

As they passed a group of troll warriors, one of them said something under his breath and spat, the spittle splattering across the cobblestones at Melantha's feet.

She skidded to a halt just shy of the spit. Heat burned in her chest, and she curled her free hand into a fist. How she longed to be a warrior to defend herself instead of having to stand there like a weakling and take their hatred.

Prince Rharreth tugged her behind him with their joined hands while the elven dagger appeared in his free hand. Icy magic and snow swirled around his fingers. "Do you wish to challenge me?"

The troll warrior shifted, then backed away. "No, my prince."

"That's what I thought." Prince Rharreth glared at the gathered trolls. "This elf is my wife. She will soon be my queen. Anyone who has a problem with that has a problem with me."

None of the surrounding trolls stepped forward, and most of them looked away as if they did not dare meet Prince Rharreth's eyes.

"If that is all, then I have my wedding feast to attend." Prince Rharreth spun on his heels and marched toward the stronghold.

Melantha trotted to keep up, holding her head high as she passed the staring trolls.

Finally, they stepped through another set of stone doors, though these were decorated with carved designs, and entered a hall that was three stories tall. Streams of light beamed from narrow, high windows. Curved openings in the far wall plunged into the mountain itself. Broad stairs led up to another set of openings that acted as the second floor.

Prince Rharreth led the way to the right hand opening into the mountain with his three shield brothers still trailing them.

Melantha braced herself for darkness, using more of her

magic to stave off any headache that stone tended to give elves.

Instead, they stepped into an expansive hall tiled with dark granite polished to a shine. Lights twinkled, set into an obsidian ceiling, giving it the impression of a starry night sky. Long tables had been set up with long benches on either side. Many of the tables and benches were already filled, and more trolls were coming in behind Prince Rharreth and Melantha.

Zavni strode around them. He raised his hand and his voice, "Behold, our Prince Rharreth of the royal warrior family of Regdrir!"

Cheers and stomping filled the feasting hall. Some of the warriors, both male and female, pounded the hilts of knives on the tabletops.

Zavni flourished his hand again. "And his bride, Princess Melantha of Tarenhiel!"

The cheers died so quickly they might as well have been strangled. The trolls glared, but none of them spoke. While they did not wish to cheer her, they did not want to offend their king-to-be either.

Prince Rharreth made his way to the long table set on the dais and took a seat in the large, throne-like wooden chair in the center. With her hand still tied to his, Melantha had no choice but to join him, sitting in the slightly smaller chair at his side.

Servants set bowls in front of them. Melantha picked up her spoon and stirred the contents of her bowl. The broth was watery, only a few vegetables and a little meat floating in it. A plate with hardtack was placed between her and Rharreth, as if they were expected to share the single plate.

She had expected something more. Not the same watery broth he had been serving her in the dungeon.

Prince Rharreth shot her a look, as if warning her not to comment.

A part of her still wanted to. But she was an elven princess. Of anyone, she knew how to suppress what she was thinking and put on a regal, serene mask.

Yet, she did not try to paste on a smile. Smiling was not her natural expression.

Melantha choked down the watery broth yet again. After the feasting, if it could be called that, some of the tables were pushed aside and trolls danced in the space. Their dances were nothing like the graceful, sweeping elven dances. The trolls stomped their feet in a rhythm as they marched around each other, and Melantha was not sure if the couples were supposed to find this romantic or if they were plotting to kill each other.

She just wanted to leave. She wanted to go home to Tarenhiel and return to the life she had before.

Instead, she was stuck here. Stuck with a near stranger as her husband. Worse, what little she did know about him was that he had fought her people for years. He had stood by while his brother Charvod tortured her brother Farrendel.

Melantha sneaked a glance at Prince Rharreth next to her. He was leaning closer to Zavni and the two of them were laughing over some inside joke between shield brothers.

The troll prince had been kind to her so far. He had fought to keep his brother from whipping her. But he had not fought to stop his brother from torturing Farrendel. Prince Rharreth claimed to have honor, yet his honor apparently only extended to certain people.

She was an elf. One of the enemy. What if he was forced

to choose between her and his people? Would he stand by and let her come to harm?

She was not sure what he would do. Considering their marriage was less than a day old and arranged for political reasons, he would probably choose his people over any minuscule duty to her.

Prince Rharreth stood and tugged on her hand. The others were pounding tankards on the table and dancing and only Zavni noticed them leaving, and his eyes twinkled as he smirked.

Melantha swallowed, her breath catching in her chest. What would Prince Rharreth expect of her that night? They were strangers. Surely he would not...

But he was a troll. Trolls were known to be barbaric.

Prince Rharreth led her from the dining hall, then up the stairs into a tunnel deeper into the mountain. The walls of the tunnel were decorated with carvings and woven tapestries that showed scenes of battles and hunts. Gemstones were embedded in the wall behind the sconces, scattering colored light into the tunnel.

It was more beauty than Melantha had been expecting to find here in Kostaria.

Prince Rharreth halted outside of a door bracketed by two sconces flickering blue light across the passageway.

Melantha dug her heels in, tugging on the hand still tied to his. "Is there a room next door for me?"

If she made it clear that her assumption was that they would have separate bedrooms, perhaps he would go with it.

He glanced over his shoulder at her, his dark blue eyes even darker in the shadows of the tunnel. "You will be safer with me."

Or so he said. She was not so sure. "I would prefer my own room."

Prince Rharreth pushed the door open. "As you may have noticed, many in my kingdom are not happy with my choice of bride. There are some who are not above killing you in your sleep. They might even consider it justice, since your brother killed my father and brother. For that reason, you will sleep in my room where I can guard you."

Melantha allowed herself to be pulled inside. Her stomach was still churning.

How had Farrendel done this? Gone through with a marriage to a stranger?

Then again, Farrendel was not as helpless as she was. Farrendel had his magic and his skills with his swords. He had been in no danger, at least not physically.

Perhaps she should be wondering how that human princess Elspeth had managed it. Melantha had always scorned her for being too happy and naïve.

But Elspeth was not so naïve that she had not known the kind of danger she had risked when marrying Farrendel. Now that Melantha was in the same situation, she better understood the kind of courage Elspeth had.

Taking a deep breath, Melantha let the door swing shut behind her and forced herself to look around the room instead of staring at the floor.

As this room was deep inside the mountain, it had no windows. But the entire ceiling was covered with diamonds and other precious gems, scattering the light from the wall sconces. A fireplace was set into one wall. It must have some kind of flue magically grown into the stone to pipe the smoke out of the mountain. Several upholstered chairs were arranged before the fire, looking like a cozy place to enjoy a book.

A large bed, piled with blankets and furs, filled most of the remaining space, its four posts made of carved stone. Clothes hung in a nook on the far side while an opening beside the nook led off into another tunnel that was probably some kind of water closet.

To hide her churning stomach, Melantha held up the hand that was still tied to Prince Rharreth's. "Can we untie this now?"

Prince Rharreth nodded and tugged on the knot, quickly loosening the cloth.

As soon as she was free, Melantha yanked her hand from his, wincing as the scab that had fused their palms together tore open. But she did not care as long as she had her hand all to herself again.

Prince Rharreth drew the elven dagger and sliced the cloth in two pieces. He held out one half to her. "A bandage."

Hardly a sanitary bandage, after it had been riding around on their hands all day. "Thank you, but it is not necessary. Unless there is a reason I should not heal myself?"

"No, as long as the scar remains. The scars on our palms show that we are married." Prince Rharreth stuffed the cloth he had offered her into his belt, then started to wrap his hand with the other half.

Melantha called on her magic, ignoring the slight headache that pounded at her temples as she used magic while surrounded by so much stone. A green glow surrounded her hand, then seeped into her, easing the lingering pain of the cut across her palm.

Melantha curled and uncurled her fingers. No pain.

She glanced up at Prince Rharreth. Should she offer to heal him too? Would he let her if she offered?

He was not looking at her as he tied the end of his makeshift bandage, tightening it with his teeth.

Melantha sighed, and somehow the sound had a bit of a growl to it. She could not allow him to walk around with such a horrid bandage. As much as she despised it, she was still a healer. "Let me. There is no need for that."

Prince Rharreth hesitated for a moment. What was he thinking? Was he worried about letting her use her magic, knowing she could harm rather than heal if she chose, though doing so would kill her along with him?

His dark blue eyes searched her face. "You would do that for me?"

"I am stuck with you now. And, apparently, you are all that is standing between me and your people slitting my throat. I do not wish for that wound on your sword hand to fester." Melantha held out her hand, then wiggled her fingers when he did not extend his hand for her to heal.

After another moment of hesitation, he held out his hand.

Melantha unwrapped the bandage, revealing the slice across the gray skin of his palm. Calling up her magic again, she touched her fingers to the cut and eased her magic into him. She had to do it carefully, working around the feel of his magic that filled him.

As her magic sank deeper into him, she sensed a lingering pain. She extended her magic, searching for the source of that pain.

His back. The lash marks from his whipping were still raw and healing. He had not shown evidence of that pain, but it had been only a week. Of course the deep wounds were not fully healed.

Then there was the wound in his shoulder where Farrendel's magic had pierced him, as well as the burns around his wrists.

Melantha poured more magic into him until she could sense that her power was working and would be enough to close the wounds. Once she was finished, she let go of his hand.

Prince Rharreth was staring at her, his brow furrowed. "I was not sure elven healing magic would work on a troll."

"I had to ease past your magic, but I have had practice doing that." Melantha eyed him, wondering if he would acknowledge the reason she had gained such practice.

"Of course." Prince Rharreth straightened. "Thank you."

"You are welcome." Melantha stepped back to put more space between them.

Prince Rharreth pointed toward the nook holding clothes. "I asked my shield sister to locate a few outfits for you."

"Linshi." Melantha hurried around the bed to the nook while Prince Rharreth disappeared down the tunnel toward what was presumably the water closet.

When Melantha reached the nook, she inspected the clothes it contained. One half was crowded with tunics and leather jerkins and trousers that obviously belonged to Prince Rharreth. The other half held two dresses and a few other tunics, shirts, and trousers. Far fewer clothes than she had at home.

Home. Her room in Tarenhiel with its view of Estyra. Would she ever see it again?

By the time Prince Rharreth returned, his hair damp, Melantha had picked out the softest of the shirts and trousers. Without a word to him, she headed down the tunnel.

After only a few feet, the tunnel took a sharp turn to the right, then another sharp turn to the left after a few more feet. After she exited the last turn, the sound of running water greeted her.

She had to walk a few more yards and take one more turn before she stepped into a chamber with a gentle waterfall washing over the far wall. The waterfall cascaded onto a flat rock before another small waterfall poured into a pool of water. Damp warmth washed over Melantha's face, and when she crossed the room and stuck her hand in the waterfall, the water was warm.

The room was lit by a soft glow of lights set near the ceiling, giving the whole place a warm, soft feeling even though it was a cave deep in the mountain.

Melantha washed and changed into the tunic and trousers.

When she re-entered the bedroom, Prince Rharreth was sprawled on the bed, and only two of the lights near the bed were still lit.

Melantha halted. There was only one bed. And he was already on it.

Prince Rharreth gestured from her to the bed. "I intend to get a good night's sleep. You are welcome to share the bed or sleep on the floor. Whatever you prefer."

Flexing her fingers, fighting the heat building in her chest, Melantha glanced from the bed piled with soft blankets and pillows, to the stone floor with only a bearskin rug to soften it. How dare he force her to choose between the bed or the floor. He claimed to be honorable, but what kind of honor was this? And after she had nicely healed him.

See if she healed him again if this was how he would treat her.

She glanced around the room. Perhaps she could curl up in one of the padded chairs by the fire?

The chair, the floor, or the bed. Which would be most awkward?

Probably the bed.

But he had challenged her. She was not about to back down now. If he wanted to make things awkward by sharing the bed, then that was exactly what she was going to do.

Her back stiff, she stalked around the bed and eased onto the far side, sticking as close to the edge as she could, all too aware of the bulk of him behind her.

He shifted, and the whole mattress dipped, threatening to roll her toward the center. Melantha gripped the edge of the mattress to stay in place.

This was her husband. Her home. Her life now.

And she was trying hard not to hate all of it.

CHAPTER
SIX

Rharreth slumped over the stone desk that dominated the long-unused study in Khagniorth Stronghold, just down the hall from the room he now shared with Princess Melantha. The shelves across from the desk still held dust and trailed cobwebs all the way to the floor, and he had yet to sort through the crumbling books stacked there.

A pile of paperwork sprawled across the desk as he tried to put Kostaria into order without the aid of whatever records his brother and father had kept.

Those record books were still buried in the ruins of Gror Grar, and between the Tarenhieli-Escarlish army still camped on the plateau and Laesornysh's magic still lingering in the stones as if seared into them, it would be a long time before the records could be retrieved.

The trolls who had tried to use their magic to clear the rubble from the road through the mountains reported that Laesornysh's magic burned too painfully for them to do anything.

How was he going to rule his kingdom when he wasn't even sure how to build his marriage? For the past two days, Princess Melantha had been hard and distant. When he suggested she tour Khagniorth or oversee the distribution of supplies in the stronghold's kitchen, she did it without a complaint.

He almost wished she would complain. That she would unleash the fire he saw burning in her eyes behind the icy mask. He had seen glimpses of that Princess Melantha when she had defended her brother Laesornysh there in the dungeon. Rharreth liked that Melantha, though he was not sure how to tell her that. Not when she was giving him this hard, serene mask from dawn until dusk.

A knock came on the door, then the stone slab opened. Zavni strolled inside, his large sword at his side, while Drurvas, the tallest of their shield band, had to duck as he sauntered inside. His battle-ax rested against his back.

"What is the report?" Rharreth focused on Zavni first.

"The invaders are in the process of pulling out. Their entire army should be gone from our soil by tomorrow evening." Zavni's mouth twisted, as if it was a struggle to stand by and allow the Tarenhieli-Escarlish army to leave unhindered. "They turned over what food supplies they no longer need, now that they are returning home."

"Good." As much as it grated on Rharreth to accept anything from Escarland and Tarenhiel, the supplies were a final gift as part of the treaty that would, hopefully, see his people through until the first trade shipment of grain and produce arrived from Escarland. Rharreth's people would starve, otherwise. "See to it that the supplies are properly distributed."

"Yes, Your Majesty." Zavni grinned and bowed.

Rharreth sighed and resisted the urge to shake his head. That title would not be official for a few more days. He had decided to wait on his and Melantha's coronation until the invading armies were gone from his kingdom.

It had been one thing to allow the elves and humans to witness the wedding. Quite another to have them involve themselves in something like the coronation. Rharreth would have a hard enough time dealing with the rumors that he was just a puppet king put there by the elves.

But Zavni seemed to get great pleasure out of irritating Rharreth by using the title.

"Drurvas, were all their weapons returned to them as specified in the treaty?" Rharreth had inspected the return himself yesterday, but he wanted confirmation.

Drurvas crossed his arms and nodded, his smirk twitching into something sour at the corners. "Of course, though I don't like just handing them over. We got those weapons fair and square. It isn't our fault that they were handed to us by traitors in Escarland. Nor does it look good, Rharreth, just rolling over to all of Escarland's demands like that. There is already talk about you being a weak king."

"I know." Rharreth scrubbed his face with a hand, glaring down at the pile of paperwork spread before him.

While he hadn't liked how his father and brother had run Kostaria, he had never truly wanted the responsibility of the crown to rest on his head. No matter what he did, there were those who would question his strength and honor.

He braced himself against the desk. "We desperately need peace with Escarland and Tarenhiel, little as our warrior families want to acknowledge it. Our people are starving. Without food from Escarland, thousands will starve this winter. Better we make peace now while we have some position of strength than go begging to them in the spring after winter has broken our people."

"We have had other hard winters in the past few years that we survived without Escarland's help." Drurvas shrugged, his fingers flexing as if he wanted to draw his ax and start the war with Tarenhiel all by himself.

Thousands had died in those winters too, even more than had died in the war at the border. But Charvod hadn't cared how many died. He had just given more speeches about how it was an honor to die for Kostaria until the entire kingdom bought into the twisted version of honor he and their father had believed.

But Rharreth had to believe that it was just as honorable to live for Kostaria as it was to die. That peace could be as honorable as war.

Drurvas and Zavni were still standing there, waiting for his answer. Rharreth faced his shield brothers. "Each of those winters weakened us. How else could Escarland and Tarenhiel defeat us in a mere week on our own home ground when they didn't even have the aid of their greatest warrior until the final battle?"

"We didn't have the aid of our greatest warrior until that battle either." Zavni raised his eyebrows as he gestured toward Rharreth. "In choosing not to kill Laesornysh outright, Charvod sidelined you, his best warrior, to guard the elf."

Beside Zavni, Drurvas's smirk dropped for just a moment before it returned in full force. While Rharreth was the strongest with magic in all of Kostaria, Drurvas was one of the best—if not the best—at hand-to-hand combat.

"Still, my point remains. We need time—and food—to rebuild our strength. Tarenhiel has gained strength through its close alliance with Escarland. Perhaps we can gain the same." Rharreth stood and met first Drurvas's gaze, then Zavni's. "That is why I handed over the weapons and married the elf princess. I firmly believe this is best for Kostaria, and I need my shield band to stand by me. Eventually, Kostaria will improve, and everyone will see that this was the right plan."

"The shield band stands by you." Zavni rested his hand on his sword's hilt.

"It is our duty and our honor." Drurvas reached over his shoulder to pat the head of his ax. "We are willing to do what it takes for Kostaria."

Rharreth could not ask for a better shield band. With them at his back, he might survive long enough to save his kingdom.

SEVEN

W hen the royal train glided to a halt in Estyra in the early morning hours, Farrendel had already disappeared from the train before Essie awoke.

Essie kept her fake smile in place as she hugged Jalissa in farewell since Jalissa was staying on the train to return to Escarland as Tarenhiel's ambassador. Perhaps Jalissa would have noticed something wrong, but her own smile was plastered in place, her movements stiff.

Essie would have questioned her, but Jalissa pulled away and returned to the train, and Essie had to check on Farrendel.

Instead of strolling through Estyra hand in hand with Farrendel, Essie found herself walking toward Ellonahshinel alone, forcing herself to admire the sight of the yellow, orange, and red of autumn painting the leaves overhead rather than dwell on the lump in her throat.

The elven capital city was even more quiet than usual. Few elves strolled the grassy paths that meandered between the shops grown into the bases of the massive trees. The swinging bridges between the shops in the first level of branches were mostly deserted of people.

Most of the able-bodied elves were either with the army or stationed at the border in the encampment run by Leyleira, shuttling supplies to the armies. Only a handful were left to keep Estyra running.

As Essie rounded a bend, the massive tree-palace of Ellonahshinel came into sight. Stairs wound up its trunk into the sprawling palace grown into the broad branches. Shafts of the early morning sunlight filtered through the leaves, which were touched with hints of orange and red.

She climbed the long flight of stairs into Ellonahshinel, then wound her way up all the branches until she finally reached her and Farrendel's suite of rooms.

The main room held a small bank of cabinets that held dishes and a cold cupboard for storing food. The other side had piles of comfortable cushions for lounging.

Across the way were three doors that each led to a tree-house style bedroom tucked into a branch.

Essie entered the first door and climbed the stairs to their bedchamber. The room itself was small, smaller than the turret bedroom she and Farrendel shared at Buckmore Cottage in Escarland. The elven bedroom was light and airy with windows set into every wall and its sides and roof formed from the living tree with a layer of magic keeping it warm and pleasant, despite the chilly fall breeze outside. The bed was curved and almost nest-like, grown into the wall, as was the mirror and even the shelves that held their clothes and belongings.

Essie glanced around and set down the small bag she had taken with her to Kostaria. The room was empty.

Stepping back outside, she walked around the small

porch that circled the room to the place where Farrendel normally exercised in the mornings.

Instead of leaping and spinning along the twigs and branches, Farrendel sat on the porch, his back to the wall as he stared at the brilliant red and yellow leaves of the forest spreading out around them.

When Essie touched his shoulder, he started and tilted his head to glance up at her with dull, almost unseeing eyes. His shorn hair straggled over his forehead, longer in the front and on one side than it was in the back.

"Do you want something to eat?" She squeezed his shoulder, trying to keep her voice cheery.

He shook his head, his shoulder lifting in a shrug, before he went back to staring at the forest.

Her smile felt brittle as she leaned over to kiss his forehead. "All right. I'll be inside unpacking if you need anything."

Perhaps space was what he needed. Some space, and the peace and quiet of his familiar home here in Estyra. Surely that was all he needed to feel more like himself.

At least, that was what Essie told herself as she unpacked, sent her clothes off with a maid to be cleaned, set up the small camp stove she'd taken home with her from the front, checked that someone had helpfully restocked their cold cupboard with food, and generally pretended to stay busy for the rest of the day.

ESSIE WOKE to the sound of screaming. She pushed onto her elbow, trying to blink herself awake. Through the heart bond, she could feel the haziness of sleep mixed with terror and panic coming from Farrendel.

The bed next to her was empty. Farrendel must never have come to bed as she had assumed he eventually would.

His cries were not coming from the porch right outside the window, but from farther away. As though he was in the other bedroom, the one where she had stayed for the first three months of their marriage.

What was he doing all the way over there? Didn't he want her help with the nightmares?

Wrapping a blanket around her shoulders, Essie forced herself out of the nice warm bed and made her way from their room, down the stairs, across the main room, and up the second set of stairs to the room that had once been hers.

When she reached the door, she knocked. "Farrendel?"

Inside, the cry cut off, and an awareness flooded the heart bond a moment before the cold block crashed down between her and Farrendel.

"Farrendel? Are you all right?" She tugged on the door.

It wouldn't budge. Was it…locked?

She tugged again, as if the door would have miraculously unlocked, but it hadn't.

What was going on? Even when they had first been married, Farrendel had never locked her out before. Not even when he'd had nightmares.

Essie pounded on the door. "Farrendel? Let me in. I can sit with you. Or we can talk."

No answer.

Essie pressed her forehead to the door, hot tears stinging the corners of her eyes. Pressure built in her chest. She wasn't sure whether she wanted to cry or scream or yell or shake him until he snapped out of this.

He couldn't help it. He'd gone through a lot of trauma as a prisoner of the trolls.

But that still didn't stop her from wanting to shake some sense into him until things went back the way they were before he had been captured. She couldn't even reach him through the heart bond. That, too, was locked tightly against her.

"Farrendel. What's going on? Please, at least talk to me. Just let me in. Please." Essie wasn't sure if she meant the door, the heart bond, or both.

Still no answer. Coming from Farrendel, that was as good as a shout for her to go away.

She pushed away from the door. Despite her best efforts, her voice came out choked. "I'll be in the main room with hot chocolate if you want it. You can come down when you're ready."

Gripping her blanket tighter around her shoulders, Essie returned to the main room and set to work gathering the supplies for hot chocolate, including milk from the cold cupboard and the cocoa mix from a shelf next to the two mugs that she and Farrendel had picked out in the Aldon Market.

That seemed so long ago now, meandering through the market with Farrendel. Laughing with him. Trying all the different flavors of hot chocolate. They had been so happy and carefree, even with the threat of war looming over them.

Hot tears traced down Essie's face, and she had to blink to see what she was doing as she lit the camp stove, warmed the milk, and stirred in the mix. When it was done, she poured it into the two mugs, took them both to the cushions along the far wall, and sat with a blanket over her legs.

She cradled her mug and waited.

And waited.

Until the hot chocolate went cold and Essie could no longer deny the truth.

He wasn't coming.

She shoved aside both of the mugs and curled on the pile of cushions. She pressed her face into a pillow, dragged the blanket over her head, and let herself cry.

She had done her best to be strong from the moment Farrendel had been captured. She had clung to hope as they fought across Kostaria. She had refused to break, no matter how much it had hurt, knowing what the trolls were doing to him.

But she wasn't strong enough for this. Losing Farrendel hadn't broken her. But getting him back just might.

THE TAPPING WAS SO light that Essie lay there for several moments, not sure if she was awake or asleep or what was making that noise. Her eyes felt caked shut, and when she finally managed to peel them open, her eyelids scraped as if they were filled with dirt.

With a groan, she pushed onto her elbow, swiping her hair from her face and blinking at the early morning sunlight streaming through the windows.

There the tapping came again, this time more insistent even though it remained light.

The door. Someone was knocking on the door.

A part of Essie wanted to just ignore whoever it was. She was drained. Scraped raw inside.

When the knocking came yet again, Essie sighed and pushed to her feet. It must be important if the elf at the door was this persistent. Most elf servants left after a knock or two if the door wasn't answered.

Her hair was a frizzy, tangled mess after her rough night. Her shirt and tunic were rumpled, and she probably had dark circles under her eyes.

She nearly tripped over the two mugs of cold hot chocolate still sitting on the floor. After picking them up, she deposited them on the table as she headed for the door.

Pasting on the most cheerful smile she could manage, she lifted the latch, pulled the door open, and froze.

Queen Rheva of the elves stood on the front porch of the main room, her long nut-brown hair loose around her shoulders and contrasting against her light green dress. Her honeyed brown eyes were soft as she swept her gaze over Essie.

Essie tried not to shift. She'd had little chance to get to know this elf sister-in-law of hers. Weylind's wife had always stuck close to Melantha and seemed busy with her queenly duties. Not to mention that her seat at the dining room table was at the far end from where Essie and Farrendel usually sat, making it difficult to strike up a conversation without shouting across the table, something Essie would have done without thinking at her own family meals, but not with this serene elven family.

After a moment, Essie forced her fading smile back onto her face. All she really wanted to do was shove Rheva back outside and slam the door. "What brings you here?"

Rheva shifted, her hands clasped demurely in front of her. "I am sorry I did not meet you at the train station yesterday. I was not sure how I would be received, and I..." Rheva trailed off and stared at the floor of the porch.

Essie had always assumed Rheva was just as aloof as

Melantha. Or perhaps as disapprovingly condescending as Weylind.

But, perhaps, she was simply shy. And Essie's loud laughter and bright smiles were most likely intimidating to someone whose culture encouraged serene, quiet behavior.

There was more to Rheva than met the eye, and, as she had with Jalissa, Essie felt bad that she hadn't taken the time to see that until now. It wasn't only Rheva's fault. Essie had never attempted to approach her either.

"Uh, would you like to come in?" Essie stepped aside, gesturing from Rheva to the room.

Rheva glided inside but didn't take a seat either at the table or on the cushions. Her hands remained clasped in front of her, and only a close inspection showed how white her knuckles were. "I came to check on you. You do not look well."

"It…was a rough night." Essie's smile turned brittle again. She was not sure how much to tell Rheva. She braced herself, drawing in shallow breaths at the pain of tears building inside her chest again.

Rheva stepped closer and, when she lifted a hand, her fingers glowed a faint green. She touched the back of Essie's hand, and a soothing coolness spread through her.

"I am sorry. I should have been here last night. Come and sit." Gently, Rheva steered Essie to the pile of cushions and nudged her to sit.

Essie reclaimed her blanket from the night before, the lump too thick in her throat for words. She had not expected this almost motherly tenderness from Rheva.

Rheva gracefully eased onto one of the cushions next to Essie. "Do you want to tell me about it?"

Essie wasn't sure why, but Rheva's gentle tone and

sympathetic words drew tears. Last night, she'd felt like such a failure as a wife because she hadn't been able to reach Farrendel. If she had only loved him more or made sure he knew he could confide in her or something, then surely she could have helped him out of this.

But there was truly nothing she could do. No amount of love or caring on her part could fix Farrendel. Not this kind of damage.

"I just wish...I just want it to be better..." Essie's words hitched. She didn't want to cry. Not in front of this sister-in-law during the first real conversation the two of them had ever had.

But Rheva shifted and put her arm around Essie's shoulders.

It was that gesture that broke down Essie's last barrier. Elves didn't normally reach out to offer hugs or comforting physical contact.

The relief of crying on someone's shoulder was almost palpable, even as it brought another stab of pain. She should have been able to cry on Farrendel's shoulder. He was her husband. That was how things were supposed to work.

But right now, Farrendel was broken, and their marriage felt shattered along with him.

When Essie had first married Farrendel, she had expected nothing. She had expected to be locked out and ignored.

Now things were different. They had been so close to being utterly, blissfully happy. Was it too much to ask that she got a nauseatingly happy honeymoon phase before things settled into the hard reality of life and marriage?

When Essie finally sniffed her way to silence, Rheva handed her a soft handkerchief. "It is all right to cry. It is not weakness to ask for help nor is it strength to silently bear what truly should not be your burden to carry. Burdens are not meant to be carried alone."

No, they weren't, even though that was what Essie normally did. She hid her burdens behind smiles and laughter and pretended everything was fine. It always seemed as though everyone else had burdens far weightier than hers, and she had never wanted to add her burdens to theirs when she was capable of dealing with them herself.

But, right now, she was thankful Rheva was there. Essie swiped at her face and blew her nose. "Thank you."

"It is the least I could do." Rheva pulled back, her gaze flicking to Essie before dropping to the floor. "I should have been the first to make you feel welcome here in Tarenhiel after your marriage, and I apologize for neglecting to do so."

Essie stared at the crumpled handkerchief in her hands. She wasn't sure how to go about gracefully accepting that apology. Simply brushing it aside as no big deal seemed too trite a response for the depth of Rheva's sincerity, yet Essie didn't want to imply that she had been truly offended when she hadn't.

Honestly, Rheva ignoring her had been one of the better responses from Farrendel's family. "I'm sure you had many duties keeping you busy, especially with how often Weylind was called away to the border."

"It was not only that, I am afraid." Rheva's tone remained stiff, but the set of her shoulders relaxed some-what. "I wished to give you and Farrendel time and space. You were already dealing with enough hovering by Weylind that I did not think you needed my interference as well."

A genuine smile tugged on Essie's face. It hurt, as if she was no longer used to smiling like that anymore. "That was thoughtful of you. I appreciate your lack of hovering." Would Rheva be offended if Essie joked about Weylind? "Weylind was a bit...much for a while."

Instead of looking offended, Rheva tilted her head and gave a soft laugh. "I am sorry. I tried to curb his hovering as much as possible. But where Farrendel is concerned, he is rather zealous in his protection."

"Wait, you mean Weylind's hovering could have been worse?" Essie had to resist the urge to hug Rheva. "I deeply appreciate any time you managed to keep him from breathing down our necks."

"You are welcome." A tentative smile tiptoed onto Rheva's face, though it disappeared after a moment to return to that liquid, searching look once again. "I do not wish for you to think I am hovering, but as Weylind is not here, I suppose it falls to me instead. How is Farrendel?"

With Farrendel's friends and even with her own family, Essie hesitated to admit the truth. She didn't want to talk badly about Farrendel to others.

But Farrendel's family knew just how bad his trauma could be. They'd been through this before. Whatever Essie said, it would not be a surprise to them. Besides, Rheva had probably guessed much of the truth, considering Essie had just cried all over her.

Essie sighed and sagged against the wall behind her. "Not good. He locked me out last night and won't let me in."

"I was afraid of that." Rheva sighed and shook her head, staring down at fingertips glowing faintly green. "He most likely will not allow me in to help him either."

What could Rheva do that Essie couldn't? Essie pointed at Rheva's fingers. "Can you help him with your magic? I didn't realize healing magic could do something about…this."

"Most healers cannot. But my father's healing magic is particularly skilled, and he has discovered a way to influence emotions." Rheva gave a small shrug, as if something like that was no big deal. "I can do it to some extent, though not to his level of skill."

Essie wasn't sure she understood how that would work. But she trusted that the elves knew what they were talking about. "Your father?"

"He is retired now, but he was the head healer at Ellonahshinel. Weylind and I met when both Melantha and I were training under my father, and Weylind started walking Melantha to Dacha's office each day." Rheva's smile grew, and almost looked…swoony.

Essie had a hard time picturing Weylind being all romantic, but he must have been at one point. Rheva had to have seen something in him to have married him.

Rheva blinked and glanced at Essie. "Anyway, since his retirement, my father has spent the past twenty years studying the way the brain works and deepening his skill. Fifteen years ago, he helped Farrendel after his rescue from the trolls. He will be able to help again."

"Really?" Essie straightened, her heart beating harder. For the first time, she had hope that something could be done to help Farrendel. "Can your father come here?"

Rheva shook her head. "His knees trouble him now, and he no longer climbs all the stairs and branches of Ellonahshinel like he used to."

"Oh." Essie slumped back against the wall. There went that idea. She wasn't sure she could convince Farrendel to even leave his room at the moment, much less walk all the way across Ellonahshinel.

"Do not fret." Rheva patted Essie's arm. "The other reason I came was that I received word that Leyleira, Weylind, and your brothers will be returning to Estyra this evening. Weylind will be able to drag Farrendel to my father's office."

Essie snorted, though there wasn't a lot of mirth to the sound. Weylind's bossy hovering would be good for something. If anyone could argue Farrendel into something, then it was Weylind.

Not to mention, Weylind would be able to use his plant-growing magic to break down Farrendel's door.

After last night, Essie was more than ready to let Weylind step in.

"Until Weylind arrives, I will stay with you." Rheva patted the skirt of her light green dress. "I put Ryfon in charge and asked Brina to help him. The practice will do them some good."

Essie relaxed against the wall. She wasn't alone. Perhaps she would introduce her sister-in-law to hot chocolate. Then, tonight, Weylind, Averett, and Julien would arrive, and maybe, finally, Weylind would be able to drag Farrendel out of this.

EIGHT

Farrendel lay on the floor of the porch, staring at the branches of Ellonahshinel that he was too weak to run or jump across like he used to.

Even if he was strong enough, he did not care enough to move, much less exert that much effort. He had slept right there on the porch the night before, not even caring enough to crawl back to bed. Not that it was truly his bed.

Night...Farrendel dug his fingers into his hair, as if he could claw out the nightmares and fog filling his head. He could not think. His head was spinning and heavy. A weight pressed him to the floor, making it hard to take more than shallow breaths even as his fingers tingled from lack of oxygen.

How was he going to face yet another night of reliving what had happened to him? Last night had been filled with terrors and pain. Would he ever escape that dungeon, or would it be forever embedded beneath his skin and torn into his mind?

A loud pounding sounded on the door at the base of the

stairs, much too loud to be Essie. "Farrendel! Open this door, or I will break it down."

Weylind. Farrendel curled tighter in on himself. He did not even have the energy to shout back.

Weylind's magic burst to life nearby, the green sense of it flooding Farrendel's senses. A crack sounded from below, then Weylind's footsteps were on the stairs. In a moment, he was pounding on the door to the guest bedroom where Farrendel had retreated last night.

This time, Farrendel gathered a lungful of air. "Go away."

Weylind strode around the porch, the floorboards creaking faintly beneath him. The boot steps halted behind Farrendel, and Weylind's shadow loomed over him.

Farrendel did not push himself upright to face his brother. "I told you to go away."

"You know I will not." Weylind's tone was hard, and Farrendel did not need to look to know he had his arms crossed.

This was not a battle Farrendel wanted to fight today. He was already so weary. Exhausted from lack of sleep and the battles of nightmares and memories that left him foggy and disoriented. "Leave me alone."

"No." Weylind's voice cracked even harder against the stillness of the treetop.

Farrendel gritted his teeth, clenching his fists. Why would Weylind not leave? Could he not see that he just wanted to be left alone?

"Farrendel, look at me."

Farrendel shoved onto his elbows, heat building in his chest. If Weylind wanted him to look at him, then fine. That was what he would do. He pushed to his feet and spun to face his brother. His head whirled, his vision blurry, and he braced himself with a hand against the wall. "I am fine."

"No. You are not." Weylind's crossed arms and scowl came into focus. "You need to eat and change your clothes, and then we need to talk."

Heat built inside Farrendel's chest. Weylind was talking to him as if he was a child. Well, Farrendel was done taking orders. "Stop. Just stop."

"Or you will do what?" Weylind's fists clenched as he took a step forward. "You can barely stand right now."

"I am fine!" Farrendel let himself yell. Magic crackled along his fingertips. "Stop hovering! I am tired of you ordering me around and constantly watching every move I make. I just need space and time and no one is giving that to me. Leave me alone!"

At the last word, magic flashed out. Weylind ducked, and a wall of branches flung up between him and Farrendel's magic.

Farrendel tried to yank his magic back, but he could not stifle it quickly enough. Weylind's protective branches were incinerated, but Weylind remained unscathed behind them.

Farrendel slumped against the wall behind him, hands shaking. Unlike Essie, Weylind was not immune to his magic. He would have been killed if he had not been fast enough.

This was why Farrendel had to stay away from others. He was far too dangerous.

Weylind slowly straightened, his hands held in front of him as if he was prepared to grow another protective wall.

Farrendel wrapped his arms over his stomach. "Please, shashon. I just need time. Please."

"I know. I know that often you can sort yourself out

eventually. But, not this time." Weylind waved in the direction of the main room, the hard expression softening into one of compassion. "Your wife is down there worried out of her mind for you. You cannot go on like this."

Essie. Farrendel hunched, sliding down the wall to sit on the floor of the porch. He was hurting her by pushing her away, yet he would hurt her if she got too close. Either way, he had no choice that did not harm her, and it killed him inside. He sighed and rested his head on his arms. "I know, shashon."

"Good." The bossy older brother tone was back in Weylind's voice. "Rheva is visiting her father right now and letting him know that you will be there to see him tomorrow morning, bright and early."

Taranath, Rheva's father, had helped last time Farrendel had spiraled this low. Seeing him was the right thing to do. For Essie's sake even more than for himself.

But something inside him still turned stubborn at being forced to go by Weylind. He raised his head and met Weylind's gaze. "And if I do not go?"

Weylind raised an eyebrow at him, meeting him stare for stare. "Then I will set Machasheni Leyleira on you."

"You would not dare." Farrendel glared back, though without any heat. His brother was playing dirty, pulling the grandmother card.

Weylind just stared back, though the corner of his mouth twitched in a suppressed smile.

"Fine. I will go." At least being angry at Weylind had cleared Farrendel's head and finally made him feel something besides the crushing numbness. A momentary reprieve, but welcome nonetheless.

Essie waited in the main room, huddled on the cushions. It had been nice to hug Averett and Julien before they had boarded the train to continue the rest of the way to Escarland, but it had hurt to try to smile and pretend she was fine even with Farrendel's conspicuous absence.

Through the opening to the guest bedroom, she could hear Farrendel shouting, something she had never heard from him before. Was it wrong that she was relieved it was Weylind who was taking Farrendel's anger right now?

After a few more moments, the shouting quieted. Then, Weylind reappeared in the wrecked doorway to the room. The set of his shoulders seemed less tense than it had been when he'd torn the door off its hinges and marched up the stairs.

Essie scrambled to her feet, her stomach still knotted. "How is he?"

"Things will get better." Weylind awkwardly patted her shoulder. "One of us will be back in the morning. You and Farrendel are not alone."

He was trying, at least, and Essie barely resisted hugging him. She had never expected Weylind would use his protectiveness for her like this. "Thank you."

With one last nod, Weylind left, softly closing the outer door behind him.

With a deep breath, Essie faced the open door to Farrendel's room. Now that she could go and talk to him, a part of her didn't want to. She didn't want to see Farrendel like this, nor was she sure how he would react.

But he was her husband. He was still her husband even

when he was dealing with trauma just as much as when he was happy.

No more stalling. Essie squared her shoulders and marched up the stairs to the guest bedroom.

She found him on the porch around the back of the treetop room. He leaned against the wall, legs sprawled in front of him. His hair straggled across his forehead, unwashed and greasy. He was still wearing the same light green shirt and trousers.

It was the most bedraggled she'd seen him, except for the moment when she'd fought her way to his dungeon cell in the now ruined fortress of Gror Grar. This seemed almost worse since, in Kostaria, she'd expected him to look awful.

Essie sank onto the floor next to him, close enough she could take his hand if he let her, but with several inches between their shoulders. She didn't say anything. For once, she didn't have the words to fill the painful silence.

After several long minutes, Farrendel sighed, his head resting against the wall behind him as he stared up at the broad, red-gold autumn leaves of Ellonahshinel rather than at her. "Essie...you should go back to Escarland with your brothers. I just make you miserable."

Essie froze, her breath catching in her throat and a weight settling painfully into her stomach. Surely Farrendel didn't mean it. "Don't say that."

"It is true." Farrendel didn't move, not even to glance at her. "It might have been better for everyone if I had died in Kostaria."

The weight in her stomach turned icy. "No, Farrendel. No. I don't know what lies your brain is telling you, but don't you dare listen." Essie rested a hand on his cheek and tilted his head toward her. "Of course, I'm miserable.

Because you're miserable. But that doesn't mean I would be better off without you. We all just want you to feel better and more like yourself."

Farrendel shook his head, burying his fingers in the short strands of his hair.

Essie wasn't sure she was getting through to him. Would her words click in his head? Or would they get pushed out by the nightmares and memories of what he had endured?

As she studied him, she frowned. Gently, she eased one of his hands from his hair and studied his knuckles. A gash ran across the back of his hand while several of his knuckles were skinned and bloody. How could he possibly have gotten hurt? It looked like he had punched someone, but he'd been alone. Had he punched Weylind?

No, these wounds didn't look fresh enough for that. Nor had Weylind been sporting any bruises on his face as though he'd been in a brawl with his brother.

Essie gently traced the length of the gash with her thumb. "What happened?"

If anything, Farrendel shrank into himself more. His hand twitched in her grip, as if he was torn about pulling free of her grip. "That is the reason you cannot be near me. I struck the wall last night during a nightmare. If I…if you…"

He was dangerous. He did not mean to be. He could not help it if he thrashed in his sleep.

But, that wasn't the real problem here. Essie rested a hand on Farrendel's cheek and forced him to look at her again. "I get that. I am glad you were thinking enough to wish to protect me. And lashing out in your nightmares is a problem we are going to have to deal with. But hurting yourself in your sleep isn't much better than accidentally hurting someone else."

Farrendel kept his eyes down, not meeting her gaze, even if his face was turned toward her.

"Why didn't you just tell me?" Essie couldn't keep the bite out of her voice. Heat filled her chest, and she barely had enough control to keep her voice at a steady, normal volume instead of yelling. "We could have talked it over. Instead, you locked me out. Without an explanation. I had to have your brother break down the door to get you to finally talk to me. That, more than you flailing in your nightmares, is the problem."

"Essie...I...I could not..." Farrendel shook his head, tugging free of her hand. His hands dug into his hair again, as if he was trying to keep his head from exploding.

Essie struggled to hold back the heat building in her chest. As satisfying as it would be to yell at him, he would just splinter even more. She'd scream into a pillow later if she needed to.

His brain was so messed up right now that he probably couldn't have thought logically enough to have sensibly talked to her earlier.

That still didn't make what he'd done right.

"Yes, you could have."

He flinched, then his eyes flashed to her for the first time, sharply silver-blue and pained. "What was I supposed to say? That I fear hitting you in my sleep? What kind of monster does that make me?"

"That's exactly what you were supposed to say! Not the monster part. You aren't a monster. You're traumatized and need help, and there's a difference. It's a difference we could have worked through if you had just talked with me." Essie's hands were shaking with all the pent-up emotions inside her.

He slumped back against the wall again with a sigh. "I am sorry."

"I forgive you. But, please, in the future, just talk to me, all right?" Essie blinked back tears, her throat going thick and painful again. Why couldn't she seem to find the end to these tears?

He tilted his head toward her, then held out an arm.

She took his invitation, curling against him and burying her face against his shirt. When he wrapped his arm around her shoulders, she couldn't hold back the tears any longer. After crying on Rheva's shoulder that morning, she should have been all cried out. But it turned out tears had a way of replenishing just when they weren't wanted.

But crying on Farrendel's shoulder felt so much better, with him warm and solid, if far too bony and thin after his ordeal in Gror Grar.

When he leaned his head on top of hers, she felt his shoulder shaking. If he was shedding tears of his own, she did not stop crying or lift her head to see. The moment felt like healing, even if the block didn't yet lift from the heart bond.

When Essie sniffed her way to silence again, she dug out the handkerchief that she had stuffed in a pocket, prepared this time. She didn't raise her head from Farrendel's shoulder as she dabbed at her eyes and running nose. "So what do you want to do about tonight?"

"I am going to have more nightmares. I will just keep you awake." Farrendel didn't move either. If anything, his arms tightened around her, as if he wasn't ready to let her go.

"You will keep me awake no matter where you or I sleep." Essie patted his chest with her free hand. "If I make hot chocolate tonight, will you actually want some?"

She assumed the movement of Farrendel's head against hers was a nod and not a shake. He squeezed her hand. "I think so."

"I'll hold you to that. If you don't come down, I'll bring the hot chocolate to you."

"I will not lock you out." He paused, his tone going from numb to holding just a hint of his wry humor. "The door is incapable of locking right now."

"Ah, yes. Your brother is very thorough when he rips a door off its hinges." And, right now, Essie was not in a hurry to ask anyone to fix it. She traced her fingers over the scabs across Farrendel's hand. "Now, if I go fetch something for dinner, do you think you could muster the energy to wash up and change?"

She would start small. Coax him to eat and take a shower. And hope that, tomorrow, Rheva's father would be able to help Farrendel.

Because, after all she'd been through fighting across Kostaria, Essie really wanted her Farrendel back.

CHAPTER
NINE

A knock sounded on their door early in the morning on the day Melantha was going to be crowned queen of the trolls. While Melantha tied the belt of her thick wool dress to make it small enough for her, Prince Rharreth strode to the door and opened it.

A troll female with mounds of wool fabric and furs and a satchel bustled inside, followed by another troll female dressed in a leather vest and skirt over wool trousers and fur-lined boots to her knees. She rested her hand on the large sword she had belted at her waist. Her white hair was piled on her head, held back with leather cords and clips that looked like they were fashioned out of bone. Hopefully those were animal bones and not elf bones, though Melantha would not put it past these people.

Prince Rharreth closed the door and gestured to the woman carrying the fur and fabric. "The seamstress is here to provide you with garments suitable for life here in Kostaria. She will also alter a dress so that it will be suitable for the coronation later today."

The woman bobbed a bow, though her eyes glittered sharp when she straightened.

Melantha nodded to the woman, keeping her expression neutral. Yet another troll who hated her.

"And this is my shield sister Vriska. She will stand guard." Prince Rharreth gestured at the female troll warrior.

The female troll glared even more fiercely than the seamstress did. Melantha did not like her chances of surviving this fitting.

"I am trusting you to guard her well, Vriska." Prince Rharreth gave Vriska a stern look.

"I am loyal, my prince and my shield brother. She will not come to harm under my watch." Vriska held her head high, meeting Prince Rharreth's gaze without flinching.

Melantha balled her fists, the heat flaring in her chest. This Vriska was everything she had always wished she could be. A warrior. Confident in herself and her abilities. Skilled with a sword and able to defend herself from anyone seeking to do her harm. The kind of warrior Melantha could have been, if she had been born with different magic.

Instead, she had been born with healing magic. If she was attacked, she could not even use her magic to defend herself. She had to be guarded at all times. Helpless and basically worthless here in Kostaria.

Prince Rharreth nodded to Melantha. "I will be back later. I have much to do before the coronation."

Then, he disappeared out the door, closing it firmly behind him.

Melantha gritted her teeth and worked to keep her serene mask in place. This was how it had been for the past few days. Prince Rharreth seemed to be all attentive and kind... on the surface.

But every day, once he had figured out something to keep Melantha occupied, he went off to see to his actual duties of running Kostaria or training with his shield brothers and sister. He made no effort to include her in those duties.

Vriska turned her back to the door and crossed her arms, sweeping a slow glare from Melantha's toes up to her head. "Rharreth could have done so much better. You are weak. You can't even protect yourself, much less fight at his side. If he's lucky, some warrior will assassinate you, and he will be able to move on to a real, troll wife."

Melantha crossed her arms and glared back, the simmer in her chest painful in intensity. There was nothing she could do but take Vriska's words, and Vriska apparently knew it. If Melantha ran to Prince Rharreth to tell him what had happened, she would only make herself look even weaker. "Will you help those assassins harm me?"

"At least not right now." Vriska smirked as she leaned back against the door. "I gave my pledge to protect you to my shield brother. That oath is binding. I will not break it or my honor."

That tree-festering honor. Prince Rharreth did that same thing, using his honor as a shield between them.

Melantha spun to put her back to Vriska. She was going to do her best to ignore the annoying shield sister. She faced the seamstress. "Well, let us proceed."

The seamstress set to work measuring and taking notes on which colors and fabrics Melantha preferred. Not that there was that much to choose from. The only colors available were a variety of dark blues, reds, and greens. And black, gray, and brown, of course. Her choices of fabrics were wool, heavy canvas, leather, or fur.

Melantha chose to have the dark red wool dress modified

in time for the coronation that evening. The seamstress promised that she and her assistants would have a few dresses and warm trousers and tunics finished shortly. Until then, Melantha would be stuck in oversized dresses.

THAT EVENING, Melantha dressed in the dark red dress, leaving her black hair to flow down her back.

When Prince Rharreth reappeared from the waterfall room, he was dressed in the same black trousers, green shirt, and matching black vest that he had worn for their wedding. He held out an arm to her.

Melantha held her head high, her back stiff, as she strode at Prince Rharreth's side through the passageways of Khagniorth to the front doors.

Outside, the stars glittered far overhead, already night-time with the short autumn days. In the courtyard in front of the palace, a small army of troll warriors waited with eight troll warriors standing in their center. These trolls carried two shields on their shoulders, four to a shield. Melantha recognized Eyvindur, Zavni, Nirveeth, and Vriska, and she figured the other three must be the rest of Prince Rharreth's shield band with an extra pulled from another band.

The first four, all trolls Melantha did not know except for Eyvindur, knelt, and Prince Rharreth climbed onto the shield, standing with his feet planted. When the shield bearers straightened, Prince Rharreth remained steady, swaying with their movements as easily as if he were standing on a motionless floor.

When the four holding the second shield knelt, Melantha stepped on top. Vriska leaned over and spat onto Melantha's slipper. The glare she sent Melantha challenged Melantha to protest the action.

Zavni sent Vriska a quelling look, but the others did nothing to defend Melantha.

Melantha held her head high and pretended the spittle had not landed on her foot and was drooling onto the inside of her shoe. She would not look weak, especially not in front of Prince Rharreth's shield band. She planted her feet and struggled not to fall as her shield bearers straightened. The last thing she needed was to take a tumble in front of everyone during the coronation. They already hated her simply because she was an elf. They would hate her more if she appeared a weakling.

Eyvindur and the trolls carrying Prince Rharreth started forward, and Melantha's shield bearers strode forward as well. Thankfully, their pace was solemn and measured, so Melantha was able to keep her balance. It was a bit like walking on the branches during a large windstorm when the gale was so strong it overpowered the magic shields and magic in the trees that kept them from swaying.

The troll army gathered around them, forming a procession as they marched through the main street of Osmana. Trolls lined each side of the street and leaned out of upper story windows. Some of them stomped and gave their howling cheer at the sight of Rharreth. He kept his expression neutral, not giving any indication he heard them.

Melantha kept her own expression blank, even as a few stones and chunks of ice were hurled in her direction. The troll warriors made no move to stop them, and Rharreth stayed facing forward so he did not see what was happening.

She would not cry out. She would not bow beneath their hatred.

The shield bearers carried them through Osmana and out the opposite gate from the one where she had entered a few days earlier, the one that led to the ruins of Gror Grar.

Outside the gates of Osmana, the stars burned brightly in the black sky above, the starlight glittering on the icy mountain peaks. The trolls, both warriors and villagers from Osmana, held torches as they marched up a trail to one of those peaks.

The cold air surrounded Melantha, and she tried not to shiver as the breeze swept down from the mountains.

The top of the mountain was a large, flat space with a single square block of stone in the center. Prince Rharreth's shield bearers halted with the shield level with the stone so that Rharreth could step off.

Melantha's shield was held next to the stone, and she breathed a silent breath of relief as she stepped back onto solid ground. With a glance at her, Rharreth knelt, and Melantha matched his movement.

The same old troll who had married them started the ceremony. There was a lot of growling and stomping. Finally, another troll presented the old troll with a smaller shield with the antler crown of the trolls and a leather diadem resting on it.

Eyvindur picked up the antler crown while the old troll intoned, "Do you, Rharreth of the royal warrior family of Regdrir, swear to govern Kostaria with all honor for as long as you live?"

"I do." Rharreth's voice was solemn.

Eyvindur placed the crown on Rharreth's head.

Then Vriska picked up the leather diadem and halted

behind Melantha. The back of Melantha's neck crawled from having Vriska behind her where she could not keep an eye on her.

"And do you, Melantha of the elves, swear to rule at King Rharreth's side for as long as you both live?"

"I do." Melantha stated as firmly as she could manage.

The cold leather with its emerald-embossed center rested against her forehead. Vriska tied the knots far too tightly, yanking Melantha's hair while she was at it. To top it all off, a wet glob of spit landed on the back of Melantha's neck.

Melantha gritted her teeth. These trolls really had quite excessive spittle.

"I present King Rharreth and Queen Melantha. Come and give your oath of loyalty."

One by one, the warriors stepped forward, pricked their right thumb on their dagger or sword or other weapon of choice, swore that they would be loyal to Rharreth, and pressed the bloody fingerprint to Rharreth's forehead. Most of them passed Melantha with either a glare or an icy stare, but some turned their head and spat, not even bothering to hide the action from Rharreth.

Each time it happened, Rharreth's eyes narrowed, his square jaw hardening, as if he was taking note of each of the disrespectful warriors.

Finally, all the gathered warriors had given their pledges.

Rharreth stood, and Melantha straightened as well. She held her head high, refusing to break under the glares, the spit, and the throbbing bruises from the stones and ice hurled at her. And now her aching skull, shooting pain both from the tightness of the diadem and the stone pressed against her skin.

TARA GRAYCE

As subtly as she could, Melantha drew on her magic and washed it over herself to soothe the bruises and headache.

No matter what these people threw at her, Melantha was now their queen. Somehow, she would have to figure out a way to endure their hatred.

CHAPTER
TEN

Rharreth balanced on a wagon near the eastern gate to Osmana. Several wagons were lined up along the road, guarded by a squad of warriors. Troll citizens pressed around the warriors in something that was coming close to a mob with a few discernible lines to the distribution point at the front wagon where Rharreth stood.

Drurvas stood just in front of the wagon, guarding the clerk who was taking down everyone's name and how much they were given to prevent people from going through the line twice or otherwise attempting to cheat to claim more food for themselves.

A stirring came from the crowd, then Zavni and Vriska pushed their way through, followed by Melantha with her head held high and that cold mask stealing the life from her face. Eyvindur and Brynjar followed her, keeping the crowd away from her.

She climbed onto the wagon next to Rharreth, and while her expression might have been cold, her eyes were blazing.

Handing off the sack of grain to Zavni, Rharreth touched

Melantha's arm and steered her to the far side of the wagon. It still wasn't very far away for a private conversation, but it was the best they would get. "Is something wrong?"

"Would it have killed you to wait for me? Or even invite me to go along?" Melantha hissed, poking him in the chest.

Rharreth held still, not sure how to react to her anger. "Your wardrobe was ready. I thought you would wish to see to the final fittings."

"Is that all you think I am good for? Wardrobe fittings and pretending I am running the kitchens when everyone knows the cook ignores me." Melantha kept her tone lowered, but her voice could have set the wagon on fire. "I am your wife. More than that, I am your queen. And as your queen, I should be standing at your side for events like this. Unless you plan to shove me aside and keep me isolated in Khagniorth for the rest of my life."

"No, that wasn't..." He reached for her arms, but she stepped back, nearly tripping over a sack of grain.

She caught herself on the edge of the wagon and glared up at Rharreth as if she blamed him for that too. "Is it not? I am an elf. I am unworthy of ruling Kostaria at your side in the eyes of your people. You have done very little to show me that your opinion is any different."

Hadn't he? He had kept her safe. He had seen to it that she had new clothes fit for a queen of the trolls. He had...

Rharreth tried to think of something else, but he could not. All the duties he'd given her had been ones that kept her occupied inside Khagniorth, yet they weren't anything that had to be done by her, specifically.

It was more that he did not know what to do with her. His father had never included his mother in ruling Kostaria.

She had birthed him two sons and fulfilled her only purpose. After that, he'd had no more use for her.

Had Rharreth accidentally turned into his father, despite his best intentions?

He tilted his head toward the crowd. "Let's discuss this later, all right? For now, my queen, would you like to join me in distributing food to our people?"

While some of the fire left her eyes, she still studied him as if she thought those might just be fancy words he was using to temporarily mollify her.

Perhaps he was. But this wasn't an argument he wanted to have in front of all of Osmana.

"Fine." Melantha raised her chin and stalked back to the front of the wagon.

Rharreth joined her and took over the task of handing out the grain and other supplies they had been given by the Escarlish army. Melantha soon caught on to the system and handed him the individual sacks after Zavni measured out the portions.

The longer they worked, the more the look on Melantha's face softened. Did she see the same thing Rharreth did when he looked out over his people? Did her heart ache at the hunger written across the gaunt faces, the skeletal arms, and the hollow eyes, especially among the regular citizens?

A group of warriors from some of the most influential families in Osmana gathered at the far side of the road, glaring toward the wagons, Rharreth, and especially at Melantha.

One of them stomped his feet and shouted, "We won't take any food given out of charity from the stinking elves!"

The other warriors stomped and howled in response.

Drurvas glanced over his shoulder, his amber eyes narrowing as if saying *I told you so*.

Still, the mothers with the young children hunched their shoulders, kept their heads down, and pressed toward the food, clutching the tiny hands of children whose stomachs were distended, their arms nothing but bone covered with too-tight skin.

They were the reason Rharreth was doing this, no matter how unpopular it made him among the warrior families.

When the next mother and child approached the wagon, Melantha held out a hand to the child but kept an eye on the mother. Her smile was softer and more genuine than anything Rharreth had yet to see on her face. "I am a healer. I can restore your child's strength and health and heal the effects of malnutrition."

The mother snatched her child away from Melantha's hand. "Keep your filthy elf hands away from my son. We don't need your help."

Spinning on her heel, she marched away without even bothering to claim the portion of grain Rharreth held out.

Melantha straightened, her eyes blazing again, her jaw set in that hard, stubborn line of hers. She muttered under her breath in a tone Rharreth probably was not supposed to hear, "Fine. Let your child die rather than accept my help. See if I care."

Rharreth found himself staring at her. She was back to angry now, but, for a moment there, she had been truly offering to help. It had made her...beautiful. More beautiful even than she had looked when she had faced down Charvod in the dungeon.

He was not sure he could name what stirred inside his

chest. Nor did he want to examine it while standing in front of an angry mob in Osmana.

Instead, he gave Melantha a nod. "Please, do not give up on all of them. Thank you for offering to help."

She raised her eyebrows at him, as if she was surprised by his response. What had she expected? That he would tell her to go back to the stronghold and stay out of the way?

Perhaps there was more truth than he wanted to admit to her accusations. He had not even considered that she could help. Nor had it occurred to him that she would want to do so.

"Please." Another voice, this one lowered and desperate, drew his gaze away from Melantha.

Another woman had worked her way to the front of the line. Her gray face was haggard, her white hair straggling down her shoulders. In her arms, she clutched a small child. Its body was so wasted, Rharreth couldn't guess if the child was a boy or girl, much less the child's age. The child's stomach was distended while its mouth gaped open. It spasmed in its mother's arms.

Rharreth's chest hurt. He'd seen this far too many times. The child was dying, its organs shutting down after prolonged starvation.

The mother peered up at them, tears glistening in her eyes. She focused on Melantha. "Is it true that you are an elf healer? Could you please help my daughter?"

Melantha knelt on the edge of the wagon and reached forward, her fingers glowing green. As soon as she touched the girl's forehead, Melantha's face twisted, as if in pain. She squeezed her eyes shut, the glow around her fingers strengthening.

Rharreth crouched next to Melantha, reaching for her but

stopping short of touching her. He was not sure what to do, and he saw the same helplessness mirrored in the mother's eyes.

Melantha shuddered, her breathing growing ragged. A bead of sweat formed at her temple.

But, the child's spasming calmed, the pallor under her gray skin retreating to a healthier glow.

When Melantha withdrew her hand, she sagged, and this time Rharreth didn't hesitate. He caught her by the shoulders, steadying her as she sucked in deep breaths.

After a moment, Melantha turned to the woman. "Your daughter is stabilized, for now. But you will need to get some food into her soon. My magic will keep her alive for only so long."

"Thank you, my lady. Thank you." The troll woman hugged her daughter, tears pouring down her face freely.

Rharreth felt the weight as Zavni set a sack of food into his outstretched palm. Rharreth held out the food. "This will help."

The woman took it, clutching it to her. "Thank you, Sire."

Melantha gestured to the pouch of grain. "Make sure to cook the grain into a mash for your daughter. Give her only small portions at first. Her body will need time to adjust to receiving nourishment. Actually, could you give it back to me for a moment?"

It was a sign of the woman's trust in Melantha that she gave the precious food back.

Melantha opened the sack, then her fingers glowed green once again. She stuck her hand inside, and green light shone from the bag. After a moment, she closed the sack again and held it out to the woman. "I infused the grain with my magic. It will help both you and your daughter regain your strength."

The woman bobbed a bow to each of them, then hurried off.

As the next mother and child stepped into line, Rharreth motioned for Zavni to see to them. Rharreth tugged Melantha to her feet and studied her face. "I did not know you could put your magic into food."

"We healers can infuse anything that was once a plant with healing properties. It is part of the close tie shared between healing magic and growing magic." Melantha gave a small shrug, then glanced over the crowd once again. "I just infused it with a little bit. It is nothing harmful, I assure you."

"I did not think it was." Rharreth struggled to find the words. He had married her for peace. He had wanted peace for the food Escarland could provide. But he had not believed that she would use her magic on behalf of his people. How could he, knowing little of how the elven healing worked, even imagine all that Melantha could do with her magic?

Between the trade for food that she brought and her power, she was more capable of saving Kostaria than he had even dreamed she was.

And he was not sure how to go about telling her that without making her mad at him.

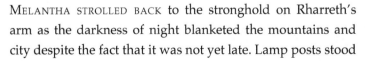

MELANTHA STROLLED BACK to the stronghold on Rharreth's arm as the darkness of night blanketed the mountains and city despite the fact that it was not yet late. Lamp posts stood along the streets, the candles inside providing some light to the streets. More light spilled from the windows of the houses they passed.

She gritted her teeth and kept her mask in place. That day, handing out the food, had been unexpected. The mix of anger and deep hurt that she had seen in the trolls had resonated inside Melantha's chest. Perhaps because it was the same thing she felt every day. Seething anger covering a festering pain that she could not heal even with her magic.

She could not heal herself, but something in her stirred to want to heal these people. Back in Tarenhiel, there were so many healers of various strengths that her magic had just seemed useless and redundant. But here in Kostaria, she was the only healer in the entire kingdom.

But she had not wanted to be a healer, had she? Then why had the fire inside her cooled when she had healed that troll child?

The fire returned when she glanced at Rharreth at her side. He had been so attentive. Giving her those warm looks, as though he found something to respect about her.

And yet, that could not be the case. Otherwise he never would have left her behind in the first place. He would not have done his best to ignore her for the past few days.

When they reached the stronghold, Rharreth asked a servant to bring a tray with supper, then he led Melantha through the passageways. By the time they reached their room, Melantha was one word away from boiling over.

As soon as the door shut behind him, Rharreth turned to face her, leaving space between them. "I promised that we would talk later."

"Yes, you did." Melantha swallowed back the heat, keeping her mask in place. She was an elven princess. An elven princess was serene. Calm. Not a roiling, seething, barely contained explosion.

Rharreth studied her face. "Why do you always do that?"

"Do what?" Melantha clasped her hands gracefully in front of her.

"Hide your true thoughts and feelings." Rharreth's deep blue eyes searched her face. "I have seen your fire. You don't have to hide it."

Oh, he thought he knew her fire. He had not seen anything yet. Melantha took a step back, her skin burning with the heat crackling inside her chest. "I will only let down my calm if you drop your own icy mask."

"I don't—" Rharreth blinked at her, as if he did not even realize he had a mask of his own.

"Do not play innocent with me." Melantha jabbed his chest with her finger. His leather vest had little give to it, and the pain that jammed up her finger only added fuel to the heat swirling through her head. "You act all kind and honorable, but in reality, you only do the bare minimum that honor demands. You rarely act with any passion or do anything that would truly risk yourself."

Rharreth gaped at her, his jaw working.

He was not even going to bother saying anything? Melantha bit back a scream, even if some of it still slipped through her teeth. "You do not even see it, do you? You have been the spare too long. Until now, your only duty was to exist. I know. I was my brother's spare until his children were born. But now you are the king. You need to do more than merely exist. And that begins with how you treat me."

"I don't—"

She was in no mood to hear his excuses or explanations. "Right now, I am barely your wife. I am definitely not your queen. If all you wish for me to be is an ice queen who stands at your side during formal ceremonies, then fine. That is what I will be. But if you want my fire, if you want me to truly be your queen, then you have to stop shutting me out and start treating me like you think this marriage is going to last longer than a month or two, depending on how long it takes for some assassin to get to me."

Melantha found herself jabbing Rharreth in the chest yet again. The pain was somehow satisfying. "You want to know why I act calm and serene? It is because that was how the elven nobility expect an elf princess to act. Well, I am in Kostaria now. Teach me how you want your troll queen to act, and that is what I will become."

Rharreth stepped closer to her again. He cupped her chin, tipping her head up so that she met his gaze. "I'm not asking you to pretend to be something you are not. I want you to be yourself. I like the fire I see in your eyes."

For a moment, Melantha stilled. His fingers were gentle beneath her chin, his face only a few inches from hers. The heat inside her twisted into something less painful and more a pleasant tingle.

What was going on? She had never felt like this before, not even with Hatharal, the elf she had been betrothed to marry.

No, Hatharal had looked at the fire and told her to bury it. He had said it was unbecoming of an elf princess.

Melantha stepped back from Rharreth's grip, digging deep for the remnants of the heat in her chest. "I will only stop pretending if you do. You claim to be honorable, but I know your honor has limits. You did not torture my brother, but neither did you protest his treatment. You allowed me to help him, but you only helped him when you thought your brother would not find out. About the only time you ever risked yourself was when you took that whipping in an attempt to spare me. Why did you even do that? Why would you stand up to your brother when you had not until then?"

Rharreth's mouth was a thin line, but his gaze was thoughtful. When she met his gaze, he gave a slight nod, as if to acknowledge the truth of her words. "You were not a captured warrior and should not have been treated as one. It is not honorable to beat the helpless."

He said the last sentence with such vehemence that Melantha knew he was not talking only about what was done to her.

His brother, King Charvod, had been cruel, and he had learned that cruelty from his father, King Vorlec. King Vorlec had been cruel enough to torture a teenage Farrendel.

Rharreth would also have been a young man at that point. While trolls lived longer than humans, they aged faster than elves, living about five hundred years instead of nearly a thousand. So Rharreth would have been around the same age Farrendel was now, though he had aged faster than Farrendel had in the past fifteen years, making Rharreth roughly Melantha's age now.

If King Vorlec had been willing to torture a teenage elf, what would he have been willing to do to a young Rharreth? What about Rharreth's mother?

Melantha remembered how Rharreth had said his father and brother often lived in Gror Grar while Rharreth and his mother lived here in Khagniorth. It did not sound like a happy family. Melantha's own family had their problems—most of them recently caused by her—but at least they had been happy growing up. She had always known her father loved her and would sacrifice anything for their family.

Perhaps that was why his betrayal of her mother's memory with Farrendel's mother had been so shocking to all of them. Even if he had spent the last ninety years of his life owning up to his transgressions and doing his best to fix what he had broken.

For the first time, Melantha understood how it was possible to fail so completely. Would she be able to restore what she had broken?

Maybe. But, first, she had to figure out how to build this new relationship. Perhaps, in learning how to build this relationship, she would figure out how to fix the ones she had destroyed.

She tipped her head up to meet Rharreth's gaze. "I know you are not your father or your brother."

As if realizing Melantha's fire had been temporarily spent, Rharreth reached toward her but stopped short of touching her. "I see how I have not expended myself as I ought when it comes to you or the kingdom. I didn't wish to appear as if I was expecting you to become something you are not. You are an elf. I don't want you to feel as if I'm trying to turn you into a troll."

It was good of him to worry about such a thing. Melantha felt something like a smile cracking the mask she had trained herself to wear. "Thank you for not pressuring me."

All those years in her home in Tarenhiel, she had tried to hide the passionate part of herself. Yet, Rharreth had taken her anger and had not flinched away. Was this her chance to stop hiding the heat and turn all that passion inside her toward truly living?

Deciding to be daring, Melantha rested her hands on Rharreth's chest, his leather vest smooth beneath her fingers.

"But I do want to acclimate to your culture. I am willing to try new clothes or new ways of thinking or doing things. This is my new home and new life. There is no point in holding back. Instead, I want to embrace it as fully as possible."

"And I promise that you don't have to pretend with me. If there is something you don't want to do or don't want to adopt, then feel free to tell me. Here, when it is just us, you are free to be angry or frustrated or whatever else. I can take it." Rharreth's mouth quirked at the corner. "I also promise that I will work to include you as my queen. You are right. This is our life now, and I've been treating you like I expect this marriage to be temporary instead of like I expect you to truly be my queen. I'm sorry for that. And I'm sorry for how you were treated in the dungeon of Gror Grar."

It was a start. A better start than Melantha had the right to expect.

Perhaps she and Rharreth had a chance to form some kind of relationship based on mutual respect. Not that Melantha was expecting a passionate, romantic love. She was not a hopeless, naïve optimist like Princess Elspeth, after all. Besides, it was not like Melantha knew how to love, if her treatment of her own brother was any indication.

But maybe Farrendel had been right. Perhaps Melantha might not find love, but here in Kostaria, she might find freedom. Just then, that seemed even better.

CHAPTER
ELEVEN

Farrendel's eyes were gritty after staring into the forest half the night. It was the closest thing he had found to rest, even after the mug of hot chocolate Essie had brought him in the middle of the night.

He should get up. If he did not, Essie or whoever Weylind sent would come here to drag him from his room.

He could either convince himself to get up, or he might end up hauled across Ellonahshinel to Rheva's father hanging over his brother's shoulder like a sack of grain.

Picturing that embarrassment provided enough energy to push onto his elbows, then to his hands and knees. His muscles and joints ached. Lying on the wooden porch was not the best way to rest or recover from those weeks of torture.

Farrendel used the wall to get all the way to his feet. So tired. Still so sore. He could barely totter around. A far cry from the flips he used to do each morning.

He could hear voices down in the main room. As he had

guessed, Weylind had sent someone. Perhaps Weylind himself had come to hover.

It took far too long to navigate the stairs. Perhaps Essie was onto something when she kept talking about adding handrails.

He stepped into the main room, past where the ruined door leaned against the wall. There, he found Essie grinning and dishing cold meat and cheese onto a plate. Across from her, Machasheni Leyleira held another plate and nibbled on a piece of cheese.

Farrendel leaned against the doorjamb. Weylind was playing dirty.

"Sasonsheni." Machasheni set aside her plate, crossed the room, and gripped Farrendel's shoulders. "You are not looking well. Come. You must sit and eat, and then we will leave. Elspetha, do you have that plate?"

Somehow, Farrendel found himself steered to the table, nudged into a chair, and a plate set in front of him. Machasheni Leyleira reclaimed her own plate, perched in the chair across from Farrendel, and nibbled daintily at her breakfast. She gave Farrendel a stern look.

He dug into his food. With Machasheni giving him that look, he did not dare do anything but attempt to finish everything on his plate.

Essie grabbed one of the cushions from the other side of the room, plopped it on the floor next to Farrendel's chair, and sat on it with her own plate of breakfast. Farrendel would have offered her a chair, but Machasheni had placed him in this one, and he did not dare move. Not to mention, Essie was grinning and seemed perfectly happy sitting on the cushion on the floor.

He was down to only a few pieces of cheese. His stomach felt tight and full for the first time in weeks.

With a smirk, Essie slipped another piece of meat on his plate.

He pointed at it. "I am not eating that."

"It's on your plate." Essie picked up one of two pieces of cheese on her plate, eyeing him as if waiting for him to look away so she could slip it onto his plate as well.

"Do not do it." Farrendel tried to glare at her, but it was hard to keep even the fake expression in place while she was smirking at him like that.

Machasheni raised her eyebrows. "I agree with Elspetha. It is on your plate. It is yours to finish."

Great. They were already ganging up on him. It would be a long day at this rate.

Still, as he forced himself to eat the last few bites and hoped his stomach expanded enough to fit it all, he felt more alive than he had in far too long. It was a small spark of life, buried beneath all his weariness and the fog still swirling through his head, but it was there.

ESSIE COULD NOT HAVE BEEN MORE thankful Leyleira had come that morning. Somehow, she'd convinced Farrendel to eat an entire plateful of breakfast with no more cajoling than a stern look. Then she had herded him out the door and through the winding branches of Ellonahshinel so skillfully that Farrendel hadn't even had a chance to balk.

All Essie had to do was trot to keep up. After a sleepless night of Farrendel's nightmares and her own worries about having to drag Farrendel to Taranath's rooms somewhere in a part of Ellonahshinel that Essie had yet to explore, it was a relief to have the matter taken out of her hands.

It took nearly half an hour to navigate the branches to one of the lower sections on the far side of the tree palace. Like Farrendel's rooms, this area of the treetop palace was quiet with only a few other treetop rooms grown into the branches in the far distance from the sprawling set of five rooms that Leyleira led them toward.

Stepping onto a porch that had two padded benches on either side, Leyleira knocked on the door, then opened it without waiting. She swept inside. "Taranath, your morning patient is here, if you can pull yourself away from your research long enough."

Essie glanced at Farrendel and nudged him to go in first. She wouldn't put it past him to make a run for it the moment her back was turned.

The hexagonal room was larger even than her and Farrendel's main room. Essie glanced around, unable to place the faint herbal smell that clung to the air. Cupboards and a wooden countertop filled half the room while the other half was ringed with shelves stuffed with jars holding a variety of pastes, creams, herbal mixtures, and mysterious liquids ranging in color from green to a bright watermelon pink.

The only breaks in the cupboards were a few padded benches grown into the wall. A wooden table stood in the center with a leather pillow at one end.

An old male elf stood near the countertop fussing with a few of the jars, his long hair completely white, though when he looked at them, his deep brown eyes were sharp and clear. "Ah, yes. Farrendel. My favorite patient."

"Since you are retired, he is your only patient." When

Leyleira glanced at Taranath, her smile was softer than anything Essie had seen on her before. "I will take a seat outside to wait, if that is all right."

"Of course, Leyleira. You are always welcome here. You know that." The smile on Taranath's face was also filled with meaning.

Essie shifted, almost feeling like she and Farrendel were the ones who should leave these two alone. She glanced at Farrendel, but he only shook his head and shrugged, as if just as confused as she was.

Sweeping gracefully across the room, Leyleira disappeared outside. The back of her head was visible through the window as she took a seat on a bench and pulled out a book.

Taranath turned to face Essie and gave a small bob of his head. "I am Taranath, Queen Rheva's dacha. I have heard much about our Farrendel's human princess."

If he'd been hearing about her from Weylind and Rheva, then she wasn't sure what he'd been told. From Weylind, it probably hadn't been good. From Rheva? Essie wasn't sure. Probably something along the lines of reserving judgment until they'd had a chance to chat, which they hadn't done until yesterday.

But Essie found herself smiling anyway. Taranath's smile was too sincere, his eyes twinkling, for Essie to stay tense and formal. "If you've been talking to Weylind, then I'm sure you got an earful."

"Yes. Quite hypocritical of him, considering his own scandal when he married my daughter." Taranath shook his head and turned away from them to start assembling jars and liquids on the countertop. "Most have forgotten the scandal now, but it was quite the to-do when the future king chose to marry the lowly daughter of a healer instead of one of the nobility."

Essie felt the tension leaving her shoulders at Taranath's rambling. She hadn't known that bit of history about Farrendel's family. It seemed none of his siblings, except Jalissa so far, was immune to causing scandal.

Though, admittedly, it was all too easy to cause a scandal in the elven court.

"But you are not here to hear such long-forgotten family history." Taranath turned and patted the exam table. "Farrendel, young elfling, let us take a look at that brain of yours."

Farrendel was still lingering by the door, shifting as if he was thinking about making a run for it. Not that Essie could entirely blame him. She would be a tad nervous about someone rooting around her brain with magic, even an elf who, presumably, knew what he was doing.

After a moment, Farrendel perched on the table, eyeing Taranath warily. With a deep breath, he lay down. But only a heartbeat later, he stiffened, his breathing going first ragged, then escalating into hyperventilating.

Essie stepped closer, reaching out to take his hand. Before she could, he bolted upright again, hunching and gasping.

"If you are going to vomit, please do so out the window. The maid just cleaned the floor." Taranath turned from the countertop and shuffled to the head of the exam table.

Farrendel hung his head, gripping the edge of the table, but his breathing steadied after a moment.

Essie took his hand, and he squeezed her fingers tightly enough to be painful. Lying on his back probably felt too much like being pinned to the floor of that dungeon cell, helpless and in pain. She glanced at Taranath. "Can he sit up instead of lying down?"

"He may feel dizzy, and I am not about to catch him if he faints." Taranath patted the table again, his fingers glowing faintly green. "I can sedate you, if you wish."

Farrendel shook his head and straightened his shoulders. With yet another deep breath, he lay back down, still gripping Essie's hand. This time, he squeezed his eyes shut, and his breathing remained too steady.

The silence felt strained, but even Essie couldn't think of something to talk about. She rested a hand on Farrendel's shoulder as Taranath set a hand glowing with green magic on Farrendel's forehead.

Farrendel flinched, but he did not seem to be in pain.

Essie cleared her throat. "You must be proud, having a daughter who became queen of the elves."

"Of course. But I was proud of her even before she married Weylind." Taranath had his eyes closed as well, as if he was seeing what his magic was showing him. "My late wife and I thought we would never have children, but then we had Rheva late in life. She has been my pride and joy ever since."

The warmth in his voice made Essie smile, even if he couldn't see it. He had the same parental pride about Rheva that Essie heard in her mother's voice about Essie and her siblings.

Was she bothering Taranath with her talking? The last thing she would want to do was distract him into making a mistake while he was using magic inside of Farrendel's head.

Taranath withdrew his hand and the green glow faded.

"All done. You may sit up, though I suggest doing it slowly."

Farrendel swung upright, and something in his expression seemed less tight and worn than it had been a few moments ago.

Taranath returned to the countertop, muttering to himself as the green glow surrounded his hand again. He filled one of the jars with the light pink liquid and stirred in some of his magic. A moment later, he did the same with a deeper burgundy liquid.

After capping both jars, he returned to the table and held the jars out to Farrendel. "Take one dose of the pink, strawberry-flavored medicine each morning. The other jar is a blackberry-flavored sedative. Take one dose before bed for at least the next week, and as needed after that. Lack of sleep just aggravates your nightmares."

Essie made a mental note of those instructions. Farrendel most likely would take them on his own, but she didn't know what to expect out of him lately.

Farrendel let go of Essie's hand to take the jars, studying them with a frown.

Taranath crossed his arms. "It is not weakness to accept help. If a warrior returned from battle missing a leg, you would not tell him that he should be tough enough to walk without the help of a crutch. He needs that crutch to restore what he lost and help him live his life. This"—Taranath tapped one of the jars—"is your crutch. Your wound from the war is to your mind, but that does not make it less real. Maybe someday you will be able to wean off the medicine, as you did before. Maybe not. But, for now, this is what you need to function."

Farrendel still stared down at the jars in his hands, but his legs swung like he was a child too short for a chair.

Taranath glanced between Essie and Farrendel before he focused, interestingly enough, on Essie. "There is something else I would suggest. It was not an option last time, but the treaty with Escarland has changed that."

Now Essie was the one frowning. "There's something in Escarland that can help? I would have thought you elves were the most advanced in regards to medicine."

"Yes, we are, though few elf healers can examine the chemical level the way I can." Taranath shrugged, as if that wasn't a boast but a statement of fact. "But, the mind is more than just chemicals. There is also your heart and your soul, which I cannot heal. Yet, without having the access to healing magic, the physicians in Escarland have made some amazing strides in that regard. Recently, I have heard of an Escarlish couple who specializes in counseling warriors who have struggles like yours, Farrendel."

Essie straightened. "My brother Julien mentioned them. At least, I think it is the same couple. Though, I wouldn't think there are too many other couples working in that field, so it must be the same people. He'd heard good things about them as well, and he was looking into whether they were legitimate."

"If they use the counseling methods I have heard about, then I believe they are. They might be able to help your mind while I help your brain." Taranath nodded sharply, his white hair sliding across his shoulders. "Years ago, I would not have recommended Escarland's primitive methods. They were based more in superstition than knowledge. But this couple seems to have done their research, and I would be interested in learning more, if you would share once you return."

"I guess we need to go to Escarland." Essie met Farrendel's gaze. "If you're all right with that?"

His rooms in Tarenhiel were his sanctuary. He might not want to leave their safety, not even to travel to Escarland.

Yet, after a few seconds, Farrendel nodded. "If it is necessary, then we should go."

Perhaps Taranath's magic was still in Farrendel's system, helping him feel more like himself, if he was agreeing to packing up and leaving so readily.

Essie gestured to Taranath. "Why don't you come with us? You could observe their methods yourself." And make sure what they were doing was not something harmful rather than helpful to Farrendel. But she didn't say that. She didn't want Farrendel to worry.

"Really? I could come along?" Taranath eyes lit up.

Essie waved at herself. "Of course. I am the princess of Escarland."

Taranath turned back to his countertop. "This will be such an opportunity."

Essie glanced at Farrendel as they stood there for a moment, ignored as Taranath bustled around, already packing.

After a minute, he seemed to remember they were there and hustled them outside, all but shutting the door in their faces as he continued muttering to himself.

Leyleira stood, her eyebrows rising in a question. Essie gave a quick explanation and ended with how they were leaving for Escarland.

Leyleira patted Essie's shoulder. "Do not worry about anything. I will have the train ready shortly."

Essie didn't doubt it. As she and Farrendel stepped onto the branch to stroll back to their rooms, Essie held out a hand to Farrendel to offer to carry one of the jars.

Instead of handing her a jar, Farrendel switched both jars to one arm, hugging one between his body and his arm, then took her hand.

Essie clasped his hand, her chest expanding with so much happiness she might skip or squeal or something. She hadn't expected him to take her hand. He hadn't been that demonstrative in the past few days, too curled up inside himself to reach out to her.

It was a start, even if he was still blocking her through the heart bond.

With a smile that stretched as wide as it would go, Essie took the jar he had been hugging before he dropped it. "Are you feeling better?"

"Yes." For the first time since he'd been rescued, Farrendel's shoulders weren't tensed. "My mind is clear, and I can actually think."

"I'm glad this was worth the walk." Essie leaned closer to Farrendel, swinging their clasped hands. She'd missed this so very much. She had missed *him*.

But at least now she had hope that things could finally start to get better.

CHAPTER
TWELVE

L eyleira turned out to be even better than her word. Within a couple of hours, she had the train waiting at the station, all of their things loaded, and had informed Essie's family that they were on their way.

They gave brief farewells to Weylind, Rheva, and Leyleira, and Weylind mentioned that they might meet Jalissa at the border. Apparently, she had been looking for a reason to turn her duties as ambassador over to someone else, and Essie and Farrendel would provide Tarenhiel with enough representation that Jalissa could return home.

Iyrinder, an elf who normally served as a guard for Weylind, joined them with a pack slung over a shoulder.

Weylind had given Farrendel a stern look. "I know you do not prefer guards. But do not fight me on this. Your human brother Averett will explain more when you arrive. But just know that we intend to keep you well guarded, especially in Escarland."

That last was said with a quirk to Weylind's mouth, rather than the heat it would have held before. He might find humor in tweaking Averett's and Escarland's failings, but he knew as well as they all did that there had been plenty of failures and gaps in security to go around.

Farrendel scowled, but he nodded and didn't protest.

As they were about to board, Illyna hurried toward them out of the bustle of Estyra. Her gaze swept over Farrendel, taking in his appearance. "Do not think you can skip out on all of us that easily. We were all worried."

Essie gripped Farrendel's hand. She did feel bad that she and Farrendel hadn't had a chance to greet all of his elven friends who had fought in whatever way they could by keeping the supply chain running or making healing balms the way Illyna had during the war.

"I know." Farrendel glanced at Illyna before his gaze dropped down to the moss beneath their feet.

Illyna dug into the satchel she wore and pulled out two jars filled with a slightly green, viscous cream. "Here. I was on my way to Ellonahshinel to give these to you, then learned you were heading to Escarland. I made more shampoo and conditioner for you, and these have extra magic in them so they should help your hair grow faster."

Farrendel stiffened, but he took one of the jars. "Linshi."

Essie took the other, since she wasn't about to let Farrendel drop her hand to take it. "Thanks once again, Illyna. I'm not sure when we'll be back, but I'll be sure to write."

After a few more farewells, Essie, Farrendel, Taranath, and Iyrinder boarded the train and were on their way. Farrendel slept most of time, a deep and nightmare-free sleep, due to Taranath's magic.

An elven boat took them across the Hydalla River and docked on the Escarlish shore where they boarded the

Escarlish train that transported them the rest of the way to Aldon.

Finally, the train screeched to a halt at the station inside Winstead Palace late in the afternoon, a full day after they had left Tarenhiel.

Essie pulled Farrendel to his feet. He seemed wrung out by the journey, but at least he didn't resist as she tugged him to the door of the train car.

As she stepped to the platform to one side of the large, stone Winstead Palace, she found her mother, her sister-in-law Paige, Averett, and Julien waiting for them. Her mother had deep auburn hair streaked with white. Smile lines grooved into her forehead and around her eyes and mouth.

Essie let go of Farrendel's hand, dashed to her mother, and hugged her tightly. The tension released from her shoulders as her mother embraced her, rubbing her back. It was all Essie could do to stop herself from bursting into tears right then and there. She murmured low enough that only her mother could hear, "It has been so hard, Mama."

"I know. I know." Her mother gave her a tight squeeze. "If you need to talk, I'm here."

"Of course." Essie blinked, dabbing at her eyes as she stepped back. She had done enough crying lately.

Her mother turned to Farrendel, where he stood shifting from foot to foot and staring at the ground as if he was thinking about fleeing. Mother held out her arms. "And you, sason? Is that the correct elven word? Do you want a hug?"

Farrendel lifted his head, his silver-blue eyes wide. "Macha." He stepped forward and hugged her tightly, so tightly it seemed to take Mother back a step.

Essie's throat tightened, hearing Farrendel call her mother the informal *macha*, something he hadn't done the last time they were in Escarland when he had stuck to the more formal *mamasha*.

Mother patted his back. "I am so glad you're safe. That you're all safe."

"We were so worried." Paige wrapped Essie in a hug. Paige's blonde hair was braided and wrapped around her head to form a crown of hair with a diamond clip tucked into the top. When she stepped back, Paige gave a small, tentative grin, as if she wasn't sure grinning was appropriate right now. "But very impressed at the way you fought across Kostaria to get your elf back."

"I was rather determined." It felt good to smile about those awful weeks. As Averett wrapped his arm around Essie in a side hug, Essie poked him while still facing Paige. "You should have seen Avie. He went into full-on king mode and bossed everyone around."

"I'm sure he did." Paige stood on her tiptoes and kissed Averett on the cheek.

Taranath and Iyrinder disembarked from the train, and Essie made introductions. Then, while servants came to collect their luggage, Essie gripped Farrendel's hand and started off through the gardens toward Buckmore Cottage on the other side of the palace from the train station.

Averett and Paige fell into step with Essie and Farrendel while Mother started up a conversation with Taranath. Julien and Iyrinder took up the rear, already talking quietly. The rapport they had built while guarding their respective kings during the war was still holding strong.

Averett glanced between Essie and Farrendel. "I have an appointment set up for tomorrow afternoon with Mr. and Mrs. Harwell. They have been thoroughly vetted and already signed non-disclosure agreements. They will come to Buckmore Cottage. Hopefully that is all right? Is tomorrow too soon?"

Farrendel's fingers tightened on Essie's hand, but he shook his head. "The sooner, the better."

"That was the impression I got." Averett studied first Essie, then Farrendel. His mouth flattened into a line, as if he could tell from each dark circle and tense muscle that neither of them was anything near all right.

"You might also notice a few extra guards around. Weylind and I agreed that both you and Essie need to be guarded more carefully." Averett frowned and glanced toward Winstead Palace, as if he still resented the fact that Farrendel and Essie had been kidnapped in his own palace. "We'll introduce you to your new guard captain later, once you're settled."

"I did hire the guard captain's sister as a temporary cook and housekeeper for you." Paige leaned around Averett, searching Essie's face as if worried Essie would find it presumptuous that Paige would hire a servant for her. "I know you'll probably want to hire your own servants eventually, and she knows her position is likely only temporary. But she has the security clearance, and I think you'll like her."

From anyone else, Essie might have resented it. But Paige was a good judge of character, and she knew Essie well enough to know the kind of servant who would best fit her.

Beside Essie, Farrendel stiffened, his stance going wary.

Essie patted his arm. "I know you aren't used to having a lot of servants around. But Buckmore Cottage is a big place and having our own cook and housekeeper will cut down on the number of servants carrying food from Winstead Palace and seeing to the Cottage on top of their other duties. It means we'll only have one person to get to know and trust instead of several."

Not all of Farrendel's wariness disappeared, but at least he wasn't quite as stiff.

They stepped from the tunnel of trees into the back garden of Buckmore Cottage. Last time they had been there, Jalissa had added her magic to the cottage, growing branches and vines. It had looked odd, combining elven and human architecture styles. It still looked odd now, though the orange autumn leaves did pop against the light blue paint of the manor house's siding.

Essie halted and drew in a deep breath. Perhaps, in this place, Farrendel would find peace of mind and soul.

Farrendel kept walking, as if fleeing her family.

"Farrendel, before you go." Julien hurried forward. "I'll be here first thing in the morning for a training session."

"Training session? Really, Julien?" Essie stepped between Farrendel and Julien. Couldn't her brother see that Farrendel was in no shape for training?

Julien crossed his arms, his gaze focused over Essie's head to stare at Farrendel. "Yes. It will be good for him."

Farrendel turned to face Julien, raising his head.

"What do you say, Farrendel?" Julien held his gaze, unflinching.

Farrendel nodded. "I will be there." With that, he spun on his heel and all but ran into Buckmore Cottage. He had apparently reached the end of his tolerance for people that day.

"Trust me. I know what I'm doing, Essie." Julien patted her shoulder before turning to Iyrinder. "I'll introduce you to the other guards and show you where you'll be bunking."

Iyrinder gave a small nod and followed Julien around

the side of Buckmore Cottage, probably headed to the small guardhouse that stood by the gate in the surrounding wall.

Mother gave Essie another hug as she passed, then she waved to Taranath. "And I'll show you to your room on the ground floor of the Cottage."

"Let me know if you need anything." Paige gave Essie another hug. "And when you're both up for it, the boys will be excited to see you again. We didn't even tell them you were coming yet, since they would beg to see you if they knew."

"We'll try to have a family supper just as soon as we can." Essie hugged Paige back, then leaned into Averett's side hug. It felt so good to be hugged again. While Essie appreciated the support of Farrendel's family, none of them hugged the way her family did.

When she finally could convince herself to pull away, Essie entered Buckmore Cottage, the memories she had with Farrendel here enveloping her. Things had been so right, before it had all gone so wrong.

Inside, Essie glanced around, then headed up the stairs. As expected, she found Farrendel in the turret bedroom that they had claimed last time. The walls were covered in a light blue wallpaper with white wainscoting. Windows were set into each wall, looking out over the garden and the large forested parkland that made up the grounds of Winstead Palace. The bed sat beneath one of the windows while a small dressing table and a mirror filled the space along the inner wall.

Farrendel sat cross-legged on the bed, staring down at his hands. His ragged hair flopped across his forehead.

Essie sat on the bed facing him. "Are you all right? I

know my family was probably overwhelming. They're just happy you're safe."

"It is not that. I love your family." Farrendel still stared at his hands. "Tonight...I am not sure if I am safe to be near."

"You didn't have any nightmares last night, on the train." Essie wanted to reach for him but didn't dare. Not yet.

Farrendel gave a small shrug. "Taranath's sedative kept me sleeping deeply. But we cannot assume that it will always prevent me from lashing out in my sleep."

Now Essie was the one staring at her hands. She didn't want to offer to sleep in another room here. While it had been bad enough back in Estyra, they had slept in separate bedrooms there before, when they had first been married and had been strangers.

But here in Buckmore Cottage, this had always been their room. Together. It seemed wrong to do anything else.

The bed was bigger than the one in Estyra. If they each slept on the far side from each other, they would probably be fine, even if Farrendel flailed in his sleep.

But Essie knew he wouldn't want to risk it.

"I have an idea." Essie patted Farrendel's knee, then rolled off the bed to her feet. "Come on. I'll need your help to carry all the pillows."

"Pillows?" Farrendel trailed after her as she strode out of the room.

With the housekeeper and Taranath sleeping on the ground floor, Essie and Farrendel had the upper floor all to themselves. Essie went from room to room, stripping the beds, settees, and chairs of all the pillows she could find.

When she and Farrendel returned to their room with their arms piled with pillows, Essie built a wall of pillows down the center of the bed, then lined the wall for good measure. Might as well protect Farrendel from another set of bruised knuckles.

When she finished, she stood back and gave a nod. "There. How's this?"

Farrendel crawled onto the bed, then sat in the center of the nest of pillows. His nose wrinkled as he frowned at the wall of pillows. "I now have my own padded cell."

Oops. That wasn't what she meant it to look like. Essie sat on her side of the bed facing him. She didn't really like the wall between them either, even if it was only pillows. But she forced cheeriness into her voice. "No, you have your own pillow fort."

She took one of the top pillows from the wall and swung it at his head, though she did it slowly to avoid startling him.

Farrendel blocked the pillow with an arm, though he didn't smile as she'd hoped.

"Ah, I see. You're not the pillow fight kind of person. Maybe you're the read-a-book-under-a-blanket kind of pillow fort person." Essie plopped the pillow back into its spot. "I'm sure that Escarlish history book you started reading last time is still around here somewhere."

That earned a twitch of a smile. But it faded quickly. "I never should have locked you out in Estyra. I should have known you would come up with a creative, better solution."

He hadn't been thinking, too caught up in whatever fog he'd been stuck in. That still didn't make what he'd done right or take away the lingering sting. Especially since, while he was no longer locking her out physically, he was still keeping the wall between them in the heart bond.

But Essie was thankful he was at a point where he could see that locking her out had been a problem. And she could forgive him. He had made a mistake, but it was not something that was a part of his normal behavior.

She leaned across the pillow wall and kissed his cheek. "Just don't ever, ever do it again."

"I will not." Farrendel reached across the pillows and clasped her hands.

The gesture was tentative, but it was a start. Surely things would only get better from here.

CHAPTER
THIRTEEN

Farrendel woke groggy and dry-mouthed. He stifled a groan against his pillow. This was the part of taking a sedative that he always hated. At least the elven magic was better than that human drug the trolls had used on him. That drug had given him nausea and a headache on top of the grogginess.

A part of him did not want to get up. That weight was back, the fog in his head telling him that he should not care about Julien or exercising or climbing out of bed. It would be so much easier if he did not move.

But Julien was waiting, and Farrendel would not put it past him to march up there and drag him out of bed if that was what it took. It seemed all his brothers were conspiring to force him back onto his feet one way or another.

Gathering the last shreds of willpower he possessed, Farrendel pushed onto his elbows, then crawled out of the nest of pillows Essie had built for him. She still slept, her hair flaming across her pillow and her breathing loud.

As he had not woken her last night with screaming, she

135

probably assumed, as she had the night before, that he had not had any nightmares.

He had. The sedative had just kept him so deeply asleep he had not thrashed, cried out, or woken. Thankfully, the nightmares themselves remained hazy as well, and he had not experienced them as vividly as he did normally.

He eased from the bed as carefully as possible to avoid waking Essie. After dressing in a shirt, trousers, and boots, he strapped on his swords. He had to tighten the straps as tight as they would go, and even then the sheathes remained too loose against his back.

After sneaking a light breakfast of meat and cheese from the kitchen and taking the morning dose of strawberry-flavored medicine, he crept out the door and entered the garden. The early morning air was crisp against his skin, a light fog blanketing the garden and the forest, and he suppressed a shiver. Maybe he should have grabbed a cloak, though he would get warm once Julien started whatever training session he had in mind.

Three figures appeared out of the mist. Farrendel reached for a sword, before he recognized Julien and Iyrinder. The third man was shorter than the rest of them, but not by much. He had a thin cavalry sword like Julien's strapped to his hip while a small Escarlish gun—Farrendel could not think of the name for it—rested in a holster on his other side. He seemed vaguely familiar, though Farrendel could not place him.

"Good morning." Julien swept a glance over Farrendel, then waved at the stranger. "This is Captain Eugene Merrick. He served in the palace guard and has been a patrol leader for Averett's personal guards for the past three years."

That would explain why he seemed familiar. Farrendel

must have glimpsed him a few times during that visit to Escarland or after his rescue in Kostaria.

"It is good to meet you and a pleasure to serve as the captain of your guards."

Captain Merrick bowed, his expression neutral.

Farrendel eyed him, not sure how to read that blank expression. Did this Captain Merrick have any prejudices against elves? Surely Julien and Averett would not have promoted him if that were the case. And Farrendel would have noted this Captain Merrick before, if he had seen him sneering behind Averett's back.

But, as the number of traitors in both Escarland and Farrendel's own family had proved, true motives could be hidden.

"Averett, Weylind, and I discussed security for you and Essie extensively on the train ride back to Estyra." Julien turned back to Farrendel, gesturing at Iyrinder and Captain Merrick. "As relations between Tarenhiel and Escarland deepen, Averett's and Weylind's personal guards will need to work together to guard their kings. Captain Merrick will be your permanent guard, but the other elves and humans on your guard will rotate from the personal guards for Weylind and Averett. Captain Merrick will be in charge of training them in working together, with input from you, of course."

That sounded like a good idea, in theory. Farrendel crossed his arms, still studying Captain Merrick. He was not sure he liked the thought of having to learn to trust new guards on a rotating basis.

Still, better to test such a plan on Farrendel where any problems a human might have with elves or an elf might have with humans would be rooted out before they were called upon to protect a visiting king.

"All of the guards will be thoroughly scrutinized, of course." Captain Merrick bobbed his head in something almost like another bow.

"We'll be careful, don't worry." Julien slapped Farrendel on the back. "Now, I was thinking we'd start with a jog around the parklands. Let's stretch, then you can set the pace."

After the four of them took the time to stretch, Farrendel forced himself to start into a jog. His muscles felt tight and weak.

Julien fell into step beside him, directing him down a path into the forest as they exited the garden. Iyrinder and Captain Merrick jogged side by side behind them.

A month ago, Farrendel could have jogged around the walled parkland of the Winstead Palace grounds without breathing hard. Now, he had to stop and walk several times, coming close to dry heaving while his side cramped.

After they finished a circuit of the forest, Julien had him do chin-ups using a low hanging branch. Then a variety of other exercises until Farrendel's arms and legs shook, and sweat trickled down his face and back.

Yet, even as he struggled to catch his breath, he felt stronger than he had in weeks.

After Essie woke, showered, and dressed, she made her way down to the kitchen. There, she found a young woman only a few years older than herself stirring eggs and flipping bacon in two different pans. The young woman glanced over her shoulder, then spun and bobbed a curtsy, her light brown hair swinging in its braid. "Good morning, Your Highness."

"You must be the new housekeeper and cook." Essie took a seat at the kitchen's work table.

"Yes, I am Miss Merrick." The young woman went back to deftly turning the bacon in the pan. "I will understand if you wish to conduct your own interview, since you were not the one who hired me."

Essie studied Miss Merrick. Her instincts weren't screaming at her, but she didn't want to trust the person handling their food too easily, not after what had happened to Farrendel last time. "Actually, there's only one question I need to ask. How do you feel about elves?"

"I have nothing against elves. My brother was on King Averett's guard detail during the recent war and fought alongside the elves. He has a great respect for them, and I look forward to the opportunity to see more of their kingdom and culture by serving you and Prince Farrendel." Miss Merrick stayed stirring the eggs, not looking at Essie as she spoke. "Neither my brother nor I are married. We are both willing to move between Escarland and Tarenhiel as necessary to see to whatever needs you might have."

If Essie were to guess, Miss Merrick was alone, except for her brother. Her desperation for this job was fueled by a desire not to be left alone while he guarded Farrendel in Tarenhiel for months at a time.

Though, Essie hadn't planned on taking the servants hired for Buckmore Cottage with them to Tarenhiel. But, they might be able to make an exception, if Miss Merrick and Captain Merrick turned out to be trustworthy.

Essie gave a practiced smile. "Willingness to travel would definitely be beneficial."

After grabbing a plate from the cupboard, Miss Merrick dished out some eggs. "How do you prefer your bacon?"

"I like it slightly crispy, but Prince Farrendel prefers it less crispy. He likes to be able to cut it with a fork." Essie took the plate after Miss Merrick added a couple of pieces of bacon. She dug into the eggs, then the bacon. Miss Merrick was a good cook, at least. "Let's start with our stay here at Buckmore Cottage and give both you and us a chance to make sure we are a good fit for each other."

"Thank you so much, Your Highness! I really appreciate it, and I will not let you down in the performance of my duties." Miss Merrick bobbed yet another curtsy. "If there is anything you would like me to do to help make Buckmore Cottage more comfortable, please let me know."

"I know you are currently understaffed, as the only staff member, so cooking will be your main duty." Essie would have to figure out how to bring up the topic of more servants to Farrendel. Perhaps she should see if there were any elves who would be interested in moving to Escarland. Farrendel might be more comfortable with them, and it would get the Escarlish people more used to interacting with elves.

Until then, Essie would probably have to work with Miss Merrick to see about getting one or two maids to help. The elves might be able to live simply in Tarenhiel, but unless Farrendel knew of a way to magically clean Buckmore Cottage, a place this size needed upkeep.

Essie outlined a few things she would like Miss Merrick to oversee and went over her and Farrendel's normal routine. Both so that Miss Merrick could have the meals ready at the right times and so that she knew not to crowd

Farrendel at the times when he needed to be alone, like his early morning breakfasts.

Essie rubbed at a scratch on the tabletop, not sure if she should mention one last thing or not. But, it wasn't something they could hide, with Miss Merrick sleeping on the main floor. "Prince Farrendel suffers nightmares, occasionally. If that happens, Prince Farrendel and I will probably go down to the kitchen to make hot chocolate. You don't have to serve us. Please feel free to go back to sleep."

Miss Merrick didn't seem too shocked. "If you would like, I would be happy to get up, make the hot chocolate, and deliver it to your room."

"You don't have to do that." Essie didn't want Miss Merrick to feel as though she had to force herself out of bed at all hours of the night, even if the thought of not having to blearily stumble down the stairs in the middle of the night sounded amazing.

"It would be my pleasure and my job."

"In that case, if you wake up, I would appreciate you making hot chocolate for us. If you don't wake up, then I won't go out of my way to wake you. How does that sound?" Essie held out her empty plate.

"It sounds like I will enjoy working for you, Princess Elspeth."

Good. Essie had learned from a young age that being a fair and kind employer usually led to more loyal and hardworking employees. Something rather important for royalty when their lives would be in danger if their employees were less than loyal.

The door opened, and Farrendel strode inside. His shortened hair stuck to his forehead while his shirt was stained with what looked to be a mixture of sweat and dirt. He limped slightly, as if his muscles were sore.

But he had a hint of a smile on his face. Maybe Julien had been right about exercise being exactly what Farrendel needed. At least here in Escarland, he could regain his strength safely on the ground under Julien's watchful eye rather than trying to resume his routine high in the treetops of Tarenhiel.

Essie stood and wrapped her arms around Farrendel's waist, so very thankful when he didn't pull away. "You are gross and sweaty."

"Then why are you hugging me?" Farrendel held his hands out, as if he wasn't sure what to do with them.

Behind him, Essie spotted Miss Merrick slipping out of the kitchen. Yes, Essie was definitely keeping her on the staff.

"Because you actually look happy, and I'm happy that you're happy." Essie stood on her tiptoes and kissed his cheek. "Now, do you want your second, after-exercise breakfast or a shower first?"

Farrendel's forehead wrinkled, then he glanced over her shoulder. "The bacon is hot right now."

Hard to argue with that logic.

Farrendel gripped Essie's hand and tried to keep his knees from bouncing. Every muscle in his body wound tight, and not just because of the stiff ache from the exercise this morning. It was taking every shredded scrap of his willpower to remain sitting on the settee beside Essie and not bolt from the room.

Buckmore Cottage's parlor was off the main entrance,

the walls a pink floral pattern while the room was crammed with plush couches and chairs and cloth-covered tables. It was a claustrophobic room even without his nerves straining to the snapping point. If he was ever attacked in this room, fighting back would be interesting, though he would have a number of items from which to launch himself.

Across the room, Taranath lounged in one of the chairs, reading through a stack of papers that represented Mr. and Mrs. Harwell's research. It must have been fascinating and on the right branch since Taranath was engrossed in his reading rather than shaking his head at inaccuracies.

That was a good thing. It had been hard enough letting Taranath magically mess with his brain, even if Farrendel now felt better than he had before.

But these Escarlish doctors were strangers. Averett and Julien and Essie seemed to trust them, but Farrendel was not so sure.

The outer door opened, then Captain Merrick walked into the parlor, followed by an older human couple. Farrendel was not sure how old they were, but the man's hair was completely gray while the woman's hair was almost entirely gray as well, with only a few threads of brown still showing.

Both of them were slightly plump and shorter than Farrendel with lines around their mouths and eyes.

They looked older and nicer and more...parental than Farrendel had expected.

After introductions and after Miss Merrick set a tea tray on the low table, Essie waved at the settee across from them. "Please, have a seat."

Mr. Harwell stepped aside and waited until his wife took

a seat first, then he sat beside her. Mrs. Harwell smiled and glanced from Essie to Farrendel.

Farrendel could not hold her gaze and instead glanced down at his and Essie's clasped hands. An awkward pause stretched into an even more awkward silence. One Farrendel had no intention of breaking. Especially since he could depend on Essie to do it for him.

"Do you want some tea? Or do you want to start..." Essie trailed off, as if she was not sure how to describe the reason they were there.

Mrs. Harwell's voice held a smile, even though Farrendel was staring down at his hands. "We'll start by explaining how we ended up doing this. About twenty years ago, our son fought in the war against Tarenhiel. When he returned, he was different. He struggled with what he had seen and done. We tried everything that was recommended at the time, including sending him to an asylum." Mrs. Harwell's voice held a quaver, but it did not break.

"It was...not good. We feared for him." Mr. Harwell's voice was matter-of-fact, even if it held a depth of emotion.

"I'm sorry." Essie's grip on Farrendel's hand did not loosen. "Do you blame the elves for your son's troubles? Or the Escarlish royal family? I'm sure my brother King Averett already asked these questions, but before we trust you, we need to hear your answers ourselves."

Farrendel managed to raise his head and study Mr. and Mrs. Harwell. Neither of them was glaring at him. But if they had lingering anger toward his people, they must have been good enough at hiding it to fool Averett.

If only Edmund were here instead of still helping the scouts keeping an eye on Kostaria. He would see right through this couple, if they had any bad intentions toward Farrendel.

"We did, at first." Mr. Harwell's voice was slightly gravelly.

"We blamed the elves. We blamed the royal family, begging your pardon. We blamed the doctors who had been unable to help. We even blamed ourselves." Mrs. Harwell reached over and clasped her husband's hand before she glanced at Essie, then Farrendel. "Out of desperation, we started our own research to find help for our son, which led us to some of the few pieces of elven knowledge on how the brain works that made it across the border. Eventually, we lost our anger and instead found our passion."

"We attended Hanford University and obtained medical decrees." Mr. Harwell gripped his wife's hand, sharing a smile with her. "Our son was our first patient, and he and his wife live here in Aldon with their three children. We have been doing our best to help others like him ever since."

"Our methods aren't always effective for everyone, but we have a very good record." Mrs. Harwell glanced toward Taranath. "Though if you have any input to offer, we would appreciate it. We can't believe an actual elf healer who specializes in the mind will be here observing. It is a great honor. Truly."

Farrendel felt his muscles relax slightly. If this couple had ever hated the elves, it had long since faded into admiration, based on the way both of them were looking at Taranath as if ready to hang onto every word he said.

Taranath tapped the stack of papers he had been perusing. "I have nothing to add besides my commendation for your work. You have accomplished a great deal without the benefit of magic to examine the brain yourselves. I am eager to see your methods in use."

"It will be difficult. The nightmares we've been told you're experiencing might get worse right at first." Mrs. Harwell's blue eyes fixed on Farrendel with a depth of sympathy. "But it does get better."

Farrendel could no longer hold Mrs. Harwell's gaze, and he focused on his and Essie's clasped hands again.

He could do this. He had dragged himself out of the darkness after torture once, though it had taken years.

This time, he had Essie to think about. He did not have the luxury of taking years to feel more like himself. For her sake, he had to fix this, fix himself, as much as possible so that he could truly live. If this could help, if he could finally feel like he was winning the constant war in his head instead of barely surviving, then this would be worth it.

FOURTEEN

Melantha strode next to her husband as they walked from the meeting room where they had spent the morning reading through petitions from Kostaria's citizens and arranging the details of starting trade with Escarland by going through Tarenhiel. It was not as straightforward as it sounded. But after seeing how desperate the food situation was in Kostaria, Melantha was motivated to make sure the next shipment of food from Escarland arrived in time.

Melantha's new wool tunic fell to her knees beneath a soft, leather vest while her toes were finally warm in her new, fur-lined boots. She wore thick leggings under the tunic and tucked into the boots. She had used several antler clips to pull her hair back from her face. The outfit was not something she ever would have worn back in Tarenhiel, but, somehow, it felt right.

Deep in the lowest level of Khagniorth, Rharreth pushed open one of a set of large, stone double doors. "This is the training arena. It's time I introduce you to the rest of my shield brothers."

Melantha drew her shoulders straight as she followed Rharreth inside.

The training arena was a vast underground space with a domed ceiling of smooth rock. Rows of stone benches circled the room while a low wall separated the sand-covered combat floor from the seating.

Seven figures, six males and one female, sparred against each other in the center of the arena. Zavni swung his battle-ax, and Nirveeth blocked it with a spear as long as Melantha was tall and thicker than her wrist. Eyvindur swung his massive sword, parrying a thrust by Vriska's sword.

Melantha did not know the other three troll warriors. One of them wielded an ax like Zavni's while the other two had large swords.

Rharreth led Melantha between the rows of seats down to the flat combat area. When they reached the edge, Rharreth put his fingers in his mouth and let out a piercing whistle that made Melantha wince.

The troll warriors stopped what they were doing and turned to face Rharreth and Melantha, resting their ax handles, the flat of their sword blades, or spears on their shoulders.

"Shield brothers and sister, this is my wife, Queen Melantha. I know some of you have already met her, but she will be joining us more often from now on." Rharreth steered Melantha deeper into the training area with a hand on her lower back. He halted in front of the first pair of troll warriors she did not know and pointed to each of them. "Darvek and Brynjar."

148

Both of them were shorter than Rharreth and held their swords easily.

The last troll warrior swaggered forward. His battle-ax on his shoulder, he stood a few inches taller even than Rharreth. He grinned and thumped his chest. "I'm Drurvas, Rharreth's shield brother and his cousin."

"Cousin?" Melantha glanced between Rharreth and Drurvas. There was a resemblance. Why had Rharreth not told her he had more family than just his brother? She had assumed he was alone, now that Farrendel had killed his one remaining family member.

"On his father's side. My father was his father's younger brother. Of course, both of them were killed by your brother." Drurvas still wore a smile, and it was hard to tell in his voice if he held any anger toward her for that or not.

"I am sorry for what the war between our kingdoms cost." That sounded diplomatic enough, right? Melantha probably should get used to others throwing her brother's kills in her face. While the trolls hated all elves, they had a particular hatred for Farrendel, thanks to the entire armies he had wiped out with his magic.

Healing that kind of rift might be beyond even her magic. She struggled to heal even her own problems with her brother.

"Thus the reason my cousin made the sacrifice to marry you." Drurvas bobbed a bow in her direction.

That was definitely an insult, said through a smile as it was.

Rharreth gave her a gentle nudge toward the seating. "Melantha, please take a seat. I believe my cousin and I need to have a sparring match."

Melantha hurried to the other side of the short wall and

took a seat several rows up, hoping that was far enough away from the training area to avoid any flying weapons. Based on the growl to Rharreth's voice, his match with Drurvas would be less than friendly.

The other troll warriors went back to sparring, though Melantha could see by the way they were giving Drurvas and Rharreth space that they too sensed the tension. Though, none of them interfered. Melantha got the sense that beating each other up in a training bout was probably the standard way shield brothers dealt with issues between them.

Rharreth drew his sword and faced Drurvas. Drurvas brandished his ax and smirked.

Then Drurvas swung his ax with a grunt, and Rharreth side-stepped, blocking with his sword.

After that, Melantha struggled to keep up with the pace of the fight. It looked like an indecipherable whirl of bodies and flashing steel to her. Spots of red soon peppered the fight, splashing onto the sand on the floor.

Melantha gripped her hands between her knees. Were practice fights supposed to involve this much blood? As long as Drurvas did not fully lop off one of Rharreth's arms or legs—or head—Melantha could heal him. But a strange tightness twisted her stomach. As if she was worried about Rharreth.

Rharreth tumbled to the ground, Drurvas's ax at his throat.

Drurvas put his boot on Rharreth's chest. "Yield?"

"Yield." Rharreth sighed, then he held out his free hand.

Drurvas removed his ax from near Rharreth's chin, rested it on his shoulder again, then took Rharreth's hand and pulled him to his feet.

Just like that, the tension was gone. Drurvas and

Rharreth pounded each other on the back. While Drurvas returned to sparring with Darvek, Rharreth strode toward Melantha. His steps were steady, as if he were unconcerned with the blood running down one of his legs, one of his arms, and from a gash across his chest. The seamstresses and tailors must do a steady business here in Kostaria if this was common practice for the trolls.

Melantha stood and met him at the short wall, magic already dancing at her fingertips. She trailed her fingers over the wound in his upper arm. "Are sparring matches always so bloody?"

"Not always." Rharreth shrugged, though he did not protest as she pressed her other hand over the slash across his chest. "But Drurvas likes to rub it in that he is the only one of my shield brothers and sister who can routinely trounce me. I can occasionally win a bout or two, but he was always the most talented of our shield band."

Rharreth's voice held something almost like pride. It was probably not the time for Melantha to admit to her misgivings about Drurvas. Perhaps she was just biased against him, now that she had watched him beat her husband in a sparring match.

She spread her magic through Rharreth, healing bruises and the gash in his leg.

Rharreth smirked, running his knuckles over her cheek. "I can see where having a healer for a wife is going to come in handy."

"Just do not get your head chopped off. I cannot fix that." Melantha stepped back, her heart pounding in an odd rhythm. What was this crackle filling the space between her and Rharreth?

He cleared his throat and put a few more inches of space

between them. He gestured toward the training area. "Would you like to learn?"

"Do you think I could?" Melantha glanced from Rharreth to the combat floor, her heart beating harder in her chest. She had thought she had given up the dream of being an elf warrior two hundred years ago when she had come into her magic. But ever since her discussion with Farrendel in the dungeon of Gror Grar, that old longing for something *more* lingered.

"I don't see why not." Rharreth's gaze swept over her. "You're small, so it would be best to start with the dagger or perhaps the quarterstaff."

"But...I am a healer. I took an oath to heal and not to harm." Melantha clenched her fists, crossing her arms in front of her as if to create a barrier between herself and temptation.

"You took an oath not to harm with your magic. That doesn't forbid learning how to wield a weapon." Rharreth shrugged, turning to the training area as if he believed the matter settled. "While I don't mind protecting you, it would be advisable for you to know how to defend yourself."

She could learn how to fight. Just as she had dreamed so long ago. Melantha hurried to keep up with him, her new fur boots making little noise on the stone.

Rharreth gave another whistle. "Training is over. Zavni, Eyvindur, please stand guard."

Rharreth's shield band stopped what they were doing and, after bowing toward Rharreth and Melantha, left the training arena, leaving Rharreth and Melantha alone.

"Here, let's find a weapon that fits you." Rharreth led her across the area to a stone door set in the wall. Inside, swords and shields hung on pegs on the wall. Spears filled barrels. Axes rested in racks. Daggers piled in a large stone chest.

Rharreth scanned the room before he walked to a barrel holding staves in a variety of lengths. "Let's start with a quarterstaff. If you don't know anything about fighting, it would probably be best to start with something without a blade, even if you could heal either of us if there was an accident."

The lack of a blade sounded good to her. Even if she was eager to learn, the part of her that had been told for years that it was inappropriate for a healer to fight had a niggling discomfort about learning the art of war. Perhaps she would be less uncomfortable if she learned a weapon like the quarterstaff. She could deal out bruises or perhaps a broken bone, but the likelihood of permanently hurting someone was small.

Rharreth pulled out several of the staves and had her hold them one at a time, until he nodded as if satisfied with the second-to-last one.

Melantha ran her hands over the quarterstaff. It was some kind of hardwood, polished smooth beneath her fingers.

"How does it feel?" Rharreth studied her, his dark blue eyes calculating, a frown creasing his chiseled face.

"Surprisingly good." Melantha hefted it, though she was not sure what a quarterstaff was supposed to feel like.

"Then, come." Rharreth took a quarterstaff for himself, this one taller than the one he had handed Melantha.

Outside in the training arena, Rharreth had her hold the staff, then he corrected her stance and her grip. After that, he taught her the basic swings.

Melantha swung her quarterstaff, and Rharreth easily

blocked. He smirked, raising his eyebrows at her. "You can hit harder than that. You won't break me. Put your shoulders and back into it and don't check your swing. It's on me to either block or take the hit. It isn't your job to spare me."

Hit harder? Melantha tightened her grip on her quarterstaff and settled into the stance Rharreth had shown her.

He faced her, his smirk widening. "Come on now, Melantha. Tap into the fire I know is in you."

This was her chance to finally lash out as she had always longed to do. With a scream of effort, Melantha swung the quarterstaff as he had shown her.

Rharreth blocked, and the shock shuddered up Melantha's fingers into her arms. But Rharreth's eyes twinkled. "Good. Again."

Melantha felt the fire throbbing through her blood, lending strength to her arms. She swung again and again, as hard as she could. Rharreth blocked each one until, finally, he ducked under her strike and swung his own quarterstaff, whacking her thigh.

Melantha let out a shriek, but she kept a hold of her staff. She whirled and struck again, and she found herself grinning.

At that moment, she felt more alive than she had in a hundred years. Maybe even longer than that. Her muscles burned with effort. Her bruises throbbed. Blisters were forming on her palms.

But her blood was singing, and the heat in her chest finally had a release. And, as the heat left, she did not feel worn or empty. Instead, she felt filled for the first time in a long time.

CHAPTER
FIFTEEN

The scream yanked Essie from sleep. She lay still for a moment, assessing the situation.

The wall of pillows remained between her and Farrendel, but he didn't seem to be flailing, or she'd feel the movement through the bed.

She pushed into a sitting position and peered over the pillows. Illuminated in the moonlight, Farrendel curled on his side in a ball, his arms over his head as if trying to protect himself. He gave another cry, curling tighter.

Essie eased from the bed, trying to move as slowly and carefully as possible to avoid startling him. She halted when she was halfway across the room, rubbing at her temples. How she hated these nightmares. She hated having to listen to them. She hated the fear they brought. Living like this was not romantic. Not healthy. This was definitely the "worse" part of "for better or worse."

Farrendel gave another cry and started shaking.

How could she safely wake him? She could shout or slam the door. Even if he lashed out with his magic, she was immune. Though, there was no telling what his magic would destroy in the room.

His magic...Essie crossed her arms and studied Farrendel. Since he was asleep, he was not blocking her through the heart bond. She could feel the distant crackle of his magic.

What would happen if she tried to use it herself? Could she stop him from using his magic when he startled awake?

Only one way to find out. With a deep breath, Essie mentally reached through the heart bond to that crackle of Farrendel's magic, gripped the blazing power, and tugged.

No blue lightning bolts crackled around her hands or burst from her fingers. His magic didn't flow into her.

But Farrendel's scream cut off mid-breath, and his whole body went rigid. With a deep, shuddering breath, Farrendel sat upright, brushing the shortened strands of his hair from his face. He met Essie's gaze, his brow furrowing. "What... did you..."

"Sorry. I was trying to wake you, and I tugged on your magic. Sort of. We haven't really talked about how I have access to your magic." They hadn't yet talked about any of the details of his capture or her battle across Kostaria. It hadn't seemed like a topic he had been up to discussing yet.

Still, the wall in the heart bond and the lack of discussion on the two weeks he had been captured felt like the last two things still standing between them.

Farrendel nodded, scrubbing a hand over his face as if he was still trying to wake up. The wall in the heart bond fell into place between them again.

Essie crossed her arms over her stomach. It was cold, standing there in the middle of the room with a chill autumn breeze rattling the windowpanes. But she didn't dare move yet. Not until the lost, wild look fully faded from Farrendel's eyes. "You don't have to keep locking me out of the heart bond. Please."

Farrendel rubbed at his chest, as if the heart bond was painful. But, after a moment, the wall eased, then dropped. A wave of pain and memories crashed into her, and she concentrated on breathing through it.

A soft knock sounded on the door, and Essie opened it to find Miss Merrick standing there in a dressing gown and holding a tray with two mugs of hot chocolate and a plate with two chocolate chip cookies on it.

"You are amazing. Thank you." Essie took the tray. How had she and Farrendel survived without Miss Merrick? For the past three nights, she had shown up right on cue with hot chocolate and cookies, and Essie suspected she had asked her brother and whoever else was on guard duty to keep the stove stoked throughout the night so that she could heat the milk at a moment's notice.

"My pleasure, ma'am." Miss Merrick gave a soft smile and a curtsy.

Essie closed the door and turned back to Farrendel. He was leaning against the wall next to the window, one knee drawn up and his hands buried in his shortened hair. Through the heart bond, Essie could feel the way he was struggling to drag himself out of the nightmare to fully wake up.

Balancing the tray, Essie returned, set the tray on the end of the bed, then carefully crawled onto the mattress without spilling the hot chocolate. After pushing aside a few of the pillows, Essie settled against the wall next to Farrendel, their shoulders brushing. She handed him a mug, then claimed her own.

Farrendel cradled his mug in both hands, staring down at the hot chocolate.

They sat in silence for a few moments, Essie sipping her hot chocolate and Farrendel just staring at his.

Finally, Farrendel sighed and leaned his head against the wall behind him. "I just want this to be over."

"I know." Essie leaned her head against his shoulder. "But things are getting better. Your nightmares have been mild compared to what they were in Estyra before we left. And, it seems I have figured out a way to safely wake you."

"Yes." Some of the tension left Farrendel's shoulders. He sipped his hot chocolate, the ache through the heart bond fading. He picked up Essie's free hand, running his thumb over her palm. "I have been so distracted that I had forgotten you used my magic. I suppose you will need to be trained to wield it."

Essie tucked her feet beneath the blanket, her arm tingling with the gentleness of Farrendel's thumb tracing across her palm. She struggled not to yawn. While it sounded nice to curl under the blanket and go back to sleep, Farrendel tended to be more forthcoming during their late night talks. "You don't have to, if you don't want to. I just won't use your magic if you don't want me to."

"My magic is too dangerous to risk you using it by accident without training." Farrendel stopped stroking her palm and clasped his fingers through hers. For some reason, the logistics of training seemed to steady him. "But, perhaps, we will not begin training right away. We both need to be ready. And we will need to ask your brother for a safe place to train where magical explosions would not cause widespread damage."

"Good point." Essie winced at the thought of accidentally

leveling half of Aldon with a magical accident. Neither she nor Farrendel would ever forgive themselves for something like that. "Lance would have a field day studying this new magical development. How did this whole magic-sharing thing happen? Weylind seemed surprised by it, so it isn't something that occurs all the time because of a heart bond."

Lance Marion was a magical engineer who worked with the Escarlish government to invent weapons. When Essie had introduced him to Farrendel the first time they had been in Escarland, Lance had found Farrendel's magic incredibly fascinating. He would be even more distracted studying this new development.

Farrendel set aside his hot chocolate to reach for a chocolate chip cookie. "I am not entirely sure what I did or how it happened."

Essie was inordinately pleased he'd chosen to give up his hot chocolate rather than let go of her hand. "Definitely sounds like something Lance would find fascinating."

Farrendel took a few bites of the cookie, then washed it down with more hot chocolate, before he set both aside. The tension returned to his shoulders and to the heart bond. "In that dungeon, I was helpless. The stone kept me from accessing my magic. But I could still feel the heart bond. Somehow, the stone could not touch that magic."

His words came hard, as if being dragged from him.

Essie squeezed his hand and glanced up at him. "You don't have to tell me if you don't want to."

At least, that was what she forced herself to say. She wanted so very much for him to open up to her.

Perhaps, with the heart bond open between them, he could sense that. He stared at the ceiling as he continued talking. "But when Melantha healed me, she put her magic between me and the stone. It gave me temporary access to my magic. I was desperate to figure out a way to store my power so that I could get to it when I needed it. So I attempted to store it in the heart bond."

"You tried to store magic inside of magic?" How would that even work? Essie set aside her mug of hot chocolate as well.

"I am sorry I was not able to ask you first before I tried it." Farrendel put his arm around her shoulders to tug her closer.

"You were desperate." Essie rested her free hand on Farrendel's chest, his shirt warm and soft beneath her fingers. If she wasn't careful, she would fall asleep right there.

"Still, you probably should have had a choice in making such an irreparable change." Farrendel shook his head, his voice going softer. "I thought I was merely storing the magic. But, instead, I think I linked my magic to the heart bond permanently. Whether it happened that first time I tried to store magic or if it happened over time or strengthened the more I used that link to store magic, I do not know. However it happened, my magic can now be accessed through the heart bond. I can still draw on it separately, but I can also reach through the heart bond for it."

"And that's how I can feel it as well." Essie nodded against Farrendel's shoulder. That made sense. And it explained why it felt like she needed his help to wield it. "Does this mean you can never be cut off from your magic again?"

"Maybe. I am not positive. It will take training and study to discover the limits of what happened." Farrendel's thumb rubbed her shoulder.

Essie hoped it was true. With his magic linked to the heart bond, it would be much harder for enemies to capture Farrendel. The Escarlish traitors had used her as Farrendel's weakness. He had not dared to use his magic when she had a gun pressed to her back. But if she could have defended herself, then both of them could have fought back. With this new ability, she could prevent Farrendel's capture from ever happening again.

WHEN FARRENDEL WOKE, sunlight already beamed through the window, splashing pools of bright light on the floor. Essie was curled against his chest, warm and breathing deeply in sleep. His arm lay over her waist while her red hair frizzed over her pillow, his pillow, and into his face.

He must have slept late after he and Essie had spent hours the night before talking about the war and what had happened to both of them during the two weeks apart.

He had already talked about what had happened to him during the counseling sessions with Mr. and Mrs. Harwell, and somehow that had made it easier to talk about it the second time with Essie. If anything, the weight pressing against his chest and mind lifted further. It still lingered, there at the back of his mind. But it was manageable now, even before taking his morning dose of Taranath's medicine.

Sometime in the early morning hours, Essie had fallen asleep against Farrendel as if worn out from all their talking. He could have picked her up and set her back on her side of the bed.

Instead, he had eased her from his shoulder where she lay, then wedged himself between her and the wall. During the night, the pillow wall had gotten shoved off the bed, and he was in no hurry to put it back. If his nightmares remained as mild as they had been the night before and if Essie's ability to tug on his magic could wake him quickly when he did have a nightmare, perhaps precautions would not be as necessary.

As much as he wanted to linger, he could hear the sounds of Julien and Captain Merrick talking in the garden below, muffled through the closed windowpanes.

He brushed Essie's hair out of the way so that he did not accidentally set his elbow on a strand and pull it. Essie stirred, but she did not wake.

Farrendel eased onto his elbow, then sat up. When that did not disturb her, he climbed off the bed, then pulled the blanket over her shoulders.

After dressing and taking his medicine, Farrendel strapped on his swords. He was now at the second hole in the leather straps. A good sign that he was regaining his strength and filling out after starving there in the trolls' dungeon.

Still, his balance and strength was not yet restored enough for him to risk climbing down the tree outside the window, so he had to take the longer route down the stairs and out the door.

In the garden, Julien, Iyrinder, and Captain Merrick were already stretching. Farrendel joined them. They glanced at him but did not ask why he was late.

After stretching, they launched into their normal jog around the forested parkland. Farrendel could now keep up with Julien and Captain Merrick without having to walk to catch his breath. Iyrinder stayed with them, though

Farrendel knew the elf warrior could have outpaced them if he wished.

Their jog ended near the pond that was set at the edge of Winstead Palace's gardens, mostly surrounded by the fringe of the forest.

Farrendel's pace slowed as he studied the pond. Yesterday, the only thing sticking into the pond was the dock. Now, a beam spanned the pond from the dock to the far side. A few feet beside the beam, a rope was strung about four feet in the air and also spanned the pond.

Julien dropped back to run next to him. "What do you think? I was trying to find a way for you to safely practice without running through the treetops. You can start with the beam, then move on to the rope when you're ready."

Had Julien realized just how much having his hair cut would affect Farrendel's balance when flipping or spinning the way he used to? It seemed he must have guessed some of it, at least.

Farrendel's long hair had helped him sense what was around him. It helped him know exactly where the branch was when he did a flip, as well as sensing when an enemy was taking a swing at his back. While he retained enough of his balance that it did not affect running or fighting on the ground, he would struggle trying to race around the treetops like he used to.

"I know the water will be a little cold at this time of year. Incentive not to fall, I guess." Julien shrugged as they halted next to the pond. "And try not to bash your head open on the beam when you fall. I looked into adding some kind of padding, but it wasn't feasible."

Farrendel waved at the trees in the direction of Buckmore

Cottage. "I have an experienced elf healer staying at the cottage."

"Good point. In that case, don't bash your head in so severely that your healer can't fix it." Julien held out a hand. "I'll watch your swords if you want to test it out."

With Captain Merrick, Julien, and Iyrinder standing guard, not to mention all of Captain Merrick's squad fanning out into the forest, Farrendel felt safe enough to unbuckle his swords and hand them to Julien. "Do not watch. It will be embarrassing enough without all of you gawking."

Julien just smirked, which was not reassuring.

Farrendel sighed and headed for the dock. If he wanted to regain his strength and his skills, he had to practice. Even if he could convince Julien to leave, Captain Merrick and Iyrinder were under instructions to watch him like he was a mouse and they were starving hawks.

Farrendel took a few practice runs across the beam. It was four inches wide, which would have been more than enough before. On his fifth time across the beam, he threw himself into a front flip.

He mistimed the landing, coming down with only part of his foot on the beam. He slipped before he had a chance to catch himself. All he could do was attempt to launch himself away from the beam to make sure he landed safely in the water instead of smashing into the wood.

The cold water closed around him, icy and piercing straight through to his bones. He flailed until he righted himself and found the surface. Spitting out water, he flopped over the beam and pulled himself onto it. He shivered and glared over at Julien. "That water is more than cold."

Julien just shrugged and smirked. "Like I said, incentive not to fall in."

Farrendel sat up and swiped his hair from his face. Gritting his teeth, he pushed back to his feet. He would never regain his strength and figure out how to balance with his short hair if he did not practice.

He practiced for an hour and landed in the pond several more times. The beam only got more slippery the more he fell in and dripped water on it. But he managed two successful flips, so that was something.

By the time he squelched back to Buckmore Cottage, he was shivering, and he could no longer feel his toes. When he stepped into the kitchen, both Miss Merrick and Essie glanced up at him.

Essie's eyes widened, and she bolted to her feet. "What happened?"

"Training." Farrendel relaxed in the warmth of the kitchen, even if he was still dripping water onto the tiled floor.

"I really question my brother's training methods." Essie stepped closer to him, though she stayed at arm's length.

Even though he was dripping wet and shivering, he felt...happy. Thanks to the exercise, the counseling sessions, and the medicine, the weight was banished to the farthest corner of his mind, making it easier to smile and step closer to Essie. He pulled her in for a hug, ignoring her squawk of surprise, and kissed her forehead. "It has been a good morning."

"Eww. You got me all wet." Essie's nose wrinkled as she glared at him, though she was not truly annoyed with him. The lightness to the heart bond and the way Essie was struggling to keep her mouth pressed into a frown instead of the grin gave away her true emotions. She wiggled out of his

165

grip and patted his chest. "Now stop dripping on the floor and go wash and change."

He gave Essie one more kiss, this time a peck to her cheek. Miss Merrick was standing right there, after all, even if the housekeeper was edging toward the door as if trying to make a graceful exit.

He had his magic back. He was getting his strength and agility back. Soon, he would have his mind fully his once again. Perhaps recovery was possible after all.

CHAPTER
SIXTEEN

Melantha swung her staff with as fierce a war cry as she could manage. Rharreth still blocked her swing easily, but he had to move more quickly than he had when they first started training.

The fire in her blood hummed, even as the painful tightness in her chest released. She let out another scream of battle fury and charged Rharreth, whipping her staff through the air as fast and hard as she possibly could.

Was this how Farrendel felt during his training every morning? If Melantha had known, she would have talked with him about it. Perhaps she would have even joined him for training.

Though, back in Tarenhiel, it would have been considered unseemly for a healer to train in fighting. Strange how Melantha had resented those social norms, even while she did her best to conform to them and even resented Farrendel when he did not—and never could because of his illegitimate birth.

Perhaps, instead of just resenting him, she had really

been jealous of Farrendel. In the end, he had figured out a way to defy all those who hated his birth, hated the way he did not fit into their society and managed to thrive anyway.

With a grunt of exertion, Rharreth parried her swing, then changed his momentum to lash back at her. Melantha moved to block, only to realize he had feinted high, then flicked the end of his staff low. He whacked her thigh, right on the spot that would have been bruised from their last training session, if Melantha had not healed herself.

She gritted her teeth and redoubled her efforts, side-stepping and bringing up her own staff. Ducking, she swung one end at Rharreth's knees before twitching the top toward his head. He blocked both easily, but at least Melantha managed to parry his fast strike in return.

Rharreth hooked a foot around hers, but she sidestepped before he could trip her. Still, he got in close, inside her guard. He looped his staff over her, pinning her back against his chest.

She squirmed, but he had caught her. She could not even free her hands to try any of the hand-to-hand combat he had taught her. She stilled, growing aware of the muscles in his arms and chest and the way he was holding her. Tight, but still gentle, for all they were training.

"Do you yield?" He spoke near her ear, his breath hot against the back of her neck yet somehow sending tingles down her spine.

Melantha had to swallow several times before she could whisper, "Yield."

His grip on her loosened, but he did not let her go.

Melantha kept her staff out of the way as she turned in his arms to face him. Held as she was against his chest, his face was only a few inches from hers. His gray skin beaded with a hint of sweat while his white hair was tousled. She probably looked a sight with sweat pouring down her face and her black hair wild about her head, yet his dark blue eyes focused on her with an intensity that she did not think came from the battle.

"You look...wild when you fight." Rharreth's voice rumbled beneath the hand Melantha had pressed to his chest. "You appear to love it."

"Strange, I know, for a healer." Melantha found herself leaning toward him. What was happening to her? For the past week, she and Rharreth had spent their days companionably enough.

But it was here in the training arena where Melantha felt alive. She could be free, with all her passion thrumming through her chest and burning hot through her veins. She no longer had to hide behind a serene exterior.

It was also when they were here that this crackling intensity between her and Rharreth was at its strongest, though she felt it at other times. When they climbed into bed and tried to ignore each other. When he handed her a report of the latest shipment from Escarland and their fingers brushed. When he asked for her opinion on how to best distribute that food shipment and truly listened to her response.

Rharreth leaned closer to her, a hand skimming up her arm. "I love that wildness."

Melantha had thought she felt this way with Hatharal. Yet, something about what she had with Rharreth was deeper.

With Rharreth, Melantha was no longer hiding behind her people's expectations of how she should act. She was free to be herself here. With him, she had blazed with fury, stormed with anger, pushed herself into fighting with abandon.

Only a few inches separated them now. Was Rharreth about to kiss her?

Somehow, that thought did not bring dread. Melantha held her breath. Somewhere, distantly, she heard her wooden staff thunk to the sandy floor as she dropped it to rest both hands on Rharreth's chest.

A loud knock rang through the training arena. Rharreth gave a growl in the back of his throat before he stepped away from her. "What?"

Melantha put another step between them, her arms cold, as Zavni stepped into the arena. Could Zavni see the way her face was flaming? Perhaps he would chalk it up to the exertion of their training.

Zavni glanced between them before he cleared his throat and focused on Rharreth. "Pardon my interruption, Your Majesties. There is a large group gathering in the courtyard. They have been asking for you...both of you."

"Really? Why would they want to see me?" Melantha bent to pick up her staff. "Unless they have gotten so fed up with the thought of an elf as their queen that they are waiting to mob me the moment I step out the front doors?"

"If that were the case, Your Majesty, we never would have let them inside the gates of the stronghold." Zavni shook his head, his shoulders rolling in a shrug. "They all appear to need healing in some way and have come to beg for your help."

Really? Melantha froze, gripping her staff.

"Thank you for coming to inform us." Rharreth nodded to Zavni before he turned to Melantha. "You don't have to heal any of them if you don't want to."

"I am their queen, and I am a healer. Both of those things make it my duty to at least attempt to heal them." Melantha rubbed her fingers over the smooth hardwood of her staff, the depth of the passion in that statement surprising even herself.

"Very well." Rharreth held out an arm to her, as if planning to escort her there himself.

Melantha stayed where she was. If she stepped outside into a large crowd and started healing people, those waiting might get restless or disorderly, depending on how desperate they were. And, from what Melantha had seen of Kostaria and the trolls living there, things were desperate for many. "Is there a place where I could meet with each person or family seeking healing individually? I would need a large table and access to some kind of juice or other beverage made from a plant in case I have to send any of them home with a more long-term healing medicine."

"There is a meeting room on the ground floor just off the entry hall that should work." Rharreth gave a sharp nod before he turned to Zavni. "Send Brynjar to fetch some juice and prepare the meeting room. Then, instruct the guards to arrange the people into an orderly line. You and the shield band will let each person or family in one at a time, escort them to the meeting room, then escort them out once they are finished. My queen will remain guarded at all times."

Melantha shook her head. "No. For the privacy of my patients, I cannot have any guards in the room with me."

Rharreth turned his hard-blue eyes on her. "This is not Tarenhiel where such delicacies are observed. You may be a healer, but you are still their queen. You will have a guard to ensure your safety. Don't fight me on this. You won't win."

Melantha clenched her fists, the simmer returning in her

chest. She was not about to let him dictate to her, especially not when it came to healing. "This may not be Tarenhiel, but I am still an elf healer, sworn to heal and bound by the rules I was trained in. They may have very personal ailments that they will not be comfortable sharing if I have a guard looming over my shoulder."

"They may not be comfortable being alone in a room with an elf either." Rharreth shot back.

That stilled her. She had not thought about that. She was used to healing other elves, who knew the rules all healers swore to obey. But these trolls, for all they were seeking her help, had more of a reason to fear her than they did to trust her. Even if she meant well, they might be more on edge and prone to overreact. The presence of a troll guard might reassure them.

But, she still was not about to back down all the way, not when Rharreth had used that tone of voice. "Fine, I see your point. I will allow one guard. But the guard must stand in the corner out of the way unless there appears to be a problem and must not interfere with my work or with the privacy of my patients."

Rharreth bowed his head in a nod, some of the fire leaving his eyes. "I also see your point. I will arrange to have the back half of the room and your exam table screened off with only Vriska stationed in the corner by you. I will remain just inside the door, but out of sight and out of earshot if the patient wishes to speak in lowered tones."

It was a good compromise. And, perhaps, the presence of their king would reassure the people that he was taking their needs seriously.

Zavni cleared his throat. "Many of them came as whole

families. Perhaps those not in need of healing could wait on the other side of the screen as well."

"A good suggestion. See to it. We will meet you at the meeting room in half an hour." Rharreth gestured to Zavni, then held out his arm to Melantha again. "While trolls respect a war-like demeanor, perhaps you would prefer to clean up first?"

Melantha swiped a strand of sweaty hair from her forehead. Another good point. She took his arm. "Yes, I would. My current state is not sanitary whatsoever."

In short order, she and Rharreth returned to their room, and Melantha cleaned up in the waterfall room. She dressed in one of her wool dresses, though she wore her warm trousers and fur boots underneath. She braided the sides of her hair to keep it out of her way, then tied the troll queen's diadem so that it rested comfortably against her forehead. It would not hurt to remind those coming for her help that she was their queen as well as an elf healer.

When she was ready, Rharreth escorted her through the maze of passageways. As they neared the entry hall, Melantha could hear the hubbub of voices even through the stone doors to the palace. How many trolls were out there, hoping to be healed? What would happen if she did not have enough magic to heal all of them?

Rharreth's shield band members were waiting in the entry hall, and they nodded to him as he and Melantha swept inside.

"Quite the crowd you have attracted. They sound eager to be healed by their benevolent elf queen." Drurvas lazily swung his battle-ax before letting it rest easily on his shoulder.

Even though his blue eyes twinkled and he was smiling,

there was something about the way he said it that still seemed like an insult.

Melantha drew herself up straighter, feeling the way the diadem rested against her forehead. "Actually, I am the troll queen."

Rharreth glanced at her, his look warm as if he approved of her response.

Zavni strode forward and gestured at a nearby doorway. "The room has been prepared."

Melantha pulled away from Rharreth and hurried into the room. A white sheet had been strung across the back half of the room, but when she pushed it aside, she found a long table that was also draped with a white sheet. A jug of juice was set on a wooden chair while a side table was piled with medical supplies.

Vriska stood in the corner, arms crossed and scowling. Her scowl deepened as her gaze landed on Melantha, but she stayed where she was.

For some reason, Melantha's heart thumped harder in her chest, her muscles relaxing at the familiar sight of a makeshift hospital room. Could it be that she had missed healing? Even though she had resented that she had healing magic and that it prevented her from fulfilling her dream of becoming a great elf warrior like her father and brothers, it was still a part of who she was.

Melantha turned, finding that Rharreth had followed her inside. He waved around the room. "Will this be acceptable?"

"Yes, I believe so. Please send the first patient in." Melantha took a station next to the table.

Rharreth left, leaving Melantha temporarily alone with Vriska. Thankfully, Vriska took her duty to be a silent guard lurking in the corner very seriously and did not so much as twitch from her angry scowl.

The first patient turned out to be a woman suffering from a chronic cough. Melantha healed the buildup of fluid in the troll woman's lungs.

The next patient was a troll family whose four children were all suffering symptoms of malnourishment. The father and mother were not much better off than the children, and Melantha eased magic into all of them to strengthen them, then sent them home with a jar of juice laced with more magic.

The third patient was a young boy whose arm had been broken in the past and had healed badly, leaving the arm weak and continually in pain. His mother accompanied him inside the curtained-off part of the room while the troll father waited with Rharreth.

Melantha considered the boy where he sat on the table, his legs swinging. She would have to re-break his arm before she could heal it properly. "Please lie down."

The boy's eyes were wide, and he was stiff as he lay down, gripping his mother's hand. He looked so lost that it tugged something deep inside Melantha's chest. In that moment, she did not want to be a screaming warrior. She wanted to be kind. Compassionate. Soothing. Right now, she was all that was standing between this boy and a life of struggle in a warrior kingdom that prized physical strength above anything else.

"Do not worry. It will not hurt. When you wake up, you will be all better." Melantha called on her magic, a green glow surrounding her fingers, before she gently placed her hand on the boy's forehead.

His eyes flickered closed, and he was asleep within heartbeats.

The mother gasped, shoved Melantha hard in the shoulder, and gathered her boy to her. "What did you do, elf witch?"

Melantha stumbled back, caught off guard by the reaction. "I just—"

Vriska remained in the corner, not moving. Not stepping in between the troll woman and Melantha, even though she was supposed to be guarding her.

Rharreth shoved the curtain aside, giving Melantha a brief glimpse of Zavni and Nirveeth restraining the troll boy's father. Rharreth circled the table in heartbeats, wrapping his left arm around Melantha's shoulder. It was a protective gesture, yet not as threatening as pushing her behind him would have been. When Rharreth spoke, his voice was level and his gaze was focused on the troll woman. "What is the problem?"

"She did something to my son! He won't wake up!" The woman hugged her son tighter, giving him a slight shake. Tears were welling in her eyes even as she glared at Melantha.

Rharreth glanced down at Melantha. "Would you like to explain, my queen?"

The emphasis he placed on the words *my queen* held a level of trust. As if he had complete confidence that she had not harmed the boy.

How could he be so sure? After what she had done to her own brother, would he not doubt her? Especially since she was an elf.

But he was trusting her with his people. More than that, he was placing his own reputation as king in her hands.

Melantha drew in a deep breath and faced the shaking troll woman as calmly as she could. "I merely sent him to sleep. He will wake up in half an hour. To heal his arm, I will need to re-break the bone, and it is common practice in Tarenhiel to put the patient to sleep before such a procedure. I am sorry that I did not think to warn you or explain first."

The troll woman stopped shaking, but she still hugged her son tightly to her and did not appear ready to set him back on the table.

Melantha met the woman's gaze. "I promise you, I will not harm him. As an elf healer, I have taken an oath that I will not cause harm with my magic. That oath is binding, so binding that my own magic would likely kill me if I broke the oath."

The troll woman stilled, as if thinking that over. But she still did not release her son or step closer to the table.

Melantha stepped out of Rharreth's grip, thankful that he had remained silent and was letting her stand up for herself. She gestured at Rharreth. "If I could have harmed with my magic, do you not think I would have done it when I was held in the dungeons of Gror Grar by Rharreth and his brother, the late troll king? But, as you can see, Rharreth is standing before you unharmed."

The troll woman's gaze finally turned speculative. She glanced from Melantha to her son, something in her expression twisting.

It must be hard, trusting a former enemy with her son's future and life. Melantha tried to put as much compassion as she could manage into her voice. "If you do not wish for me to heal him, I will wake him before you leave."

The troll woman drew in a deep, shuddering breath, then

she eased her sleeping son onto the table. She kept her grip on her son's good hand. "Please heal him."

Melantha stepped closer to the table, calling on her magic again. "Very well. As I said, I will have to break his bone again so that I can heal it properly. Please do not be alarmed if you hear the bone snapping."

The troll woman's gray skin paled, but she pressed her mouth into a thin line and nodded.

Melantha rested her hand on the boy's arm. As she sent her magic into him, she could sense the place where the bone had regrown at an angle instead of straight. Clenching her magic around the spot, Melantha snapped the bone cleanly.

The troll woman flinched, but she did not react or lash out at Melantha again.

Pouring more magic into the boy's arm, Melantha nudged the bones back into their proper alignment, then encouraged them to heal more quickly than they would on their own.

When she was satisfied, she pulled her hand away and met the woman's gaze. "Your son's arm will be fine now. It will still be healing for the next day or so, so I will bind it in a splint. But in two days, you can remove the splint, and his arm should be completely healed."

"Thank you, Your Majesty." The troll woman remained where she was, gazing down at her son, as Melantha found items for a splint in the pile of medical supplies on the end table and bound the boy's arm.

Rharreth remained where he was, standing near the table with stiff shoulders. Vriska still had not moved from her post in the corner.

When Melantha stepped back, the troll woman gently picked up her son and cradled him to her chest. She bobbed something almost like a bow. "I am sorry for my reaction earlier."

"It is forgiven." Melantha gave a nod in return, though she did not bow. She was the queen, after all.

Though, it had been a good lesson in the need to explain herself further. These trolls were not used to how an elf healer worked.

Rharreth held the curtain open for the troll woman, then glanced to Zavni. "Wait a few minutes before sending in the next one."

Zavni nodded, then escorted the troll family from the room.

Rharreth turned, the set of his shoulders going stiff. He glared at Vriska then stalked around the table toward her. "Why didn't you protect the queen?"

"She was not in danger." Vriska waved her hand, meeting Rharreth stare for stare.

"Your performance was unacceptable. You are relieved of your duty." Rharreth's dark blue eyes burned as he jabbed a finger toward the door.

Vriska gave Melantha a glare as she sauntered past, as if she was not repentant in the least.

When Rharreth faced Melantha, his shoulders were still stiff, though the burning light had retreated from his eyes. "I will remain here with you, unless a patient finds it uncomfortable."

This time, Melantha was not going to argue. It was reassuring, having Rharreth's solid presence at her back rather than Vriska's glaring.

Melantha healed ten patients. Then fifteen. By the time the last troll left, she had healed thirty-seven trolls. Her head ached from doing so much healing while surrounded by stone, and she leaned against the table as she poured some of her magic into her temples to relieve the pain.

Strong hands settled on her shoulders, and she glanced up to find Rharreth studying her with dark blue eyes, his forehead knotted. "Are you all right? Has all that healing taken a toll on you? I told you that we could refuse the last few, if it was too much."

"I am fine. I actually have plenty of magic left, if more show up." Melantha's tense shoulders relaxed, both from the warmth of his hands and her magic easing her headache. "It is just the stone."

"I did not realize the stone affected you. You never seemed to be bothered by it the way your brother Laesornysh is." Rharreth cupped her chin, turning her face side to side as if searching for hints of pain.

"I am affected, though not as strongly as he is. I still have access to my magic and thus can heal myself from the headache." Melantha shrugged and let herself lean into Rharreth. While she still had plenty of magic left, she was weary after training and then expending more magic than she had in a long time. He was satisfyingly solid and warm in this place of cold stone.

Rharreth's mouth flattened into a thin line. "I am sorry. I did not realize living in this stronghold was still hurting you."

"It is not. I can heal myself." Melantha waved a hand to brush aside his concerns. They did not have any other choice. All houses were made of stone here in Kostaria. There were not enough trees to waste them on buildings, especially when the trolls could just mold the stone into whatever home or stronghold they wanted.

Rharreth nodded and stepped back, though he did not

completely let go of her nor did the thoughtful look leave his eyes.

The outer door creaked open again, and Zavni stuck his head inside, visible around the edge of the curtain. "The last one has left, and…oh, sorry, Your Majesties."

When Melantha glanced up at Rharreth, he was glaring at Zavni. His voice held a hard edge to it when he ordered, "Please step outside and guard the door. See that we are not disturbed."

Zavni smirked and bowed. He was still smirking as he shut the door behind him.

Were the tips of her ears growing hot? Melantha swallowed. Whatever Zavni was thinking, it was not like that. Surely Rharreth just wanted to talk, right?

Yet, why was she not entirely repulsed by the idea that he might want to do more than talk?

Rharreth's hands settled on her waist as he faced her once again. His expression was grave as he studied her. "We'll leave this room set up like this. I don't think this will be the last time it is needed. Will you be all right healing if more people come?"

"Yes, though I will probably want to make sure I take the time to heal my own headache between patients." Melantha found herself resting her hands on his chest again, leaning into his steadiness. "Do you really think more will come? The ones who came today were those brave enough to actually risk asking for help from an elf healer."

"Yes, but once word spreads, those who feared to ask for your aid will be more likely to seek healing. More than that, word will spread throughout all of Kostaria. The sick and injured will travel to Osmana for your aid." Rharreth's frown deepened, as if the thought worried him for some reason.

"Then I will just have to pace myself. You have seen the strength of magic in my family. I might not have Farrendel's power, but I am strong." Melantha straightened her spine, lifting her chin.

"I do not doubt your strength, but the reaction of the warriors." Rharreth's forehead furrowed, and he seemed to be gazing past her shoulder. "Once, it was seen as the honor of the warriors to protect the helpless and the weak. But, over time, that honor became a duty that the warriors performed while sneering at the weakness of those they protected. Now, the warriors have become the elite of our society, lording their power over those who don't have the magical or physical strength to stand up to them. It shouldn't be that way."

"No, it should not. But what does that have to do with my healing?" Melantha eased a few inches back from him to better see his face.

"Because you strengthen the weak and give them a source of help apart from what the ruling warrior families condescend to provide. You will threaten the power of the warrior elite, even as you gain the loyalty of the common people." Rharreth swiveled his gaze back to her. "It is not a bad thing. It is the change Kostaria needs, a change I didn't have the power nor the will to enact before. But it will be dangerous, for both of us."

"I see." Melantha searched his face, realizing that statement was really a question. He was giving her a choice. If she wanted to remain safe, he was willing to back down and return to the kind of prince he had been. The one who only pushed for small changes when it would not endanger him overly much.

If she wanted to pursue this, then he was willing to fight for change at her side. Or, perhaps, she would be fighting at his side. Together, they would be in for a fight.

It would be a change for the better. Right now, the troll warriors still pushed to return to war. Because war gave the warriors power and a purpose. Without the war, their power diminished.

Yet, the war caused suffering to the common trolls in Kostaria. All the ice and magic they had been wielding across their kingdom year upon year was destroying the very land. The people were starving and hurting, and no one currently in power seemed to care.

Honor without compassion was meaningless. Duty without love was nothing. War without the purpose of peace was just empty bloodshed. Focusing on war, honor, and duty while despising compassion, love, and peace had warped troll society.

That needed to change, or the trolls would destroy themselves.

Strange how much Melantha cared about that. After seeing the suffering of the common trolls while she was healing their sick and wounded, she could not turn a blind eye to what was happening.

Perhaps it was because she had done much the same thing in herself. She claimed loyalty to her kingdom and her family, yet it had been without a true depth of love. Instead, she had just focused on bitterness to the point where she had been a cold shell covering a burning hate. She was determined to change, and maybe she could work that same change in Kostaria.

Melantha lifted her chin and met Rharreth's gaze. "I am willing to fight this battle, if you fight it at my side."

"You are my queen. Of course I will fight at your side as you fight at mine." Rharreth's mouth tilted, something smoldering in his dark blue eyes.

Why did talk about fighting turn her insides to mush? She had never felt this open and soft with anyone before, even as he saw her hard edges for what they were. "I suppose I will have to train even harder now. Too bad my magic is utterly useless for fighting."

Rharreth released his relaxed grip on her waist and stepped back, regarding her. "That magic you did when you sent the boy to sleep. Could you do that on anyone?"

It seemed like a random change of topic, but Melantha shrugged. "Yes, I just have to be touching them. I..." She trailed off, her mind spinning as she saw what Rharreth had already recognized. "I can put anyone to sleep, and sleep is not harmful."

Even if she did it against their will, it technically was not harming them and thus not against her healer's oath. She would not wish to employ such methods all the time, but if she had to defend herself, sending someone to sleep was arguably better than killing them as she would have to attempt to do with a weapon if attacked.

"Show me. Send me to sleep." Rharreth gestured at himself, the smolder in his eyes returning to calculating.

"You might want to sit down. I do not wish to be crushed when you collapse on me." Melantha called on her magic yet again, feeling its comfortable soothing feeling against her fingertips.

Rharreth sat in a chair and glanced up at her. "How does this..."

Melantha trailed her fingers over his temple, sending her magic into him. He slumped in the chair, his head lolling.

She let him sleep for a moment before she placed her hand on his forehead and sent her magic into him again.

He shifted, then blinked up at her as if trying to bring his eyes back into focus. Then, he shot to his feet, gripping her shoulders. "That was incredible. I did not expect that you would be able to knock me out that fast. This will be very useful in battle."

"I still have to touch someone to use it, but, yes, if I can touch an enemy, I can make them sleep in seconds." Melantha stared at her hands. After all these years of resenting her magic, she could finally use it in battle as she had always longed to do.

Her magic was not useless, and she was no longer helpless.

CHAPTER
SEVENTEEN

I n the training arena, Rharreth faced Vriska, gripping his sword and trying to keep his anger in check. It was just the two of them. Melantha was arranging her new healing room to her satisfaction, and the rest of the shield band had been tasked with guarding her.

But Rharreth needed to have it out with Vriska. Her actions toward Melantha had been unacceptable for some time, and her failure that day had placed Melantha in danger.

Vriska faced Rharreth, a stubborn set to her jaw, her eyes flashing.

"You failed to protect my wife. As was your duty to your queen and to the wife of your shield brother." Rharreth advanced on Vriska.

She held her sword in an easy grip. "If she were a troll warrior worthy of standing at your side, she wouldn't have needed protecting. Don't you see that?"

"If she had been a troll warrior, she wouldn't have been able to heal all those people." Rharreth whipped his sword at Vriska's head. She parried and turned the movement into a strike of her own. Rharreth blocked, pressing his taller height for the extra leverage it gave him. "More than that, Melantha is my wife. Your disapproval isn't going to erase the vows I spoke."

"Maybe not. But I would think the disapproval of your shield band would keep you from falling in love with her." Vriska ducked away from his attack, taking a few steps back to give herself space. "Don't think we all haven't noticed those looks you've been giving her. It is disgusting the way you look at that elf."

Rharreth gritted his teeth, and it was an effort not to turn his strike into something more deadly. "She is my wife. Would you have me remain in a cold and loveless marriage? What kind of wish is that for your shield brother? Besides, not all of the shield band disapproves. Nirveeth and Eyvindur are more or less neutral. And Zavni heartily approves."

Vriska parried his thrust and turned her grunt of exertion into a huff. "Zavni is a foolish, hopeless romantic, and we all know it. He's just brainless enough to support your marriage to an elf."

"More like loyal enough." Rharreth swung his sword harder, satisfied when Vriska stumbled back a step under the force of his blow.

"I am loyal, Rharreth. I would gladly give my life at your side if it were necessary." Some of the stubborn look faded from Vriska's eyes as she parried yet another blow. "You are my shield brother. That's why I'm worried about you. I'm worried about what your loyalty to this elf bride of yours will do to you and your reign."

If Rharreth didn't believe that, he would have taken

Vriska off guard duty long before this. But he needed to hear her out now, much as he didn't like it. He backed off, letting Vriska get in a series of strikes as she unleashed her anger and questions.

Vriska's voice was almost pleading, her eyes focused, as she swung her sword and her words. "What were you thinking when you agreed to marry her? Did you really think Kostaria would accept her? That they would eventually allow your half-elf children to inherit the throne? Why didn't you even discuss it with your shield band before you allowed the elf king to bully you into marriage to his disgraced sister? We could have come up with a different way to appease the elf king that would not have sacrificed the rest of your life or your honor."

If Rharreth told Vriska that the idea to marry Melantha had been his, not King Weylind's, would he lose Vriska's loyalty completely? He definitely wasn't about to tell her that he had volunteered to marry Melantha because he had already begun to fall in love with her, there in the dungeons of Gror Grar, though he had not been able to name the depth of the emotion at the time.

"What's done is done, Vriska. I cannot change the fact that I am married to Melantha." Rharreth caught her sword with his and struck with the right force, knocking the sword from her hand. He pressed the blade to her throat, meeting her gaze. "Now I need you to trust me. I know what I am doing. I know the danger it places me in. But I firmly believe that not only is this the best way forward for Kostaria, but it is the only way. Now, do you yield?"

Vriska met his gaze, her jaw working. Finally, she blinked and sighed. "Yes, I yield."

It was not as wholehearted as Rharreth would have

wished, but he withdrew his sword, wiped it clean on his trousers, and sheathed it. "Good. You are still relieved of the duty of guarding Queen Melantha until such time that you redeem your honor where she is concerned. Understand?"

"Yes, Your Majesty." Vriska kept her eyes down, a hint of a growl to her voice, as she sheathed her sword as well and stalked from the arena.

Rharreth crossed his arms as he watched her go. The thought of Melantha being in danger—of losing her—sent a stab through him unlike anything he had ever felt before, even when he had faced Laesornysh and been sure the elf warrior was about to incinerate him. Without his shield band's support, could he protect Melantha from the storm that would come?

CHAPTER
EIGHTEEN

E ssie sat at the small, white-painted dressing table in their turret bedroom, braiding her hair. No reason for anything more complicated since she had no plans to leave the palace grounds that day. Essie partially swiveled in her seat to see Farrendel. "Paige is coming over shortly to go over a list of social engagements. I am thinking about taking on some of her duties while I am here. Would that be all right?"

Farrendel's hair was still wet from his shower after his exercise with his bodyguards and Julien that morning, and he was fiddling with the buckles of the straps holding his swords across his back. At her question, he met her gaze, his forehead scrunched. "You do not need my permission for either of those things."

"I know. But if I take on more royal duties in Escarland while we are here, it will change our schedule and create more busyness." Essie shrugged as best she could while still braiding her hair. She turned back to the mirror to finish the last of it. "I'm asking for your opinion on it, and I guess it is considered more polite to phrase it as a question instead of just saying, *I'm taking on more royal duties* without getting any input from you whatsoever."

"Ah." Farrendel halted behind her chair, meeting her gaze in the mirror. "Would you expect me to attend any of these functions with you?"

"No." At least, not for a long while. Essie knew Farrendel was far from ready. "That's why Paige is coming over. We're going to divide up the work and brainstorm which ones I can feasibly attend by myself or with her or my mother without anyone starting to gossip about you not attending. Things like visiting the widows' and orphans' home, or a few of the hospitals, or stuff like that. It was a lot of the things I was doing before marrying you. Averett and Paige do more of the official royal duties where people want someone with more clout than the youngest royal sibling. Paige and Mother have taken on a bunch of my engagements since I married you, but I thought it would be nice to alleviate some of their burden while I'm here."

And while Farrendel was so busy. He had his morning exercise sessions, and Julien was talking about adding sword training in a week or two, once Farrendel had regained more of his strength. He also had counseling with Mr. and Mrs. Harwell, and Lance Marion was sure to send an invitation so that he and Farrendel could go back to studying—well, experimenting with—Farrendel's magic some more.

Essie had no intention of sitting around twiddling her thumbs while Farrendel was gone. She might as well resume her own schedule. If she and Paige could arrange it so that Essie's royal duties fell into those times when Farrendel was busy, she wouldn't have any less time with him than she already did.

Farrendel nodded, though his gaze had swung from her to studying himself in the mirror. "If I do not have to attend, then I think you should take on whatever you wish. You like people. You are already restless, and it has only been a week. Besides, it would probably be best to remind your people that you are still their princess. You did not get much of a chance to do that when we were here last."

Trust Farrendel to see the political ramifications as well as the personal ones.

Still, Essie grinned as she tied off her braid. It would be good to return to the charities around Aldon. She had missed that work, even if she'd found other ways to be useful around Estyra working with the elves wounded in the war.

Farrendel was still studying himself in the mirror, reaching up to touch the ragged ends of his hair. The scrunch returned to his forehead while a frown creased lines around his mouth.

His intense expression caught her attention. "Is something wrong?"

Farrendel straightened his shoulders, his forehead smoothing and his jaw tightening. "I want my hair cut."

"Pardon?" Essie turned in her chair again, then stood. She studied Farrendel's stiff muscles and narrowed silver-blue eyes. "Did someone say something about it?"

Ragged and uneven since it had been hacked off with a troll's knife, Farrendel's hair looked awful. But Essie had been careful not to say anything. She hadn't been sure Farrendel would want anyone to touch his hair again, not even to straighten out the strands while it grew.

He clenched and unclenched his fingers, not meeting her

gaze. "I cannot keep seeing this." He gestured to his reflection in the mirror. "Can you cut my hair?"

If only Essie could, but cutting hair was not something she had ever learned as a princess. If she attempted it, she would just make him look worse.

She tried to imagine asking some Escarlish barber to trim Farrendel's hair. Even though he seemed determined, Farrendel would freak out if a stranger got anywhere near him wielding a pair of shears.

But, there was one person who might be able to help.

Essie stepped closer to Farrendel and brushed the ragged ends of his hair from his forehead. "Sorry, but I don't have the skills myself. Would you be comfortable with my sister-in-law Paige trimming your hair? She used to cut her father's hair before she married Averett, and she still trims Avie's hair whenever he doesn't have time to call in a barber to do it for him. If you would like her to help, I can ask her when she's here."

Farrendel shuddered as he released a long breath, but he nodded.

"All right." Essie stood on tiptoe and kissed Farrendel's cheek. This would be hard for him, but hopefully it would help if he didn't have to look at such a visible reminder of what that troll king had done.

"Just sit down right here." Paige waved to the chair set on the brick patio outside the doors of Buckmore Cottage. It was a mild autumn day, mild enough that none of them would get too chilly during a haircut outside.

Bertie and Finn both sat on the patio, playing with their

wooden elf warriors that they had been given last time Farrendel and Essie were there. Essie sat on a bench near them, gripping the wooden versions of herself as she attempted to keep her nephews busy and keep an eye on Farrendel.

Farrendel edged toward the chair as if it were a device of torture. He perched on it, his back as straight as his sword. He flinched as Paige flung an oilcloth cloak around him.

Paige snugged the cloak tight, then wrapped a cloth around Farrendel's neck. "Don't worry. This won't hurt. I cut Averett's, Bertie's, and Finn's hair all the time. Did you have any thoughts on how you want it to look?"

"I do not know." Farrendel's eyes were wide, and he glanced at Essie.

Essie set down the wooden figurines, since both of the nephews had been distracted by the haircut, and turned back to Paige and Farrendel. "Something like how you usually cut Averett's hair, I would think. Longer at the top and shorter at the sides, trying to keep it as long as possible while still getting it even."

Paige nodded. "I can do that." She pulled a comb and a small, silver pair of scissors from a pocket. She gently pushed on the back of Farrendel's head. "Tilt your head forward."

He did as instructed, though Essie could see his hands were clenched on the armrests of the chair with a white-knuckled grip.

Bertie scrambled to his feet and shuffled across the bricks before he stopped a few feet in front of Farrendel. He glanced from Paige to Farrendel, still hugging his wooden elf warrior. "Farrendel getting a haircut?"

"That's Uncle Farrendel, and, yes, he's getting a haircut.

Just like I give to you boys." Paige combed the hair at the back of Farrendel's head, then she snipped the ends with the scissors.

Farrendel's breath caught, but he did not flinch away even as Paige kept combing and cutting. Essie could not imagine how hard that must be for him to sit still for this.

Bertie regarded Farrendel with a rather grave expression for a three-year-old. "Mama says we gotta sit still or she'll cut our ears off."

Farrendel went rigid, his gaze snapping first to Bertie, then to Essie. Something almost like terror flashed in his eyes, as if he really believed his ears were in danger of being sliced off with Paige's scissors if he so much as breathed too deeply.

"Don't worry. I only tell that to the boys to stop them from squirming." Paige combed another section of Farrendel's hair, her gaze never wavering from her work. "Your ears are safe."

Farrendel's shoulders didn't exactly relax, but he didn't look about ready to snap from tension either. After a few more moments, he squeezed his eyes shut, and his breathing returned to that rhythmic, too steady pace that told Essie he was struggling to remain calm.

Paige halted and gestured with the scissors. "Here, Essie. Why don't I show you what I'm doing? That way, you can trim his hair in the future as it grows out."

Essie wasn't sure his hair would need more trimming. With the magical elven conditioner, it wouldn't get split ends. But it might grow out uneven or need a trim to keep it looking nice at various lengths. Essie stood and joined Paige. "Sounds good."

While Paige worked, she explained what she was doing.

Essie did her best to memorize the instructions, and she could see by the set to Farrendel's shoulders that hearing what was going on was helping him as well.

Paige eventually handed over the comb and scissors to Essie and observed while Essie took over. Essie's stomach was tight, nervous that she would mess everything up. But Paige's voice remained calm as she talked Essie through each snip of the scissors.

After a few more minutes, Paige took the scissors back, finished the last few cuts, and tipped Farrendel's head back and forth. Finally, she stepped aside and turned to Essie. "See anything I missed?"

Essie cradled Farrendel's face in her hands. When she tilted his chin up, his eyes were wide, almost pleading. She could feel the slight tremble to him, as if he was barely holding it together.

A quick inspection showed that Paige's haircut was impeccable, as always. "Looks good to me. Very good." Essie pressed a kiss to Farrendel's forehead, hoping that would help him remain calm.

When she straightened and rested a hand on Farrendel's shoulder, he was still trembling. It was too slight to be noticeable, but he was so tense he was about ready to break. Essie faced Paige, forcing a smile. "Thanks for your help and for doing such a good job."

"You're both welcome. Will you be coming to supper tonight?" Paige gathered her supplies, whipping the canvas off Farrendel quickly enough to send the cut hair flying off to the side so that it didn't land on him.

"Maybe." Essie wanted to spend the time with her family, but she wasn't sure if Farrendel would be all right after this experience.

"I hope we'll see you then. I'm sure Averett and Julien will be eager to see the new haircut." Paige's smile didn't slip, though her eyes seemed knowing as she glanced at Essie. She rounded up Bertie and Finn, then herded them down the path headed for Winstead Palace.

When they were out of sight and earshot, Farrendel shot to his feet. He managed to take one step, his breathing going from ragged to hyperventilating. "Essie...Essie...I..." He sank to the ground, wrapping his arms around his knees and resting his head on his arms.

Essie knelt in front of him and gripped his upper arms firmly, giving him a point of contact to ground him as Mrs. Harwell had suggested. She wasn't sure if this was helping him, but it did help her to feel she could do something instead of just sitting there. "Take a deep breath. That's it. Now breathe out slowly."

It took several minutes, but Farrendel's breathing steadied.

She eased to the patio bricks next to him, close enough that their shoulders were touching. Yet, when she traced her fingers down his back, he flinched and she stilled.

"No, do not stop," he mumbled against his arms, still breathing rhythmically.

She ran her hand up and down his back in a soothing rhythm. His shuddering calmed back to a slight tremor, then stilled altogether.

After a long, exhale, he finally lifted his head, though he did not yet glance at her. "Does it at least look better?"

Essie gently cupped his chin and turned his face toward her. His silver-blond hair was still slightly tousled, though it was still trying to part down the center as it had when he wore it long. With his hair short, his ears looked slightly too big, but in a cute, adorable way. His face appeared even more finely angular without his hair framing it.

She ran her fingers through the short strands of his hair, tousling it even more, and smiled. "It looks good. Are you ready to see it?"

Farrendel's shoulders tightened, but he nodded.

Essie dug the hand mirror she'd taken with her from her pocket without getting all the way up. She held the mirror out to Farrendel.

He took it gingerly, as if he expected the mirror to slice his hand. He held it out and studied his reflection. His nose wrinkled, as if he was not sure he liked what he saw.

Essie leaned her head on his shoulder so that she was looking in the tiny mirror with him. "I know you probably don't like it and will want to grow it out as soon as possible. And, I won't mind. I've always liked your long hair. But I love *you*, no matter the length of your hair, and I think you look just as good with short, Escarlish hair." She kissed his cheek. "And, since this is the only time I will probably ever see you with short hair, I'm going to enjoy it while it lasts."

"It...does not look as bad as I thought it would." Farrendel tilted his head, as if he was still trying to get used to his new reflection. "It is an improvement, at least."

"And you'll have options to style it. You can wear it tousled like this." Essie brushed her fingers through his hair again, making it stand on end. His hair was still soft and silken, even when short. "Or you can slick it down." She smoothed his hair down, giving him bangs. Knowing her rather neat and tidy husband, that was probably the style he would choose. "Just don't let it part down the middle. That looks weird with short hair."

The wrinkle on his nose deepened.

"Just figure out a style that feels like you when you look in the mirror. That's what matters." Essie patted his chest, leaning her head against his shoulder again. "And remember that I love you, all right? No matter what."

Farrendel set down the mirror, took her hand, and kissed the top of her head. "I love you too, my shynafir."

Essie swallowed at the lump in her throat. His fierce heart. It was the first time he'd called her that since he'd been rescued. She snuggled closer to him, letting the warm silence wrap around them for a long minute.

Then, she shifted, growing aware of the cold bricks seeping dampness from the ground into her through her clothes. She patted his back with her free hand. "Um, nice as this is, my rear end is going to sleep. Next time, when we want to have a romantic moment, let's sit somewhere softer. Like an actual chair. Or even a carpeted floor."

Farrendel made a noise in the back of his throat.

Then, he laughed.

It was such a pained, croaking sound that Essie didn't even recognize what it was at first. He sounded like he was choking. Or sobbing. Or possibly dying.

She pushed away from him, studying him as his laugh descended into ragged gasps. "Are you still laughing? Or hyperventilating again?"

"Not...sure..." Farrendel gasped as he hunched over, shuddering under the force of his laughter, or whatever it was.

"That wasn't even that funny."

"I know." More shuddering laughter.

Essie patted his shoulder. Yes, Farrendel really would be all right. Eventually.

FARRENDEL TRIED to remember not to touch his hair yet again as he and Essie strolled hand in hand along the path from Buckmore Cottage to Winstead Palace. Captain Merrick, Iyrinder, and a few of the other guards had scouted the path and were following in the trees, but they were staying discreetly out of sight. "Are you sure my hair looks all right?"

"Yes." Essie squeezed his hand, a trace of her laugh in her voice. She nudged him as they walked. "Stop obsessing. People will start to think that you're vain."

He tried not to grimace. Essie had assured him that his hair looked nice. That should have been good enough for him.

Essie swung their linked hands. "Are you going to be all right? We don't have to go inside Winstead Palace if you don't want to."

"I will be fine. I asked Taranath to fill me full of his healing magic, so I should not get a headache or feel the effects of the stone." Farrendel felt great with all the healing magic pumping through him at the moment.

Still, he found himself tensing as they stepped through the doors into the large, stone palace. The walls closed around him, but he did not feel the weight of them the way he normally would.

"Is it working?" Essie's eyes were focused on him, her forehead wrinkled.

"Yes." He smiled, and it felt more natural than forced.

Essie led the way to the dining room, where her family had already assembled. Farrendel found himself gripping her hand tighter. Not that he was scared of her family, not anymore.

But he was still nervous, much as he knew he had no reason to be.

When they entered the room, Bertie and Finn squealed and raced around the table toward them. "Aunt Essie!"

The two children barreled into Essie's legs, and Farrendel used his grip on Essie's hand to steady her under the impact. She hugged each of the nephews with her free hand.

They glanced over at Farrendel and waved their hands in the air, saying something in their high-pitched, garbled toddler language. He glanced at Essie. "Translation?"

"They want you to do more of your sparkling magic like you did last time." Essie patted Bertie's back. "We have to eat dinner first."

The two little boys made whining sounds but trudged back to their seats.

"Notice anything different?" Essie gestured at herself and Farrendel.

Farrendel braced himself as Essie's mother, Averett, Paige, and Julien turned to them.

Averett groaned. "Not this game, Essie. You know we can never guess right. It isn't something like you got a new haircut, is it?"

Wait, they could not tell that *he* was the one with the new haircut? Farrendel shifted, dropping his gaze down to the table instead of looking at them.

"Not me. Farrendel." Essie patted his chest, and it took everything in him not to flinch.

"Oh." Averett drew out the word. "Right, should have seen that."

"See. That's how you know it's a good haircut." Essie

201

grinned up at him. "When it looks so right on you that people don't even notice."

That eased some of the tension from his shoulders. He had seen the truth of that, the past few days. His hair, so obviously hacked off with a knife, had been glaring any time he looked in the mirror. While it was still a shock seeing his hair short, he could get used to this Escarlish style. Probably. Especially while they were here in Escarland where all the males wore their hair short.

"It looks very good." Essie's mother's voice was warm. "You did a good job, Paige."

"Yep, definitely looking good, little brother." Julien slapped Farrendel's shoulder as Farrendel took his seat at the table with Essie's brother on one side, and Essie on the other.

Farrendel found himself relaxing. He had told Essie that he saw Aldon as his home as much as Estyra. Yet, sitting there now with Essie's family as the servers set an unseasoned steak in front of him, it truly felt like home. A place he could relax and feel safe.

The feeling lasted all the way through supper and as Essie's family gathered in her mother's sitting room.

Farrendel sat on the carpeted floor, shooting out harmless sparks of his magic to the squeals of the nephews as they chased each spark.

Essie was sitting across the room, ensconced between her mother and Paige as they chatted so rapidly that he had no hope of keeping up with the conversation.

But, Farrendel had been hoping to talk to Julien and Averett. He glanced between them, waiting for a lull in their conversation about some law going through Parliament before he spoke. "Is there a place I can go to train Essie in how to use my magic? It would need to be free of other people where it does not matter if we cause a few magical explosions."

Averett frowned. "Essie still has use of your magic? That was not a one-time thing?"

"No. I may have accidentally linked my magic to the heart bond. She has use of my magic and thus should be trained." Farrendel sent another shower of sparks into the center of the room, causing another round of giggles from the nephews. "There is no rush. She is in no danger of magic spontaneously leaking from her, since she has to purpose-fully reach for it through the heart bond."

"I will see if you can use the army's bomb range. It won't matter if you magically destroy a few things there." Julien leaned his elbows on his knees. "But it might take a week or two to get something arranged. And to convince the army brass to give the two of you space, at least for the first few training sessions. I might have to promise that you'll do a demonstration for them, possibly let them see how much ordinance you can incinerate with your magic."

That was to be expected. The bulk of the Escarlish army had seen a demonstration of his magic when he destroyed the fortress of Gror Grar. They likely had not realized how much he had lost control and how much danger they had been in.

"That would be acceptable. As long as they give Essie and me space while we are training, I would be willing to give a demonstration with my power." Farrendel shrugged. While it would give the Escarlish generals an idea of the strength of his magic, it would also give Farrendel the opportunity to learn about Escarland's weaponry and figure out how much of it he could take out.

Not that he would end up fighting Escarland, thankfully. But, other human kingdoms would soon have modern weapons similar to the ones Escarland currently had. And Tarenhiel did not have treaties with those kingdoms.

Averett's forehead remained furrowed, and his gaze searched Farrendel's face. "Will practicing with your magic hurt Essie?"

Farrendel shook his head, the movement feeling strangely light without his long hair trailing down his back. "No. She is bonded to my magic now. It cannot hurt her."

And, she would be less likely to hurt someone else with it, if she was trained. That was a guilt he would do his best to make sure she never carried. While she had fought at his side—and had killed when necessary—she was not a warrior.

Farrendel glanced to where she sat across the room. She was grinning broadly, laughing at something Paige had said. Her green eyes were twinkling, her freckles less pronounced in the lamplight, though her hair was a deep red in the warm glow.

How he loved her. It was almost painful in his chest, yet it filled him so completely. He never would have guessed, when he had been desperate enough to agree to an arranged marriage with a human, how absolutely perfect his life would turn out to be thanks to her.

CHAPTER
NINETEEN

elantha gripped Rharreth's arm as they strolled the length of one of the streets of Osmana. This road wound up the valley, the houses on either side built directly into the mountain.

They had been visiting Osmana twice a week for the past two weeks, making the time to talk directly with their people. Rharreth was talking about traveling the kingdom in the spring, possibly late winter so that the dog sleds could still travel easily, to introduce them to her. Melantha found herself more and more excited about exploring Kostaria at his side.

Troll men, women, and children lined the road. Most pushed forward, barely held back by the shield brothers and sister who guarded Rharreth and Melantha.

But others peered from windows or through the crack between door and frame, their gray faces blending in with the stone of the mountains around them. At least most of the faces were less gaunt than they had been when Melantha had first arrived. More hope shone in their eyes. More smiles were visible, though most of the trolls stared at her blankly as if they did not dare show any emotion.

And yet, when Melantha looked at them, she felt something deep within her chest. A heat so intense, so painful, it almost felt like the simmer of anger that had haunted her for so long. This heat did not consume and destroy. It gave life and warmth and drove her to pour herself out for these people.

Love. A burning compassion she had not felt back in Tarenhiel, perhaps because she had spent so much time secretly resenting everybody and everything that she had never tried to give of herself the way she was doing here in Kostaria.

Or, perhaps, because she had not truly known how to love the way she was learning to now. Love was not something that strove to earn another's affection or give only for what one could get back.

Love was self-sacrificing without expectation of any reward. It was healing when all she could expect were glares and suspicion in return. It was feeling compassion for these people, even as some still shouted and spat at her as they passed, though the spitting and shouted expletives were growing fewer among the common people in Osmana. In this particular side street, at least, the crowd remained either silent or pressed forward as if eager.

Rharreth stopped to talk to several citizens, and Melantha paused as well as one troll woman pushed her way to the front of the crowd, gripping a boy's hand in hers. It took a moment for Melantha to recognize her, with her wide smile and the way the boy was bouncing as if he wanted to run and play.

The troll woman bobbed a bow. "I wished to thank you once again, Your Majesty, for what you did."

"I am glad he is healing well." Melantha studied the boy's stance, seeing with satisfaction that he was not favoring either arm. He would grow strong and sure, and that would save him from being an outcast in this kingdom that so valued strength.

But, perhaps, that just meant there was more work for her to do to ensure that those she could not heal, those who were weak and crippled and did not fit what was deemed the norm, would also not be outcasts. If there was a way to do such a thing. Such prejudices were a thing of the heart, and even if she and Rharreth passed good laws, they could not change hearts.

Her own heart had already been changed. In Tarenhiel, she had perpetrated keeping her own brother an outcast. Here, she would do better. She had to do better.

The troll woman was still staring at her, as if expecting something. Or perhaps waiting to be given permission to do something. Finally, the woman bowed her head, giving a lower bow than she had before. "If you ever need anything that is in my power to give, my queen, my service is yours."

Melantha blinked, not sure how to take such a solemn oath of fealty. For that was what it was. In Kostaria, service was not a thing to be bantered about lightly. "Thank you," was all she managed to say before she had to trot to keep up with Rharreth as he began walking again.

"You are winning them," he said in a low voice as she caught up and threaded her arm around his once again.

"Will it be enough, do you think?" she whispered back between a smile and a wave for those being held back by Zavni and Nirveeth.

There had been reports that many among the warrior families were not happy with their elf queen, and far less thrilled with all the healing she had been doing. No one had made any overt threat, but a report from Rharreth's scouts and spies among his own people said that some of the warrior families had been secretly meeting together in small groups to discuss the state of Kostaria.

It was not a good sign that they were meeting behind their king's back rather than presenting their concerns in person as they ought.

"It might." Rharreth paused for a few minutes to talk to another troll family before they moved on and continued their conversation. "Hopefully we will convince them to join our side when they arrive for the Winter Solstice Feast in a few weeks."

In this place of stone and ice and snow, the Winter Solstice Feast was a big event all over Kostaria, but especially here in Osmana. On the Solstice, longest night of the year, at least one member of all the warrior families gathered to celebrate with their king. This would be the first time in over a hundred years that the troll king's Winter Solstice Feast would be held in Khagniorth Stronghold inside the walls of Osmana instead of at the fortress of Gror Grar where Rharreth's brother, father, and grandfather had preferred to hold court.

More than that, this Winter Solstice Feast would be one planned by Melantha, an elf. Planning such events was always the duty of the queen, no matter what kingdom or race, and Melantha had insisted even when Rharreth offered to do it for her this year.

As the road wound its way to the farthest height of Osmana where a wall was built out of the top of the mountain, Melantha could see over the lower sections of the wall into the surrounding mountains.

While the road winding from Osmana had been cleared, the rest of the destroyed mountaintops and the ruins of Gror Grar lay just as they had since Farrendel had laid waste with his magic.

Melantha squinted. Was that a faint, blue glitter to that section of mountains? "You have not even started rebuilding Gror Grar. I would have thought rebuilding the fortress would be a priority."

Rharreth's hand settled on Melantha's shoulder. "We can't. Your brother expended so much magic, it is embedded into the very stone, making it nearly impossible for all except the strongest troll to work magic in that section of mountains. I can still use my magic, but it is incredibly painful. Your brother has ensured that Gror Grar will never be rebuilt in our lifetime." Rharreth's fingers tightened on her shoulder, his voice lowering. "I am happy to have an excuse never to rebuild that place. It once served a purpose to defend Osmana, but it had turned into a place that embodied everything that has gone wrong with our way of thinking."

Something warm and satisfied, perhaps even pride, filled Melantha at seeing the ruins of Gror Grar left where they had fallen. That was the strength of her brother's magic on display for every troll to see every day from Osmana. Maybe the sight of those ruins would remind all who saw them why peace with Tarenhiel was so necessary.

After one last glance at the ruins of Gror Grar and the faint glimmer of Farrendel's magic, Melantha let Rharreth tug her down the next road as they greeted more of their people on their way back to Khagniorth Stronghold.

By the time they returned, night had fully fallen. Melantha kept a firm grip on Rharreth's arm so that she could tilt her head back while walking, gazing at the deep darkness of the sky filled with a myriad of twinkling stars, far more than she had ever seen in Tarenhiel. Even in the winter, the dense branches of the trees blocked parts of the sky, and it had never felt as vast as it did in Kostaria.

"Come." Rharreth gave her a smile as he slid her grip from his arm to his hand and led the way through the passageways of Khagniorth Stronghold. "I have a surprise for you."

Melantha hurried to keep up with his long strides, her hand feeling small clasped in his. Yet, the warmth of his calloused fingers around hers felt increasingly right each time he held her hand.

She had been expecting him to lead her to a section of Khagniorth Stronghold that she had yet to explore—the passages were seemingly endless. And, with the trolls' ability to just grow a few more tunnels deeper into the mountain the same way the elves could just grow another room out of the tree, the stronghold was always expanding.

Yet, instead of a new passageway, Rharreth led her up the main staircase, down the familiar hallway, and halted at their bedroom door. There, a kitchen maid was waiting, holding a tray with covered dishes. Rharreth claimed the tray with a nod of thanks, then juggled both the tray and opening the door as he strode into their bedroom.

Melantha's stomach clenched, her palm going sweaty in his grip. What was his surprise? She was not so sure she would like it.

Rharreth glanced over his shoulder at her, and his white

teeth flashed against his stone-gray skin. "Don't look so nervous. You'll like this."

Still carrying the tray in one hand, he strode past their bed, then placed his hand against the wall. White, icy magic swirled around his fingers. With a grinding of stone, an opening appeared in what had previously been a blank, definitely solid stone wall. Stairs formed, disappearing up until a tiny section of sky pierced with stars appeared in the opening far above.

"How did you...never mind, I know how." Melantha shook her head, blinked, then stared at the set of stairs before her. "Have those stairs always been there? Or did you just create them?"

"Both." Rharreth's smirk widened. He was enjoying her bafflement.

Before she had thought about what she was going to do, Melantha lightly swatted him on the arm, then froze as she realized what she had done. That was not a gesture she would have felt free to do before. Nor was it something she would have done if Rharreth had been an elf. Elves were not given to such physical displays of affection. At least, elven royalty were not.

Rharreth's deep blue eyes twinkled in the starlight as he led her up the stairs. "I built these stairs years ago, but I always put the stone wall back over the entrance to keep it my own little secret. I've been waiting for the right evening to show you."

He had been planning this for a while? Melantha's chest unknotted, and instead she was filled with warmth.

As they neared the top of the stairs, a gust of wind whipped through the opening, and she snuggled the collar of her fur coat tighter. Her breath misted in front of her face as they stepped through the opening onto a broad ledge near the top of the mountain.

Their back was to the outer wall while the mountain around them dropped on the other sides. Before them sprawled Osmana, tiny curls of smoke marking the various dwellings and warm torchlight filling windows and dotting the blackness like a sea of stars below to mirror the one above. Beyond the town, the snow-capped mountains glittered in the light of the stars as far as she could see. To the southeast, the section of mountains infused with Farrendel's magic held a hint of a blue glow that was more noticeable at night.

A pile of furs and blankets were spread on the ledge in the nook formed by the outer wall and two low walls that blocked the wind.

Rharreth gestured with the tray. "The perfect place to watch the northern lights. They should be spectacular tonight."

"Really? How can you tell?" Melantha hurried across the ledge and snuggled into the layers of fur and wool.

Rharreth sat beside her, close enough that his body warmed the blankets beside her. "I can sense the mountains, the northern lights, and things like that. I rarely ever get lost, even in a snowstorm."

"That's a helpful talent." Melantha tucked her toes closer to him. Even in her fur boots, her toes had gone cold during their walk through Osmana.

Rharreth set the tray in the space in front of them and took off the metal covers, revealing bread and a roast, steam still wafting from the meat. "The hunters brought in several caribou today."

Melantha's mouth watered. She had been used to dining

on venison often in Tarenhiel, where the game was plentiful. But in the frozen land of Kostaria, meat, like everything else, was in short supply. "Thank you for saving us a feast for tonight."

Rharreth's grin just widened, and he pulled out a bottle of elven juice and two glasses from where they must have been tucked alongside the blankets near the wall. "I thought you might appreciate a taste of your homeland."

"Thank you." Melantha leaned forward, then halted, not sure what she had been about to do. Had she been leaning in to kiss his cheek? She cleared her throat and looked back to her plate of food. "Let me guess, no one else wanted it?"

"Well, none of the warriors wanted to trade their mead for the 'sissy elf drink,' but I hear that there were plenty of takers among the common citizens. Don't worry. I set aside some for your hospital before trading any away."

Hopefully, more trolls would begin to appreciate something made by elves, even a simple thing like juice. It would break down the barriers that had existed between the trolls and the elves for centuries.

Rharreth poured a glass for each of them, and they dug into the food before it cooled in the frigid mountain air.

As Melantha set aside her empty plate, the first shimmer of bright green streaked across the sky. In the past weeks in Kostaria, she had caught glimpses of the northern lights, and she had seen faint flickers of them occasionally in Tarenhiel. But, sitting at the top of the mountain with Rharreth with nothing but the open sky above them, the lights seemed more magnificent than anything she had yet seen.

More colors formed shifting, glowing patterns in green and pink, tracing ribbons across the sky. The bright colors painted across the mountains, turning the snow pink, then green, then a glowing pink again.

Melantha snuggled closer to Rharreth and, feeling daring there in the darkness with only the brightness of the stars and the northern lights illuminating them, she leaned her head on his shoulder.

After a moment, he wrapped his arm around her shoulders, tucking her closer against him.

Melantha rested a hand on his chest, tucking her cold fingers beneath his coat to warm them against his soft shirt and hard chest. Cradled against him, she felt safe. Not just physically. But here, with him, she was safe to be herself. She could be angry. Passionate. Shout. Yell. Break into a thousand pieces.

But she was also safe to love. To feel compassion all the way to her bones. When anger and bitterness had started crowding out everything else from her chest, she had forgotten how to feel anything. She had become a hollow shell. The image of a perfect elven princess on the outside, but nothing but seething emptiness inside.

As she watched the northern lights blaze across the sky, she felt filled in a way she had not in decades. Perhaps, in learning to open her heart to Rharreth and his people, she might be able to learn to love her own family again the way she ought to have loved them all along.

Melantha tilted her head to look at Rharreth. From this angle, she was looking at the square line of his jaw, his white hair brushing over his tapered ears. The colors from the sky played across his skin and his hair, shining in his eyes. "Thank you for tonight."

He shifted as he glanced down at her. A smile softened the line of his jaw. "You're welcome."

"I can think of one thing that would make it better." Melantha reached up and traced her hand along his jaw. She was free to be herself, and she was not going to hold back.

Rharreth cradled the back of her head as she leaned closer. "Are you sure?" His voice was a brush of a whisper across her face.

"Yes." Melantha's own voice was a whisper.

She was not sure if she kissed him. Or if he kissed her. She wrapped her arms around his neck and let herself feel. Deeply. Tenderly. With every fiber of her being and beat of her heart.

RHARRETH WOKE to the first rays of the rising sun shining against his eyelids. Cold frosted against his hair, his face, and his ear, but the thin layer of ice didn't bother him since his magic protected him.

Melantha lay cradled in his arms, the sunlight shining against what little of her long, black hair he could see over the blanket she had pulled over her head to ward off the cold. She still slept, breathing evenly and deeply.

Was this what love felt like? Something deep and almost painful at times inside his chest?

He'd had no one to show him what it should look like. If his parents had ever loved each other, that love had been long gone by the time he was old enough to remember. His mother had loved him. But had his father? His brother? Once, he'd thought they had. Now, he wasn't sure.

He wanted his relationship with Melantha to be different than what he'd grown up witnessing. He wanted any children they might have to grow up with a better family. A loving family.

Could he manage it? Could she?

Rharreth tucked Melantha closer to his side, protecting her from the cold morning air. Last night gave him hope that she would fight for that future just as hard as he would.

CHAPTER
TWENTY

Farrendel spun and blocked a strike from Iyrinder, then ducked behind the shield Julien held. Julien took Captain Merrick's sword across his shield, striking out with his own sword.

Farrendel gripped the edge of Julien's shield and used the leverage to launch himself up and over, pushing off from the shield as Julien gave it a shove upward.

Iyrinder twisted and propelled himself off the ground, but he was a second too slow. Farrendel kicked his sword aside, then caught his wrist on his way down. He hooked a foot behind Iyrinder's knee and took him to the ground.

Iyrinder rolled before Farrendel could pin him, and Farrendel could not pursue him since Captain Merrick was swinging his sword at Farrendel's head.

Farrendel raised a sword to block, then rolled to put himself behind Julien and his shield once again.

Julien grunted as he blocked Captain Merrick's swing and Iyrinder's leap. He stabbed toward Iyrinder, but

Iyrinder twisted out of the way, stumbling for just a moment.

But the moment was enough for Farrendel. He launched off the ground, using Julien's shoulder for leverage. He planted a solid kick to Iyrinder's chest, and Iyrinder fell heavily to the ground. Farrendel did not let him recover and this time placed a foot on his chest and a sword to his throat.

With his other sword, Farrendel stabbed toward Captain Merrick, sending him off balance as he tried to block both Farrendel and Julien.

Julien shoved Captain Merrick farther off balance with his shield and leveled his sword at Captain Merrick's chest.

Captain Merrick shook his head and huffed something like a laugh between his panting breaths. "Now that Prince Farrendel has his strength back, the two of you are tough to beat, even when he doesn't use his magic."

"I am not yet entirely at full strength. And my flips were still off." Farrendel released Iyrinder and sheathed his swords.

Captain Merrick snorted as he rolled to his feet. "Glad to know we'll just get walloped even worse here in another week or two."

Iyrinder stood and brushed himself off. "It is to be expected when fighting Laesornysh."

Not so expected, after what Farrendel had been through. But with his strength and balance returning, he might eventually feel like Laesornysh again.

Julien swiped at his forehead. "As fun as this has been, I have a full schedule today. I'll see you all again this time tomorrow." He gave them each a salute, then shouldered his weapons as he headed toward Winstead Palace.

Captain Merrick and Iyrinder remained where they were, staring at Farrendel. Waiting for him to make the first move to walk back to Buckmore Cottage, since they were his guards.

Farrendel cleared his throat and faced Captain Merrick. "Would it be possible for me to go into Aldon today?"

"Of course." Captain Merrick sheathed his sword, then reached for the revolver he had set aside when they began their practice fight. "That's why I'm here. So that you can safely move about at your pleasure. Where would you like to go, Your Highness?"

Perhaps having guards was not so bad after all. Farrendel shifted. "I would like to visit Lance Marion's workshop."

Even though Farrendel had been in Aldon for a month, he had not yet ventured outside the palace grounds. Essie, of course, had been going about Aldon nearly every day for the past two weeks, which was how Lance had figured out that she and Farrendel were back in Escarland. Ever since, Lance had sent multiple messages a day, asking Farrendel to come to the workshop whenever he had time.

"That could be arranged. Do you want fanfare or would you rather travel incognito?" Captain Merrick studied Farrendel, then glanced at Iyrinder.

"The less fanfare, the better." Farrendel suppressed a shudder. The last time he and Essie had visited Aldon Market and Lance Marion's workshop, a large crowd had gathered, someone shot at Farrendel, and things had come very close to turning ugly. He did not want a repeat of that experience.

"Incognito it is, then. Meet me at the guardhouse after you've washed up and are ready to leave. I'll have a disguise for you." Captain Merrick turned to Iyrinder. "I suppose you need to come too?"

"I am under strict orders from my king never to let his brother out of my sight whenever he steps foot outside of Buckmore Cottage." Iyrinder gripped the hilt of his sword, probably wishing he had his bow ready to hand, as that was his preferred weapon.

"I will figure out something for you as well." Captain Merrick frowned, as if a disguise for Iyrinder would be tougher.

Then again, Iyrinder did not have an Escarlish haircut like Farrendel did. Farrendel resisted the urge to touch his shortened hair. That was a good thing about wearing his hair short. He could pass more easily among the Escarlish people.

As Farrendel strolled back to Buckmore Cottage, the early winter breeze sliced through his light clothes. With his sweat drying on his skin, he would start shivering if he did not get inside soon. The sky was clouded over, threatening to rain, perhaps even sleet, before long.

When Farrendel entered Buckmore Cottage, he found that Essie had already left for her engagement at the orphan's home or hospital. He was not sure which one it was that day.

After a shower, he made his way to the gatehouse, where he found Captain Merrick and Iyrinder already waiting. Miss Merrick was also there, talking with Iyrinder.

Iyrinder wore brown Escarlish trousers and a baggy off-white shirt, both of which were inferior quality compared to the fancy Escarlish party clothes Farrendel had worn before. Miss Merrick was in the process of tying back Iyrinder's chestnut hair at the base of his neck.

"Prince Farrendel, good. I think these should fit you relatively well." Captain Merrick held out a stack of Escarlish clothes, including brown trousers and a not-quite-white shirt of some rough material Farrendel had never worn before.

Farrendel located the water closet. Not an ideal place to change, especially since this one was not as clean as he would prefer, but it would do.

When he was dressed in the Escarlish clothes, he exited the water closet while keeping a tight grip on the waist of the trousers. They were so large on him that if he let go, his trousers would be down at his knees. The shirt billowed around him, even though he had tucked it into the trousers as was customary in Escarland. The sleeves would have been the right length, but the shoulder seams drooped halfway down his upper arms since he did not have the shoulder breadth of the person for whom this shirt was designed.

He appeared much as Essie had when she had borrowed his clothes on the day they married, except that she had managed to be adorable while he was just pathetic.

Thankfully, Miss Merrick had left, and only Iyrinder and Captain Merrick remained in the guardhouse to see how ridiculous he looked.

"You look like a gangly youth trying on his father's clothes." Captain Merrick shook his head. "Hopefully people will assume I'm your older brother rather than your father. I'm not that old."

"If you were an elf, you would be old enough to be my father." Farrendel shrugged, causing one of his sleeves to droop even more off his shoulder.

"Your generations must get interesting." Captain Merrick held up what looked like a rope and a Y-shaped belt. "Here, tie this rope to tighten the waist, then these suspenders will keep your trousers from falling down."

Suspenders? Farrendel took the items with one hand, not daring to release his trousers even for a moment. That was when he noticed Iyrinder had a rope tied around the waist-band of his trousers. The suspenders were buttoned to the trousers with one strap in the back that branched into two straps going over his shoulders.

Farrendel held it up. "Do these suspenders help carry weapons?"

"Nope. They just hold up your trousers. Since I'm assuming you don't want to end up with your trousers around your ankles in front of half of Aldon, that's a pretty important job all on its own." Captain Merrick stepped forward, holding his palms up. "Would you let me assist in getting them on? The back can be tricky."

Farrendel let Captain Merrick help him get the suspenders attached. They kept the trousers where they were supposed to be, while the rope tightened some of the bagginess.

He could not take his swords, but he hid a knife in his boot and a dagger along his back where it was covered by a wool coat.

Iyrinder took a coat and put it on over his hair, flipping up the collar as Captain Merrick instructed. When Iyrinder put on a slouch cap, the tips of his ears and his long hair were covered. As long as no one looked too closely to notice his elven skin tone and features, he would blend right in.

Farrendel took his own slouch cap. It was soft with a small brim in the front and a band around the bottom. When he put it on, he made sure his ears were tucked into the band. The ends of his hair stuck out from under the cap, and in the reflective surface of the glass windows, he looked like a human lad off to find work at a factory.

When Captain Merrick was satisfied with their disguises, they left the palace grounds through the gate by Buckmore Cottage. Captain Merrick was also dressed as a laborer, as were the two other human guards he had tasked to go with them, though they had small, Escarlish guns hidden beneath their coats.

While Captain Merrick and Iyrinder stuck close to Farrendel, as if they were merely three human brothers, the other two guards stayed at a distance, keeping a wary eye on their surroundings while pretending they were not with them.

Unlike last time, when all eyes had been on Farrendel and Essie as they rode through the streets, this time no one even gave him a second glance. It was reassuring, if a little nerve-wracking, as he had to shove through the crowd at Captain Merrick's heels. People bumped him with their shoulders and jostled him with their elbows. Sometimes they apologized, but often they went on their way as if such invasion of personal space was normal.

The noise of all the talking people, rumbling carriages, tramping feet, and street hawkers shouting about their wares assaulted Farrendel's ears to the point he wished he had stuffed them with moss before leaving the palace.

His heart was pounding harder, his breathing growing ragged. Maybe this had been a bad idea.

Farrendel clenched his fists and tried to take calming breaths. He could not afford to dissolve into panic in the middle of this crowd.

Just when he was not sure if he could keep it together any longer, they popped out into a quieter side street.

Farrendel leaned against the brick wall of a building, gulping in lungfuls of air and trying to pretend his hands were not shaking.

Captain Merrick did not comment while he and Iyrinder waited for Farrendel to piece himself back together.

When Farrendel felt steadier, he nodded, and they continued on their way.

Lance Marion's workshop was a large brick building set among a number of other massive brick buildings that were most likely factories or warehouses, though Farrendel could not tell which. Lance's shop was unmarked, and one of the unassuming wooden doors was propped open, as if Lance had no fear that anyone would try to rob him. Perhaps they would not dare, considering Lance's reputation for causing magical explosions.

Captain Merrick nodded to Farrendel. "We will remain just inside the door."

"Thank you." Farrendel appreciated that he could relax while spending time with Lance, knowing that Captain Merrick, Iyrinder, and the two other guards were making sure no one could attack him.

When Farrendel stepped inside, the cluttered space felt strangely cozy. Piles of random bits of metal, half-finished devices, and weapons were stacked haphazardly around the cavernous space. The towers of junk were so tall that Farrendel could only see a small section of the building at a time.

A distant mechanical beeping sound came from the far corner, then the scrambling of boots on the paved floor.

A young man, who looked only a few years older than Farrendel, careened around a pile of junk. He wore baggy, grease-stained clothing with the sleeves of his gray shirt rolled to his elbows. A pair of goggles pushed onto his fore-head was the only thing taming his disheveled, light brown hair. His gaze was glued to a small device in his hand. It held a couple of dials and a red, flashing light.

"Farrendel!" Lance grinned, still not looking up from his device. "I see you are still maxing out the range of my magical sensor, even though I increased the top end of the range exponentially during the war. What do you think of my new model? It has a flashing light instead of a beep when it is activated. During the war, it let us know when an attack was coming, though I had to keep the sensors away from your brother since his presence would set them off."

Farrendel felt his muscles relaxing further. Lance did not comment on his hair or how he was dressed. He did not even seem to notice. Even better, he did not ask how Farrendel was or how he was feeling.

It was oddly nice to be treated as if nothing had happened.

"Come on to the back. I have a whole bunch of magical power cells you can fill with your magic, if you would like. I had to blow up the other one. Could you feel it when it went off?" Lance led the way through the piles of metal items, only glancing over his shoulder briefly as he asked the question.

"Yes. I was able to gather much of the magic back to myself. It boosted my access to my magic when I was surrounded by stone." Farrendel had to duck under a beam that was precariously balanced between two towers of junk.

"Fascinating! Human magicians cannot retrieve their magic like that. It is not so connected to them the way elven magic appears to be." Lance rounded one last junk pile, and they reached the far corner where he had his main workspace.

Here, a device sat in the corner, walled off from the workbench and tools. That was where Lance had human magicians—and Farrendel the last time he was here—fill magical power devices. Tempered glass barriers provided protection in the event of magical explosions. Along one wall, a bunch of empty power devices sat in a row while a small device with a metal stove coil on top sat on the workbench.

Lance strode over to it and picked it up. "I got a start on the heating device Essie requested, but I'm not finished yet. I was thinking we could try to power it with your magic. That way, you could replenish it yourself when needed. No sense for you of all people to have to buy magical power cells when you have enough magic at your fingertips to power all of Escarland for a year."

"If we can get my magic to refrain from blowing up the device, it would be acceptable to use it as the source of power." Farrendel stepped closer to the device, spotting the space where the power cell was supposed to go. Would they be able to contain his magic in such a small device?

If they could pull it off, it would be a dream come true to use his magic for something besides killing. He had never been able to power things in Tarenhiel. Most elven technology used growing magic, a living energy that just got killed off when paired with Farrendel's power.

"Oh, sure. We just need to find the right metals that will conduct your magic rather than be incinerated by it. Or a way to dampen it to make it less volatile and more manageable." Lance tugged the goggles down from his forehead to cover his eyes. He picked up a second pair of goggles from the workbench and tossed them to Farrendel.

"Here. You'll want to put these on, and then we can get to work."

Farrendel caught the goggles, then took off his hat and coat and set them on a nearby chair. The goggles were much easier to put on when he did not have to worry about them getting caught in his long hair, though he still had to ensure that the tips of his ears were not pinched in the strap.

Perhaps it was Lance's absentminded enthusiasm, but Farrendel found himself telling the inventor something he had only told Essie. "Stone dampens my magic."

"Does it? We'll have to experiment to determine how much and if it could steady your magic enough to use in the power cell as I am envisioning." Lance started flipping switches and pushing buttons on the large device set behind a protective wall. The magic-storing device whirled to life.

Unlike most people, Lance was not plotting how to use that new information to trap Farrendel. He just wanted to study the phenomenon as an interesting facet of magic.

Farrendel settled the goggles more firmly over his eyes, then he strode around the barrier toward the small, protected area next to the magical storing device. "Do you need me to put one of the empty power cells in the device?"

"Yes, please! All of those cells along the wall are designed to hold your magic. I've been making them ever since I got back from the war." Lance gestured toward the row of magic-storing devices.

Farrendel raised his eyebrows as he retrieved one and settled it in place according to Lance's instructions. Lance must have been working night and day to get so much done in the past month.

As Lance called instructions, conducting his experiments and taking notes on how Farrendel's magic reacted,

Farrendel found himself relaxing as he only did when he was with someone he trusted.

It was strange, in this place of gears and grease and human inventions, that he would find himself truly belonging.

CHAPTER TWENTY-ONE

E ssie resisted the urge to scrub her palm against the sturdy trousers she was wearing. The whole three-hour train ride northeast out of Aldon, she had struggled to hide her nerves. Not that she was fooling Farrendel since he could feel her jitters through the heart bond.

Now, she and Farrendel stood deep in the bomb range of Fort Charibert, the sprawling army base named after the first Escarlish king. Here, Escarland's army trained and tested new weaponry. A few scrub trees and patches of grass valiantly attempted to grow on the range despite the bombardment the acres routinely suffered. A thin layer of snow blanketed the range, smoothing out the battered ground.

At least Averett and Julien had convinced the army to clear the range for the day. Essie could not imagine having an audience for this first lesson in using Farrendel's magic.

Farrendel took her hands, giving her a soft smile. "Do not

be nervous. We will start with small amounts of magic. There is nothing within a two mile radius that your army would mind if we accidentally destroy."

"Except for each other." Essie swallowed and swiped her palms on her trousers. The sweat just made her fingers feel colder.

Farrendel gave a huff that was the equivalent of an eye roll. "I am immune to my own magic. You cannot hurt me if you lose control any more than I can hurt you."

Very true. Still, she couldn't help but be nervous. The first time she'd used Farrendel's magic, she and Jalissa had been about to be overwhelmed by a troll ambush. It had been terrifying, both the near-death experience and wielding that much power. Then, in the final battle, she had helped Farrendel bring his magic under control, and she had gotten a taste of its sheer vastness. Did she even have a hope of wielding that much power?

But, for all her nerves, Farrendel did not seem to have the same jitters. For the past week, he had been spending a great deal of time with Lance Marion on days when he didn't have counseling with Taranath and Mr. and Mrs. Harwell or wasn't training all day with Julien.

The days with Lance seemed to give Farrendel a new confidence about his magic, something Essie had never seen in him before. It was as if, for the first time, he was truly coming to appreciate his magic instead of the fear-bordering-on-hatred that he used to show when it came to his power.

"We will start slowly. I promise. After all, we elves come into our magic slowly as we mature, and that gives most elves time to train and learn control before they have access to their full power." Farrendel started to let go of her hands, but she reflexively tightened her grip.

Perhaps she was just trying to delay the inevitable, but something about what he'd just said struck her. "Wait, when we were first married, you mentioned that elves aren't considered fully mature until they are one hundred fifty to two hundred years old. Since you are only a hundred and five, does that mean you could still get more magic?"

"Maybe." Farrendel froze, his gaze dropping to their clasped hands. "I think I already *have* come into more magic since I married you. Thanks to the elishina, I have begun to mature faster. I have more control and more power than I had even a few months ago, and I do not think this is all due to the additional practice with my magic with Lance or linking my magic with the heart bond, though that seems to be part of it."

Essie tightened her grip on his fingers. This was the first time they'd had proof of this effect of the heart bond, the one that would give her a longer life and Farrendel a shorter one. She'd always assumed the first sign would be that she would noticeably not age. It had never occurred to her that Farrendel would show evidence of aging faster first. "I'm sorry."

"Why are you sorry? I am not." Farrendel lifted his gaze to hers, a hint of a smile tipping up his mouth. "But, yes, it is possible that I am not at my full magical strength yet. I started to come into my magic only twenty years ago, after all."

More magic. Essie could hardly imagine it. He couldn't fully control the magic he currently had. "Who trained you?"

"My father, as much as he could." Farrendel gave a small shrug. "Normally, elven parents teach their children the basics even before they gain magic of their own. Once they do, elves are apprenticed to someone with the same magic. But, there was no one to teach me. I mostly figured out how to use my magic on my own during battle."

A flash of something hot filled her chest. Sure, the elves had been desperate. But it still seemed foolhardy to send an untrained boy with Farrendel's level of power into battle. He would have had his magic for less than five years at that point.

No surprise that he had been captured. Of course, he hadn't had the magical strength to rescue himself or save his father during the rescue. And no wonder he always seemed scared of his magic, when he'd had no one to teach him how to properly use it.

"But do not worry. You have me to teach you." Farrendel tugged his fingers from hers. Tiny bursts of sparks formed above his palms, the same ones he formed for the nephews. "Hold out your hands."

Essie did so, hoping he couldn't see how much her fingers were trembling.

Farrendel gently slid his hands under hers, his palms warm against the backs of her hands and the magic a gentle tickle. As he did, she could feel him push the magic toward the heart bond, as if asking her to take control of it.

With a deep breath, Essie mentally reached for the magic and took it from him. Her sense of the magic sharpened, and she concentrated on keeping it at its contained sparkle.

"I am going to add more power to the heart bond." As soon as he finished speaking, Farrendel handed over yet more magic.

Essie held her breath, but the sparks on her hands didn't leap out of control. The magic in the heart bond stayed there, as if waiting for her command.

"Now try to increase the sparks into full bolts of magic curling around our hands." Farrendel's voice remained as soft as the fizzling sparks in her hand.

As soon as she tugged on the magic, it leapt to her, as if eager to burst out. The sparks in her hand exploded in a blue-white flare before she cut the magic off. "Sorry. Sorry. That didn't work right."

"I would consider it a success that it only mildly exploded rather than blew up with so much force we were knocked off our feet." Farrendel shrugged, a grin now tugging at his mouth. "Try again."

Essie tugged on the magic again, and this time she was able to get more controlled bolts to twine around their hands and up her arms.

Farrendel talked her through more practice, creating a shield of the crackling magic, and shooting it out in a specific direction. Essie found it easier than she was expecting, but that could have been because Farrendel only gave her a portion of magic each time so that she never had to work with unmanageable amounts.

After an hour, Farrendel halted them, studying Essie. "Would you like a break?"

"No, I'm fine. It was such a hassle to get this set up, and a long train ride out here. We need to make the most of the time the army is giving us." Essie straightened her shoulders, though she probably wasn't fooling him. He could sense through the heart bond the way her eyes were going dry and a throbbing starting at her temple from how hard she was concentrating.

His silver-blue eyes searched her face for another moment, before he pulled a piece of paper from a pocket. "When I talked over how I accidentally melded my magic to the heart bond with Lance, he gave me a list of questions to pinpoint some of the limits. Now that you are more comfortable with my magic, we could go through this list. It should be less taxing."

"That sounds better than more practice. And probably more useful." Essie plopped down onto the patch of ground that had been cleared of snow thanks to all the magical practice incinerating it.

Still, the ground was damp, and moisture quickly started soaking through her trousers. But, they didn't have much of a choice since they still needed to stay far away from civilization—and thus chairs—that could be destroyed.

Farrendel's nose wrinkled as he grimaced down at the ground for a moment before he also sat. Then he held up the paper and read off the first item. *"Can Essie use your magic directly or does it have to be put in the heart bond first?"*

"That is a good question." Essie closed her eyes and mentally reached out to the heart bond, then through it toward Farrendel. The distant crackle of his magic was less distinct than when he placed magic in the heart bond. With a deep breath, she gave a tug on the magic, trying to draw on it. "I'm tugging on your magic, like I've been doing to wake you from your nightmares. But I can't seem to actually use the magic directly."

"Let me try something." Farrendel's voice was absent-minded, as if he too had his eyes closed as he concentrated.

A moment later, Essie mentally fell backwards as Farrendel's magic suddenly released, flooding through the heart bond into her. A crackle burst around her, more and more magic gushing through her.

She scrambled to try to control it or stop it, but it felt like she was trying to plug a running faucet with her fingers. "Farrendel!"

The magic cut off as abruptly as it started.

"That answers a few of Lance's questions." Farrendel's voice was level, almost satisfied, rather than panicked as Essie felt.

She opened her eyes, cocking her head. "Really? What did you make of that? I was mostly just freaking out."

Farrendel smoothed the paper, his mouth pressed into a thin, thoughtful line. "You can use my magic directly from me, but I need to...give you permission, I guess? I think I have been subconsciously releasing the magic to you when I have been putting it in the heart bond."

"That makes sense." Essie reached out and rested a hand on his knee. "I wouldn't want to just steal your magic from you."

Farrendel rested his hand on hers. "I have more than enough magic for both of us. It is yours to use, and I will never wish to keep it from you."

Maybe he did not mind sharing his magic. He might even be a little relieved not to have to carry the burden of it alone. But, Essie wouldn't want to just take magic from him, as if she had the right to use him however she liked. He'd already had two troll kings torture him with the most extreme version of that mindset. "I know. And thank you for that trust."

"Still, I would prefer that you could use it without my permission, in case I am ever unconscious and you need to defend yourself or me." Farrendel's frown deepened, and he stared down at the piece of paper.

Ah, now she understood his logic. Of course that would be his worry. "I take it another question on that list is whether I can use your magic even if you are incapacitated due to stone and troll magic?" Essie gripped one of his hands in both of hers.

"Yes." Farrendel stared up at the overcast sky for a long moment. When he spoke, he seemed to be thinking out loud, as much as he was speaking to her. "If I give you permission to use my magic when I place it in the elishina, then perhaps if I store a power there, you will always have access to it. The magic seemed more...stable after it was in the heart bond than when you use it directly from me."

"Yes, it does seem less overwhelming when I draw it from the heart bond. Perhaps because it doesn't have the full scope and power of your magic behind it?"

"Or, maybe, the heart bond does something to the magic. Makes it steadier, somehow?" Farrendel shrugged. "I guess I will have to experiment to see how my magic feels to me if I run it through the elishina before I use it rather than tapping on my magic directly."

"Go ahead. We're here to experiment, after all." Essie let go of his hand, then leaned her elbows on her knees. Besides, if Farrendel was experimenting, then she could sit and watch and take a break.

Farrendel pushed to his feet and took a few steps away from Essie before he drew on his magic. Perhaps it was all the practice or she was simply concentrating hard enough on his magic, but she could feel him use his power in a way she hadn't before.

Magic twined around him, crackling and filling the air with a tingling sensation, like the moment before a lightning strike. He sent a blast toward the sky, exploding it with a boom that shivered through the dirt. Sparks of magic rained down, fizzling into the grass.

Once the magic had dissipated, Farrendel drew on it again, but this time he dumped it into the heart bond, filling Essie's chest with a faint fizzing feeling, before he tugged the magic back out.

Magic burst into the air around him again, and he whipped it into a whirlwind before letting it explode outward.

Essie blinked as the magic whipped past her face, tingling against her skin. When her vision cleared, Farrendel was sitting down across from her again.

"Well? What's the verdict?" Essie leaned forward.

"It does not seem to make a difference for power, and I think I can reach through the heart bond and use my magic the same way you do. It takes more concentration for me to access it that way, but..." Farrendel's forehead furrowed, and his gaze was unfocused. "I wonder if that was how I drew on my magic there in Kostaria while I still had stone inside me. Or, that was how it began. Once it started to pour out, it unleashed in a torrent that even the troll magic could not stop."

Essie resisted the urge to shiver, and not just because the damp earth beneath her was chilly. Farrendel had come far too close to destroying their own armies when he had lost control of his magic. He normally kept such a tight grip on his power. What if she messed up and lost control? She could accidentally destroy half of Aldon if that happened.

She let out a long breath. That was why she was training. Besides, as long as she just drew on the magic that Farrendel placed in the heart bond, it should be more or less safe.

Farrendel went back to staring at the sky again. "If I can reach my magic through the heart bond, perhaps I can no longer be cut off from it, though I guess we will not know unless we experiment with stone laced with troll magic."

"Not something I really want to test." Essie grimaced. If she closed her eyes, she could still picture Farrendel as she had found him, pinned to the stone floor in a puddle of his own blood. She wasn't sure she could handle watching a troll wrap him with stone and magic, even if it was just an experiment.

"I would rather learn the answer in a safe experiment than in a life-or-death situation." Farrendel rubbed a thumb over the puckered scars on the inside of his wrist. "With trade opened with Kostaria, I can probably send a message to Melantha to have Rharreth lace some stone with his magic, then send it along with the next ice and stone trade shipment. I am sure Lance can figure out a way to experiment with it."

"That sounds sensible. But only when you're ready, all right?" Essie reached across the space between them to squeeze one of his hands. His idea for experimenting sounded much better than what she had been envisioning. Still, there was no reason to rush things. Surely Farrendel wouldn't need to fight trolls again anytime soon. And, even if he did, he would have the might of both the Tarenhieli and Escarlish armies to back him up. "What is the next item on Lance's list?"

Farrendel picked up the paper from where he had dropped it on the ground. "Looks like we answered a bunch of these. Here is one we have not: *Can we use my magic at the same time?* I think I already know the answer, but we might as well be thorough. Lance will quiz me relentlessly tomorrow and might drag you into his workshop for more experimenting if we are not."

"He might try anyway, even if we're thorough. I'm sure he will just think of more questions that need to be answered." Essie shrugged and patted his arm with her free hand, since she was still holding his hand with the other.

There was still some magic in the heart bond, so she drew on it to create a few small bolts of magic.

Farrendel held up his hand, magic twining around his fingers as well.

"Yep, we definitely can use magic at the same time. This might be the most useful skill. I can hold a shield or something while you do your whole attack thing." Essie thought about the ambush they had suffered near Lethorel. She could have kept up a magical shield around their group while Farrendel attacked. It would have freed him to concentrate on winning the battle.

She would have to practice until she could confidently wield his magic. She didn't want to become a warrior or fight like Farrendel did. But if she could prevent him from being captured or killed, then it would be worth it.

Would this magic sharing have happened if not for Farrendel's capture and torture? Leyleira had mentioned that heart bonds themselves could be strengthened through difficulties. Perhaps linking his magic with the heart bond wouldn't have worked if he'd tried it earlier since it was their separation that had strengthened the heart bond to what it was now.

Maybe there had been no other path to get where they were than the one that they had walked. But, Essie was going to do everything in her power—and apparently everything in Farrendel's magical power—to make sure that he never suffered torture ever again.

As the early darkness of late fall settled over the bomb

range, Essie and Farrendel strolled hand in hand toward the army base and the waiting train that would take them back to Aldon. There, they found Averett pacing and Julien leaning against the wall of the train station. The entire pack of guards, including Captain Merrick and Iyrinder, waited a few paces away.

As they approached, Averett hurried toward them, his gaze flicking over Essie as if searching for injuries. "We could see the magical explosions even from here. Are you all right? How did it go?"

Essie glanced past Averett toward Julien. "You had to physically restrain him from going to check on us, didn't you?"

Julien pushed away from the wall. "Yes. I finally convinced him that he would get himself blown up if he stumbled onto the bomb range when you weren't expecting it."

"Thank you, Julien." Essie stretched to give Julien a side hug without letting go of Farrendel's hand.

"Anytime." Julien patted her back, then stepped away.

Averett was shifting from foot to foot behind Julien, doing his whole hovering overprotective older brother routine.

Essie grinned and turned to him. "And, yes, Averett. I'm fine, and it went well. See." She held out her hand and drew on the magic Farrendel had left in the heart bond. Bolts of magic twined around her fingers.

Farrendel held out his free hand as well, sending matching white-blue bolts around his hand and arm.

Averett started, blinking at Essie's hand. "I'm not sure I'll ever get used to seeing that. It's a good thing you didn't have magic when we were children. You would have zapped all of us out of existence at one point or another."

"Edmund definitely wouldn't have survived. Not with all his teasing." Julien crossed his arms, as if trying to pretend he was less shocked by his little sister using magic than Averett was.

"You weren't much better." Essie cut off the flow of magic, and she sensed when Farrendel did the same. "Now let's get back to Aldon before it gets too much later. I think I'm going to regret the fact that we only took the seating car and not the sleeping car as well."

Farrendel tugged her closer to him as they all started walking toward the train. "You can nap on my shoulder, like you always do."

"Even if it means I will be wide awake when we get home and will talk a mile a minute while you're trying to go to sleep?" She patted his chest.

He tugged her closer still, his voice going soft as he gave her a tiny smile. "Even if you end up in one of your nonstop giggling fits."

Julien gave a soft groan as he stepped up the metal stair into the train. "Now I'm going to regret that we didn't bring the sleeping car. Please tell me the two of you aren't going to be all cuddly all the way home. Three hours is a long ride when we can't escape."

Essie smirked as she climbed into the train, still gripping Farrendel's hand. Farrendel obligingly followed in her footsteps, as if half-hoping her brothers would overlook him in their teasing.

When Farrendel settled onto the end of one of the benches, Essie curled up beside him. After they ate a light supper, Essie took him up on his offer to nap against his shoulder. Despite her brothers sitting across the way, Farrendel put his arm around her shoulders, and Essie found herself smiling against his shirt.

She had missed this. Cuddling with Farrendel. Embarrassing her brothers. Everything that made life so very good.

As the train trundled toward Aldon, she let herself doze. Farrendel's voice rumbled beneath her ear occasionally as he joined in the low murmur of her brothers' conversation, though Essie didn't try to stay awake enough to listen.

When they arrived, Averett and Julien headed for Winstead Palace while Essie and Farrendel, with their escort of guards, walked through the darkness of the gardens until they reached Buckmore Cottage.

"That was a good day." Essie ran her hand up the smooth handrail as she strode up the stairs. She glanced over her shoulder as she reached the hallway at the top. "We'll have to schedule another practice session soon. I'm determined to learn to wield your magic."

"You did very well." Farrendel's mouth quirked as he joined her in the hallway, then pushed open the door to their turret bedroom. Moonlight shone through the windows, dappling the floor with patterns from the shadows of the bare tree branches outside.

"Are you sure you're all right with me using your magic? It must be strange, sharing it like this. It wasn't something you were expecting would happen." Essie rubbed her upper arms. She had to be absolutely sure Farrendel was all right sharing his magic. She would never want him to feel like she was just using him.

"My magic has always been too much for one person. Perhaps it was always meant to be shared." Farrendel reached out and gently held her, stepping closer. "More than that, when I see you use my magic, it...I cannot hate my magic when you wield it."

"You should never hate your magic. It is a part of you." Something about this moment made her feel bold. Essie stood on her tiptoes to kiss his cheek, wrapping her arms around his neck. "I have always loved your magic, just as I have always loved your scars. Because your scars and your magic are a part of you, and I love you. All of you."

"And I love you. Your red hair." He cradled her face and kissed the top of her head. "Your freckles." This time, he kissed her cheek. "Your chatter. All of you."

Essie was melting from the inside out. If he kept on saying sweet stuff like that, she was going to be an Essie-shaped puddle on the floor by his feet.

He slid his hands to her shoulders, then wrapped his arms around her waist, cradling her close with his hands gentle against her back. "There, in Gror Grar, I promised myself that if I ever was rescued, I would stop holding back with you and love you fully. I have not kept that promise as I should have."

"You had a lot to sort through. And..." Essie trailed her fingers down his neck to the loose collar of his shirt, tracing the length of one of his scars. As she'd known he would, he flinched, though he did not pull away as he had before. She searched his face. "You're still flinching."

He let out a sigh that brushed against her hair. Instead of letting her go as she had expected, he held her tighter, holding her gaze. "I am fine, Essie. Truly. Flinching is such an instinct that perhaps I will always do it. But, I know, right now, that it is you. I know I am not in that dungeon. I am here. I am with you. And I am *fine*."

Then, he kissed her. Tenderly. Slowly. The kind of kiss that promised more.

Essie held onto him, kissing him back as she had longed to do since she'd rescued him. She was ready. He was fine. And they were married. It was high time they acted like it.

TWENTY-TWO

Melantha sat in the front row of the benches surrounding the fighting arena as two shirtless male troll warriors faced off against each other.

Outside, the snow lay thick and heavy on the ground. The darkness of this, the shortest day of the year, pressed down onto the mountains, leaving only a sliver of daylight.

Inside, the room was so packed with trolls that Melantha had shed her layers of fur and wool until she was down to a light dress for the first time in this place of ever-present cold stone and even colder ice. Troll warriors had come from all over the kingdom to celebrate the Winter Solstice Feast in Osmana. Not even the blizzards and several feet of snow had deterred them.

Would the trolls be able to tell that an elf had planned their celebrations? She was not sure if she wanted them to notice a difference or if she would rather they did not to prove that she could adapt to their customs.

A cheer reverberated around the room, booming off the stones so loudly it took all of Melantha's training in calm serenity not to flinch. Down in the combat field, one warrior tumbled on the ground, having been tossed by his opponent.

Rharreth reached over and rested a hand on her arm, though he did not look away from the fight. Perhaps he had noticed her flinch.

Melantha made sure her spine was straight, her expression blank. As subtly as she could, she touched the dagger belted at her waist. Over the past weeks, Rharreth had added training with the dagger to training with the staff. She still preferred the staff, but there was comfort in having the dagger near to hand when surrounded by so many troll warriors.

The Winter Solstice celebration began with several hours of fighting bouts. Apparently, trolls could not properly feast until after they had fought many, many bloody and sweaty matches while shirtless, for the male warriors, or wearing tight, sleeveless tunics, for the female warriors. Either way, it was as if they wanted to show off as much muscle and blood as possible.

At least, that was Melantha's way of looking at it. Rharreth had explained that warriors could earn honor and prestige, by winning matches before all the warriors of the kingdom at these Solstice bouts.

The troll warrior placed a boot on his thrown opponent's throat, pointing his sword at the fallen troll's eye. "Do you yield?"

The troll on the ground could barely move enough to tilt his chin in a nod and croak something that was probably *yield*, but Melantha could not hear it over the roar that was even more deafening than the one before it.

She would never last at this rate. Keeping her magic buried inside her, she carefully called up some of it and stuffed it in her ears. As the magic deadened the shouting and stomping of hundreds of feet, Melantha had to resist sighing in relief. So much better.

Several more bouts progressed in the same fashion. Two warriors stepped into the ring. They beat each other up until blood and sweat flowed freely. Then one was slammed down or overpowered or eventually tired and was finally forced to yield.

Zavni had a bout with a female troll warrior, who almost seemed to be flirting with him as much as she was fighting, though Melantha could not tell if Zavni's good humor was him flirting in return or just Zavni being Zavni.

Nirveeth and Eyvindur each had bouts as well, though Melantha noticed that only one of Rharreth's shield band accepted bouts at a time. They did not challenge each other. Perhaps they were under orders not to leave Rharreth and Melantha short-handed. Or, maybe, they fought together so much in training that challenging each other was no real challenge at all.

Either way, the members of the shield band occupied the bench behind Rharreth and Melantha, guarding their back from the other troll warriors gathered around the arena.

A challenge was called out that Melantha could only vaguely hear, and Drurvas stood up, giving an answering shout. After shucking his shirt and dropping it onto his bench, he strode down the last two benches, then hopped into the arena, swinging his battle-ax as easily as if it were made of air instead of iron.

His opponent's grin slipped a little bit, as if realizing that he might have miscalculated in challenging Drurvas. Perhaps he had thought he would gain honor in a well-earned defeat against one of Kostaria's best warriors.

With a yell, the challenger charged, his sword raised.

Almost carelessly, Drurvas batted aside the sword's swing with such force that it knocked the sword from the other troll's hand, then kicked his opponent in the knee, sending him to the ground. Drurvas put his battle-ax to the kneeling troll's neck almost lazily. "Yield."

The challenger swallowed. "I yield."

When Drurvas lifted his ax, the defeated troll scrambled on his hands and knees to retrieve his sword, as if he did not dare take the time to so much as stand, then he half-crawled, half-ran from the combat arena.

If an honorable defeat had been his goal, then he had failed. Even Melantha could see that, and she was only just learning the troll customs when it came to honor.

Drurvas strolled to the center of the arena, his ax resting on his shoulder. He turned, his gaze focusing on Melantha.

Her breath caught in her throat. She could not be challenged, could she? She was not a warrior, even if she had been training. If Drurvas had made short work of that troll warrior, then he would humiliate Melantha.

Surely he would not do that. He was Rharreth's cousin and shield brother. To humiliate Melantha would humiliate Rharreth.

Drurvas's mouth tipped into a smirk, as if to remind Melantha of what he could have done, before his gaze swiveled to Rharreth. "I challenge King Rharreth."

A hush fell around the arena. All eyes turned to stare at Rharreth and Melantha.

Melantha tensed. Drurvas had crossed a line, though she did not know what it had been.

Beside her, Rharreth stiffened, but his face remained impassive. A long, deadly silence stretched before he pushed to his feet. If anything, the hush deepened with the sign of his acceptance of the challenge.

He unbuckled his black leather vest and dropped it to his seat. His dark blue shirt followed a moment later.

Melantha caught her breath as he turned to her, the muscles in his arms and chest flexing as he took the antler crown from his head and held it out to her. "Guard this for me, milady."

She took the crown, clutching it tightly. Were her ears burning? Her whole face felt hot, and she was not sure where to look, whether at her hands or at Rharreth's very muscled, very near chest.

Swallowing, she tried to think of something to say. This seemed like a moment she should say something bold and regal, as a queen of the trolls ought.

Instead, Rharreth turned away and marched down into the arena while she sat there mutely, the tips of her ears blushing red as if she were a young girl instead of a queen.

Rharreth drew his sword, swinging it easily as if unworried about facing one of the few trolls who could match his fighting skill.

If this had been a contest of magic, Rharreth would have trounced Drurvas. Magic was banned for these bouts, and that meant all Rharreth had were his sword and his fighting skills.

Sitting behind Rharreth's empty seat, Zavni leaned forward, his face more serious than Melantha had ever seen. He put his mouth close to Melantha's ear. "It is considered dishonorable to challenge the king. He is above such bouts. Nor should Drurvas have challenged him, as a shield brother."

This was wrong, and all the trolls sitting around there knew it. Now Melantha knew it too.

Her fingers tightened around the antler crown. What was Drurvas thinking?

Down below in the arena, Drurvas swung his ax with a grunt. Rharreth parried the ax and dodged to the side.

"Does he mean to humiliate Rharreth?" Melantha whispered back, though she kept her eyes glued to the fight in the arena.

"It is because of you." Vriska's voice hissed in Melantha's ear. "You are no warrior. You cannot fight at our king's side. You make our king weak, and Drurvas is showing that."

"Vriska." Zavni's tone cut sharp. "You must not speak to our queen that way."

Melantha stiffened and half-turned in her seat, trying to watch the fight while keeping Zavni and Vriska in her line of sight.

"Even if it is true? You know it. I know it. Even Rharreth knows it." Vriska's mouth curled as she glared at Melantha.

Melantha clenched and unclenched her fingers around Rharreth's crown. Vriska was everything Melantha was not. She wore a sleeveless tunic, showing off her brawny, well-muscled arms. She sat straight, carrying a sword the size of Melantha's arm as easily as if it were the small dagger Melantha wore. Vriska's white hair was festooned with braids and woven bits of leather and antler beadwork. A true troll warrior, who would fight at the side of her husband.

But Melantha was not helpless. She would not back down. If she did, then she would make Vriska's accusations true.

Zavni opened his mouth, probably to defend her again,

but Melantha held up a hand, her gaze focused on Vriska. "I may not be a warrior. If I stepped into that arena, you would trounce me."

As she spoke, Melantha drew on her magic, keeping it just below the surface. She leaned closer, then jabbed Vriska's bared arm. "But do not mistake my inability to fight as weakness. I am not helpless."

With the last word, she blasted her magic into Vriska. Vriska's eyes flickered closed, and she slumped.

Zavni caught her, then lowered her to the bench. He glanced, eyes wide, from Vriska's limp form to Melantha. "What did you do?"

"Just sent her to sleep. She will wake up in a few hours." Melantha waved, trying to appear nonchalant. Inside, a part of her was trembling. She had never tested this ability apart from her work as a healer and that one time on Rharreth. But, she could use it to defend herself if needed...if she was close enough to an enemy to touch them.

A roar went up around the arena, and Melantha swiveled around to face the fight just in time to see Drurvas's battle-ax score a line of red across Rharreth's chest as Rharreth stumbled backwards.

Melantha's stomach churned, and she returned both hands to gripping Rharreth's crown. Surely Drurvas would not go so far as to seriously injure his cousin, no matter what point he was making. He was still a loyal troll. One of Rharreth's trusted shield brothers.

As Drurvas swung again with his ax, Rharreth stumbled another step back, this time losing his balance and falling to a knee.

Melantha could not help the gasp. All it would take

would be for Drurvas to miscalculate a swing, and he could easily separate Rharreth's head from his shoulders.

But before Drurvas could change the direction to swing at Rharreth once again, Rharreth's sword darted up and out, catching the ax and using the last of its momentum to send Drurvas off balance.

With his sword still locked at the place where the battle-ax's head met the shaft, Rharreth came up from a crouch, the elven dagger Melantha had gifted him during their wedding now in his hand. He pressed the point of his blade to Drurvas's throat. "Yield."

Drurvas smirked, going still.

Melantha held her breath. Drurvas probably could jerk away from Rharreth, free his ax, and keep fighting.

But would he? He had made his point. Surely he would take this opportunity to gracefully yield the fight rather than keep pushing until he gained the victory over Rharreth. It did no good to anyone to publicly humiliate his king to that degree, not after he had already done enough damage by calling him out for a match.

"I yield." Drurvas stepped away before Rharreth moved, showing just how easily he could break free.

The hush returned to the arena, as if the trolls were not sure if they should cheer over this strange ending to a tense match.

Drurvas swung his battle-ax so that its handle rested on his shoulder once again. He grinned and gestured to Rharreth, "Our mighty warrior, King Rharreth!"

The trolls surged to their feet, stomping and howling cheers and war cries.

Melantha frantically stuffed more magic in her ears, deadening the noise once again. She also jumped to her feet and clapped, though she did not try to replicate the way the trolls were roaring and shouting.

Rharreth held up his sword and bobbed his head in something that was not deep enough to be a bow but was instead an acknowledgment of his people. He then sheathed his sword and strode from the arena, bounding over the wall to land on his feet facing Melantha. His mouth quirked. "You look like you were worried."

"I was." Her mouth was going dry, her ears heating in another blush. Even with his white hair plastered to his forehead with sweat and blood running down his chest from multiple gashes, he looked...he looked good.

He gently gripped her upper arms, tugging her closer.

Tingles ran down her spine as Melantha stood on her tiptoes and kissed him. Even as she melted into his kiss, she rested her hands on his chest and called on her magic. By the time she stepped back, breathless, the gashes on his chest were healed, all except for the new, gray scars.

The gathered troll warriors had gone silent, and Melantha ducked her head, her ears burning, as she felt their eyes on her and Rharreth.

Zavni gave a whoop and stomped his feet. A few other troll warriors followed suit, and cheers filled the room. They were not as hearty as the cheers for the fighting bouts, but at least it was not a tense silence either.

Rharreth gave a wave, and then he took his seat on the bench once again, tugging Melantha to sit beside him.

As the cheering grew louder as the next two troll warriors sauntered onto the sand-covered combat floor, Rharreth leaned closer to her again, tipping his head toward the still unconscious Vriska sprawled on the bench behind them. "What happened to Vriska?"

"A lesson."

"Ah." Rharreth's smile returned as he faced the arena once again.

Melantha's smile widened, something melting inside her. Rharreth knew her well enough that no long explanations were needed. She tucked her hand inside his larger one and leaned against him for the rest of the bouts, drawing in his warmth and strength.

And, strangely, she did not feel a burn to join a bout there in the arena. She enjoyed training with Rharreth, and something about the exertion of pushing her skills with her hardwood staff made her jubilant for the rest of the day afterward.

But she did not feel drawn to battle the way she thought she would. Fighting was raw and bloody and brutal, even in these controlled bouts.

Perhaps she was more a healer than a warrior after all.

RHARRETH STRODE down the center of the great hall, a large room with a black obsidian ceiling that sparkled in the light of the torches lining the walls and the candles set on each of the tables filling the space. Boughs of greenery decorated the tables at a safe distance from the candles while more greenery hung around each of the doorways.

At his side, Melantha held her head high, the queen's diadem resting against her forehead.

A few of the warriors sneered at her when they thought Rharreth's back was turned, but none of them did anything so obvious as spit at her. One warrior sloshed his drink onto her as they passed, but it was hard to tell if he had simply imbibed too much mead or had spilled on purpose.

Rharreth glared at him long enough to let the warrior know not to attempt such a thing again and let the matter drop. He had no wish to destroy all of Melantha's preparations by causing a brawl in the middle of the great hall.

On the tables, plates of roast caribou and fresh bread baked with grain from Escarland filled the room with delicious scents. A better feast than had been enjoyed in Kostaria in many a Winter Solstice.

When he reached their table on the dais, Rharreth stood behind his chair and curled an arm around Melantha's waist.

She smiled up at him, a vision in her layers of fur and long black hair streaming down her back.

Rharreth picked up his mug filled with mead and raised it high. After a moment, Melantha did the same.

A clatter filled the room as the warriors surged to their feet, holding out their foam-topped mugs.

Rharreth drew in a deep breath, speaking loudly enough that everyone in the room would be able to hear him. "To our warriors! May you fight with honor and strength all your days!"

A howling cheer filled the room, accompanied by the stomping of feet.

Rharreth sipped from his mug before he held it out again. It took several seconds before the hall quieted enough for him to give another toast. "To Kostaria! May our kingdom know better and greater days ahead!"

This toast too was received with cheering and stomping.

Rharreth glanced at Melantha again, tucked against his side as she was. He was not sure how this toast would be received. But he was going to make it anyway. When the room fell into semi-silence again, Rharreth held out his mug a third time. "And to my wife, Queen Melantha. May the peace and healing she brings to Kostaria strengthen us as we have never been strengthened before."

A hush so silent, so tense fell across the great hall that Rharreth could hear Melantha catch her breath beside him.

Before the silence dragged on too long, Zavni stomped his feet, banged his mug against the table hard enough to send mead sloshing onto the tabletop, and let out a hooting howl.

Eyvindur, Brynjar, and Darvek joined him. Then Drurvas and Vriska were also cheering and stomping, though less enthusiastically than Zavni.

Soon, more and more of the warrior families were joining in. It was hard to tell from the dais who was doing so out of genuine support and who was cheering simply because they did not want to be seen publicly dishonoring their king by ignoring his toast.

He was sure a few weren't cheering. But they at least had the decency to attempt to hide it rather than making a big display out of their disapproval.

It was a start. Looking over at the crowd of warriors cheering for Melantha, Rharreth had hope that maybe, just maybe, his wife would find acceptance by his people.

CHAPTER
TWENTY-THREE

T wo and a half months after they arrived in Aldon, Essie woke to find Farrendel already up and gone, his half of the bed cold, as usual.

Stretching, Essie sat up and peered out the window. Outside, winter had fallen over Escarland, several inches of fresh snow covering the trees, the gardens, and the roof of Winstead Palace, visible through the bare branches of the trees. Essie could not see Farrendel in the trees or in the gardens, but perhaps he and his guards were at the training field or running their circuit around the parkland.

The past two months had been some of the best of her life. Farrendel had been happier than she'd ever seen him. He'd stayed busy working with Lance, training with Julien and Captain Merrick, and teaching her how to use his magic.

Farrendel had been doing so well that Taranath had returned to Tarenhiel a month ago, leaving three months' worth of doses and telling Farrendel to check back in at the end of that time. Mr. and Mrs. Harwell now only had a session with Farrendel every other week, and they were talking about going down to checking in with Farrendel once a month unless he felt he needed more counseling.

While Farrendel was busy, Essie enjoyed her royal engagements in Aldon. It was nice to be able to resume her work with the hospitals, the women's shelter, and the orphanage. She also added a few veterans charities to her list and helped Mr. and Mrs. Harwell start a foundation to raise money to reach more soldiers in need of help. Taranath also agreed to help in this endeavor, and they were expanding his help to Escarlish soldiers and Mr. and Mrs. Harwell's help to more elves besides Farrendel.

When she wasn't busy arranging foundations and charities, Essie trained with Farrendel's magic. She was now skilled enough that he had given her a set of exercises to practice, even when he couldn't join her in person. Some of the minor practice she could do in the parkland at Winstead Palace.

Her control over his magic was improving. Her marriage was wonderful. Life was good.

Smiling, Essie got up and dressed, taking the time to brush her hair, though she left it down the way Farrendel liked it. And the way that she liked it, now that the elven conditioner made it behave in sleek and shiny strands.

The window latch creaked, and she turned in time to see Farrendel swing through, the folded top of a paper bag clutched in his teeth, probably to keep his hands free while he climbed the tree. He landed on the carpet, leaving behind clumps of snow.

Essie pushed to her feet and crossed the room as he took the paper bag out of his mouth. She wrapped her arms around his waist, ignoring the cold of the snow on his Escarlish style wool coat. "Good morning, my love."

He grinned and held up the paper bag. "I got this for you."

"You didn't have to. You've been showering me with gifts lately." Essie took the paper bag anyway, even as she gestured toward the roses he had somehow managed to find for her last week. They were still blooming strong, and she was beginning to think they must have been sent all the way from Tarenhiel and filled with elven magic to keep them so beautiful for this long.

"I like making you smile." He kissed her, just a quick peck, before he stepped back to remove his wool coat, tossing it onto the back of a chair, revealing his white shirt, brown trousers, and gray suspenders.

She tugged on one of the suspender straps. "I still can't get over the sight of you in suspenders."

He looked adorable, with his silver-blond hair roguishly tousled, his wide grin, and his Escarlish suspenders holding up his trousers. While he'd had slightly better-fitting Escarlish clothes made, they were still purposely loose and ill-fitting to complete the look of his disguise.

"They are not as bad as I thought at first." Farrendel tugged off his snow-covered boots, then he perched on the end of the bed, sitting cross-legged. "Now, open the bag already."

"Fine, fine. If you insist." Essie sat opposite him on the bed, then unrolled the folded top of the bag, avoiding the teeth marks he'd left on the paper. Inside, two cinnamon rolls rested on napkins. Her mouth instantly watered, and she snapped her gaze back up to Farrendel. "Are these from the Sixth Street Bakery? Really?"

"Of course. It is your favorite bakery in Aldon." Farrendel's tone seemed almost smug in that knowledge.

Essie fished out the two cinnamon rolls, handing one to him before she cradled hers. Farrendel must have raced back to Buckmore Cottage from the bakery to get it back to her still warm and sticky like this, especially with the weather as cold as it was outside. "You have become really comfortable wandering Aldon."

"It is less overwhelming, now that I have grown used to it." Farrendel was still smiling as he took a bite of his cinnamon roll.

Essie bit into hers, closing her eyes as the sweetness burst across her tongue. These cinnamon rolls were pure, edible bliss. "Thank you for this. The perfect breakfast."

"I am glad you like it, even if it is not very substantial." Farrendel contemplated his own cinnamon roll, as if he was torn between enjoying it and resenting it for being all sugar and nothing healthy. "And it is messy to eat breakfast in bed."

"I know, right? So much fun." Essie grinned and tried not to wolf down her cinnamon roll too quickly. "I might even lick my fingers when I finish."

Farrendel huffed, the closest thing he ever gave her to an eyeroll. As he chewed his last bite, his expression turned thoughtful, flattening his mouth and furrowing his forehead. "Being here in Escarland, spending time with your family, has made me see some things more clearly."

"What are you talking about?" Essie reluctantly popped the last bite into her mouth. If only she didn't have to finish it.

"When we were first married, all I could think about was

how I hoped you would not change my life. I did not want an intrusion into my sanctuary. I thought that was what I needed to stay sane. I did not consider what you would need or want." Farrendel stared at his hands, sticking and unsticking his fingers together. "I did not think I could adapt to anything else."

"I was a stranger. Of course that's what you were worried about. It wasn't like I was unselfishly thinking about you when we got married either." Essie would have reached out to him, but her own fingers were sticky, and he would not appreciate it. "I was mostly thinking about the adventure and getting to explore Tarenhiel."

"Yet you still went into the marriage expecting to adapt to elven culture. You expected to give up your home, your people, while I gave up nothing." His mouth flattened into an even tighter line.

This time, Essie did reach out and take his hands, stickiness and all. "That's what is expected in a marriage alliance."

Farrendel stared down at their clasped hands, going on as if he hadn't heard her. "Perhaps it would be expected for a marriage alliance like Melantha's. She is now queen of Kostaria. She had to give up her home, her people, and her place in Tarenhiel's line of succession."

Essie tried not to react to the mention of Melantha. Farrendel spoke her name without flinching. If anything, his voice still held warmth and affection, and Essie wasn't sure how to feel about that.

Sure, Melantha had saved Farrendel's life. She had also been the one to put it at risk in the first place. Perhaps it was good that Farrendel had forgiven her, but Essie wasn't going to let Melantha put him in danger ever again. Was it wrong that she was a tiny bit glad that Melantha was now tied to Kostaria and there would always be distance between her and Farrendel?

Essie shrugged and stuck to the topic they had been discussing. "That's how marriage alliances have always been done. That's why my brother pushed for a second marriage alliance."

"Yes, but it does not have to be that way. Not for us." Farrendel held up their joined hands, finally looking up to meet her gaze. "We are the bridge between our kingdoms. If you were given to Tarenhiel, then I was given to Escarland just as much. I see that now."

Essie blinked at him, her mind whirling. Why had she never put that together? She had come close, a few times, but she had still overlooked what Farrendel had seen, perhaps because he had not been raised with the culture of a marriage alliance ingrained in him the way she had.

She and Farrendel were free in a way most marriage alliance couples weren't. They were both far enough down the lines of succession that they were in little danger of ever inheriting a throne.

Essie squeezed his hands. "What you're saying is that we are not tied to only one kingdom but could serve both. That's what we have been doing. We have been encouraging trade. We have been visiting charities on both sides of the border. We have shown that our two kingdoms can work together."

"Yes, but we can do more." Farrendel gestured at himself —from his Escarlish haircut now long enough to brush his collar to his suspenders and human outfit—with their clasped hands. "Look at me now. I have learned that I can adapt. It might take me longer and in my own way, but I can do it. I am happy here, more than I ever thought possible."

"That's good. I want to visit my family often." Essie leaned forward and kissed his cheek. When she leaned back, she decided she wasn't going to mention the fact that she had accidentally smeared cinnamon roll frosting on his face.

"Time with your family is precious and short. Far shorter than the time I have left with my family. A hundred years from now, I do not want us to have any regrets." He met her gaze again, his posture strangely tense and stiff, as if what he was about to say meant a great deal to him. "I do not want to merely visit your family. If you agree, I would like to split our time between Tarenhiel and Escarland. We can make our home in both kingdoms."

Essie's breath caught in her chest, her fingers tightening on his until it was probably painful. "Do you mean that? Truly?"

"Yes. And, when we are in Tarenhiel, we will have to invite your family to stay with us. Perhaps we can have more rooms grown below the lift by our set of rooms so that your family can stay on the forest floor where they will be more comfortable." Farrendel's gaze searched her face, as if worried about her reaction. "What do you think?"

"It…" Essie couldn't manage to get any more words out. Instead, she let go of Farrendel's hands so that she could fling herself forward and hug him instead. "I think it's wonderful!"

Farrendel's arms went around her, though she could feel the way he kept his hands, still sticky from their breakfast, away from her. Unlike the way she had buried her sticky fingers in his hair. She pressed her face against his shoulder, feeling the burn of tears against her eyelids.

When she had married Farrendel, she had expected to give up her home, her family, her people, in order to fully adopt his. Yet, here he was giving all those things back to her. Even better, he was telling her he was willing to adopt her family, her home, her people as his.

It was the best present he had given her—outside of the gift of his heart and himself. Better than all the roses and cinnamon rolls in the world.

Farrendel huffed a laugh, then pulled away from her. "Do you have any plans for today?"

"Nothing I can't cancel, why?" Essie sat back, gathering the paper bag and their napkins.

"Would you like to come with me to Lance's workshop? I have some things I would like to show you." Farrendel glanced down at his hands again before peering up at her.

This also meant a lot to him. He must have something he desperately wanted to show off. And, after wondering for months what he did all day over at Lance's, Essie wasn't about to turn him down. "Of course I'll come. If I take a pen and paper, I can start brainstorming ideas to make living in two kingdoms actually feasible. Before we go, I suppose we should wash our hands."

"Yes." Farrendel hopped to his feet, his nose wrinkling as he glared down at his fingers.

"And your face and your hair. I got you thoroughly sticky." Essie smirked at him as she also slid to her feet, holding up her hands to avoid touching the blankets.

Farrendel's nose wrinkle deepened, and he all but raced to the water closet.

WHEN THEY REACHED Lance's workshop, Farrendel gripped Essie's hand and dragged her past the piles of junk and inventions toward the back of the spacious building.

As they reached the cleared workshop area, Essie managed to get in a wave toward Lance, who barely even glanced up from the device he was fiddling with while sitting at his workbench, as if he were so used to Farrendel's comings and goings that having him show up was no big deal.

Last time Essie had been there, Lance had one workbench crammed into the space behind the protective brick-and-tempered-glass wall.

But now, a second workbench sat behind the wall in a larger, cleared space. Essie would have known which work-bench was Farrendel's even without knowing it was new, based on the fact that the second one was spotless and organized.

A shelving unit was set up along the wall, and each shelf was packed with row upon row of magical power cells. The tiny windows into the power cells glowed blue with Farrendel's distinctive magic.

"You have been busy." Essie waved at the shelving unit.

"Yes, though that is not what I wanted to show you." Farrendel tugged her toward his workbench, then let go of her hand to pick up a device. It was the size of a hatbox with a stove coil on top and a base that held a small magical power cell glowing with Farrendel's magic. A knob with a dial was attached to the base. Farrendel held out the device, all but beaming. "It is the heating device you requested from Lance. He and I made it. It runs on my magic."

"Really? That's amazing!" Essie took the device but nearly dropped it when it was heavier than she was expecting. After turning it over and examining it, she handed it back to Farrendel. "How does it work?"

Farrendel set it on the workbench. "It is simple. Just turn this knob. The farther you turn the knob to the right, the hotter the coil gets. All the way to the left turns it off." He gestured at a pile of parts on his workbench. "I am making a second one so that we can have one in our room in Buckmore Cottage and the other in Ellonahshinel. I actually finished this first one about a month ago, but we wanted to continue testing it to make sure it was not about to overheat and set something on fire or explode."

"There were a few explosions in the prototypes." Lance set aside his tools and pushed his goggles onto his forehead. "But Farrendel's idea of stone dampeners was the key to making a power cell with his magic truly work."

"Your idea?" Essie glanced from Lance to Farrendel. She couldn't imagine Farrendel wanting anything to do with stone.

"Oh, yes. Turns out Farrendel has a knack for magical engineering. Did you know he can weld with his magic? Definitely comes in handy for some of the finicky projects, and his magical welds are incredibly strong." Lance grinned, waving from the heating device to the magical power cells. "Really, it is a shame we can't actually sell his power cells for broader use. Just think of what could be powered with his magic. There is so much potential."

Farrendel frowned, studying Lance.

Essie patted Farrendel's arm. "Yes, but it is discouraged for Escarlish royalty to own and run businesses. And the liabilities if one of the power cells did malfunction and explode wouldn't be good for the public image."

"Well, yes, that. But also he is not a certified magical

engineer, and you have to have a certification to sell magi-cally engineered devices." Lance shrugged, then gestured at the heating device on Farrendel's workbench. "If you're concerned about public image, then it would probably be best if you only used that for personal use. It is safe, but even the safest devices can sometimes have problems. The Escarlish press would be all over it if King Averett were injured from a device powered by elf magic and in part created by someone not certified in magical engineering."

"Right." Essie frowned. She hadn't thought of that. "Though, if you would be willing to list Farrendel as an apprentice, that would help, even if it put you in more hot water. You are certified as a master magician and magical engineer yourself."

"True, true. And, with all the testing we did on this device, I'm sure it's safe. There isn't that much that could go wrong." Lance heaved a sigh. "It is just such a shame that we cannot put Farrendel's magic to more use. Enough power to fuel all of Escarland, and we can't use even a bit of it."

"The Escarlish magicians would be thankful, if they knew. They would be rather annoyed if Farrendel single-handedly put all of them out of business." Essie leaned closer to Farrendel. He had a strange look on his face as he stared at the heating device. She wrapped her hand around his arm. "Besides, elves are not given to the Escarlish drive to accumulate massive amounts of wealth. Isn't that right, Farrendel?"

When Farrendel didn't react, Essie nudged him. "Farrendel?"

He started and glanced up, his gaze flicking between the device and Essie before settling on Lance. "What would I need to do to obtain a certification?"

"You would need to get a degree in magical engineering, then pass the certification test." Lance leaned against his workbench, his expression more focused than Essie was used to seeing. "I went to Hanford University. I was the youngest magical engineer in Escarland. That was how I met Prince Edmund. A few of our classes overlapped, and he thought I could be of use to the Escarlish army."

"And I eventually met Lance through Edmund." Essie shrugged. "I took a couple of classes at the university, though I never got a specific degree."

"I got my magical engineering degree with a dual emphasis in engineering and magic so I am a master engineer and a master magician, even though I don't have magic myself." Lance was nodding, still studying Farrendel. "I didn't think to mention a degree before, not when we were just experimenting with your magic. But now that I've seen its potential...I think you could do great things with your magic, and a magical engineering degree would make it possible. I'm not sure how it would work with you being an elf rather than a human magician. The professors would probably have to come up with a special track just for you."

"Would a degree be something you would be interested in?" Essie turned to Farrendel. Until seeing how at home he was in Lance's workshop, she hadn't realized how serious he was about melding his magic with Escarlish mechanics. "You could, you know. If we're going to split our time between Tarenhiel and Escarland, we can plan our schedule around your classes. The professors might even be willing to set up some of your classes as correspondence courses where you could do the work in Tarenhiel."

"Do you think they would?" Farrendel placed his hand

on her back, then withdrew, as if he wasn't sure what to do. "Could I even enroll at an Escarlish university?"

"You're a prince of the elves. If you apply, they would fall over themselves to enroll you. It would be a feather in their cap to have foreign royalty studying with them." Essie clasped Farrendel's hand. "Why don't you think it over? You don't have to make a decision today. Take the time to figure out if this is the dream you want, and if you decide that it is, then I will support you wholeheartedly, all right?"

"Thanks, my shynafir." Farrendel leaned over to kiss her temple.

When Farrendel had talked about splitting time between Tarenhiel and Escarland, this was not what Essie had imagined. But if Farrendel wanted to try his hand at taking university classes, then she wasn't going to stand in his way.

Even if he took a few classes and realized he didn't like it, he could always drop out. It would not look that great for the public image, but that would be only a minor scandal. It would be worth it even then. Essie wanted to encourage him to try new things. Even if he failed. Even if he found out he didn't like it. Trying things and taking risks was a part of truly living.

Essie spent the rest of the afternoon curled up in one of the wooden chairs, alternating between jotting down dreams about the future and watching Farrendel as he perched cross-legged on the table and fiddled with his latest project. He seemed so happy, smiling and laughing and occasionally shouting over at Lance to request one tool or another.

Watching it, Essie found herself adding other dreams and ideas to her paper than she had been expecting. Not just additional rooms on the floor of the forest for her family to visit, but also a workshop for Farrendel where he could tinker without worrying about blowing up a section of Ellonahshinel.

This was everything she had ever dreamed about and more. More, because it was real. It was raw at times. Gut-emptying hard.

But so, so good.

TWENTY-FOUR

Melantha started awake to a heavy hand over her mouth and Rharreth's voice harsh against her ear. "Melantha, grab your knife."

She clawed her way awake, fumbling for the troll dagger Rharreth had given her at their wedding, which she had left on the table near her side of the bed. "What is going—"

The clash of metal against metal sounded from outside their door. Shouting. A cry of pain.

Their door burst open. Melantha only caught a glimpse of Zavni's back and crowding trolls swinging swords and axes at him before Rharreth gripped her elbow and physically tossed her off the far side of the bed.

She shrieked as she fell, but she landed on her stomach, the fur rug breaking her fall. Her elbow and wrists ached from the impact. She lay there a moment, trying to catch her breath and her bearings. What was happening? Who was attacking? Why?

It did not matter. Right now it was time for action.

Melantha pushed to her feet, grabbed the knife from the

table, and whirled to face the clashing of weapons as she drew the knife from its sheath.

Rharreth had joined Zavni and parried a sword thrust with only the elven knife and his magic for protection. He was not dressed for battle. The muscles in his back strained beneath the loose shirt pulled taut across his shoulders while his bare feet scuffed across the fur rugs as he and Zavni were pushed back from the sheer weight of bodies pouring through the doorway.

Rharreth's sword and belt hung from a peg next to their closet, a sign of how secure Rharreth felt in his own home.

With a deep breath, Melantha darted across the room, bashing her hip against the bedpost in her haste. She was not dressed for battle either, not in her loose, gray nightgown. At least it was flannel and not some flimsy thing.

Her fingers closed around the leather of Rharreth's sword sheath, and she fumbled to draw the sword. He would be too busy fighting to draw it himself.

A cry of pain came from behind her. Melantha whirled, Rharreth's sword in one hand, her dagger in the other.

One of the trolls attacking Zavni stumbled back as Zavni withdrew his sword from the attacking troll's stomach. Rharreth yanked Zavni back, then blasted a wall of ice, blocking off the door and the attacking trolls.

"Nirveeth?" Rharreth asked, not taking his gaze away from the wall of ice, even as he added more ice to reinforce it.

"Dead." Zavni's mouth pressed into a tight line. Only then did Melantha notice the red soaking the side of his tunic and down his right leg.

In the near darkness of a room lit only by the light of the torches in the passageway filtering through the ice wall,

Melantha hurried across the room and held out Rharreth's sword. When he sheathed his dagger and took the sword, she called on her magic and touched her hand to Zavni's side. She did not have time to think about Nirveeth, Zavni's tall, almost silent shadow, lying dead outside that wall of ice.

"Put on something warm." Rharreth did not look at her either as he kept guard over his temporary wall. From the other side came the sounds of their attackers chipping away at the ice with their swords and axes. Sections shuddered under assault of magic, but none were able to overpower Rharreth's magic. Yet.

There was no time for dressing properly. Melantha raced back to the closet nook, grabbed a dark gray, wool dress, and put it on over her nightgown. She tugged on trousers underneath her dress, then shoved her feet into wool stockings and her fur-lined boots.

As she clasped her fur cloak around her throat, the wall of ice blasted apart, shooting shards of ice across the room and sending Rharreth and Zavni stumbling.

Melantha shrieked and shielded her face. Ice stung her hand and the exposed skin of her forehead.

When she dared to lower her arm, Rharreth had regained his balance and had magic swirling around his left hand, the sword still in his right and the elven dagger in his belt.

A line of troll warriors poured into the room, but they did not charge. Not yet. Instead, they parted, allowing a figure to stride through their midst, his face shadowed in the faint light of the torches in the passageway, his ax resting lazily on his shoulder.

"Drurvas," Rharreth growled, flexing his fingers on his sword's hilt.

This was not a random attack. This was a coup.

She did not need gloating from Drurvas to figure that out. Drurvas was Rharreth's cousin. The only reason there could be for him launching an attack on Rharreth in the middle of the night was if he planned to take the throne for himself.

Melantha did not have time to stand there, frozen in place. Locating a leather pack in the back of the closet, she started stuffing Rharreth's warm clothes into it, along with anything else she thought would be helpful. For what, she did not know.

"Rharreth, you have been deemed unworthy to rule Kostaria." Drurvas's voice rang hard against the stones. "You are weak."

"Why? Because I have married an elf and brought peace to Kostaria?" Rharreth's snort was loud in the confined space. "You would not think my elf bride was weak if you had ever seen the numbers she has been able to heal with her magic. She has shown me that there is more to strength and honor than the ability to make war. There is great strength in compassion. In healing. Yes, even in peace. Peace, not war, is what our people need right now, and I will fight with everything in me to obtain that for them."

Melantha turned as Rharreth finished his speech. He faced the crowd of troll warriors, his shoulders straight, his head held high.

Some of the attackers shifted, but most were still stone-faced. A few glanced over at Melantha, their eyes hard.

She was the reason for the coup. If Rharreth had married someone like his shield sister Vriska or another of the female troll warriors, he might not be in this situation. The warriors might have tolerated a temporary peace treaty with Tarenhiel, but they did not want an elf as their queen, nor did they want the more permanent peace with Tarenhiel that she represented.

Drurvas shook his head, swinging his ax down from his shoulder. "The fact that you believe that just shows how unworthy you are to be our king. You will weaken Kostaria. It is with a heavy heart that we must take this action."

Did any of his followers really believe that?

This was not about preserving Kostaria. This was about power. Drurvas had seen an opportunity to seize the throne, and he was taking it.

Drurvas lunged forward, swinging his ax. Rharreth stepped to meet him, blocking with his sword. His magic clashed against an answering blast from Drurvas.

The other troll warriors rushed at Zavni and Rharreth, raising swords, axes, and daggers. More magic filled the air, and Rharreth was hard-pressed trying to single-handedly block it.

Melantha growled and charged forward, setting the pack of supplies on the bed as she passed. These trolls claimed honor, but then they charged fifteen to two, as if a mass assassination was somehow honorable.

They hated Farrendel's assassination of Rharreth's father, but at least Farrendel did it one on one.

Zavni grunted, blood welling from his left side near his hip. His stumble backward gave the troll attacker an opening to Rharreth. Trying to fend off magical attacks with one hand and Drurvas's ax with his sword in the other, Rharreth shifted, but he could not block the oncoming strike.

Melantha let the fury in her chest fill her as she leapt forward, a war-scream bursting from her. She knocked aside the oncoming sword with her dagger, as Rharreth had shown her.

As she had practiced with Rharreth, she used the shorter length and thus quicker recovery time of her dagger to strike at the troll's chest, expecting him to block her thrust.

But, he must have been too shocked at her attack to move. Her dagger hit resistance but still crunched into the chest in front of her. Blood spattered, and the troll collapsed, dragging the dagger from Melantha's hand.

She stumbled back, her lungs feeling like they were frozen inside her chest. Her stomach gave a sudden lurch, and she doubled over, vomiting onto the floor.

Even as she heaved until nothing came out, that fiery heat filled her chest. She had always had a tough stomach. It came with being a healer.

But this...this was different. This was gory and bloody and the smell...her stomach was heaving yet again.

She did not have time for this. She gritted her teeth and willed her stomach to settle. This was a battle. She did not have time to huddle in the corner, helpless and as weak as these trolls thought her to be.

She rushed into the battle again, this time unarmed. Dodging a sword swing and using Rharreth as a shield, she called on her magic, reached over Rharreth's shoulder as he blocked an attacker's strike, and pressed her fingers to the enemy's hand.

The troll collapsed at Rharreth's feet, asleep. He was immediately replaced by another attacker, and Melantha waited for her chance, timing it and grazing the troll's neck with her fingers. He, too, went down.

The third troll was more wary, but Rharreth managed to get him in an arm lock, using his body as a shield even as Melantha sent him to sleep.

But the attacking trolls kept coming. Drurvas himself

pressed forward with troll warriors on either side of him. Even more troll warriors were packed in the hallway behind him, just waiting for their chance to attack their king.

Melantha sagged, even as she managed to send another attacker off to sleep. There were too many. At any moment, they would be overrun and killed.

A sword grazed her arm, and she cried out, yanking her arm back behind the shield of Rharreth's body.

With a growl, Rharreth stumbled back into her. He dropped his sword and held up both hands, magic building in icy swirls around him. With a crack, ice blasted at the attackers even as stone shot from the floor, the walls, and the ceiling. One thrust of ice knocked Zavni backwards just before the stone slammed into place, once again blocking the attackers.

"We need to move." Rharreth picked up his sword with one hand, then pushed her toward the far wall with the other.

Melantha grabbed the leather pack from the bed as she stumbled past, her brain catching up to Rharreth's plan after a second.

The hidden staircase. They could get outside that way, then climb down the outside of Khagniorth Stronghold. Perhaps they could find shelter somewhere in Osmana while they assessed the situation and rallied those warriors still loyal to Rharreth.

Melantha shrugged into the pack as she ran across the room, reaching the far wall only a moment before Rharreth and Zavni.

Zavni was limping, a hand clutching at his side. But he gave her a tight smile as she glanced at him, and by the way the blood was slowing, she could tell that the magic she had pumped into him earlier was still working.

Rharreth pressed a hand to the wall. Icy magic surrounded his fingers before the opening began to appear.

A crack sounded from the wall behind them. Melantha glanced over her shoulder, stifling a gasp at the sight of a similar but smaller crevice appearing in the stone behind them. Drurvas's magic might not be as strong as Rharreth's, but he had multiple trolls to help him.

"Go." Rharreth pushed her through the narrow opening to the stairs.

She raced up the steps, slipping and bashing her knee, before she kept on going. She could hear Rharreth and Zavni at her heels, but she could not turn around to check on them.

Cold stung her nostrils and the back of her throat as she stepped onto the ledge where she and Rharreth had spent many an evening gazing at the stars and northern lights.

Only when she stood on the fur blankets where she and Rharreth normally sat did she finally turn around to look for Rharreth and Zavni. As she turned, her gaze caught a glint on the dark wall far above. That glint was not normal. That wall was supposed to be dark and empty.

But, no, there was a hulking shadow up there, with a small, moving shadow behind it. Moonlight gleamed on something long and shiny. Something cracked loud and sharp, a puff of smoke wafting from the end of that shining barrel at the same time as a rock shattered off to her left.

A gunshot. A gun barrel swinging toward her.

Not just a gun barrel. The large, multi-barreled muzzle of an Escarlish repeater gun.

A whole line of shattered rocks worked toward Melantha across the ledge, the gunshots echoing against the night sky, ringing in Melantha's ears so loudly that it nearly drowned out the thunder of her own heartbeat.

She could not move. Her feet were frozen to the rugs beneath her. Even her last breath was frozen inside her chest.

Then a broad back clad in only a loose, off-white shirt appeared in front of her. Rharreth shuddered, as if under multiple impacts. Something punched into Melantha's shoulder.

But Rharreth still raised his hand. A blast of ice shot out, headed for the repeater gun on the wall.

Melantha did not have time to see if the ice reached the ambusher. Rharreth spun, and his arms wrapped around her. Then they were falling, tumbling. Off the ledge. Down the mountainous slope of the outside of Khagniorth Stronghold.

Cradled inside Rharreth's arms, one of his large hands protecting the back of her head, Melantha gripped his shirt and tried to tuck herself tighter against him. The pack she wore protected her back and shoulders, but her breath was still knocked from her as Rharreth's weight settled on her as they rolled. Her legs and feet scraped over the stones.

Then, with a final jolt, they came to a stop in a scrape of gravel and cloud of dust.

For a moment, Melantha could only lie there, gasping for breath. Pain throbbed in her shoulder, across her back and legs.

Warm and wet stickiness was spreading over her hands where they clasped against Rharreth's shirt. Beneath his shirt, his heartbeat was stuttering.

No, no, no. Melantha pushed upright, frantically examining Rharreth in the faint moonlight. Blood soaked the front of his shirt. He was gasping, blood trickling from the corner of his mouth. More blood shone on the back of his head.

There was no time for finesse. At any moment, his heart could stop or enemies would pour from the stronghold to hunt them down. She called on her magic, pressed her hand to his chest, and shoved her magic into him as if she intended to keep him alive through sheer brute force.

Brute force might be what healing him would take. Through her magic, she could see the concussion and slight crack to his skull, the multiple bullet wounds piercing his chest and shredding lungs and organs, and the broken ribs and other cracked bones. With the bullets still inside him, she could not heal him all the way, but she could at least keep him alive.

More gravel slid down the slope, and Zavni stumbled to a halt beside her. Blood coated his side and his face. "I closed the stone again, and Rharreth took out the repeater gun. But Drurvas will get through my magic in moments."

"I know. We need to get him out of here." Melantha gripped Rharreth's arm, as if she could physically pick him up herself.

Zavni knelt, grimacing as if even that small action was painful. Then he rolled Rharreth, lifting him across his back, gripping his arm and leg. With a grunt, Zavni shakily pushed to his feet.

He would not have the strength to haul Rharreth far. Melantha stood, swaying and willing away her sudden dizziness, and pressed a hand to Zavni's arm. She shoved magic into him, healing and strengthening. With her magic in him, he would feel physically stronger than he actually was, enabling him to do more.

He grunted and glanced to her. "Where to now, my queen?"

Where should they go? Where would they be safe?

Rharreth was in no shape to go back into the stronghold and try to rally those still loyal to him. Drurvas had planned well, setting up an ambush in case the attack in their bedroom failed.

The only weapons they had were Zavni's ax and Rharreth's elven dagger still secured to his belt.

They needed a place to heal and plan. They could trust no one, and she was still a stranger here. Who could she ask for help?

She straightened, remembering a day weeks ago walking the streets of Osmana. Perhaps Melantha could not trust any of the troll warriors, not even any of Rharreth's shield band except for Zavni. But she could, maybe, trust a family who owed her their son's life.

"This way." Melantha stuck to the shadow the moonlight cast at the base of the wall. She avoided the sections of unblemished snow, trying to walk only on the stones or patches of ice where they would not leave footprints. There was nothing she could do about the drops of blood Rharreth and Zavni were leaving.

Melantha hurried along the dark, empty streets. She had only been here once. During daylight. What if she picked the wrong house? What if she remembered the wrong street?

She simply could not make those mistakes. Rharreth's life depended on them finding shelter, and soon.

She turned down the side street, walked a few houses down from the wall, and glanced around, trying to picture it as she had last seen it, packed with people barely held in check by Rharreth's shield band.

This had to be the right place. It simply had to be.

With a deep breath, she knocked on the door.

Nothing happened. The street remained empty and dark. She could not hear anything besides her and Zavni's heavy breathing.

She knocked again, harder this time. She did not dare raise her voice to call out. While the people in this home—assuming Melantha found the right place—were probably trustworthy, the others on this street might not be.

A few more long seconds passed. Melantha raised her hand to knock again but halted when shuffling came from inside.

The door cracked open. Just wide enough to show a sliver of face and the shine of a knife clutched in the male troll's hand. "Who goes there?"

She could not see enough to recognize the face, and the voice was gravelly with sleep and muffled by the door. But, at this point, it was too late. This troll had seen them, even if he did not yet recognize them thanks to the darkness.

"Please, sir. There has been an attack. King Rharreth and I need sanctuary for the rest of the night." Melantha kept her voice low, and she gestured to Zavni behind her.

Zavni turned, putting Rharreth's face more in the light. It was difficult, with him hanging across Zavni's shoulders.

But the eye peering through the crack between door and jamb widened, and moments later, the door was flung open. "Come in, Your Majesties."

Melantha hurried inside, then waited for Zavni and Rharreth. As soon as they were inside, she yanked the door from the troll's hand and shut it, barely stopping herself from slamming it.

Lights flared, and a troll woman appeared in the tunnel

that led deeper into the mountain, a candle in her hand. She stood there, blinking, as if she could not understand what she was seeing.

This was the right place. Melantha sagged against the table set in the center of what she could now see was the kitchen, complete with a fireplace molded into one wall and cupboards along the other.

Melantha bolted upright. "We need to cover the windows. Please. And no use of magic. We cannot give any indication that we are here."

The troll man pulled ragged curtains across the windows. The woman disappeared for a moment before she returned with blankets clutched in her arms. Together, she and her husband covered the windows, using the benches from around the table to press the blankets tight against the walls.

When the woman finished, she turned, taking in Rharreth draped across Zavni's back and dripping blood on her floor. "Put His Majesty on the table."

While Zavni eased Rharreth down onto the table, the woman lit more candles and lamps while her husband stoked the fire.

Melantha braced herself against the table as she reached a trembling hand toward Rharreth. She needed to heal him. Her vision blurred, her head spinning. Her whole body was aching.

Next thing she knew, she was blinking up at the ceiling. Zavni knelt on one side, the troll woman on the other.

The woman frowned, her forehead furrowed. "You are bleeding, milady."

She was? Melantha fumbled to rest a hand on the most painful spot—her shoulder—and her fingers touched warm, fresh blood. When she called on her magic, she finally sensed the bullet wound in her shoulder. One of the bullets from the repeater gun must have gone all the way through Rharreth to hit her. Her magic told her the bullet was still lodged next to her shoulder blade.

Rharreth. Melantha struggled to sit up. "I need to—" She trailed off as her head spun again.

The troll woman's hand pushed into Melantha's upper chest. "You need to rest. You are weak from loss of blood."

"But Rharreth..." Melantha reached upward for the table, fumbling to try to touch Rharreth's hand. She needed to check on him and make sure he was still alive.

Zavni glanced from the tabletop, then back to Melantha. "He seems stable enough. For now. You cannot help him until you help yourself first. You are our only healer."

Right. Of course. She needed to have a clear head to surgically remove the bullets from Rharreth. She would do him no good if she was dizzy and passing out.

"What about the use of magic, Your Majesty?" The troll woman's grip tightened on Melantha's arm.

"Healing magic is not like other magics. It can only be performed through direct touch and thus can only be sensed with direct touch." Melantha forced herself to concentrate. "I...I will need to dig the bullet from my shoulder and heal myself. I might need to rest afterwards. Could...could you make Rharreth comfortable by the fire?"

"Of course, Your Majesty." Zavni and the troll man moved Rharreth while the troll woman used a stack of furs and blankets to cushion the hearth and lay over him.

Melantha slowly pushed to a sitting position, leaning against the table leg. This couple was probably using every rug, fur, and blanket they had in their home, and Melantha and Rharreth would leave most of them blood-stained and worse for the wear when they were done.

The troll woman returned to Melantha's side. "What do you need? Where can I help, milady?"

"Could you please help me onto the table?" Melantha gritted her teeth as the woman pulled her to her feet, then aided her as she eased onto the table.

How was she going to perform surgery on herself? She had never had reason to do so before.

Could she ask this woman to do the digging for her? Yet, one look at the woman's work-roughened hands and wide-eyed expression sent a pang through Melantha. She did not like the thought of those untrained hands probing her shoulder.

No, Melantha would have to do it herself. "Do you have a mirror? Or some shiny object? I will also need my medical kit from my pack."

What had happened to her pack? Zavni or the woman must have taken it off when Melantha passed out.

Melantha returned to staring at the smooth, domed rock of the ceiling, even as she listened to the troll woman rummage in a cupboard, then in Melantha's pack. Lying down steadied her head, and the magic she eased through herself soothed the aches from her various bruises.

When the troll woman returned to her side, a leather satchel in her hand, Melantha caught her arm. "What is your name? I am sorry I did not take the time to ask before."

"Inersha, Your Majesty. And my husband's name is Mymrar. We are of family Verdrun." The troll woman smiled, then held up the pack. "Where would you like this?"

Melantha talked Inersha through laying out the supplies on a bench, then cleansing the instruments she would need.

Inersha cut her dress around the injury and cleaned the wound while Melantha gritted her teeth.

She was probably being more cautious than necessary, but she would need all the magic she could get for Rharreth. She could not waste it fending off an infection in herself because she decided to do everything with magic instead of taking the time to clean the wound beforehand.

Then, while Inersha held a metal frying pan, Melantha used both a slim knife and a pair of tweezers to dig inside her shoulder. It was difficult trying to find the bullet in the vague reflection on the worn pan. Not to mention, what little she could see was all reversed in the mirrored surface.

She found the bullet mostly by feel, tears heating her eyes as she finally withdrew it. "Could you please look to see if any more pieces of my dress or other debris are in the wound? I cannot see well enough in the reflection to be sure I have everything."

Inersha took the tweezers and the bullet from Melantha, then leaned closer to examine the wound. After a few moments, she nodded. "I don't see anything, milady."

Melantha pressed her hand to her shoulder and eased her magic into the wound. Her magic knit the muscles and torn skin, erasing the pain.

When it was done, Melantha let out a long sigh. She was tired, but at least her mind was clear. She pushed to a sitting position, then straightened. The dizziness did not return, thankfully.

As much as she wanted to rest, she glanced over at Rharreth. His breathing was far too shallow, his gray skin paling until it was almost the same shade as hers. He could not wait while she took a nap.

Melantha swung to her feet, steadying herself for a

moment before she turned to Inersha, Mymrar, and Zavni. "Could you please lift him onto the table?"

Rharreth gave a small moan as Mymrar and Zavni picked him up and placed him on the table.

Melantha recleaned her tools, then got to work.

It took much longer to dig all of the bullets from Rharreth than it had the one from her shoulder. While several of the shots had gone all the way through, like the one that had struck her, many others had not. She had to examine every single bullet hole to pick out the pieces of his shirt from each wound.

Once all the wounds were clean, she pieced together bones and muscles with her magic. She healed Rharreth's organs and placed more of her magic inside him to continue to restore his strength.

When she was finished, she sagged against the table, her hands trembling.

But she had done it. She had saved Rharreth and gotten them to a safe place, at least for now.

"Zavni, could you see to it that he is made comfortable by the fire again?" Melantha faced Zavni, then noticed the blood staining his clothing. "Right, you are injured. I can heal you as well."

"I am not badly injured, not after you healed me earlier. I can wait. Rest, my queen." Zavni gave her a bow, and something in that heartfelt gesture brought a lump to Melantha's throat.

Somehow, she had gained the loyalty of this shield brother, even if the rest of Rharreth's shield band had turned on the both of them.

"Your Majesty, you can take our bed. We will gladly sleep out here." Inersha bowed, gesturing toward the pile of rugs and blankets, the ones that had already been stained with Rharreth's blood.

Melantha shook her head. "Thank you for the kind offer, but it would be best if Rharreth stayed by the fire. The extra warmth will make it easier for his body to heal."

Mymrar straightened. "I will stand guard for the rest of the night to allow you and your guard to rest."

"I can stay awake. I am fine." Zavni patted the sword at his side, but Melantha could see the weariness around his eyes and pulling at his stance. He needed rest as badly as she and Rharreth did.

"Zavni, take the offer and rest. If you sleep by the door, Mymrar can easily wake you at the first sign of trouble." Melantha forced herself to push away from the table and walk on trembling legs to Zavni's side. "You need to be well rested when Rharreth wakes and we decide on our next move."

"Very well." Zavni nodded. When he helped Mymrar once again lift Rharreth from the table to the nest of blankets by the fire, Zavni's hands were shaking, and his face strained into tight lines.

When Rharreth was settled, Melantha eased under the blankets with him, resting her hands against his back.

As she closed her eyes and tried to sleep, those moments of the attack in their bedroom played against her eyelids.

She had always believed that, if she were placed in the position of having to fight, she would find that she was tough. That she was secretly a warrior.

Yet, when faced with a battle, she had hated it. She had fought because she had to, just as she had there in the dungeon when she had tried to prevent the trolls from taking Farrendel to his death. Back then, she had not had a weapon, and she had been so frantic to get to Farrendel that she had barely noticed the blood as she had scrambled toward Farrendel's cell.

This time, she had been in the thick of the fight. She had been covered in the blood and gore.

And she had found herself vomiting in the corner rather than fighting.

While she loved the release of the practice fights, she hated the real thing. Perhaps, contrary to what she had always believed about herself, she was not a warrior. She did not want to end up in battle ever again if she could help it.

She was a healer. Healing was her war, her battle. And she would fight it with every scrap of magic she possessed.

TWENTY-FIVE

Rharreth blinked at the fire burning a few feet in front of him. His chest was still sore, but he could breathe freely. Something he had not expected when he had jumped in front of that repeater gun to shield Melantha.

He could feel her now, her warmth pressed against his back. He had no memories of what had happened after he had flung the two of them from the top of the stronghold.

But somehow, she had found a safe place for them. She had healed him. She had shown courage worthy of the best warriors.

Stifling his groan, Rharreth pushed upright. He was growing warm between the fire and Melantha and all the blankets and furs piled on top of him.

"Look who is awake."

Rharreth turned to find Zavni sitting on a bench beside a table, eating a thin porridge.

On the other side of the table, two children, a boy and a girl, were staring at Rharreth, wide-eyed. The boy, Rharreth recognized. Melantha had healed his arm, months ago now.

A troll woman filled a bowl from the pot set on the table, crossed the room, and held out the bowl. "It is good to see you looking well, Your Majesty."

"Thank you." Rharreth cradled the bowl. "And thank you for taking us in."

"It is our honor to serve and protect our king." The troll woman's voice was fierce, though when she glanced at her children, her mouth tightened.

It must be hard, knowing that her actions could endanger those she loved.

How bad was the situation? How much danger were Melantha and Rharreth in? Surely most of his people remained loyal.

But there had been too many warrior families involved last night. If Drurvas hadn't had support, he would have set up his ambush far more secretly.

Instead, he had not cared who would witness him commit treason and attempted regicide.

That was not good. It meant enough of the warrior families supported Drurvas that they were willing to either look away when he committed treason or participate with no fear of repercussions. They were utterly sure that Drurvas would succeed in his coup.

Footsteps sounded on the step outside. Zavni eased to his feet, hand moving to the sword at his waist.

The woman hurried around the table and placed a hand on each of her children's shoulders.

Rharreth set aside the bowl of gruel and pushed to his feet. Where was his sword? His weapons? He could not remember what had happened to them.

A knock came on the door. Three quick raps, a pause, then two more knocks. The rhythm was too purposeful to be anything but a signal.

Zavni relaxed somewhat, though he still cautiously pushed aside the blanket draping one of the windows to peer outside, something he would not have dared do without the code assuring him that it was probably safe. Only then did he unbar the door and swing it open.

Cold air flowed in, and at Rharreth's feet, Melantha stirred, rubbing at her eyes.

A man stepped inside, followed by Vriska.

Melantha bolted upright, gripping the blankets around her as if she planned to somehow turn them into a weapon. "What is she doing here? We cannot trust her."

Rharreth reached down to rest a hand on Melantha's shoulder. He was not sure what to think either. He had often seen Vriska and Drurvas talking before the coup.

Zavni shut the door, bolting it again. "I understand. She is not the member of the shield band I was expecting to come."

"I know. I know you don't trust me. You have good reason not to." Vriska's voice was shaking, and her face was drawn in a way Rharreth had never seen. "I never thought this would happen. I didn't realize. I'm sorry."

Melantha snorted. "I have been there, done that, said that. You are going to have to do a whole lot better to convince us."

Rharreth squeezed her shoulder, then held out a hand. She took it and let him haul her to her feet. Only then could he see that her dress was thoroughly bloodstained, its shoulder ripped. Rharreth leaned against the wall next to the fireplace and gave Vriska a stern glare. "Explain."

"I knew Drurvas wasn't happy. I wasn't happy. But I didn't think...I didn't think this would happen." Vriska was shaking, but she held Rharreth's gaze steadily. "Nirveeth and Darvek are dead. The others are in hiding. But right now, Drurvas thinks I'm on his side. I'm the only one who can move about freely."

"How do we know we can trust you?" Melantha's voice tightened. "I have betrayed my people. I have convinced myself that what I was doing was right. But it was not. And I have learned that no amount of groveling or work can earn redemption. So if you are here to try to earn your way back into our good graces, then forget it. But if you are here to confess without any expectation or feeling that you deserve restoration, only then will I be willing to hear what you have to say."

Vriska drew in a shuddering breath, her gaze swinging to focus on Melantha before she ducked her head. "You are correct. Honor is not trying to earn back what I lost by my actions. Honor is confessing, even knowing the consequences."

Melantha eased closer to Rharreth. The set of her spine softened. Only fractionally, but Rharreth could tell.

Vriska stared down at her hands for a moment before she straightened her shoulders. "I failed you, my king." She glanced to Melantha. "And I failed you, my queen."

That eased the lines on Melantha's face, though her mouth remained tight.

Rharreth felt the tension easing in his shoulders as well. His chest and back were aching from standing, so he pushed from the wall and took a seat on one of the benches. Melantha sat next to him, twining her fingers with his underneath the table where the others couldn't see.

He squeezed her fingers, hoping she could tell how very thankful he was for all she had done the night before.

Rharreth met Vriska's gaze. "How bad is it?"

"Not good. Drurvas has total control of Khagniorth Stronghold after spending the night killing or subduing anyone who showed any hint of loyalty to you." Vriska glanced at Zavni, who had taken a position leaning against the door. "Those who survived have fled the stronghold and are in hiding."

"Mymrar here heard about them this morning, and I sent him to make contact as quietly as possible." Zavni nodded to the man, the stranger. It must be his house that they were sheltering in.

The man was standing to the side with his wife, the children no longer in sight. They must have quietly sent their children to play in one of the bedrooms.

"The surviving shield brothers are all wounded. They had to fight hard to get out of the stronghold, once they realized His Majesty was already dead or apprehended, and the best way to help was to escape." Vriska shook her head, the bones braided into her hair rattling. "I was not with them last night. Drurvas seemed to think I was on his side, and once I realized what was going down, I played into his belief, knowing I would be able to help more from the inside than if I fled with the others. I was actually able to aid some of the last few escaping. I had just gone to the place they were staying to warn them that Drurvas plans to attack them there."

Rharreth gripped Melantha's hand tighter. Drurvas had planned well and gathered his allies with skill. Except for the fact that he had failed to kill them, Drurvas had won.

"Your orders, Your Majesty?" Vriska met his gaze. "I need to return to Khagniorth Stronghold soon. Drurvas thinks I am locating your supporters in order to turn them over to him. I need to have something to tell him."

What could they do? What should he say? Drurvas had backed them into a corner. Perhaps Rharreth could rally the warriors loyal to him, but that would take time. Drurvas had the advantage of being organized and prepared.

Beside him, Melantha straightened, then glanced at Rharreth. "We need to go to Tarenhiel. Ask my brother for sanctuary."

"No." Rharreth shook his head, unable to look at Melantha. She sounded very sure, but she did not know the culture of Kostaria well enough yet to know why her suggestion would never work. "If I take back my throne with the help of the elves, then I will never have the loyalty of my people. I will look like the weak king that Drurvas accused me of being, and I will never keep my throne."

"I know. But a prolonged civil war is not going to help Kostaria. Maybe Drurvas eventually wins. Maybe you do. But in the end, Kostaria loses. The people lose." Melantha's eyes flashed, her voice tight and simmering, as she gestured behind her to the man and woman. "You need to figure out how to stop him quickly. To do that, we need help."

She had a point. Rharreth had been fighting for peace for months. He had seen the improvement in the life of his people, even in the short time since he had signed the peace treaty with Tarenhiel and Escarland. Fighting Drurvas in the streets of Osmana would undo all that hard work.

He needed to back Drurvas into a corner until it came down to just the two of them. No armies. No large loss of life. Just strength against strength. Only if Rharreth won such a contest could he retake his throne and regain the loyalty of those warrior families who were currently siding with Drurvas.

"I will have to challenge him to a Dulraith." Rharreth glanced between Vriska and Zavni. Both gave a solemn nod, as if they had already realized that.

"What is a Dulraith?" Melantha glanced around at them, her forehead wrinkled.

"It is a traditional duel to solve aspersions cast upon a warrior's honor." It was a lot more than that, but Rharreth didn't want to divulge all the details yet. It would only make Melantha worry if she knew.

"A Dulraith would solve the problem, but you cannot fight him here. Not while he is surrounded by all those warrior families he has swayed to his side. He would kill you before you even have a chance to challenge him." Zavni sighed and crossed his arms. "Many of your strongest supporters live outside of Osmana."

"We need to buy time so that he doesn't kill all of your supporters in Osmana before you have a chance to rally those loyal to you." Vriska glanced over her shoulder at the door. "He will search the city for you."

"We will fight for you, Your Majesty." Mymrar stepped forward. "Many of those you have helped would fight for you."

Rharreth turned to better face the couple. "I thank you for your willingness to fight, but you are not warriors. I don't wish for my people to be slaughtered for my throne."

How was he to protect his people? How could he buy time? He squeezed Melantha's hand. More importantly, how did he protect her? If he lost the Dulraith, she would be killed.

But, if Rharreth waited to challenge Drurvas until they

were by the border with Tarenhiel, Zavni or one of the other remaining loyal shield brothers could spirit her across the border. If her brother would grant her sanctuary, she would be safe, even if Rharreth lost.

It was the best plan he had, even if he did not like asking the elves for anything. "Perhaps you are right. We flee to Tarenhiel. But, we have Vriska tell Drurvas that is our plan. He will gather his warriors and will give chase instead of spending his time purging Osmana."

Vriska's jaw tightened, but she nodded. "I will tell him tomorrow. I can buy you a day to get clear of Osmana. But what if he catches up? You will be able to move quickly, but..." Vriska's gaze flicked to Melantha.

Melantha was not a warrior, nor was she a troll. She was more susceptible to the cold. Would she have the strength for the journey ahead?

As if sensing their scrutiny, Melantha's spine went even straighter, her chin lifting. Reminding Rharreth with her bearing that she was strong, even if it was not in the same way as the troll warrior women. Melantha had her magic, and that might prove to be more useful than a resistance to cold.

Rharreth rested his free palm against his chest, where her magic was busy healing the last of his wounds. Her power had already proven invaluable.

"Tell Drurvas that we will be sticking near the train tracks. It is a more level and easier route, even if it is slightly longer. It will make sense, and he will use the train to move his army to the border." Rharreth tapped the table, as if a map was spread in front of him.

Zavni and Vriska nodded, as if they both could visualize

that same map. Melantha glanced between the three of them, but she didn't interrupt.

"Melantha and I will take the direct route and cross the border at Argar Point. That is rough country, but we can find shelter at Gozat Stronghold halfway there. Zavni, I know your father Ezrec will remain loyal to me. He has counseled for making peace with Tarenhiel for years." Rharreth pointed to a spot on the table along the invisible line that was the Tarenhieli-Kostarian border. "Zavni, I want you and all of the warriors loyal to me to spread the word quietly to meet me at Argar Point. But be careful. Our plan will fall apart if Drurvas catches wind of this."

"Drurvas was bold last night. He made his move, and he committed all his resources to it, expecting complete success. He had no backup plans if you survived the night. Because of that, the lines have been clearly drawn between his supporters and yours." Vriska shrugged and headed for the door. "Zavni, I will do my best to stay in touch and alert you to anything I learn from within Drurvas's inner circle. Now, I had better leave, otherwise Drurvas may suspect."

Zavni stood aside and let Vriska leave, locking the door behind her.

The woman stepped forward, her head high. "Your Majesty, we will spread word among our neighbors that you are alive. Once you have left, of course. We have no wish to bring danger to you. But the people need to know you live."

"Once again, I thank you. You are correct. The people need to know." Rharreth nodded his head toward her. "Drurvas will spread lies that I am dead. Failing that, he will continue to spread lies about my weakness and unworthiness as king, especially once he hears that I am fleeing to Tarenhiel. He will use that as evidence."

It would look bad, fleeing to Tarenhiel. But Melantha was right. They had no choice. Not if they wanted to take this fight to the border and away from street fighting in Osmana that would only harm the innocent people of Kostaria.

And, somehow, the thought that others might think him weak or unworthy didn't sting as it once had. He knew his own strength. He knew what he was doing was right. He could live with the consequences.

"We will tell the truth." The man stepped up next to his wife and rested a hand on her shoulder.

Rharreth did not deserve their loyalty. He had failed them. He had failed all of Kostaria. He had known Drurvas was restless and not happy with the direction that Rharreth was taking the kingdom. He had seen the signs, but he had chosen, once again, to do nothing, believing that Drurvas's loyalty as a shield brother would be enough.

"Thank you." Melantha stood and gifted the woman with one of her rare smiles, the ones that lit her face and redrew the hard lines into something softer, kinder.

Rharreth was not sure she even realized the effect that her genuine smiles had. Perhaps because she seemed so reluctant to betray such emotions to others. Even if she never felt comfortable showing emotions before strangers, Rharreth would take whatever genuine emotion she wanted to grant him. Her anger. Her passion. Her tears. And, yes, her joy. An emotion she had struggled to feel when he'd met her.

Melantha turned to him and rested a hand on his shoulder, the smile still on her face. "I know we just woke up, but we ought to rest. You are still healing, and I assume we cannot leave until we have the cover of darkness."

"Please, take our room." The woman gestured behind her.

"We could not possibly put you out…"

The woman gestured at the kitchen, something almost like a twitch of a smile on her face. "No disrespect, but I need my kitchen. You will be putting me more out if you keep blocking my fireplace from use."

Melantha gave her deep, throaty laugh and nodded. "Of course."

Rharreth was not going to argue. He needed a few moments alone with Melantha even more than he needed rest.

After gathering up the stack of furs and blankets from beside the fire, the woman led the way into the rest of the house. The passageway was carved deeper into the mountain, the walls smoothed with loving care even if they remained empty of fancy sconces, the floor bare of rugs. Several rounded doorways opened on either side of the passageway. Instead of doors, they were closed with worn furs.

This family didn't have much. They didn't even have the full privacy of doors. Yet Rharreth would have preferred a childhood here in this cozy, small home carved from the mountain than the one he'd had in Khagniorth Stronghold, never measuring up to the cruelty and strength of his older brother and forever stuck between trying to please his hard father and his loving but helpless mother.

The woman entered the first room on the right, setting the stack of blankets and furs on the empty mattress. Had she and her husband given up every single blanket they owned for Rharreth and Melantha the night before?

"Let me know if there is anything you need, Your

Majesties." The woman bobbed a bow before she left, letting the fur door covering fall closed behind her.

No sooner had the fur settled than Melantha stepped into his arms, holding him tightly enough it was almost painful against his healing ribs. She buried her face in his shirt, and he cradled the back of her head. It took a long moment before he realized her shoulders were shaking, the front of his shirt dampening with her silent tears.

"I nearly lost you. If one of those bullets had hit your heart instead of your lungs...if my magic had not been enough..." Melantha was shaking harder.

"I know." Rharreth pressed his face against her hair, breathing her in. That moment, when he had seen the muzzle of the repeater gun swinging toward her...it had been the deepest, rawest panic he had ever felt.

Nothing else mattered. Not his honor. His throne. His status as a strong and worthy king of the trolls. He would sacrifice all of it for her.

He cradled her face in his hands, swiping away her tears with his thumbs. "I promise that, no matter what happens, I will keep you safe. If I have to choose between my throne and keeping you safe, I will choose you. I will give it all up. My throne. My kingdom. My people. If that is what it takes."

Melantha blinked up at him, her tears drying as her jaw hardened in the way that told him he was about to feel the brunt of her unleashed stubbornness. "You will not choose me over your kingdom. Even if you are tempted, I will not let you. We took an oath to our people, and it is our duty to uphold that, even if it puts you or me or both of us in danger."

"I know. I know we discussed this when you started healing large numbers of the people, but..." It was hard to remember his oath, his determination, his duty with the memory of gunshots in his head.

Rharreth eased his fingers into her hair, hoping she couldn't feel the tremors coursing through him. When had she become so precious to him? When had she become his weakness?

He now understood how those Escarlish traitors had been able to use Princess Elspeth to capture Laesornysh. If someone threatened Melantha...Rharreth would surrender in a heartbeat if that was what it took to save her.

Instead of leaning into his hand, Melantha stood straight and met his gaze, her eyes filled with fire. "I know the cost of putting emotions above duty to my kingdom. Because of my own bitterness, I betrayed my kingdom and my brother. I am not going to let you make the same mistake, not even for me. We will fight together, and together we will take back our throne and protect our people."

The fire in her eyes stirred the heat in his own chest. This was why he had fallen in love with her. She called him out when he was weak. The same way he called her out on her weakness. They were far stronger together than they ever had been alone.

"You're right." Rharreth pulled her closer. She was soft and small in his arms, yet filled with a strength and fire that would refine both of them. "Thank you for being a compass when I waver. And a stone wall when I am being stubborn."

Because of her, he would never again stand by while an injustice was done. He would not keep his head down and go along with what was happening because he did not have the courage to take the consequences of doing what was right.

Because of him, she wouldn't linger in bitterness until it

consumed her. She would never again be so focused on fitting into what was expected of her that she forgot how to live in full, passionate intensity.

Melantha leaned into him, giving him that soft, yet somehow dangerous smile of hers. "Of course I am right. Now, are you going to kiss me already? Because I believe that is what you are supposed to do to celebrate surviving a coup by your evil cousin."

He chuckled. He definitely wasn't going to argue with that.

CHAPTER
TWENTY-SIX

Kneeling on the floor in front of a trunk, Farrendel swayed with the rhythm of the Escarlish train as it steamed across the countryside, headed toward Fort Charibert and the bomb range. The snow-covered fields flashed by outside the windows of the sleeping compartment. Early morning sunlight glinted on the fresh layer of snow, making it sparkle like a thousand diamonds had been scattered across the fields.

The trunk was crammed into the little floorspace there was in the compartment, beside the head of the bunkbed set into the train car's wall.

Essie sat on the end of the bed, and she leaned over as he opened the lid. "I've never seen you wear fighting leathers. Every fight I've seen you in has always been an ambush or a rescue when you haven't had time to properly dress and prepare. I'm sure it looks impressive."

"This will not be a real fight either." Farrendel reached for the folded tunic that lay on top. It was made of leather lined with padding to absorb minor blows. Metal plating covered the chest and shoulders in such a way that it remained flexible as he moved.

It was easier to focus on his fighting leathers rather than the demonstration he had agreed to do for Escarland's military generals, Parliament, and Essie's brothers. Averett and Julien did not bother him, but the thought of having a whole bunch of generals and members of the human Parliament staring at him while he used his magic was enough to make him want to jump off this moving train.

"No, I guess this isn't a real fight. But there will be a lot of magic and explosions and I'm looking forward to it." Essie grinned and reached out to rest a hand on his shoulder. "Don't be afraid to show off. That's why you're dressing up, after all. You're going to strut out there in front of all those members of Parliament and those generals and blast off so much magic you'll leave even the toughest of them quaking in their boots."

Leaving them quaking in their boots sounded like something he could do. But what if he lost control of his magic, the way he had in Kostaria? Averett, Julien, those generals, all those people...they expected him to unleash his magic as he had never dared before, except when pain and torture had driven him nearly out of his senses.

"Farrendel." Essie gave a sigh, then her hand rested against his cheek and tilted his face to look at her. "You will be fine. With our practice and the heart bond, you have figured out techniques you haven't tried before. But, more than showing off, more than impressing everyone, I want you to enjoy using your magic. I want you to wield it like you love it."

Love his magic? The very thought seemed so foreign, and yet...

There were all those times he had watched Essie use his magic, and he could not hate it then. It was beautiful in her hands.

But in his hands? In his hands, his magic was deadly. Destructive. Dangerous. With his magic, he had killed armies. He had blood on his hands and on his magic.

That was something he was not sure he could ever love.

But he gave Essie a small nod before he pulled away from her touch and returned to unpacking the leathers. Halfway down the trunk, canvas covered more items on the bottom, but he left that in place for now.

He dressed in the tunic, clasped a wide belt around his waist, and buckled his swords across his back. He pulled on fingerless, leather gloves, then tightened bracers on his wrists and arms.

With his leather armor in place, he felt steadier. More prepared for this demonstration.

When he turned back to Essie, her grin had softened into a smile that twinkled in her eyes. She stood and swayed with the rhythm of the train as she strode across the tiny space. She rested her hands on his chest, running her fingers over the leather and metal. Standing on her tiptoes, she leaned in and kissed him.

He held her, kissing her back. Her hands trailed through his hair, which was now long enough to just brush the collar of his tunic.

"You look rather good in your armor." Essie murmured, her lips brushing his cheek. "My dashing, deadly elf warrior."

Deadly elf warrior. That was the look he was going for. The last time these generals saw him, he was half-naked and losing control of his magic. Impressive, but not his best.

The Parliament members had not seen his magic at all besides the little burst he had let loose in the Parliament chambers.

All of them needed to be impressed to further solidify the new defense alliance. When he used his magic, he needed them to imagine what it would be like to fight with him on their side and picture the continued benefits of a long-term peace and alliance with Tarenhiel.

And, why they should never, ever think about trying to manipulate that treaty to be anything other than fair to both Escarland and Tarenhiel. Tarenhiel was not weak and not groveling at Escarland's feet, much as it had appeared that way.

"You are going to scare all of them witless." Essie smirked and stood on her tiptoes to plant one last kiss on his cheek. "We're probably getting close."

His chest tightened again, and not just at the thought of this demonstration. He could not put off revealing what was on the bottom of the trunk any longer. A gift for Essie, but not the normal type of gift he would get for her.

He let her go and knelt on the floor in front of the trunk again. He opened the lid, then glanced up at Essie. "I have something for you. But I am not sure you will like it."

"Now you have me curious." Essie joined him on the floor, squished shoulder to shoulder with him to fit in front of the trunk in the small space. She pulled back the canvas, revealing another padded leather tunic, smaller than his and without the extra metal armoring. Her gaze shot to his. "You had fighting leathers made for me? When? How?"

He stared down at the leathers rather than hold Essie's gaze. "I sent a message shortly after we started training. The dressmaker in Estyra has your measurements and worked

307

with the armorer to tailor it for you. I know you do not wish to become a warrior or ever have to use my magic in battle, but I thought if you were in that situation again because of me, I would want you protected, as much as you can be."

Essie's hand moved to rest on his, squeezing his fingers until he finally looked at her. She smiled and leaned into him. "Thank you. I love it, and more than that, I love the care behind it."

"I know. But I do not want you to feel I am trying to change you or turn you into a warrior when that is not what you want to be." Farrendel struggled to hold her gaze. She had loved him as he was, even as she managed to push him to be better without ever forcing him. He wanted to give her the same in return, but it was not as easy to find that line as Essie made it seem.

Instead of looking away as he had expected, Essie laughed and took his hands in both of hers. "I have realized that your greatest weakness in battle is not stone. It isn't me. It's the fact that you are so ridiculously overpowered. You've always walked into battle alone, trying to use as little magic as possible for the task at hand to avoid destroying everything in sight, including your allies. Your greatest weakness is fear of your magic. Your fear and others' fear."

He struggled to breathe, tension pulling all his muscles taut. Of course he feared his magic. Everyone, even Weylind, feared Farrendel's magic. How could they not, after seeing what he could do?

"You have never had anyone who could stand with you, watching your back. Until me." Her smile softened, and she let go of his hand to trace her finger over the scar on his cheek. "If this is what it takes to keep you safe and let you wield your magic as you have never been able to before, then that's exactly what I'll do. And I'll do it without a shred of reluctance. No, I don't want to become some magic-wielding warrior destroying armies. That's your job. But I can protect your back and protect your allies, just like I'm going to do today for this demonstration. That's now my job."

He leaned into her hand. "Essie…"

"Don't try to talk me out of it." She gave him a quick kiss, then turned back to the trunk. "I think matching outfits is a great idea. Here, hold the mirror while I braid my hair, then you might have to show me how to actually put all this stuff on."

Farrendel found himself relaxing as he held the mirror while Essie deftly twisted her hair into a single braid down her back. Then she pulled on the padded leather tunic and buckled on the belt. Farrendel helped her lace the bracers while she put on her own fingerless leather gloves.

Finally, he pulled out a rifle sling that buckled to the shoulders of the tunic and the belt. Straps distributed the weight across her shoulders and back, making it a much more comfortable way to carry her gun than a single strap across the body.

Essie reached onto the top bunk, retrieved her rifle, and twisted to slide it into its new sling across her back. When its weight settled against her shoulders, she bounced on her toes, as if testing how it felt. "Your armorers know what they are doing. This is so much better. I didn't even realize how uncomfortable my gun's weight was until now. I could wear it like this all day."

"That is the point." Farrendel retrieved his own swords from where they had been stashed next to Essie's gun. When he buckled on his swords, reinforcing straps distributed the weight across his back.

The train gave a piercing whistle, then lurched as the brakes squealed.

Farrendel winced and braced himself against the wall. "I think we are here."

"Yes." Essie patted his chest, which turned into bracing herself against him as the train shuddered to a halt. "You're going to do great."

He could not think of a response besides holding her more tightly against him. It was not very comfortable, with both of them wearing fighting leathers, but he did not care.

When the train came to a stop, Essie led the way from the sleeping compartment and into the seating car. There, Averett and Julien were pushing to their feet, though Averett froze partway up, staring at Essie.

Julien grinned and strode forward, then made a spinning motion with his hand. "Looking good, little sister. Very tough. I'm almost scared of you."

Essie turned in a circle for him. "Only almost?"

Julien reached out and gave a gentle tug on the end of her braid. "You're still you."

Farrendel lingered in the shadows of the doorway, not sure if he was ready to step off this train.

Averett straightened and strode toward them. His gaze swept over Essie's new armor, but he focused on Farrendel. "I know this will seem intimidating once we step off this train, but you have nothing to worry about. You can't fail. This isn't a test."

It felt like one. At least the weight of his swords on his back was reassuring as was the shield that his leather armor provided.

Perhaps he had been wrong in telling himself this was not a battle. If it was a battle, even a different kind of battle, then he could reach for the steadying cold that he felt when walking into a war.

He was Laesornysh. He let the cold settle around him, even as the heart bond remained warm inside his chest. It was a strange feeling going into battle both icy and warm. He would have expected the juxtaposition to unbalance him, but, instead, he felt steadier than ever before as if he had always needed both.

With the ice flowing in his veins, he strode from the train behind Averett with Essie keeping pace at his side.

Outside the train, the familiar bustle of the Escarlish army base stretched around the platform. Long wooden buildings stretched into the distance while men in the light gray army uniform hurried back and forth. Those who were farther away were so busy they did not even glance toward the train or notice their king disembarking.

The train platform itself was packed with people. Men in the basic Escarlish outfit of trousers and shirt made of good quality fabric clustered on one side of the platform while a group of older men in Escarlish uniforms waited on the other. All of them gave low bows as Averett stepped onto the platform, and continued bowing as Essie and Farrendel, then Julien, joined him.

Farrendel refused to let himself shift under the scrutiny of so many people. He was Laesornysh. He could kill everyone here with a flick of his fingers. Why should he be scared of anything they thought of him?

As Iyrinder, Captain Merrick, and Averett's personal guards poured from the train cars, the pack of generals hurried forward.

General Freilan, the top general in Escarland's army, bowed to Averett. "Your Majesty." The bow was cut short as he quickly turned to Farrendel, his eyes gleaming, his smile wide. "Prince Farrendel. It is an honor and pleasure to meet you again. Your magic was a wonder to behold, and we are all looking forward to witnessing such a magnificent display again."

Farrendel barely kept himself from rocking back on his heels. He was not the best at reading and understanding people, but this general—all of the generals, actually—was staring at him as if he was someone they highly respected and admired. That had not been the case the last time he had seen General Freilan, when Averett had been interviewing him about the missing Escarlish weapons.

What had changed? He had never done anything to earn that respect. All he had done was get captured, helplessly endure torture for a few weeks, then lose control of his magic and nearly kill an entire city filled with people. Hardly anything admirable.

"Yes, I'm sure it will be memorable." Essie slipped her hand into Farrendel's, giving him a smile.

"Let's head to the bomb range." The general gestured in the direction of the familiar open space before he led the way in that direction.

At the bomb range, a line of Escarlish repeater guns was set up at the edge of the field. At the far end, a set of larger guns was also trained on the field.

Farrendel knew the strength of his magic, but that long line of shining guns was intimidating. He had nearly been killed by just one of those guns. Now fifteen of them were trained on where he would be standing.

Several Escarlish soldiers stood by each of the repeater

guns and the larger artillery guns, and all of them straightened and gave salutes, not relaxing until the generals saluted in return.

General Freilan gestured to the line of weapons. "All of the guns have been elevated so that they will be firing thirty feet above your head. It will still seem uncomfortably close, but you will be in no danger."

Except if any of the Escarlish soldiers had the idea to lower the guns to point directly at him.

Some of Farrendel's thoughts must have shown on his face, because General Freilan gave another gesture, this time in the direction of the men still standing at attention by the guns. "They have all been told exactly what will happen to them if they even think about letting those guns fall below the ordered elevation. Same with the artillery guns, which are set to fire fifty feet over your head. That flag over there marks the spot where you should stand to ensure you are safe by our calculations."

Farrendel studied the field, where a blue flag flapped about a hundred yards away. He was not sure how much he trusted their calculations or these Escarlish soldiers. But that probably was not the point. He would have to trust his magic to protect him.

That, and the fact that Averett was present. It would be hard to prove that the death of an elf prince was accidental with the king, a whole bunch of generals, and the members of Parliament watching the whole proceedings.

General Freilan gave a slight cough in the back of his throat. "While none of us doubt your control of your magic, we would appreciate it if you do not lash out at the guns or destroy any of the munitions too close to our firing line. We want to keep this safe on both sides."

It would be bad if any of the Escarlish spectators or soldiers were injured.

"I will not destroy any of the guns." Farrendel glanced at Essie beside him.

Essie squeezed his hand, then turned to General Freilan. "As you will see in a moment, I have the ability to use Prince Farrendel's magic, and I will be providing a shield over our heads to ensure that no shrapnel comes our way."

General Freilan nodded, his gaze sharpening as he studied Essie. The magic sharing caused by the heart bond was not a secret. Some in the Escarlish army had seen it during their fight across Kostaria, and Essie had explained that rumors tended to fly among the army so that everyone knew at least some of it.

"In that case, let's get started." General Freilan gestured to Essie, Julien, and Averett. "Your Majesty, Your Highnesses. You and your guards can stand back here."

As the others moved away to their assigned place, Essie remained beside Farrendel. She gave him one of the part mischievous, part flirtatious smiles that made him think about kissing and holding her close and made the tips of his ears warm and probably turn pink.

She rested her hands on his chest, then stood on her tiptoes to give him a quick kiss.

Was she trying to distract him? How was he supposed to concentrate and be his cold, deadly Laesornysh self with her kissing him like this?

Essie rocked back to her heels and patted his chest. "Like I said before, go out there, show off, and have fun."

Fun was not something he would associate with his magic, not in this most deadly, potent form.

But, for her sake, he nodded and spun on his heel. He

strode across the field, the back of his neck prickling with the feeling of so many eyes focused on him. But he kept his head high, his back straight, as he gathered the icy cold he used when going into battle.

At the flag, he halted, pulled two bits of moss from a tiny pocket in the side of the leather tunic, and tucked the moss into his ears to deaden the noise. With all those Escarlish guns and ordnance, things were going to get very loud in a few minutes.

With a deep breath, Farrendel turned around to face the long line of gleaming Escarlish guns pointed in his direction. Even though he knew those muzzles were pointed at the sky rather than directly at him, a shiver still shot into his stomach.

This was what he would have been facing had he not married Essie and secured the peace treaty between Escarland and Tarenhiel. Instead of a mere fifteen repeater guns and five artillery pieces, there would have been far more pointed into Tarenhiel. As he had feared, the Hydalla River would have run red with blood.

Instead, it had been Kostaria's snow stained red. These glinting guns had pierced through the trolls' ice and blizzards to route their armies.

General Freilan waved, probably to ask if Farrendel was ready.

Farrendel gave a sharp nod and bent his knees, keeping his body loose. He called on his magic, dumping a bunch of it into the elishina, before he let more of it flood into the air surrounding him.

Seconds later, he felt the tug as Essie drew on the magic in the heart bond. A crackling shield of his magic filled the air above the heads of the observers.

The soldiers behind the repeater guns tensed, then the air cracked with a harsh, deep chatter.

Farrendel extended his magic higher into the sky until he could sense it incinerating the bullets flying well over his head.

More of the repeater guns chattered, and he could feel some of the bullets getting through. He was not using enough magic to stop all of them.

He was still holding back, using as little magic as possible. Wielding it like he feared it.

He drew on more, letting it pour from him in a crackling tower extending far into the sky, even as he still kept it under tight control.

The bullets from the repeater guns were incinerated in bursts of hot metal. The air was choked with the scent of over-heated iron and the sulfur stench of gunpowder.

One of the large cannons near the end of the line boomed. The shot peppered Farrendel's magic. Grapeshot, if Farrendel were to guess. While the smaller, exploding shot was probably effective against massed troops, it was actually easier for Farrendel to incinerate.

The next cannon down the line boomed, rocking back under the force of the explosion. This one was a solid iron ball, and he could not incinerate that much iron instantly, even if it started melting around the edges. Instead, he was able to use his magic to repel the iron ball to redirect it to fall to the ground well away from himself.

The last gun in line roared, recoiling. This was one of the experimental ones, and it spat a larger, bullet-shaped shell.

Farrendel could sense that the shell was covered with human magic. Something to help it be more lethal or pound through stone better. He could not get too good a sense of it before his magic burned the human magic away as if it were nothing.

Still, the shell flew through Farrendel's magic quickly, too quickly for the layers of his magic to halt it. It landed far behind him, exploding with such force that it shook the ground beneath his feet.

Several more shells burst through his magic, exploding far behind him. He could melt them or redirect them, but he could not entirely stop them.

Not with the little bit of magic he had let free of his tight control.

Some great elf warrior he was. He was holding back the repeater guns, but anything bigger was shredding through his magic.

Averett had said this was not a test. Yet, somehow, it still felt like one, and he was failing.

Through the heart bond, Farrendel could feel exasperation coming from Essie. Across the distance, he could see her shaking her head and laughing under her breath, as if she was telling him, *I know you can do better than this. Stop holding back.*

How could he stop holding back? What would happen if he unleashed his magic here?

More exasperation from Essie. More explosions as shells got past him.

Yes, this demonstration was a way for the Escarlish army to pit their weapons against the might of the elves and see what they would need to do to counter his magic.

But it was also a chance for him to test his magic against their weapons. Hopefully, he would never have to fight Escarland, but another human kingdom could end up with similar weapons, and Farrendel might have to fight them.

If that happened, he would have both the Tarenhieli and Escarlish armies at his back. His brother. Essie's brothers. Those shells would be killing them if this was a real battle. He had to release more of his magic.

Not just more. All of it.

Essie was protecting the observers and the army base with a crackling layer of magic. The land was empty for miles around. If ever he was going to attempt to use his magic at full strength without holding back, now was the time.

Besides, he had the heart bond, and he had Essie. If things got out of hand, she could stop him as she had in Kostaria. He would not be alone in wrestling his magic back into submission, if it came to that.

Farrendel braced himself, took a deep breath, and let go.

There was an explosion. In his head. All around him.

Time slowed down. His senses crackled. He could feel every bolt of his power shivering through the air.

Magic gushed from him until the very air he breathed was choked with energy. He could feel his hair standing on end, blue lines wrapping around him, racing down his arms, twining around his hands.

One of the guns boomed, and Farrendel could sense the shell gliding through the air. While his magic was not substantial enough to physically grip the shell, he wrapped the shell with his magic as if it was a strong electricity.

The momentum was too much to stop, but Farrendel turned its trajectory and whipped the shell toward the ground. It exploded off to his side, throwing up a fountain of dirt and debris as the ground beneath his feet vibrated.

Still more magic burst from him until it felt like his chest was tearing apart under the force.

That old surge of fear was back, panic tearing at the back of his throat. He had to stop it. Get it under control.

The magic was burning through his fingers, out of his chest. He was not sure he could stop it if he tried. His magic was unleashed, and it would not want to be stuffed back into confinement.

Instead of trying to rein it in, he redirected part of it so that the magic burst into the heart bond rather than exploding outward. The crackle filled his chest, but the pressure of his magic eased, as if it was no longer clawing to be released now that he had given it an outlet.

He straightened and faced the line of guns again. The repeater guns were still chattering away, but their bullets were incinerated so quickly he could not feel them. They were mere sparks of light among the glittering blue tornado roaring around him.

More of the bigger guns went off, and Farrendel caught each shell, smacking them down to the ground with such force that dirt showered into the air before it too was incinerated.

And still the magic roared. It whirled around him, swirling far into the sky above and flooding the bomb range all around.

He was at the center of a raging storm of his fully unleashed magic, and yet he was in control. Any part of his power that threatened to spin out of his control, he nudged into the heart bond where it calmed down before either he or Essie tugged it free again.

This was working. He nearly laughed as he reached out and plucked one of the shells from the air only yards from where it had been fired and drew it into his whirl of magic, letting it spin safely around him, before he finally squeezed with his magic, burning through the shell until it exploded high above his head.

Still his power surged forward, eager for release. And he let it. All of it. People could probably see the column of his magic rising into the sky as far away as Aldon.

This time, he laughed. He let the magic twine around his fingers, playing with it as it burst around him.

He could no longer see the observers or the bomb range. All he could see was the whirling hurricane of magic exploding around him.

And all of it—*all* of it—was in his control.

All of it except for the tug in the heart bond where Essie drew on his magic, holding a shield over the observers. Any time his wild power touched her shield, she turned the energy or drew it into her shield to strengthen it.

He was not sure how it was possible that she could interact with magic he was already wielding. Perhaps it was all their practice, and he subconsciously released his magic to her when he felt her tugging for control of it. Maybe his magic itself somehow recognized her, as if knowing it now belonged to her as well.

Two people. One magic.

He surged the magic into a vast wall between him and the guns. He formed it into towers and battlements. He let it collapse into a flood along the ground, twining it around each of the spindly pine trees that had somehow survived in the bomb range. If he wanted, he could incinerate those pines with a pinch of his fingers. Or he could ease his magic along the trunks, outline every twig and needle without singeing so much as a pinecone.

After several minutes, he drew the magic back toward him, spinning it into a tornado around him once again.

He felt a stir, and then Essie was walking toward him through the storm of magic, her bright red hair tugging free of the braid whipping in the magical gale. From the tug on the elishina, he could still feel the shield of his magic that she was holding over the observers behind her, ensuring their safety.

The guns had fallen silent. He was not sure when. He had been so deep inside his magic that the guns had become inconsequential.

Essie stepped into the eye of the storm where he stood, and he reached for her, gripping her hands and pulling her toward him. She was staring up at the blue storm, and he tipped his head back as well, taking in the vortex of magic. "You were right, Essie. It is beautiful."

"Yes, it is." She wrapped her arms around his waist.

"Can you feel it? I am in control." The joy bursting through his chest was too much to contain just standing there. He held Essie tightly and spun the two of them, his magic twining tighter around them. "I am in control."

She laughed and held on tightly, not letting go even as he set her feet back on the ground. "I always knew you could do it."

Then, she kissed him. And Farrendel did not care that they had an audience, though it was doubtful anyone could see them inside the white-hot glow of his magic. He dug his fingers into her hair, deepening the kiss, drawing her in, holding her tightly. He pulled away enough to murmur against her hair, "My magic is beautiful, but you are far more beautiful."

"Flatterer." Essie pulled back even more and patted his chest. "Save those thoughts for later, husband of mine. Right now, I think it is about time to wrap up this demonstration.

When I left, even the generals were starting to look a little green, and the Parliament members were downright terrified. I think a few of them are huddled on the ground sobbing."

Right. The demonstration. His magic.

He drew his power toward him, until it was a star surrounding him and Essie. The magic came more willingly, as if now that he had let it run rampant, it was no longer as wild and desperate for freedom.

With a deep breath, he grabbed most of it and dumped it into the heart bond. Essie released the magic she was wielding, and that magic too went back into the heart bond.

The rest of the crackling tornado of magic he tossed into the sky and exploded into a burst of harmless sparks that floated down like glittering blue snowflakes. Might as well end with a showy grand finale.

As the sparkling magic nipped against his skin before vanishing, he finally looked down to the line of observers standing behind the Escarlish guns.

The Parliament members were all on the ground, arms over their heads as if they expected Farrendel's magic to fry them at any moment. On the other end, the generals were downright gaping.

In the center, Averett and Julien were grinning. They were also the only two standing straight and tall, as if they had full confidence in Farrendel's magic or in Essie's wielding of it to protect them.

Holding Essie's hand, Farrendel strode toward the line of observers. Instead of feeling tired from working so much magic, he felt awake and alive. Whole in a way he had not been in a long time.

TWENTY-SEVEN

A s Farrendel, still gripping Essie's hand, reached the others, Averett and Julien nodded to him but were too busy shaking hands and speaking with the generals to say anything to them.

Farrendel hung back as the generals approached, bowing and murmuring versions of, "Thank you for such an awesome display."

In the background, one of the Parliament members was bowing to Essie. More like groveling, as he said, "Thank you —*thank you*—Princess Elspeth for marrying that elf."

Thankfully, Averett and Julien hurried things along, and they soon had all of them disengaged from the generals and Parliament members, who would take a separate train back to Aldon once the royal train had departed and been given enough of a head start.

As soon as they were in the privacy of the royal car, the door shut behind them, Julien body-slam-hugged Farrendel, knocking the breath from him, before pounding him on the back hard enough that Farrendel was glad he was wearing his padded fighting leathers.

"That was awesome!" Julien gave him one last pound on the back before stepping away far enough to grip Farrendel's shoulders, giving him a shake in his exuberance. "That was even better than I was expecting, and we all saw how powerful you were in Kostaria."

Farrendel managed to extricate himself from Julien and took a seat next to Essie on the settee along one wall of the train car. From now on, he was going to wear his leather armor whenever he was around Essie's overly exuberant brothers.

Averett dropped into one of the cushioned chairs, sprawling. "I *love* being right. It felt so good—so good—to go up to all those members of Parliament and say, *I told you so.* Parliament has been so sure this whole time that making a treaty with Mongalia was the better option. The generals wanted to team up with Mongalia and finish the war with Tarenhiel that Father started. But *I* pushed for a diplomatic meeting with Weylind. *I* refused to consider war until after we explored all our options. *I* had read the reports and rumors about Farrendel's power."

Averett gestured toward Farrendel, and Farrendel straightened, reaching out to clasp Essie's hand. She leaned against him, the leather of their padded armor squeaking, her smile warm as she tilted her head up to look at him.

"I knew Mongalia only wanted to get their claws into Escarland and any treaty would be an imbalanced one. I knew we would be better off keeping Mongalia out of our affairs and gaining peace with Tarenhiel another way. I was *right.* And it feels so good." Averett pumped his fist, rocking

forward and back in the chair under the force of his celebration.

Around them, the train shuddered as it chugged into
motion.

Essie gripped Farrendel's hand with both of hers. "You
can't take all the credit. After all, I'm the one who argued for
the marriage alliance once it was a real possibility. And I
have been right in pushing for closer relations with
Tarenhiel."

"She's got you there." Julien had taken a seat in the other
chair, sprawling much like Averett so that their legs filled the
space around the coffee table in the center.

"Aw, come on, Essie, Julien. Let me bask in my triumph
for a few minutes." Averett settled deeper in the chair, only
flapping his hand in Essie's direction lazily. "Being king
mostly stinks. It is just a long list of problems that everyone
expects you to fix even if you can't. When things go wrong,
you get blamed, even if it wasn't your fault. But you never
get the credit when things actually go right for a change."

All reasons Farrendel was thankful he was the youngest.
He had never been in any danger of inheriting the throne,
not that he was sure the elven nobility would even allow it
should such a tragedy come about. Much better to be the
youngest prince, able to quietly live his own life rather than
the one the crown forced upon those who wore it.

Averett folded his hands over his stomach. "So I'm going
to enjoy it. I'm on a roll, with peace with Tarenhiel, a victory
in the war with Kostaria, and the booming trade, especially
for Escarland's farmers, that has come about because of it.
Any time Parliament gets testy, I'm going to rub their noses
in this for the next ten years."

"Ten years." Farrendel raised his eyebrows at Averett. That was hardly a long time. A mere decade.

"Ah, right. I forgot. That isn't that long to you elves. Given how long you and Essie are bound to live, my great-great-grandchildren will still be rubbing my rightness into the noses of Parliament." Averett leaned back with a contented sigh. "Farrendel, you are officially the best brother-in-law I have."

Essie rolled her eyes. "He's your *only* brother-in-law."

"He can still be my favorite." Averett tilted his head back, closing his eyes. "Unless I adopt Weylind as a pseudo brother-in-law."

The thought was so ludicrous Farrendel snorted, the sound rough in his throat and loud enough to be heard above the clattering of the train wheels against the rails.

Julien's and Averett's gazes shot to Farrendel, eyebrows lifting.

Farrendel shrugged, ducking his head. He was still getting used to laughing. No surprise that the others were still getting used to it. "Weylind would hate that."

"While being secretly happy, though he would never admit it." Averett smirked, his gaze focused on Farrendel as if he meant more than just Weylind.

Farrendel found himself grinning as well. Weylind would outwardly hate Averett treating him like a brother, but Essie had told him how her brothers and Weylind had bonded during the fight across Kostaria. It would be good for Weylind to have a friend.

"After that display, I'm thinking you should get Weylind over here and host a joint Tarenhieli-Escarlish diplomatic meeting with Mongalia. I've heard the elves have had trouble with Mongalia harassing ships headed for their ports along the mouth of the Hydalla. Not as bad as the problems you were having with us, but it still should be dealt with." Julien shrugged as he gestured at Farrendel. "And Mongalia has been rattling its sabers, thanks to our strengthened alliance with Tarenhiel."

"Good idea. If Weylind and I present a united front—with a little flashy magic from Farrendel—it would convince them to back off because they don't want to mess with the combined might of Tarenhiel and Escarland." Averett gave a satisfied nod, as if that reality was a foregone conclusion. "You know, with Tarenhiel and Escarland working together—maybe with Kostaria's help, if the alliance warms to that point—we can command just about anything we want in treaty negotiations. We are on the verge of a golden age for Tarenhiel and Escarland, mark my words."

Julien leaned over and smacked Averett's shoulder. "You are drunk on being right. It's making you talk grandiose nonsense."

"Thank you, Julien. I was going to smack him if you didn't." Essie leaned her head against Farrendel's shoulder, hugging his arm. It was not comfortable since his wrist pressed against the hard surface of her wide belt, but he did not pull away. If anything, Essie gripped his arm tighter as she glanced at her brother, laughter in her voice. "Avie, please don't turn my husband into your personal intimidation weapon."

"Only when it is also in the best interest of Tarenhiel." Averett shifted in his chair, as if getting more comfortable against the cushions. He turned back to Farrendel, the humor in his eyes fading. "Back when we were on the brink of war with Tarenhiel, I was glad you were the only elf warrior with your magic. Now I'm wishing there were more. Are you sure more elves don't have magic like yours?"

Farrendel shook his head, dropping his gaze back to the arm Essie was hugging. "Not right now. It is a rare magic that runs in the royal family and some of the other noble families. It was how they became the nobility, long ago."

"Makes sense." Julien leaned his elbows on his knees. "I've heard stories about the great elf warriors of the past. I'm sure you know far more."

Averett, Essie, and Julien all turned to Farrendel, staring at him as if waiting for him to share a story.

He opened his mouth, shut it, tried to find the words. Finally, he drew in a deep breath and forced himself to speak. "You have all seen the Gulmorth River Gorge that separates Tarenhiel and Kostaria."

"Yes. We had to fight our way across it when attacking Kostaria." Essie's mouth flattened, as if she was seeing that battle again.

It was strange, hearing about a war in which he had no part. Normally, Farrendel would have been at the front ranks of an invasion into Kostaria. Instead, he had spent the entire war pinned to the floor.

As much as he hated bloodshed and fighting, missing the entire war was much worse.

He cleared his throat and forced himself to tell the story rather than dwell on the memories. "That gorge was created by the last great elf warrior with magic like mine. This was over a thousand years ago, when the great rift happened between us forest elves and the mountain elves, as the trolls were called back then. To protect Tarenhiel from the warlike and vengeful kin in the north, this warrior used his magic to split the earth along what was then little more than a stream and created the gorge, though such expenditure of magic killed him. It was five hundred years before the trolls were able to use their ice and stone magic anywhere near the gorge, and Tarenhiel enjoyed peace for hundreds of years thanks to his sacrifice."

"Now I see why your magic is rare. Those who have it tend to get themselves killed off." Averett met Farrendel's gaze, something in his tone almost like a warning.

Essie's grip tightened on his arm. "Please tell me there is at least one story of an elf warrior living a long, happy life."

"If they lived a long, happy life, they usually did not make it into stories." Farrendel had to work to keep his serious expression in place rather than let the smile break free.

"Huh. Who knew you elves were such morbid story-tellers?" Essie huffed and nudged him again. "You'll just have to be the one to change that, I guess. Because I want a really long, really happy life with you."

Farrendel studied her, not sure how to go about joking about a shortened lifespan. "By elf standards, I will die at a rather young five hundred years or so thanks to the elishina."

By the way Essie grimaced, he was not sure she found his statement as ironically humorous as he did.

She rolled her eyes. "Fine, fine. Point taken. We are probably going to be an elf legend. Love. A bit of tragedy. An early death, by elven standards. Our life has all the makings of a story you elves apparently enjoy. All I ask is that we get a chance to grow old together instead of you getting yourself killed in some battle."

Across the way, Julien and Averett were starting to shift like they were uncomfortable with this conversation.

Farrendel cleared his throat again. "There's another legend about elf warriors. One that has to do with the founding of Escarland. Thousands of years ago, two great armies of elves fought, and their magic was so great and so destructive that it razed the forests in what is now Escarland and parts of Afristan and Mongalia. The ground itself was so destroyed that it was hundreds of years before humans moved onto the land and began to eke out a living from the ruined soil."

"We humans are a tenacious lot." Essie patted Farrendel's chest, tipping her head up to give him a smile.

"The warriors who survived the battle became the elven nobility, and my ancestor was crowned the new king of the elves, thanks to the strength of his magic." Farrendel gave her a small nudge in return, not that she would be able to feel the light tap of his elbow against her side through the fighting leathers she was still wearing. "So not all of the great elf warriors have tragic endings."

"Just most of them, apparently." The wrinkle still would not leave Essie's forehead, even as she seemed to be forcing a smile.

Had his story about the elf warrior dying young rattled her that much? He had not meant to give her another worry when it came to him or his magic.

"I've heard that story. It is told to explain how Escarland has so few true forests and is mostly open farmland still today." Averett glanced at Julien. "Do you remember that summer after I learned the story from my tutor? We spent hours digging in the palace garden, trying to dig up old weapons or artifacts from the battle. Little did we know that such things would have been long gone after thousands of years or far too deep for us to find with our little shovels."

"That was a great summer. When we weren't digging, we were whacking at each other with our shovels, bucket-helmets on our heads, pretending to be great elven warriors, until Father had to pull us apart because our play fight turned real." Julien's mouth tilted, as if the memory held both happiness and pain.

Farrendel could understand that. His own memories of his father were a lot like that.

"Why don't I remember that summer?" Essie lifted her head from Farrendel's shoulder.

"This was before the war. You were just a baby. Edmund was only three, so he probably doesn't remember it either, though Mother and Father told us to let him tag along." Averett shook his head, laughing under his breath. "Julien and I were five and seven. We thought it was such a trial to have to let our three-year-old brother toddle after us, under the watchful gaze of the nanny or Mother or Father, of course."

"It's so tough being the youngest. I missed out on all the fun when you were growing up." Essie nudged Farrendel with an elbow, her gaze searching as if she was not sure if he would find the memory of his childhood painful or some-thing humorous. "Though, I guess it was probably even worse for you. All three of your siblings were adults by the time you were born, and Weylind had even been married for a number of years."

Farrendel had dwelled too long on the painful memories of his childhood, and he had told Essie far too much of the loneliness and hard times. It was time he told her a few of the good memories and learned to laugh at his childhood the way she did about hers. He leaned closer, as if about to confide a dark secret. "Yes, but that meant that I was doted upon by my father and my siblings to the point I was absolutely spoiled."

Essie snorted out a laugh that turned into a cough, as if his humor had taken her so off guard that she had forgotten how to properly breathe. "You? Spoiled? Somehow, I can't picture it."

"Weylind never could tell me no." Farrendel leaned forward to rest his forehead against hers. "After all, he could not bring himself to refuse me when I agreed to marry you."

With both Julien and Averett shaking their heads in the background, Essie laughed and wrapped both arms around Farrendel. "You're right. Who else but a very spoiled youngest sibling would be able to talk their stubborn king of a brother into agreeing to something as crazy as this marriage alliance idea?"

CHAPTER
TWENTY-EIGHT

Melantha woke cocooned in Rharreth's arms, buried beneath layers of furs and blankets. She groaned and tugged the blankets tighter around her. "I do not want to get up. I have a feeling this will be the last time I am warm for a long time."

Rharreth's chuckle rumbled in his chest, and his breath heated the back of her neck. "Probably. But fleeing to Tarenhiel was your idea."

"Do not remind me." It had sounded so simple when she had proposed the plan that morning, but now the realities were sinking in. There would be no train to carry them across the frosty miles between Osmana and the Tarenhieli border. No fires. No comfortable shelter. Just whatever they could carry on their backs.

She did not doubt Rharreth's strength. But what about her own? What if Vriska was right? Was Melantha strong enough for this?

She would have to be.

Rharreth pushed himself onto his elbow, then flung back the covers.

Cold air washed over Melantha, and she stifled another groan before she forced herself to get up as well.

She and Rharreth dressed, and thankfully Melantha had managed to do a good job of grabbing their warmest clothes and boots during those frantic moments during the attack. When they exited the troll couple's bedchamber, they found Inersha stuffing leather-wrapped food into a bag while Mymrar and Zavni were kneeling on the floor, packing more items.

Inersha stuffed one last item in the haversack, then she held it out to Melantha. "I baked travel bread and packed as much smoked meat as I could."

Melantha took the pack, feeling its heaviness. Surely the couple did not have this much food they could spare. "This is too much. We cannot take all your food."

"Please take it, milady. It is our honor to provide for your journey." Inersha bowed, her hands clenching and unclenching as she smiled almost tentatively at Melantha. "I sought out my neighbors, the ones I know are loyal, and they provided food as well. I did not tell them exactly why I needed the extra food or for whom, though I am sure they might have guessed some of the reason. They gladly gave what they could."

Rharreth bowed to Inersha. "We thank you and thank your neighbors. It seems that there are those with honor left in Kostaria."

Mymrar straightened, his mouth pressed in a tight line. "It is because you have shown yourself to be an honorable king, and we know what the alternative will bring for our families. Drurvas has already sent squads of those loyal to him to confiscate food from the citizens so that he and his men may feast. We would rather give our food to your cause than have him snatch it to fatten his own belly."

Rharreth's jaw worked, and Melantha clenched her fists at the heat burning through her chest. She and Rharreth had worked so hard to feed the starving people of Kostaria. They had lived on the same rations that were distributed to common people and had enforced the same restrictions on the warrior families, even if they had not liked it.

And now Drurvas would undo all of that, right during the dead of winter when such measures would cause mass starvation among the people.

But he did not care. All he cared about was his own power, just as the warrior families backing him only cared for their power. They wanted starvation to drive Kostaria into a desperate war once again because war gave the king and the warrior families more power, esteem, and standing.

Melantha glanced between the troll couple, her back straight. When she spoke, her voice was low and held even more of the taut, flaming emotion than she had meant to display. "We will fix this. I promise you that we will not allow Drurvas to triumph."

The couple both gave even deeper bows, their faces tightening with such a mix of devotion and determination that Melantha wanted to tell them that she did not deserve such loyalty. Rharreth might, but not her.

But, she held herself back. Rharreth needed his citizens' loyalty more than ever right now, and Melantha was not going to protest when they gave it, no matter how undeserved. While she could never prove herself worthy of it, she could give her all in gratitude.

Zavni buckled the larger pack closed and held it out to

Rharreth. "These are all the supplies we could put together for you. We also procured a set of skis for each of you."

"Skis?" Melantha glanced from Zavni to the pair of long, flat boards that Mymrar picked up from where they had been leaning against the wall by the door. The skis were polished and lacquered smooth with one tip curled upward. One side held what looked like a leather buckle where they could attach their boots. "I thought we were going to take snowshoes?"

Her stomach churned just looking at the foreign skis. She had mastered snowshoes, since those were used in Tarenhiel occasionally and all the time here in Kostaria for even basic walks around Osmana after a large snowfall.

But she did not know how to ski, and this seemed like a bad time to have to learn, considering their lives depending on speed and secrecy.

Rharreth glanced over his shoulder at her as he shrugged on the pack. "I was going to teach you, once you were fully comfortable with snowshoes and we had a day to ourselves. Skis are easier and faster for long distances. Don't worry. It is easy to learn, especially since you already have a good sense of balance."

"We have two sets of snowshoes, if you would like to take them, Your Majesty. Some of the paths you will be taking will be too treacherous for skis." Mymrar nodded toward where the snowshoes hung from a peg by the door.

Rharreth hesitated, probably knowing just as well as Melantha that they would be taking this couple's only sets of snowshoes. But after a moment, he nodded. "Once again, we thank you."

He did not promise to return the items or offer recompense, and Melantha finally understood enough of troll culture to understand why. This couple was offering their food, their snowshoes, and everything else freely because it was the honorable thing to do. To offer money in return would only shame their gift. It would be as if Rharreth were trying to buy something that could only be given.

Instead, when Rharreth regained his throne and when he was able to return these items, any money or gold or recompense that he paid them would be done in gratitude, not because he was trying to earn anything from them.

Perhaps if Melantha had understood the concept of free gifts and gratitude better, then she would have treated Farrendel better. She would not have seen love as something filled with taking and earning, but instead would have realized that love was expressed by freely giving and showing gratitude for what was given.

Zavni helped Rharreth secure the skis and their accompanying poles across his back. "Are you sure about this, Rharreth? A blizzard is descending out of the mountains. It will be a rough night for travel."

"It will be rough, but a blizzard will hide our tracks. We have no choice but to risk it." Rharreth took the snowshoes from the peg. Zavni secured them to Rharreth's pack as well.

Melantha settled the pack of food on her back, buckling the additional straps across her upper chest and around her waist to keep the haversack secure and distribute the weight. When Inersha offered a red wool scarf with a matching hat, Melantha took the items, wrapped the scarf around her neck, and put on the hat without argument about taking more items from this generous couple.

With the fire crackling in the hearth, her face was burning, and she would start sweating if she did not step out into the cold soon.

After donning his own, smaller pack, Zavni opened the door, and he, Rharreth, and Melantha stepped into the night-time street. Melantha gave the couple one last nod before the door closed behind her.

An icy wind whipped down the street and clawed against the exposed skin of her cheeks and nose. The air was so cold that it burned the inside of her nose and stung the back of her throat. The sky above was a dark expanse of clouds, not a hint of stars in sight. The wind carried something frosty and heavy. The coming blizzard Zavni had mentioned.

Melantha pulled the hood of her parka over the red, woolen hat and tied the leather strap at the chin to keep the wind from yanking the hood off her head. Once her hood was secure, she tugged on her fur-lined mittens.

Silently, Zavni led the way along Osmana's outer wall, avoiding any pools of light cast by homes or the torches of guards patrolling the wall above.

Not far from the main gate, they reached a section of wall where Eyvindur was waiting, also carrying a pack. He bowed to both Rharreth and Melantha before he waved up at the patrolling guards.

These two guards must have been ones still loyal to Rharreth, because they lowered a rope. They pulled first Rharreth, then Melantha, and finally Zavni and Eyvindur to the wall top. They then lowered all four of them to the ground on the far side, one by one with Rharreth the last to leave Osmana's wall top. As he stepped from the loop at the end of the rope, he gave one last look at the wall above, as if memorizing his city before he left for the final time.

It would not be the final time. Melantha would do everything in her power to make sure of that. Their people needed Rharreth too much for them to fail.

After a quick whispered conversation with Zavni that Melantha could not hear, Rharreth led the way, followed by Melantha. Zavni and Eyvindur took up the rear. The two shield brothers stepped in Rharreth's tracks as if to obscure just how many people had left Osmana during the night.

After circling around the main gate, they entered the land surrounding Gror Grar that had been seared with Farrendel's magic. Even Melantha could feel it, still sparking through the ground beneath her feet.

Once they were well out of sight of Osmana and standing in the gully beneath the shadow of the ruins of Gror Grar, Rharreth halted and turned to them. "I believe this is where we part."

"If all goes well, we will lead Drurvas and his army on a merry chase." Zavni grinned before he clasped Rharreth's forearm. "Stay safe, the both of you."

Rharreth clasped Zavni's forearm in return, then did the same with Eyvindur. "We will meet you at Argar Point in a week. A week and a half at the most."

Zavni and Eyvindur both bowed one last time before they turned and set out in the direction of the train tracks that ran near Gror Grar. If Vriska told Drurvas the false direction, hopefully he would believe the two sets of mostly obscured tracks heading along the rails were Rharreth and Melantha's.

When they were alone, Rharreth turned to Melantha, his eyebrows lifted, a question in his dark blue eyes.

Melantha lifted his chin. "I am no weakling, Rharreth. I am strong enough for this. Now, lead the way."

With a nod, Rharreth turned toward a gully splitting off

from the main trail. Melantha followed him inside, the dark stone walls rising above her. In places, ice drooled down the rock in giant icicles that looked like a frozen waterfall. The snow inside the gully was not deep, so they trudged along in their boots without stopping to put on either the snowshoes or skis.

The gully narrowed to a mere crevice, half-filled with rubble from Farrendel's magic. Mountains rose on either side of them, their peaks shattered and flattened.

Melantha clambered over several boulders and shattered pieces of the rock wall before she and Rharreth entered a section that widened once again.

Rharreth halted and turned. Icy white magic swirled around his fingers before he sent a blast of snow past Melantha, obliterating the tracks they had left.

Once that was done, he pressed his hand to one of the walls. He grimaced, lines digging into his forehead and around his mouth, as more of his magic sparkled around his fingers. The stones of the crevice groaned as they started to fill in the gap, though they still glowed faintly blue with Farrendel's magic.

Her brother's magic still in the stones must be why Rharreth was straining to make them move.

Melantha set her hand over Rharreth's. Touching him, she could sense the battle of magics, and she added her own magic to the mix, easing it between Farrendel's burning, crackling magic and Rharreth's cold, blustery power.

Stone snapped into place across the crevice, jagged edges and jutting ledges forming to give it a natural look. For a final touch, Rharreth added a dusting of snow and a layer of icicles trailing down the rocks.

Rharreth pulled his hand away. "Thank you. That was

much easier with you shielding me from your brother's magic."

"You are welcome, though…" Melantha glanced from him to the rock wall. "I thought you were not going to use your magic in case Drurvas could sense it."

"I did not dare use my magic in Osmana, but here your brother's magic is so strong that it will obscure any traces of my magic to those chasing us. And, since I am the only one able to even work magic in this section of Kostaria, it is unlikely he will suspect that I wiped out our tracks or put this wall in place." Rharreth set off again down the gully. "We must keep going. I won't dare use magic again until we are well away from Osmana."

As Melantha marched after Rharreth, the first snowflakes began to fall. Soon, the snow fell harder and muffled the crunch of their boots.

Finally, Melantha and Rharreth stepped into a valley. Mountains at their back separated them from Osmana while more jagged peaks rose in the distance in front of them.

"This is a good spot to teach you to ski." Rharreth reached behind his head to fumble with the straps holding the skis and poles onto his pack.

Melantha helped him unstrap them, then she watched as he showed her how to put them on. The wooden ski was thinner than her foot as she strapped her boot into place. One strap went over the toe of her boot, pinning her toes to the ski. The second strap went from the first strap and around her heel to keep her foot from slipping out of the first but leaving her heel free to move up and down.

Balancing on the first ski while she put on the second was harder than it looked. Once the leather straps were secure, but not pinching, she balanced on the skis while she claimed the poles from Rharreth. The skis felt slippery beneath her, as though they would slide out from under her at any moment.

When she tried to turn to fall into line behind Rharreth, she crossed the front of her skis and nearly fell. It was strange, having her feet attached to something so long and bulky.

"I will break the trail. Your skis will follow the tracks left by mine. Slide the ski forward with your toes, keeping the ski on the ground, then put your weight down on your heel and glide all in one motion. Then repeat with your other foot. Your poles give you an extra push and help steady you." Rharreth shuffled forward a few steps, showing her the motion he was talking about. "Your skis will glide forward more easily than mine since I'm breaking the trail, so try to leave enough space between us that the front of your skis don't keep running over mine. Understand?"

"I think so." Melantha shuffled one foot back and forth, trying to get the feel of the ski beneath her. She would just have to learn as she went, and hopefully she would get the feel of it quickly.

Rharreth slid forward, the snow giving a crunch each time his skis sank in at the end of each gliding step. He left two parallel tracks behind him, and Melantha placed her skis in the tracks and pushed forward.

She wobbled, catching herself with the poles. Gritting her teeth, she called on every scrap of balance she possessed and pushed forward. The ski glided in the track. She leaned her weight into the movement, letting the momentum carry her as she slid her other foot forward.

The skis made a soothing shushing sound against the snow, and the gliding motion felt like a elven dance. It was the most peaceful, relaxing thing she had been asked to do since she had arrived in Kostaria.

Within seconds, she caught up to Rharreth, the front of her ski clattering as she ran up and over the back of one of his. "Sorry."

He staggered, her ski acting as an anchor on the back of his, before he righted himself. "A few stumbles are to be expected."

They continued on in silence, the only sound the whisper of their skis and the muffled softness of the falling snow.

The wind picked up, the snow falling harder until Melantha had to blink against the flakes to make out Rharreth ahead of her. His ski tracks were half-filled in with snow by the time she glided over them, and her progress slowed as the new snow made gliding harder.

After they had been traveling for an hour, Rharreth halted them for a small break while he tied a short length of rope to his waist, then had Melantha tie the other end to her waist.

After two hours of travel, Melantha's legs burned from the effort, and this was no longer the most relaxing thing she had done in Kostaria. After three hours, she was panting, and she called on her magic to give her strength. Her nose ached with cold even with her scarf pulled up to under her eyes, and mucus was dripping onto her upper lip.

But she refused to ask Rharreth to slow down or stop. They had to put as much distance as they could between themselves and Osmana.

What if Drurvas got to the border first? Would he invade Tarenhiel? What if Weylind was not prepared for such an attack, thinking the peace treaty with Rharreth was still in place?

Melantha called on her magic, using it to give strength to her legs and warm her numb fingers and toes. She had to keep going. Not just for the innocent citizens back in Osmana. But for the innocent citizens of Tarenhiel who must be warned that danger was coming to their border once again.

"Are you all right?" Rharreth's shout was muffled by the whipping wind and lashing snow. Melantha could barely see him only two yards ahead of her.

"Fine." As she felt the tug on the rope when he resumed, she put her head down and kept shuffling her skis forward.

The gale blasted harder until she had to lean into it to keep from being knocked over. The snow stung against her eyes until she squinted to see. Her world narrowed to the tips of her skis shuffling through the fresh powder, the cold slicing through her layers faster than her magic could warm her, and the constant tug on the rope that told her Rharreth was still ahead of her, giving her a direction to follow.

Hopefully Rharreth knew where he was going. Melantha had no sense of anything. Even the sky and the ground were lost in the whirling, swirling tumult of wind and snow.

It could have been hours. It could have been days, for all she knew. Maybe the darkness lightened into day, but the clouds pressed hard to the ground, snow choking the air.

The end of her ski clacked into something, and she fell to her knees as she went from gliding forward to a halt within a split second. She braced herself on her hands and knees, her arms sinking up to her elbows in the snow.

A crunching sound came from in front of her, then Rharreth was leaning over, balancing on his skis as he gripped her arm and pulled, helping her get back to her feet. When she was upright, he still did not let go. His eyebrows were rimed with snow, his gray skin shiny with a layer of ice. "We should rest for a while. You look about done in."

"I can keep going." She reached for more of her magic, trying to stop her legs from shaking. She could not be weak. She reached for his face, her fingers sliding over the layer of ice covering him. "Are you all right? Your face is covered with ice. Do you have frostbite?"

"I am fine. Thanks to my magic, I can cover myself with a thin layer of ice to protect myself from the snow and wind, and I don't get frostbite from it." His smile was soft. "Not something that would work for you, I'm afraid."

"No." Melantha shoved more magic into her face, trying to stay warm as another gust of wind buffeted her, driving stinging snow into her cheeks.

"I know we have to cover a lot of ground, but we also need to pace ourselves. You can't tell, but it is morning. We have been traveling for hours. We should rest." Rharreth glanced around them, as if trying to pierce the impenetrable whirl of snow and white that surrounded them. "Hopefully the blizzard will abate by the time we are ready to continue."

"All right." Melantha was not going to argue when he put it that way. It made it sound as though he was not stopping because she was too weak but because he, too, needed a break.

Rharreth removed a glove, and magic poured from his fingers. Snow mounded into a small hill. A small doorway big enough for Rharreth to crawl through opened in the side.

"We are going to stay inside a snow house? That does not sound very warm." Now that she had stopped, the wind felt even colder. Even with her magic, she was still shivering.

"Snow insulates, and it will be warmer than you expect." Rharreth knelt and unbuckled her skis for her. Once she was free, he helped her step out of them, then motioned toward the door. "Crawl inside. I will follow."

Melantha sank onto her hands and knees again and crawled through the tunnel. Inside, the snow hill was hollow with a domed ceiling and a flat, packed-snow floor. While the floor still seeped cold through her clothing, it felt warmer sheltered from the wind as it was.

A clatter sounded as Rharreth pushed their skis and poles to her. Then, he shoved his pack ahead of him as he crawled inside. He closed the opening until it was only a small hole to let in air. Finally, he removed the layer of ice from his face by turning it into snow and whirling it away with his magic.

He began to unbuckle the straps holding his pack closed, and Melantha reached out shaking hands to help. He shook his head, his fingers still swift and sure despite the cold. "No, rest. I've got this."

Melantha curled against the side of the snow wall, tucking her hands inside her sleeves to try to warm up her fingers.

Rharreth pulled several furs from the pack, along with a thick, woolen blanket. He spread the furs on the floor, then took off his snow-covered outer parka and fur-lined pants until he was down to his wool tunic and trousers. He sat on the furs as he tugged his pack within reach. "Come."

She did not need any urging. She shivered harder as she shucked her outer layer, sitting on the furs to take off her boots without touching the snow with her woolen stockings. Since the hat had been protected by the parka hood, she left it on to keep the top of her head and tips of her ears warm. Then she slid under the blanket and burrowed next to Rharreth, his body warming hers.

He reached over her and whisked away the snow from their outer clothing with his magic. When the parkas and fur-lined pants were free of snow, he spread all of it on top of them, and Melantha relaxed under the added layer of warmth.

Leaning over her still more, he grabbed the pack she had set aside, digging around until he pulled out one of the leather-wrapped packets of food. As he folded back the layers, revealing a loaf of fresh bread, Melantha's stomach rumbled and gurgled. Rharreth grinned down at her and held out the loaf. "We burned a lot of energy today, between keeping warm and all the exertion."

Tucked against him, that sounded almost romantic, even if it was just a fact about how they needed to keep up their strength.

She tore half the bread from the loaf, then tucked all but one hand under the blanket as she ate. "How far do you think we have come?"

"Not as far as it seemed, since the blizzard slowed our progress. If the weather lets up, we should make better time, especially once your muscles get used to the travel." Rharreth settled in behind her, wrapping his free hand around her waist.

She relaxed against the hard warmth of his chest, tucking her feet against his leg to warm her toes. Once she polished off her bread, she tucked both hands under the blanket and let her eyes fall closed, trying to ignore the ache in her leg muscles.

Rharreth had been right. This was cozier and warmer than she had expected. Heaving a deep sigh, she let herself drift off to sleep as the blizzard howled around their snow shelter.

TWENTY-NINE

Essie laughed as Farrendel all but dragged her by her hand down the slush-covered street toward the Aldon Market. He was walking so fast that all of the guards except for Iyrinder trotted to keep up. "Slow down! The market isn't going anywhere."

Farrendel eased his pace, glancing over his shoulder at her with the most sheepish grin she had ever seen on his face. "Sorry."

"I know, I know. You're just a little eager to see the magical engineering fair." Essie shook her head and fell into a much more comfortable stroll now that Farrendel had slowed down. "But it will still be there whether we get there in one minute or in five."

Around them, wet snow, melting in the winter sun beaming down on a cloudless day, piled along the edges of the street and slid from porch roofs onto the heads of those passing by. The street was covered with two inches of slush that sprayed onto those walking on the sidewalks every time a carriage rumbled past.

The sun was only a brief reprieve from winter. Clouds were gathering on the northwestern horizon, showing that another round of snow and cold was on its way for that evening.

A few of the people passing by stopped to wave or stare, and Essie made sure she gave them a smile and wave in return. Thanks to the surrounding guards—or perhaps the swords that Farrendel was wearing with their hilts visible above his elven cloak—most people gave them plenty of space.

Except for his shortened hair brushing his collar, Farrendel was dressed as an elf today. She had decided to go with a warmer Escarlish dress in the new, slimmer style of skirt that was becoming fashionable. She had trousers underneath the dress for added warmth, and both the trousers and the skirt hid the derringer she had strapped to her leg just above the top of her boot.

Not that they were expecting trouble, but she now appreciated the wisdom in being prepared. After all, Farrendel kept a portion of magic in the heart bond at all times in case either of them needed to use it in an emergency. She had gotten used to the constant crackle burning inside her chest.

Ahead, the large, red brick building of the Aldon Market filled an entire city block. A steady stream of people moved in and out of the doors, and Farrendel and Essie joined them, their guards keeping them in a bubble of space.

Finally, they stepped inside, and warmth washed over Essie's face, stinging against cheeks that had gone numb from the cold even on this sunny day.

The lower floor held all the normal booths arranged in long rows with spacious aisles for the crowds to meander. An upper floor covered the back half of the building while the front half remained open all the way to the glass and steel trusses that formed the ceiling of the market. This upper floor was often filled with artists displaying their wares or taking commissions.

But, for this weekend, it had been rented by Hanford University for a magical engineering fair they were hosting to show off new inventions by past students, showcase current students' projects, and recruit new students.

Farrendel's grip tightened on her hand as he set off at a brisk pace once again. "Lance said he would be here first thing in the morning, and he is going to introduce me to the professor who mentored him at the university. He thinks this professor would be willing to work with me, if I decide to enroll, since I would need a customized program."

Essie smiled as she trotted once again to keep up with him. When was the last time she had seen Farrendel this excited? He just about chattered her ear off that morning.

But she did not mind listening for a change. Not when Farrendel was this happy. He kept saying *if,* but she could tell it was really *when* he enrolled. Adding university classes would make their lives even more complicated, but they would make it work.

Farrendel took the stairs two at a time, and Essie laughed under her breath as she struggled to keep up. She could imagine Weylind shaking his head in bewilderment if he saw Farrendel now.

When they reached the top, another set of booths and tables met them. These were filled with bunches of gadgets and gears and glowing magical power cells. University professors wearing official-looking black robes strolled from table to table while students leaned forward to explain their projects or inventions. Escarlish citizens wandered from display to display to marvel at the innovations that could change their lives.

Averett would be coming later to make an official speech about inventions and progress and whatnot, but Farrendel had been bouncing off the walls since before daybreak. He was not about to wait until that evening.

"Prince Farrendel! Princess Essie!" Lance waved from his place behind one of the first tables. It was a sign of how respected he was that his table and display were placed in such a prominent position. A black-robed professor, his brown hair flecked with gray and smile lines marking his face, stood near Lance's table.

Essie placed her free hand on Farrendel's arm, her tight grip holding him back from racing across the space.

He glanced down at her before he lifted his gaze back to Lance, and his stride turned more sedate and princely.

When they reached the table, both Lance and the professor bowed before Lance gestured. "Prince Farrendel, Princess Essie, this is Professor Harrington."

"It is a pleasure to meet you both, especially you, Prince Farrendel. I have heard a lot about your magic from Mr. Marion." Professor Harrington's gaze flicked over Farrendel, as if searching for visible signs of Farrendel's power. After a moment, he turned back to Lance. "You said that you had an invention you would show me when Prince Farrendel arrived?"

"Not so much as an invention but a power cell." Lance reached under the table, which was covered with a black cloth that draped all the way to the floor. After a moment, he set one of the power cells filled with Farrendel's blue, crackling magic on the table.

This power cell was only about the size of his palm, far

smaller than any other magical power cell Essie had ever seen. It was metal and glass in the center, but stone capped each of the ends with metal wires protruding through.

Professor Harrington picked up the power cell, turning it over in his hands. His forehead furrowed and deep grooves cut into either side of his mouth as he studied it.

Farrendel leaned closer to Essie, his fingers tight on hers. Through the heart bond, she could sense his excitement from earlier churning into nerves as he watched the professor assess his and Lance's work.

You will be fine. He will be impressed. She sent those thoughts in Farrendel's direction through the heart bond. Even though he would not hear the actual words, the sense of them would echo through their bond.

"This is good work." Professor Harrington peered first at Lance, then at Farrendel. "This is your magic? What is this power cell capable of powering?"

While Farrendel nodded, Lance launched into a technical explanation about magical sensors and power levels and stuff that was gibberish to Essie.

This was her cue to leave. She was prepared to be a supportive wife when it came to Farrendel's growing interest in magical engineering, but if she stayed there, Farrendel would look to her to do the talking, and this was something he needed to do himself.

Standing on her tiptoes, Essie kissed Farrendel's cheek. "Have fun. I'm going to wander for a while."

Farrendel gave her a nod, though his gaze only flicked to her for a moment before latching back on Lance.

Behind her, Captain Merrick murmured, dividing up the guards. As the guards moved into position, Essie set off among the tables of inventions. She peered at a few of them,

giving compliments and listening to some of the short explanations. She took enough time that she wouldn't appear
rude, but she didn't linger. She would do more of that in the
evening when she came back with Averett and Farrendel for
the royal family's official visit to the fair.

Once she had spent sufficient time in the upper story, she
made her way down to the shops on the main floor, Captain
Merrick and the guards he had chosen leading the way or
trailing behind in their assigned positions.

Her first stop was the booth that sold Farrendel's favorite
hot chocolate mix. She and Farrendel had tested many of the
flavors offered at the booths, and the double chocolate
supreme they had tried on their first time in the Aldon
Market was still their favorite.

The girl running the booth today curtsied as Essie
approached. "Princess Elspeth. Is there anything I can help
you with?"

Essie scanned the packages of hot chocolate, finding the
right one. There was only one left since hot chocolate was
especially popular now that it was the middle of winter.
She picked up the package. "Do you sell this in a larger
size?"

"Not in the shop, but if you would like to place a custom
order of anything, I would be happy to see that it is delivered to the palace tomorrow morning." The girl gave the
perfect, practiced smile that Essie recognized. There probably wasn't a whole lot of difference between a job in
customer service and the role of princess. Both involved a lot
of smiling even when people were being downright unrea-
sonable.

Essie gave the girl one of her own practiced smiles in
return. "In that case, yes, I would like to place a custom

order, though delivery by tomorrow evening would be fine. I am not in a rush."

First thing in the morning would mean someone would have to work overnight to get an order to the palace on time. Hopefully giving them the whole day would mean they would not have to work extra hours or go too far out of the way for her.

The girl took down the details of Essie's order, and she did not even blink when Essie ordered ten pounds of hot chocolate mix. Essie gave instructions to have the order delivered to the Buckmore Palace gate and paid before she left to wander the market once again.

By the back wall, she found a booth selling pottery and ceramics, including everything from flowerpots and vases to bowls and plates and mugs.

Right in the front sat a mug with two elf ears sticking out on either side. The whole mug, elf ears and all, was white but veined in vibrant blue that was clearly meant to be a representation of Farrendel's magic.

When the woman running the booth noticed the direction of Essie's gaze, her face paled, and she reached for the mug. "I'm sorry, Your Highness. No disrespect to your husband was intended. My husband is in the army, and he fought in the war and told me about your Prince Farrendel's magic. I came up with this design, and it has been selling quite well in my husband's army unit. I never meant any disrespect, truly."

"It's all right. I think the mug is hilarious." Essie snatched it up before the woman could take it away. Farrendel would absolutely hate it, which was exactly why Essie was going to get it. "Has this really been selling that well?"

The woman's spine relaxed a fraction. "Yes, it has, Your Highness."

"Good. I'm glad to see any sign that the old prejudices against elves are fading." Essie dug out more money and paid for the mug, letting the woman wrap it in paper before Essie carefully placed the mug inside her cloth shopping bag.

With one last smile for the woman, Essie set off into the market once again. While she adored the mug, it probably wasn't the best gift to thank Farrendel for the set of armor he'd given her. She should find a mug he would actually like.

She found the perfect thing a few aisles down. It was a giant beer stein, but it would work just as well as a hot chocolate mug and Farrendel would probably never know the difference unless she told him.

But what caught her eye were all the tiny gears set into the side of the stainless-steel stein underneath a layer of glass. When the stein was picked up and tipped back, a metal ball rolled along a maze of channels, moving the gears and pressing down on levers as it worked its way toward the top. When the stein was tipped upright again, the ball fell back to the bottom, often taking a different path than the one it had before so that as a person drank from the stein, the metal ball meandered around the entire outside.

It was masterful craftsmanship, making all those tiny gears turn so smoothly along the side of a round mug, and definitely something Farrendel would find fascinating as well as useful for giant amounts of hot chocolate.

After she paid, she had to struggle to keep her princess smile in place instead of smirking as she imagined the look on Farrendel's face when she showed him her new mug.

Farrendel clasped his hands behind his back and tried not to rock back and forth on his heels as he waited for Professor Harrington's verdict on the power cell. He struggled to keep his breathing even, his chest going tight.

This was the kind of thing he would have to learn how to handle if he wanted to take classes at Hanford University. His work would be judged and evaluated on a regular basis, not something he had faced since he was a young elfling still learning to read and write.

"Hmm..." The professor perched a set of spectacles on his nose and continued his inspection even more intently.

What was he even looking at? The power cell was not that complicated, though it had modifications to allow it to store Farrendel's particularly powerful magic.

Finally, Professor Harrington looked up, focusing on Lance. "This is good work. You were in new territory, melding human engineering and elven magic like this."

"Thank you, professor." Lance grinned, and he pulled another device from under the table. "If you think that's fascinating, take a look at this."

The device was another of his magic sensors, and, as soon as he flipped on the switch, the red light started flashing frantically. The needle on the dial immediately shot all the way to the far side.

Farrendel tightened his clasped hands behind his back, trying to appear nonchalant as he waited for Professor Harrington's reaction.

The professor's eyebrows shot up as he glanced from the device to Farrendel.

Lance sighed, tapping the dial. "I still haven't managed

to craft a sensor that can detect the upper range of Farrendel's magic. I'm not sure it is possible, not if I want a device that still has any degree of accuracy to it."

"I see..." Professor Harrington regarded the power cell again, his mouth falling into that frown.

Farrendel resisted the urge to take off his cloak, even though he was feeling hot and choked as he waited for a response. Any response. Lance had assured him that Professor Harrington would be impressed since it would exhaust even a strong human magician to call up the amount of power contained in that small magical device. Yet, for Farrendel, that power felt so little he could fill a hundred of those devices and not feel the strain.

With a nod, the professor set the magical power device on the table and faced Farrendel. "Mr. Marion mentioned that you were considering enrolling in Hanford University. If that is the case, please know that I would be happy to work personally with you to craft a magical engineering degree."

Farrendel forced himself to exhale slowly as the tension left his shoulders and chest. Both Lance and Essie had assured him that there was no way Hanford University would turn him away, not when it would be good for their reputation to have an elf prince studying there. Not to mention the potential access to elven knowledge that it would give them. But surely it could not be this easy, could it?

He kept his expression blank. It would not do to appear too eager, and he had a few probing questions to ask.

He just had to talk. Form words. Not freeze and panic.

He could do this. He had, after all, mentally practiced all of these questions and possible answers and scenarios a thousand times in his head the night before. After all that mental practice, surely he could manage to sound coherent during the real thing. "I have duties in both Tarenhiel and Escarland. Is that something you could work around?"

"Certainly. Escarlish royalty and even some Mongalian and Afristani royalty have studied at Hanford University in the past. We understand the demands on your schedule, and we are willing to do whatever necessary to accommodate you." Professor Harrington pulled off his spectacles, folded them, and placed them in an inside pocket of his robes, patting the front of his robe for a moment before he met Farrendel's gaze. "As I am sure Mr. Marion explained, a magical engineering degree has either an emphasis in engineering or an emphasis in magic, though occasionally some choose to take a dual emphasis as Mr. Marion did. Most students with magic focus on the magical side of things."

Farrendel nodded. As Lance had no magic of his own, it would probably make sense if Farrendel focused on magic, especially since learning to better use his magic was one of his goals for taking classes. "If I take one emphasis, I can always add the other later, correct?"

"Yes, that certainly can be done, if neither money nor time is a concern. Which, I would assume is the case for you." Professor Harrington regarded Farrendel with the same studying look he had given the magical power cell.

Lance crossed his arms, huffing a breath. "I, for one, would appreciate if you got your degree before I am too old and gray to actually invent stuff with you."

"Right." Farrendel relaxed enough to jab a thumb at Lance. "Apparently that is my only concern timewise for how long it takes."

"Then I believe there should be no trouble in taking as

many or as few classes as you wish, as your schedule permits." Professor Harrington turned a severe glare on Lance before his official tone returned to his voice, his expression smoothing. "As you are not some untrained magician having to spend years learning the spells to craft your magic, most of your magical classes will be self-driven and could be done as correspondence courses. You would only need to visit the university in person a handful of times over the semester for evaluation. You could spend your summers in guided self-study to research elven magic in the great library of Estyra and practice magical exercises to see which prove beneficial to you."

Farrendel raised his eyebrows, studying this professor. He was being very accommodating and taking a lot of extra work onto himself, even if he pretended it was not that much.

The professor shrugged and something almost like a grin crossed his face. "I will admit my generosity is not only out of the goodness of my heart. I will be reading your findings and will thereby gain firsthand access to knowledge about elven magic and secondhand access to the legendary library of Estyra. Trust me, Escarland's academia has been lining up to be the first to step foot in that library once King Weylind allows such a thing. Yes, I'm hoping to put myself first in line by helping you, but that doesn't mean that I won't do my best in guiding your classes."

Farrendel felt the last of his tension draining away, now that he knew what this professor was angling for. "I intend to speak to my brother about promoting more of an exchange of information between Tarenhiel and Escarland. Some among the learned in my kingdom are just as eager for the knowledge that can be found at places like Hanford University."

"Excellent. I look forward to such opportunities to share knowledge in the future." An actual smile creased Professor Harrington's face. "As for your particular case, I would advise that you take the basic magical theory and history classes that all the magical engineering students take, though those classes too most likely could be done as correspondence courses. The engineering classes would have to be done in person, so I would suggest scheduling those for a time when you plan to be in Escarland for an extended period."

It sounded overwhelming. Definitely challenging.

But, it was a chance to learn how to use his magic to create and invent instead of only to kill and destroy. He had already seen the results of the practice in the precision and control he had gotten by working with Lance. What more could he be capable of if he gained yet more confidence in his control over his magic?

"I am still considering my options, and I will have to talk it over with Essie—Princess Elspeth." Farrendel kept his tone as neutral as possible. It was much easier to talk when he could use the same *I need to talk to Princess Elspeth* line whenever he needed a noncommittal answer. If he could only memorize the perfect answer for every conceivable question, then he would never have to panic during a conversation ever again.

"Of course. Thank you for your time, and I hope you enjoy the rest of the exhibition." Professor Harrington nodded, then shuffled off to the next booth where he was soon in discussion with the young woman standing behind it.

"That went well." Lance's grin was splitting his face as he shut off the magical sensor and stowed it and the power cell under the table once again. "Before it gets busy, why don't I show you around and introduce you to a few more people?"

Farrendel shifted, the tension churning his stomach once again. Looking at all the tables and inventions sounded interesting, but meeting more people did not.

Lance strode around his booth and set off down the aisle without waiting for Farrendel's response. He was two booths away before he glanced over his shoulder. "You coming?"

It seemed he did not have much of a choice. Farrendel hurried to catch up, his guards keeping pace. As he and Lance strolled among the booths, Farrendel tried to ignore the stares that were cast his way. He was not sure if it was his elven ears or clothes or swords that were making people stare. Possibly all three.

Thankfully, Lance did most of the talking as he introduced Farrendel to numerous people and discussed the various inventions, giving Farrendel lots of time to observe and listen. Besides his own interest in magical engineering, Weylind would want to know what inventions Escarland was developing.

After about an hour when they had worked their way to the back corner, Farrendel heard Essie's light step behind him, and he managed not to jump when she wrapped her arms around him from behind.

"Guess who." Essie's voice was muffled against his cloak as she leaned her forehead against his back.

He patted her hands where they were clasped over his waist. "I heard you coming and recognized your step, you know. That is the only reason I did not draw my swords and face my attacker."

She laughed and hugged him tighter. "Of course."

He tugged on her hand, pulling her around to face him. Glancing around, he retreated so that he could place his back to the wall near the corner. Their guards stationed themselves facing outward, and the barrier of bodies formed something almost like privacy.

"You look happy." Essie kissed his cheek. "Did you have a good discussion with the professor?"

"Yes." It was somewhat shadowed near the wall, and with the guards shielding them from view, Farrendel dared to rest his hands on her waist. "I think...I would like to enroll in Hanford University. I know it will make our lives even more complicated, but if I can learn even one thing about my magic or how to better control it..."

"It would be worth it." Essie rested her palms on his chest. "Besides, there's no rush. You can afford to take a class at a time. It doesn't matter if you take a decade to actually earn the degree. After all, what is a decade to an elf?"

She had a point there. Even giving half his lifespan to Essie, he would still likely live to five hundred or so, as long as he was not killed off first. A decade was not that long to work toward something that would aid in better wielding his magic the rest of his life.

He tugged Essie closer to him, though not too close, considering they were still in public. "Thank you for encouraging me in this. Is there anything you wish to pursue so that I can return the favor as a supportive spouse?"

"Well, if you're going to be attending Hanford University, then maybe we should start a scholarship for any elves who want to follow in your footsteps and get a degree there. Or, maybe it would be better to start with setting up an exchange program for both elves and humans to study in the other kingdom. And, maybe scholarships for soldiers from both kingdoms who will be looking for a new career now that a more lasting peace has been established." Essie paused long enough to take a breath, grin, and pat his chest. "After all, you're going to be fabulously wealthy once you get your degree and you and Lance start selling your magical power devices and other inventions. We'll have to do something with all that money since it is terribly gauche to earn loads of riches while still in the line of succession."

Farrendel waited for several seconds to make sure her chatter had wound down before he responded. "I see. You wish for me to be dutifully supportive while you give away all my money."

"Exactly. You've told me several times how little you care for your princely wealth. You'll never miss it. Besides, it is my princessly wealth that will be paying your tuition, so you'll owe me." Essie's grin widened, and she held up the canvas shopping bag she was carrying. "Now, do you want to see how I did my duty as a princess and supported the local economy today?"

Her smirk was the mischievous one that made him wary. He eyed the bag. "Yes."

"I ordered ten pounds of your favorite hot chocolate. While we have given my family gifts, we haven't given your family anything from Escarland yet. I'm thinking hot chocolate and mugs, though I might need your help picking out the mugs." Essie leaned against the wall next to him, still gripping that shopping bag and grinning, a sense of anticipation coming through the heart bond.

He kept a wary gaze on her and that shopping bag. "If

you are planning to give away my hot chocolate, then I do not believe ten pounds will be enough."

"Ten pounds is a massive amount of hot chocolate. You can share." Essie gave him one last smirk before she fished in the bag for a moment, pulled out a package wrapped in brown paper, and held it out to him. "I got a surprise for you."

He took it and gingerly unwrapped the paper, revealing a white mug with blue, jagged lines veined through the ceramic. If that was all, it would have been acceptable. But a pair of tapered elf ears stuck out from either side. The mug was not even shaped like a face. It simply had ears jutting from each side.

Biting back his first response, he glanced from the mug to Essie. If she had been staring at him wide-eyed and anxious, as if hoping he would like it, then he would have done his best to find something truthful but tactful to say.

But she was biting her lip, her mouth twitching as she fought to hide her smirk. She was teasing him. No reason to hold back any of his thoughts.

He held up the mug. "This is hideous."

"I know, right? So horribly tacky. But in that quirky, in-your-face way that almost makes it adorable." Essie reclaimed the mug, smiling down at it.

He studied the mug. Nope, it was definitely hideous. "I do not see anything adorable about this mug."

"I knew you would hate it." If anything, Essie's grin widened. "That's why I got it for me, not you."

Farrendel shook his head, leaning more comfortably against the wall behind him. Only Essie would purposefully buy something he would hate just to tease him. Why did he have a feeling that mug would make an appearance whenever Essie was in a particularly teasing mood?

She re-wrapped the mug in the paper once again, returned it to the bag, and pulled out another, larger package. "This is your mug."

After her last surprise, he was not sure what to expect as he warily peeled back the layer of paper. But instead of a tacky mockery of elf ears, this mug was large and heavy. The entire outside was covered in gears and levers underneath a protective layer of glass. As he turned the mug over in his hands to get a better look at the gears, a metal ball rolled along a maze, rotating gears and pushing levers as it went.

Now this was more like it. He felt a smile tugging on his face as he swiveled the mug first one way, then the other, watching as the metal ball clinked along its pathways.

"Why do I get the feeling I'm going to regret giving you a mug that makes annoying sounds?" Essie's grin was still in place, even as she shook her head.

"You really should have thought of that before giving it to me." He met her gaze and tipped the mug again, just for good measure.

She rolled her eyes and heaved a sigh. "That's it. That mug is banned from the late-night hours."

"Very well, as long as your mug is also banned. If I am awake in the middle of the night, the last thing I want to do is see that monstrosity." Farrendel tried to keep his expression blank, but it was difficult with her grinning at him like that.

"I guess that's only fair." Essie held out her hand. "Let's put it back in the bag, then we can pick out mugs for your family before heading back to Buckmore Cottage. I wouldn't mind a few hours to ourselves before we have to get all fancied up and head back here for the official royal duties tonight."

He handed the mug back to Essie. Once it was safely stowed in her bag, he clasped her hand and strolled into the crowd, their guards fanning out to surround them.

As they strode down the stairs, he nearly came to a halt as a thought struck him. "Were there any more of those mugs? The ones with the elf ears? Was there one in green instead of blue?"

"No, this one was the last I saw, but I am sure the vendor would be willing to do a custom order." Essie glanced up at him, eyes sparkling with the late morning sunlight streaming through the skylights overhead. "Why? Change your mind and want one of your own?"

"No." His chest almost hurt with the grin he was trying to hold back. He leaned closer to her, lowering his voice even though no one was paying any attention to them. "I want to get one for Weylind."

Essie snorted, then gripped his hand tighter. That smirk was back on her face. "Oh, yes. We definitely need to get one for him! The disgusted look on your face was hilarious, but his expression will be priceless."

CHAPTER
THIRTY

Rharreth tromped doggedly upward, leaning into the blizzard's gale as he navigated the steep trail up the side of the mountain in his snowshoes. They had switched to snowshoes at the base of the mountain since this path was too narrow and steep for someone as inexperienced as Melantha to traverse on skis, even with her elven grace. They both still gripped their ski poles for extra balance.

They had been skiing, snowshoeing, and trudging southward for three days. And, for three days, the blizzard had yet to relent. If anything, the weather had gotten worse. The wind whipped with such force that it was hard to breathe, even for Rharreth. The snow was so thick that he could not see either the drop off to his left or the rising mountainside on his right. He was navigating by the sense that his magic gave him of the ice all around and the stone of the mountain beneath him.

The rope connecting him to Melantha tightened, and when he glanced over his shoulder, she was nothing but a gray shape barely visible in the tumult of snow. She hunched, struggling to place one snowshoe in front of the other. Even as he watched, she did not set her foot far enough forward and instead placed one snowshoe partially on top of the other.

She staggered, tripped, and fell to her hands and knees. Unlike some of her earlier falls, she didn't immediately push herself to her feet. Instead, she remained hunched like that, as if she was considering not getting back up.

In this weather, stopping was the same as dying.

Rharreth trudged back to her, lifting each snowshoe in the stomping motion that planted them firmly in the snow with each step. When he reached her side, he knelt and reached for her.

As he gripped her upper arms, he could sense her magic pulsing through her even through the layers of her clothing and his mittens. When she glanced up at him, her eyes were glowing faintly green, and even the exposed skin on her face had a green, magical cast to it.

Where she did not have the physical strength or endurance, she was pushing herself forward on magic alone. Much as her brother Laesornysh had during that final battle in Gror Grar when, even as he was dying, he had fought thanks to the illusion of strength Melantha's magic had given him.

But, like Laesornysh, Melantha would eventually collapse once the strain of pushing her body past its limits was too much to sustain.

Based on the way she was trembling, she was close to that point now.

"We cannot stop now." Rharreth had to shout to be heard over the howl of the wind gusting through the mountain pass. The cold cut straight through his layers of clothing, and only his magic's protection kept him warm.

"I know. I just need to rest. Then I can keep going." Melantha's voice was raw and shaking almost as much as she was. Her scarf had slipped down, and the mucus from her running nose had frozen onto her upper lip.

It was so intensely cold that any water in their canteens was frozen solid. Any food in the pack she still carried was hard and frozen. In this weather, even his snow shelter would not be enough to warm her.

She needed a fire, and soon.

Rharreth glanced over his shoulder, trying to make out anything of the path before them. Surely they were nearing Gozat Stronghold, the home of Zavni's parents, a warrior family sure to remain loyal to Rharreth. If Rharreth had kept his bearings, Gozat Stronghold should be just over this mountain and in the valley below.

If he was going the right direction. If his sense of the mountains had not steered him wrong in this murk.

He just had to get himself and Melantha there. Somehow.

He tightened his grip on her shoulders and felt the surge of her magic as she attempted to give herself more strength. "I will carry you."

She shook her head and leaned on him as she struggled back to her feet. Once standing, she swayed, knees nearly buckling. "No. My weight will tire you more quickly. I can keep going."

No, she could not. "I will be fine. I will carry you for a while, just long enough for you to regain some strength." At least, that was what he told her. If he had to, he would carry her until he too collapsed. Even then, he would crawl until he could crawl no farther if that was what it took to get her to someplace safe and warm.

After one shivering moment, Melantha nodded. She did not resist as he took off her pack and buckled it onto the top of his. He added her snowshoes and poles as well so that he now carried both packs, her poles and snowshoes, and both sets of skis.

He unbuttoned the front of his parka, ignoring the frigid bite of the wind as it tore through him.

Melantha took off her mittens, stuffed them inside a pocket, then wrapped her arms around his neck underneath his parka. He picked her up, and she wrapped her legs around his waist.

He tucked her inside his parka as best he could, though it was not large enough for him to rebutton it. Then, he lengthened the straps of his pack as far as they would go so that the strap that used to go around his chest now went around Melantha's upper back and pinned both her and the open flaps of his parka in place. He threaded the strap around his waist under her legs, then over her lower back so that she was securely held to his chest while leaving both of his hands free.

Melantha settled her head against his shoulder, her face all but covered between his parka and hers. She mumbled something, but he could not hear it over the screaming wind. Her fingers slackened at the back of his neck as she relaxed into the straps that held her.

Rharreth put his mittens back on, then gripped his ski poles. Now that he was carrying so much weight and unable to see his feet thanks to Melantha blocking some of his view, he needed the extra balance the poles gave him more than ever.

With a deep breath, he set out once again. His snowshoes sank deeper into the snow, thanks to the added weight, and it was more of a struggle to lift each foot higher to plant his next step.

But he kept on, foot after foot, yard after yard, as the mountain trail grew ever steeper. The blizzard raged, lashing him with snow and ice, nearly choking him with the gusting cold.

As he fought the wind, the ever-deepening snow, and the steep grade of the mountain trail, his breathing grew ragged, and the muscles in his legs burned.

Melantha's cold fingers touched the back of his neck, and her magic flooded into him. Strength surged through his muscles.

Rharreth ducked his head to put his mouth closer to Melantha's ear so that she would be able to hear him over the roar of the storm. While most of her was tucked against him, her feet and toes dangled on either side. Even in her boots, her toes must be nearly frozen, and the strap running underneath her legs to hold her against him was most likely cutting off circulation to her lower legs. "You should concentrate on keeping yourself warm, especially your toes."

"I am fine." Melantha murmured. She didn't so much as lift her head or open her eyes.

She wasn't fine. But there was nothing Rharreth could do except keep forging onward.

His foot plunged farther than he had been expecting, and he nearly fell. Only his grip on his ski poles kept him upright.

The trail was sloping downwards. Finally.

Closing his eyes, he sent a blast of his magic down the

trail, slicking the snow into an icy ramp that followed the contours of the mountainside.

He eased into a sitting position in the snow, reaching around Melantha to take off his snowshoes. Then, gripping the snowshoes in one hand, he wrapped both arms over Melantha. "Hold on tight."

She gave a small, weak nod, and he was glad she was securely strapped to him.

Then, he pushed off. He slid over the ice, gaining speed the farther he went down the mountain. The wind whipped past his face, and Melantha's arms tightened around his neck.

The ramp veered around a turn, and Rharreth had to throw up an even larger wall of ice on the side to keep himself and Melantha from flying off the edge.

He squinted into the whirling snow, letting go of Melantha long enough to press his hand to the ice. With his magic, he sensed how close they were to the valley floor. A forest was coming up, and both he and Melantha would be killed if they struck a tree at this speed.

Trying to direct the ice to go around the trees, he coated the ramp ahead of them with a foot of the fresh powder to slow them down. As they flew into the powder, snow blasted into Rharreth's face, and he had to squeeze his eyes shut. He hunched to try to shield Melantha as much as possible as she clung to him.

With another blast of power, he created a mound of fresh powder in front of them. They hurtled into it with an explosion of snow.

Rharreth slid from the ice onto a patch of ground that was almost bare, dragging him to a halt. Spruce and pines rose all around, sheltering the spot where he sat.

He tipped his head down toward Melantha. All he could see of her was the top of her parka as she had her face completely buried against his chest. "Are you all right?"

"You are insane," she mumbled against him, shifting to peek up at him before she returned to pressing her face against his shirt.

"It was faster than walking." Rharreth strapped his snowshoes back on, gathered his feet beneath him, and gritted his teeth as he strained to stand, weighed down as he was. His legs burned, but he straightened.

After taking a few deep breaths to steady himself, he set out down the trail once again. The thick stands of spruce and pine provided some relief from the clawing wind and biting snow.

He trudged for what felt like several more miles. Large clumps of snow fell from the trees above, shaken from the branches by the whipping blizzard. The tree trunks were all plastered with a layer of snow.

Against him, Melantha had gone still, her grip slack around his neck. Only the steady rise and fall of her chest against his assured him she was still alive. Though, in this cold, sleep could very well become deadly.

"Stay with me. I need you to hold on for just a little longer." He was not sure she heard him. If he did not get her warm soon, he might lose her.

He forced himself to keep going. He waded through snow up to his knees even with the snowshoes helping so that he did not sink in farther than that. His legs were shaking. His shoulders throbbed under all the weight hanging from him.

He had to rest, but he did not dare stop. He would beg the first person he found for shelter, no matter the risk.

Was that a light? He squinted at the spot where he thought he'd seen a glint.

Yes, that was a light. Either that or he was hallucinating.

Rharreth staggered forward, gaze fixed on the flickering, orange-yellow light. As he neared, a shape formed out of the tumult of white. A large stone wall rose before him, set with towers rising into the sky. More lights showed where a village sprawled up the mountainside from the wall where he stood.

If he was right, then this was Gozat Stronghold, the fortress-village that Zavni's warrior family oversaw. If he was wrong and this village was ruled by a family that supported Drurvas, then Rharreth and Melantha likely would die.

But Melantha was on the verge of dying now. For her, Rharreth was desperate enough to risk it.

He shuffled alongside the wall until he found a gate. Holding his ski poles in one hand, he pounded a fist on the gate.

Something scraped, then a small stone was pulled out, leaving an opening. The gray, ice-covered face of a guard peered through. "What is your business at Gozat Stronghold?"

Rharreth braced himself against the door. He had made it. "We are weary travelers seeking shelter. I am a shield brother of Zavni of the warrior family Rindrin."

The guard studied him, then craned his neck as if trying to get a good look at Melantha. With her face and black hair hidden, the guard would not be able to tell she was an elf, though she was still smaller and slighter than a troll woman.

Hopefully the guard would assume she was a child rather than realize whom they were. While Zavni's parents would be loyal, Rharreth could not say the same for the entire village.

The guard nodded, and the window closed. A moment later, the massive stone gate creaked open enough that Rharreth was able to slip inside.

Another guard was waiting with the first. This guard nodded to Rharreth. "Please follow me. I will take you to the stronghold."

Still holding both poles in one hand, Rharreth wrapped the other over Melantha's back. She had not even stirred at the sound of voices. That could not be a good sign.

The guard led the way down the main street of the village. No one else was strolling the streets due to the evening hour and the raging blizzard.

The Rindrin family stronghold was a large, three-tiered tower set into the mountainside near the center of the village. The gate guard spoke with the guards at the door, then they nodded and let Rharreth and Melantha enter while the gate guard spun to return to his duty at the gate.

Inside, warmth washed over Rharreth, and one of the guards had to lean his weight against the door to shut it against the gusting wind.

They stood in a stone entrance hall with mounted heads of caribou and elk filling the walls among paintings of various members of the warrior family fighting in famous battles from Kostaria's history. A large, stuffed great white bear from the far north stood in the very center of the room.

A spiraling staircase curled up one wall, leading to an upper tunnel into the mountain while the openings to Rharreth's left and directly ahead of him led to more passageways.

One of the guards waited with Rharreth while the other left, presumably in search of Zavni's parents.

While he waited, Rharreth kept his head down. He did not want anyone recognizing him before he had a chance to talk with the couple.

Footsteps scuffed in the passageway above, punctuated by the tap of wood on stone. A moment later, the guard reappeared with two more people behind him.

Zavni's father, Ezrec, walked with a limp on his wooden leg, having lost his left leg below the knee during a battle against Tarenhiel. He refused to use a cane, but instead stalked along on his wooden leg with all the determination of a white bear intent on its prey.

His wife, Lerrasah, wore her long white hair in numerous tiny braids with colored yarn braided into it. She had tied back the upper half of her hair, holding it back with a leather band. A long scar ran across her face from the top of her forehead, over her right eye, and down onto her cheek, showing that she, too, had been a warrior for Kostaria.

"Welcome, traveler!" Ezrec's voice boomed through the entry hall as he and Lerrasah strode down the stairs. "What is the word of the trouble in Osmana? Zavni managed to send us a brief ice message, but he did not give any details."

Rharreth faced them and drew back the hood of his parka, giving them a good look at his face for the first time. "Zavni assured me that you would remain loyal, despite the trouble."

"Your Majesty!" Ezrec stumped down the stairs faster, nearly falling as he reached the bottom and tried to hurry to Rharreth and bow at the same time. As he drew closer, his gaze fell on Melantha. "Pardon. Your Majesties. Of course. My stronghold is yours."

"Please, Queen Melantha has nearly succumbed to the cold." Rharreth let the ski poles clatter to the floor as he yanked off his mittens, then began to fumble with the buckles that kept Melantha tied to him.

"I'll see to her, Your Majesty. Never fret." Lerrasah hurried forward, and, once Rharreth undid the last buckle, she took Melantha from Rharreth's arms. The warrior woman carried Melantha easily, cradling her as she would a child.

As Lerrasah turned and strode toward the passageway across from him, Rharreth took a step, a part of him wanting to protest at the thought of Melantha being taken out of his sight, helpless and alone.

But he trusted Lerrasah. She would not let any harm come to Melantha.

"If it pleases you, Your Majesty, I have a fire going in my study. You can warm yourself while you apprise me of how I can best serve you." As he spoke, Ezrec helped divest Rharreth of the packs, the skis, the snowshoes, and his parka.

Rharreth rolled his shoulders, trying to relieve the cramping ache that had set in. "Thank you. Please lead the way to your study. It has been years since I had occasion to visit Gozat."

Ezrec strolled up the stairs once again and entered the first door on the right. Inside, Rharreth strode straight for the fire burning in the hearth formed into the stone wall. He pulled one of the padded chairs even closer and leaned forward, extending his hands toward the fire.

Warmth. Even with his magic making him more impervious to cold than Melantha was, he had still suffered the effects of the extreme, frigid temperatures.

Ezrec sank into the chair across from him. He did not speak, even though he must be impatient for details on the coup.

Rharreth kept his gaze on the fire as he began to talk, explaining his escape thanks to Melantha's healing magic. He then spoke of their plan and the reason he and Melantha had been fleeing by themselves through the blizzard.

Sometime during the telling, a servant brought mugs of hot cider and plates of roast caribou, which Rharreth ate gratefully. He had gone far too long without a decent meal.

The lines around Ezrec's mouth deepened as he listened, especially when Rharreth got to the part about Zavni's attempt to lead Drurvas in the wrong direction. But he did not interrupt.

When Rharreth was finished both eating and talking, Ezrec leaned back in his chair, nodding. "I think it is safe to assume that you have lost any pursuers, due to the blizzard. Drurvas will not be able to move his army through this storm. Even the train will be stuck until it clears. Take the time you and your queen need to rest, Your Majesty. When you are ready, my warriors and I will provide an escort to Argar Point."

Rharreth nodded. "Your loyalty and honor are appreciated, and I would welcome the provision of your warriors for the rest of the journey."

Ezrec gave as low a bow as he could manage while sitting down. "I know it must feel like most of your kingdom has turned against you. But there are many of us who still are loyal and, yes, even support your choice of peace with Tarenhiel and taking an elven princess as a bride. You and your queen will change Kostaria for the better, and I intend to do everything in my power to make sure you, my king, are given that chance."

Rharreth felt Ezrec's trust and loyalty settle across his shoulders like a heavy, armored vest, its weight both a burden and a comfort.

There, during the coup, it had seemed as though all of Kostaria had revolted against him and Melantha. But that was not the case. There were still the common citizens who would sacrifice their only pair of snowshoes for him. Some warrior families still remained loyal and ready to give their all to make sure he retained his throne.

A knock came from the door, then it swung open. Lerrasah stepped inside, closing the door softly behind her.

Rharreth shot to his feet. "How is Melantha? Did she wake?"

Lerrasah shook her head. "She has been warmed, and I did not see any signs of frostbite. But she has not awakened."

"I will go to her." Rharreth nodded to Ezrec before he followed Lerrasah from the room.

She led him down the passageway for only a short distance before she pushed open a door. "Here is your room, Your Majesty. Please let us know if there is anything you require."

Rharreth gave her a nod of thanks as well, but he did not linger. He stepped inside and closed the door behind him.

The room was smaller than their bedchamber in Khagniorth, but it was no less cozy. The domed rock ceiling was perfectly smooth obsidian that sparkled in the light of the gas lamps set on either side of the bed and the fire roaring in the hearth.

Melantha's pale face peeked above the layers of wool

blankets and furs on the bed, her black hair streaming across the pillow. One of her hands gripped the blankets, and her fingers were pale without any signs that she had suffered frostbite.

Yet why did she not wake? He skimmed the backs of his fingers across her cheek, feeling the soothing warmth of her magic still glowing strong inside her. Hopefully that meant she'd had the sense to set her magic to healing herself before she had succumbed to sleep. If that was the case, then this sleep would be restful, not the deadly sleep of the cold from which she would not wake.

It concerned him, how much he had grown used to the comfort and security provided by her magic. Unless either of them was shot directly in the heart or had their heads taken from their shoulders, she could heal them. It had made him feel as if the two of them together were invincible.

But who would heal her if she couldn't heal herself? If this was the deadly sleep brought on by the cold, then she would never survive the rest of the journey to Tarenhiel to find another healer. Nor would she last long enough for him to fetch a healer back for her.

Surely she would wake. The lack of frostbite was a good sign that her magic had been working inside her even after she had fallen asleep in his arms.

Sitting on the edge of the bed, Rharreth pulled off his boots and stockings, both of which reeked after three days without a fresh pair of socks. With the fire heating the room to a temperature that already had him sweating, Rharreth yanked off his shirt as well before he slid under the covers next to Melantha.

He wrapped an arm over her waist and tucked her close against his chest.

She let out a sigh and snuggled closer, as if appreciating his added warmth even in her sleep.

A good sign, that she was responding to touch.

Rharreth let himself relax. It had been a long journey to get here, and he needed rest as much as she did.

Tomorrow he would worry about retaking his throne and protecting Melantha and facing the remaining length of the journey before them. Tomorrow would be filled with worries and pain.

But, tonight, he would rest.

THIRTY-ONE

Essie had a bite of eggs halfway to her mouth when Julien burst into the kitchen of Buckmore Cottage, Farrendel trailing behind him with that bewildered furrow in his forehead.

Julien was grinning from ear to ear. "The pond is frozen. All the way frozen this time. The guards tested every inch of it and deemed it safe to allow the royal family on it." He didn't even wait for her response before he ducked back out the door.

"Yes!" Essie stuffed the rest of her eggs into her mouth as quickly as possible, gesturing to the stove where Miss Merrick was keeping Farrendel's breakfast warm. "Hurry up and eat!"

The bewildered look remained on Farrendel's face, but he claimed a plate from Miss Merrick, sat beside Essie at the table, and ate his eggs and breakfast sausage.

She gathered their warm clothing while Farrendel ate. He had no sooner popped the last bite into his mouth than she shoved his cloak, warmer socks, hat, mittens, and scarf at him. All things he left behind for his morning exercises since he stayed warm enough that he didn't need them.

She hopped up and down as she put on one wool stocking, then the other.

Farrendel raised his eyebrows. "What are you so excited about? Is there an Escarlish tradition about frozen ponds that you have not shared with me yet?"

"Maybe it's new, maybe not. Have you ever been ice skating? Do elves do that? Or is that just a human thing?" Essie sat to tug on her boot.

Farrendel laughed, and the sound came out clear instead of haggard and rusty, for once. He gave a gentle tug on her braid. "Of course, I have been ice skating before. We elves invented it thousands of years ago, back when elves and trolls were still two branches of the same people. You humans are not the only ones to invent things, you know."

"Oh." She should have realized that. She laughed and tapped his chest. "Well, then, I shall expect you to be exceptional at it, like you are at everything."

He just grinned and clasped his cloak around his shoulders, adjusting it so that the folds fell around the swords he had strapped to his back.

When they were bundled in their warm clothing, they hurried outside and headed for the pond. Julien was already there lacing on his skates, sitting on the beam that had once been Farrendel's practice beam. Large snowbanks surrounded the pond where the servants had shoveled the snow.

"Did you find an extra pair for Farrendel?" Essie fished through the pile of skates to find hers.

"He can use Edmund's. I think they will be only a little big. Or, if they are too large, Mother's pair might fit. She's planning to come later, and even if she does, she said she doesn't plan on skating." Julien tilted his head toward the pile. "So I brought both sets, just in case."

With Farrendel leaning over her shoulder, Essie sorted through the skates, setting aside Paige's and Mother's sets. "Is this Edmund's pair?"

"Nope. Those are mine." Averett's voice came from behind Essie.

She glanced over her shoulder to see Paige and Averett strolling down the path from Winstead Palace. Ahead of them, three-year-old Bertie and one-year-old Finn raced through the snow, giggling as they fell into Essie, hugging her.

"Auntie Essie!"

"Aun'ee Esssee!"

No sooner had Essie hugged them with her free hand than they turned and flopped against Farrendel.

"Ncle Farrennel!" Bertie gave Farrendel a wide grin.

Finn shouted something that was probably Farrendel's name, but it was so garbled it was hard to tell.

With lots of laughter, they all got their skates on, buckling them onto the bottoms of their boots. Farrendel's foot was just long enough to fit into Edmund's skates.

Julien swept Bertie up and placed the boy on his shoulders. Bertie squealed and gripped Julien's ears with his mittened hands, grinning and kicking as Julien sped off across the pond.

Finn was too little to want to sit on anyone's shoulders, so Averett held his hands and skated with Finn shuffling his boots on the ice in front of him.

Essie started off on the ice slowly, getting the feel of being on skates again. Paige joined her, and they set off around the pond.

Paige's purple hat was pulled tight on her head while a matching purple scarf was tied around her neck. She glanced at Essie. "It has been nice having you here. But you will probably return to Tarenhiel soon, won't you?"

"Probably." Essie reached out a hand to steady Paige as she wobbled.

Farrendel whipped by them, as light and graceful on skates as he was when spinning and flipping through the air on the spindly tree branches. He spun in a circle around Julien and Bertie, shooting off a handful of his sparks high in the air, making Bertie giggle.

A smile tugged on Essie's face. "Farrendel is himself again, and it would be good to spend some of the winter in Tarenhiel." The elven forest must be lovely, all frosted with snow. Essie didn't want to miss seeing it. "But we'll be back. We're planning to split our time more evenly between Tarenhiel and Escarland, so you won't be able to get rid of us that easily."

Paige smiled and wrapped Essie in a one-armed hug. "Good. Three months with nothing but letters was far too long."

Yes, it had been, though Essie had been so busy getting to know Farrendel and her new home that the months had probably seemed a lot shorter to her than they had for Paige.

Ahead, Julien and Farrendel halted for a moment as Julien passed Bertie from his shoulders to Farrendel's. Bertie's grin grew even wider as he gripped Farrendel's pointed ears as tightly as he could with his mitten-covered hands. He whooped as Farrendel set off, this time at a slower pace.

Essie couldn't help but admire the way Farrendel's movements were strong and sure, his balance perfect even with the additional weight on his shoulders. He was himself again, but more himself than he had been since she married him, with a broad smile and a chuckle that she could occasionally hear above Bertie's squealing and the slice of the skates against the ice.

"It is good to see him having so much fun." Essie skated more easily as she got the feel for the ice beneath her.

"He will make an excellent father someday." Paige gave her a grin and one of those knowing looks.

"Someday." Essie tried to give a nonchalant shrug. She and Farrendel hadn't even been married a year yet, and they had spent most of that time figuring out how to even be married. It was a little soon to start seriously thinking about children as more than a *someday* thing.

Farrendel skated up to them, holding Bertie out to Paige with that disgusted wrinkle creasing his nose. "Um, here, you take him."

Shaking her head, Paige took Bertie. "Let me guess. A dirty diaper."

Farrendel gave a small shudder, as if he was thinking about rushing back to Buckmore Cottage to toss himself in the shower.

Laughing, Paige skated away, carrying Bertie. On her way to Winstead Palace, Paige retrieved Finn from Averett, and Averett grinned as he raced across the pond toward Julien.

Farrendel held out his hands to Essie. "Would you like to go faster? I will not let you fall."

"Is that a promise?" Essie took his hands, and he whirled her around so that her back was to him. With an arm around her waist, Farrendel glided into motion once again.

Wind whipped through Essie's hair as they picked up speed, far faster than she would have dared with her own skills. But, with Farrendel's steadying grip on her waist and his sense of balance, she didn't worry about falling. Instead, she tossed back her head and laughed, giving in to the exhilaration of flying across the ice.

Farrendel twirled the two of them. He spun her, and she found herself facing him, her hands on his chest.

He scraped them to a halt, his skates shaving slivers of ice. Across the pond, Averett and Julien were shouting as they raced each other.

Essie shook her head, patting Farrendel's chest. "Yep. Exceptional, as always. And a bit of a showoff."

If anything, his grin widened.

But after a moment, the expression faded, a furrow forming on his forehead.

Essie glanced over her shoulder, then turned fully around.

Her mother was strolling toward them from the direction of Winstead Palace, bundled in her winter coat, hat, scarf, and mittens.

Farrendel's brother Weylind strode at her side, his thick cloak waving with the breeze of his passing. Essie had to hand it to him. Even here in Escarland, Weylind could still make a dramatic entrance.

Weylind halted on the edge of the pond, his mouth curving into a dignified smile.

"Weylind! Shashon!" Farrendel skated across the pond and, without a moment's hesitation, hugged Weylind.

Essie skated close enough to hear Weylind's *oof* as he

stood there, arms at his sides as if he was not sure how to respond. Over Farrendel's shoulder, he gave Essie a glare that clearly said *You broke my brother.*

Smirking, Essie just shrugged.

As if realizing what he was doing, Farrendel stiffened, then pulled back, giving Weylind the elven shoulder-clasp hug instead. "Shashon, what are you—"

Averett and Julien flashed past Essie, both of them skating backwards, heading straight for Farrendel and Weylind.

"Look out!" Essie wasn't sure if she was trying to warn Farrendel or warn Averett and Julien. Or possibly Mother who was standing off to the side.

Averett glanced over his shoulder, his eyes widening. His arms flailed as he tried to stop, but he only succeeded in falling into Julien. While Julien kept his feet, the two of them were still careening too fast.

Farrendel had just enough time to turn around before Averett and Julien crashed into him, sending him plowing into Weylind. Together, the four of them disappeared into the snow bank in a puff of snow and a tangle of flailing limbs.

"Are you all right?" Essie skated over to them as quickly as she could, but even before she reached their side, she could hear laughter coming from the snowbank. Even Farrendel seemed to be laughing, smushed under Averett and Julien as he was.

Essie wasn't sure about Weylind. All she could see of him was black hair trailing in the snow and one hand and arm sticking out of one side of the brother pile as if grasping desperately for help.

Still chuckling, Averett rolled off the top of the pile to sit in the snow at the edge of the pond. "Sorry. We were racing backwards and didn't see you."

Julien extricated himself next, crawling to sit on the other side of Averett. "Well, I say they shouldn't have been just standing and talking where we were racing."

Essie shook her head as she halted next to them. "Really? Racing backwards?"

Mother crossed her arms and huffed, though she didn't comment on Julien's and Averett's reckless behavior.

Farrendel shoved off Weylind and brushed snow from his hair. "You did not invite me to race."

"Of course not. You would win too easily." Julien fished around in the snow until he pulled out his hat. He shook it, flinging snow in all directions.

Next to Farrendel, Weylind eased upright and brushed the snow from his clothes, face, and hair with dignified flicks of his hand, his expression almost too carefully blank. Only the faintest twitch at one corner of his mouth gave away his suppressed amusement. "Of course. We elves are far superior."

Averett shook his head, chuckling. "Keep telling yourself that."

Essie held out a hand to help Farrendel to his feet, but Farrendel didn't seem to notice.

Instead, he was focused on Weylind, the laughter fading from his voice and eyes again. "Shashon, what are you doing here? Is something amiss in Tarenhiel?"

Weylind braced himself with hands pressed against the snow, his jaw tightening. When he spoke, he glanced toward Averett rather than looking at Farrendel. "It can wait. For now, there is nothing any of us can do."

Farrendel's shoulders went stiff, his face hardening. "Weylind…"

Essie's chest tightened as well. Weylind wasn't the type to travel to Aldon on a whim. Whatever his reason for coming, it couldn't be good.

"Truly. There is nothing you can do. We will discuss it later." Weylind's voice was firm, final, as he met Farrendel's gaze. "Right now, I do believe you should enjoy the rest of this morning."

With that, Weylind scooped a handful of snow and threw it right into Farrendel's face. Before Farrendel could do more than blink, Weylind was on his feet. He dashed a few yards away before he paused, bending to form another snowball.

"No fair!" Farrendel fumbled to unbuckle his skates, each of his shouted words punctuated by snowballs pelting him in the back of his head. "I am still wearing skates!"

Weylind just smirked and tossed another snowball, hitting the back of Farrendel's neck.

Squirming due to the snow that was probably going down his back, Farrendel flung aside his skates, leapt to his feet, and took off after Weylind.

"Huh." Next to Essie, Julien gestured toward Weylind and Farrendel. "I thought those elves didn't have any sense of fun."

"I think they just forgot how to use it for a while." Essie shrugged, then bent to unbuckle her own skates. "I guess we might as well join them."

At the edge of the forest, Farrendel had almost caught Weylind. But as he lunged, a root burst from the ground and snagged his foot. Farrendel face-planted into the snow once again. He came up swiping his face. "No magic! It is against the rules!"

"I made the rules. I can break them." Weylind whipped another snowball at Farrendel.

Farrendel rolled, dodging the snowball, and sliced the root with a bolt of magic. He took off after Weylind once again. Were they still having a snowball fight? Or a real fight? Essie wasn't entirely sure anymore.

She craned her neck as she worked at the buckle on her skate, glancing at Averett and Mother. "Did either of you know Weylind was coming?"

Mother glanced over to Averett, her expression somber.

Averett's grin dropped from his face. He unbuckled his skates, then stepped out of them. "Yes. But as Weylind mentioned, the explanation can wait."

As he straightened, Essie noticed too late that he held a snowball. She tried to dodge, and the snowball clipped her shoulder. "Avie! What was that for?"

"Well, I can't let all of us gang up on Weylind. I suppose, in the interest of diplomacy, one of us ought to be on his side." Averett dashed a few steps away before he reached for another snowball.

"Then it's younger siblings versus oldest!" Julien elbowed Essie as he reached for the snow.

Mother raised her hands, hurrying off to the side. "I'm a neutral party."

Laughing, Essie entered the snowball fray. She and Julien chased Averett, trying to hit him with snowballs. When Paige and the nephews returned, Paige joined Averett's and Weylind's team while Bertie and Finn tossed handfuls at anyone they came across, including Essie's mother, accompanied by a lot of laughter and squealing.

The fight ended when Farrendel launched himself off a tree trunk and tackled Weylind into a snow drift. Both of the nephews seemed to think that was a great idea, so they flopped on top of Farrendel in a fit of giggles.

Once everyone was cold, snow-covered, and tired, Averett, Julien, Weylind, Farrendel, and Essie trooped into Buckmore Cottage while Paige, Mother, and the children returned to Winstead Palace.

As Essie waved to Paige before entering Buckmore Cottage, she had the feeling that today would be the day she and Farrendel returned to Tarenhiel.

NOW THAT THEY were sitting in the parlor of Buckmore Cottage, warming from the heat of the fire and waiting for mugs of hot chocolate to be served, Farrendel tried not to let nerves twist his insides into knots.

But it was hard, with Weylind sitting there not speaking about whatever brought him to Escarland, even as he exchanged somber glances with Averett.

Weylind would not have made the journey for anything trivial. Why would he not explain and get it over with?

With Essie in the kitchen with Miss Merrick, silence cloaked the parlor. Farrendel clenched and unclenched his fists, glancing from Averett to Julien, and finally to Weylind where he sat in one of the overstuffed chairs near the fireplace.

Julien opened his mouth, then closed it again, as if deciding against whatever topic he had been about to broach.

"We bring hot chocolate!" Essie strolled inside, her hands behind her back.

Miss Merrick followed with a tray filled with mugs,

steam wafting from them. She headed for Averett first, holding out the tray.

But Essie strode straight to Weylind, that smirk on her face telling Farrendel exactly what she was going to spring on his brother.

She grinned at Weylind. "Welcome to Escarland, Weylind. This is an unexpected pleasure. Farrendel and I had planned to bring gifts from Escarland to your whole family when we returned to Estyra, but it seems we can give your present to you now. Farrendel picked this out *especially* for you. We are so fortunate that it was delivered last night."

Weylind raised his eyebrows and glanced at Farrendel.

Farrendel pressed his mouth into a line, trying to suppress his own smirk. He had not imagined doing this with most of Essie's brothers watching, but it seemed Essie had other ideas.

With her too-innocent smile, Essie brought her hand from behind her back and presented Weylind with the green-streaked mug with its jutting elf ears. "This is for you."

Weylind blinked, eyebrows shooting up even farther. One corner of his mouth twitched down, but he seemed to be valiantly trying to hide his grimace. "It is..." He trailed off, as if searching for the right word.

Farrendel did his best to keep his expression blank. Weylind appeared to be under the impression that this gift was in earnest. It was almost comical, watching Weylind open and close his mouth like a landed fish, trying to find something genuine and tactful to say about that awful mug.

He might as well take pity on his brother. "That mug is a monstrosity, is it not?"

The set of Weylind's shoulders relaxed, and he gave a tiny shake of his head. With a huffed laugh, he glanced at

Essie. "I see you have reawakened Farrendel's sense of humor. I hope you are prepared to deal with the consequences. I spent hundreds of years hoping for a brother when all I had were two younger sisters. But then I gained a little brother, only to discover he was the most annoying one of the lot."

Farrendel finally let himself give in to the smirk. Whatever Weylind's reason for being here, it was good to hear that teasing tone in his voice again. Weylind had been treating him like fragile glass for so long, Farrendel had almost forgotten what it was like before.

"I had nearly the same problem. I was convinced that a sister would be better than the two annoying little brothers I had, but then Essie came along, and, well, you know Essie." Averett waved in Essie's direction, smirking.

"Very funny." Essie set the ugly elf ear mug on the end table next to Weylind, then retrieved a different mug from the tray Miss Merrick held out. She turned back to Weylind. "This is your real gift. Hot chocolate in a mug that is yours to keep."

This mug was a rich, earth brown with a large, spreading oak tree embossed onto the side underneath a shiny glaze. The tree was not an exact match for Ellonahshinel, but it was the closest they could find here in Escarland.

Weylind took the mug, giving a nod, mouth twitching into a genuine smile. "Thank you. This is far better than that...that..." He glanced at the mug on the table next to him, mouth curling. "That thing."

Farrendel could not agree more. He claimed his own mug from the tray, the dark blue one he had picked out the first time he was in the Aldon Market.

Essie sank onto the settee beside him, cradling her own

dark green mug in both of her hands. "You were right. That horrified look on Weylind's face as he tried to think of something nice to say about that mug was worth the purchase."

"Yes." Farrendel sipped his hot chocolate. It was thick and rich, just the way he and Essie liked it. As he took another sip, he eyed Weylind and drew in a deep breath. While the teasing was all well and good, it was about time Weylind explained his presence. "Shashon, what brings you to Escarland?"

Weylind's fingers tightened on his mug, his mouth pressing into a thin line once again. He glanced at Averett before his gaze focused on Farrendel. "Our scouts have reported that there has been a coup in Kostaria."

"What?" Farrendel's grip tightened on his own mug as he forced himself to remain sitting. "Is Melantha all right?"

"We do not know." Weylind's shoulders hunched a fraction as his gaze swung down to the mug he held in his hands. "All we know is that King Rharreth's cousin has claimed the throne, and King Rharreth and Melantha have disappeared."

This time, Farrendel surged to his feet, the hot chocolate sloshing over the rim of his mug onto his hand before he set the mug down onto the glass-topped end table. "Then we have to go."

"Farrendel, there is nothing any of us can do." When he lifted his head, Weylind's dark brown eyes held pain, as if he blamed himself for sending Melantha into this situation. "We cannot forcibly depose the usurper and place King Rharreth back on the throne, even if we knew where he was. His people would never accept him if we meddled in Kostaria that way."

Farrendel paced across the parlor, his magic crackling

inside his chest, begging to be released. "We still need to find Melantha. We need to help her. Why did we waste so much time this morning? We should have boarded the train first thing."

"We do not even know if she is still alive." Weylind's voice roughened, his gaze falling to the floor.

Farrendel felt something inside him shaking at the thought of Melantha, killed at the hands of the trolls. How had they done it? Shot her through the heart? Stabbed her so many times she could not heal herself fast enough? Pinned her to the wall with stone and taunted her before she was eventually killed? If she had been killed, it would have been a cruel death.

Surely it was not true. He had already lost his father. Weylind, Melantha, and Jalissa had lost their mother. The trolls could not steal yet another member from this family. Not after he had fought so hard to prevent that very thing from happening ever again.

The war was supposed to be over. Melantha was supposed to secure peace and find happiness.

He clenched his fists, his blood heating with the burn of his magic. He never should have left Melantha there in Kostaria. He should have fought harder to see her pardoned and returned home to Estyra where she belonged.

If she was alive, he would find her, even if he had to scour all of Kostaria to do it. If she was dead, he would avenge her death as he had once avenged their father.

Essie stood and placed a hand on Farrendel's arm, as if hoping she could soothe his hurt with just that touch. Through the heart bond, she yanked on his magic, calming the frenzy that had been on the verge of lashing out. "Calm down. We don't have enough information, and it will do no one any good, least of all Melantha, if you go tearing off into Kostaria without all the facts."

"There is still a good chance she is alive." Averett's voice was calm, holding enough command that it drew Farrendel's focus away from the heat building inside his chest. Averett held his gaze. "You know as well as I do that if she and King Rharreth had been killed, the usurper would have paraded their bodies in the streets. He would make sure everyone knew they were dead. Both to solidify his throne and to revel in his victory. As far as we know, he hasn't done that."

Melantha was alive. Farrendel had to keep believing that.

When Essie gave a tug on his arm, he let her steer him back to the settee. He sank onto the cushions next to her, trying to gather his thoughts into something cold and logical. "When do we leave?"

Weylind shook his head, shoulders still hunched. "I am not asking anything of you, especially not after what Melantha did to you. Like I said, there is nothing you or anyone can do until we know more. Perhaps it would be wise to move warriors into position at the border, in case the usurper decides to resume the war. But, even then, I will not ask you to return to fighting. Not if you do not wish to do so."

And there Weylind went, again treating him as if he was fragile.

Farrendel met Weylind's gaze, feeling the ice of battle filling his veins. "She is our sister. I am not going to just sit here, waiting for word. I will help in any way I can."

"The royal train is taking on coal and water as we speak, and the tracks are being cleared for an afternoon departure back to Tarenhiel." Averett set aside his mug and leaned his elbows on his knees. "We also have a regiment of soldiers mustering to reinforce the men we left stationed at the Tarenhieli-Kostarian border with your warriors. Julien and I intend to go to Tarenhiel with Weylind. If Kostaria attacks, it will break the treaty not only with Tarenhiel, but with Escarland as well."

"Then we are all going." Essie slipped her hands into Farrendel's, squeezing his fingers. Her spine was sword-straight, her chin lifting as if daring Farrendel to question her need to go along.

But he knew all too well why he needed her at his side. She gave him the ability to use his magic at a strength he had never dared before. Still, he did not like the thought of bringing her into danger, not when they had no idea what they might be facing.

"Hopefully by the time we travel to Tarenhiel's northern border, the scouts will have more news to share." Now it was Julien glancing at Averett and sharing a knowing look. "We can make better plans on how to proceed then."

Better plans, perhaps. But Farrendel already knew what he was going to do.

He did not care what Weylind said. He was going to find his sister. He had promised her that if she needed help, he would come.

Even if he had to tear Kostaria apart to do it.

CHAPTER
THIRTY-TWO

S omeone was in the room with her, and it was not Rharreth.

Melantha was not sure how she knew either of those things. The presence in the room did not so much as scuff a boot on stone or breathe loudly. Yet, she knew someone was there by the way her scalp prickled, a chill racing down her spine.

She lay still, trying to keep her breathing even. What should she do? Should she scream? She did not know where she was, besides that the mattress beneath her was soft and blankets over her were warm. Was anyone close enough to hear?

The dagger Rharreth had given her at their wedding was lost in their bedchamber at Khagniorth Stronghold. Nor did she have her hardwood staff. Not even Rharreth's elven dagger.

That left her only one weapon. She called on her magic, keeping it just beneath the surface.

A hand pressed over her mouth. Her eyes flew open, and

a shape loomed over her in the hazy darkness, the silhouette barely discernible as a person.

"Queen Melantha," the stranger hissed. "I need to speak with you."

The voice was not the guttural, troll's version of the language they shared with the elves. Instead, it was elvish, and such a perfect elvish that Melantha could barely pick out the faintest trace of some foreign accent. She only heard it because she was looking for something wrong.

"I am…"

Melantha did not wait for him to explain further. She lunged and managed to catch his wrist, touching his skin. She shoved her magic into him.

"Wha…" The stranger only managed the one syllable before he slumped, collapsing onto her legs across the bed.

Melantha sat up, staring at the figure pinning her to the bed with his weight.

The door opened, sending a shaft of lamplight pooling into the room. Rharreth stood in the doorway, holding a lamp high. His gaze swept over the room, catching first on her, then on the man sprawled on the bed.

In the light, Melantha got her first good look at the man who had invaded her room. His brown hair had a slight curl to it, and it was cut short enough to reveal his rounded, human ears. He looked vaguely familiar, though she could not place him.

What was a human doing here in Kostaria?

Carrying the lamp, Rharreth hurried inside, shutting the door behind him.

Melantha gripped the edge of the blanket over her, only now realizing she was dressed in a thick, flannel nightdress that was not hers. And she had a strange man lying across her bed. "This is not what it looks like."

"This appears to be a human spy who was attempting to make contact with you, but you knocked him out with your magic." Rharreth set the lamp on the bedside.

"Then, it is what it looks like." Melantha smoothed her fingers over the blanket, staring at the human rather than at Rharreth. Would Rharreth think she had been spying for Tarenhiel all this time? Would it make him doubt her? "But, I promise you, I have not been spying for Tarenhiel or Escarland. I do not know who this is or why he was trying to talk with me."

"I know you are not a spy." Rharreth's response was quick. Trusting.

Melantha breathed out, the tension relaxing from her shoulders.

"Besides, I also recognize him." Rharreth picked up the man by the back of his shirt and deposited him in one of the chairs by the fire. "This is Prince Edmund of Escarland. I have heard rumors that he's involved in their intelligence office. How long will he sleep?"

"Um…" She had not been thinking of anything besides knocking the intruder out when she had shoved her magic into him. Flexing her fingers, she concentrated on the pulse of her magic. "For a long while. I was thinking more about defending myself than any finesse."

Rharreth's craggy face creased in a wider grin than she had seen on him since the coup. His dark blue eyes glittered with respect and approval.

He sat on the edge of the bed and traced the back of his hand along Melantha's jaw before digging his fingers into her hair, sending tingles down her back. "You are amazing,

Melantha. Even as you were succumbing to the cold, you had the sense to set your magic to healing yourself. It saved your life, not to mention all your fingers and toes."

Melantha leaned into his hand, resting one of her hands on his chest, the fabric of his shirt warm beneath her fingers. "If I had been a troll, I would not have fallen asleep from the cold. I could have kept going. I would not have—"

"Don't talk like that." Rharreth's fingers tightened at the back of her neck, still buried in her hair. He leaned closer until their faces were only a few inches apart, his breath soft against her face. "I asked for this marriage of alliance because I saw the fire in you, and it drew me. I thought you might be the one elf who had the fire to survive in Kostaria. But, I fell in love with you for your softness and compassion. I love your magic, and the way that you make me believe that, together, we will be able to heal my kingdom and its rift with yours."

"Rharreth…" Melantha breathed his name, tracing her fingers up his chest to his neck.

He trailed light kisses along her jaw to her cheek, murmuring in her ear, "I love you because you are an elf, not in spite of it."

Then he pressed his mouth to hers, and she dug her fingers into his tangle of thick, white hair.

This was love. So much better than the cold, emotionless relationship she had with Hatharal a hundred years ago. Hatharal had just wanted her for her title, her position.

But Rharreth loved her for herself. For both her fire and her compassion. With him, she could be fully herself, without fear, without holding back.

Freedom. Farrendel had told her that he had found freedom with his human princess. Melantha now understood what he had meant, now that she tasted the freedom of loving and being loved for herself.

And, with every breath in her, she would do her best to gift that same freedom to Rharreth. She loved him for his unwavering sense of honor that was tempered by the kindness that drove him to do his best for his people.

She pulled back from Rharreth to press her own line of kisses on his jaw. "And I love you. I love your kingdom and your people. I know we are headed for Tarenhiel, but Kostaria is my home."

He needed to know that she was not pining for her homeland or her people. Not anymore.

Beneath her fingers something in him relaxed, as if he truly had been concerned about that.

Kostaria was her home, and it stirred a deeper love and sense of duty than even Tarenhiel had. Or, perhaps, she had finally figured out what loyalty and duty and love actually meant.

She might not be as brawny, hardy, and impervious to cold as a troll woman, but that did not mean she was helpless. She would figure out her own way to survive in this icy kingdom. More than that, she would thrive.

Rharreth pulled back farther, sighing, and shot a glance toward the Escarlish prince-turned-spy. His jaw hardened. "He should be questioned, but if he is going to be out for a while, then you should dress and eat. Your health is most important."

Melantha also sighed and leaned against the head of the bed. Romance and kissing would have to wait. They had duties to attend to. She started to get out of bed, then halted, sending her own glance at the Escarlish spy. "I trust my magic, but I think I would feel better if he was tied and blindfolded."

"Right. So would I, now that you mention it." Rharreth stood, fished out his ragged, bullet-torn shirt, and drew his elven dagger to cut it into strips. Once he had enough strips, Rharreth tied the spy's hands, then wrapped a blindfold over his eyes. "There. He's secured. If you're all right here, I'll fetch food for you."

"Thanks." Melantha slipped out of bed as Rharreth left. She found that her gray woolen dress had been laundered and some of the rips repaired.

By the time Rharreth returned with a plate of steaming roast caribou and fresh cornbread, Melantha had dressed and brushed out the tangles caused by the blizzard that even the last of her elven conditioner had not been able to prevent.

When she sat down to eat, her stomach was gurgling and rumbling. The warm food banished the last remaining sense of cold, and she savored each bite, finally taking the time to fully assess her surroundings. "Where are we?"

"Gozat Stronghold. We arrived yesterday." Rharreth sat in the chair across from her, his gaze flicking to the sleeping Escarlish spy before focusing on her. "You slept so long we were worried that you were going to slip away, succumbing to the cold."

"I am sorry for worrying you." Melantha shoveled in the food, telling herself that it should not matter that she had not been strong enough.

"At least you are small enough that you are easy to carry." Rharreth's mouth quirked into a smile, though his eyes were still shadowed.

"I guess that is one benefit to being an elf." Melantha

chewed the last bite of the caribou and pushed aside her plate. She eyed the sleeping spy. "I suppose we should wake him."

"Yes." Rharreth drew the knife again and pushed to his feet. He approached the chair where he had dumped the spy. "Go ahead."

Melantha called on her magic, then touched the human's temple. As soon as she pulled away, Rharreth reached out with his free hand and tugged her behind him.

The Escarlish spy-prince did not so much as groan or stir. There was only a slight change to his breathing to show that he was awake. "I underestimated you, Queen Melantha."

"What reason did you have for approaching my wife, spy?" Rharreth rested a hand on the human's shoulder, touching the blade of the knife to the human's neck.

The spy did not stiffen, even with a knife to his neck and Rharreth's voice rumbling over him. "Nice to meet you again, King Rharreth. I approached your wife for information about what happened in Osmana and to find out your plans for taking back your throne, but I didn't want to reveal my presence. As that is now not a consideration, I can discuss your plans with both of you."

"Why would I share my plans with you? You were caught spying in my kingdom. I have every right to execute you." Rharreth's voice deepened with a hint of a growl.

This Escarlish prince was made of stern stuff. Either that, or he was very good at bluffing. He did not so much as flinch at the threat, even though he remained blindfolded and bound.

Instead, he leaned his head against the back of the chair, as if getting comfortable. "I am Prince Edmund of Escarland, and as far as I am concerned, I was simply visiting and enjoying the sights in your beautiful kingdom. Nor do I really think you want to risk the political ramifications with Escarland if you executed me, no matter what I may or may not have been doing."

Rharreth's jaw remained tight, and he did not remove the knife from the spy's neck. "I can still use your presence here to humiliate Escarland and force your brother to cooperate."

"You could do that, though I doubt my little adventure in your kingdom would severely hurt Escarland's political standing. Nor will threatening me gain you anything from my brother. He will simply deny he had any knowledge of my whereabouts." Prince Edmund gave a shrug, looking for all the world like he was discussing this over tea instead of while tied to a chair, blindfolded and helpless. "Besides, Tarenhiel and Escarland trounced you in the recent war, and that was while your people were united and you had Laesornysh tucked away in your dungeon. Do you really want to find out what would happen if you incited a war with Escarland when we have Laesornysh fighting at full strength and your kingdom is in shambles from a civil war?"

The muscle at the corner of Rharreth's jaw worked, and his fingers flexed on the knife as if he was barely stopping himself from using it on this far-too-confident human prince.

Melantha rested a hand on Rharreth's arm, sending some of her most soothing magic into him. While this human prince was tweaking Rharreth's pride, he was speaking the truth with his bluff. They had enough of their own problems without causing another war with Escarland and Tarenhiel.

More than that, they needed Escarland's grain and produce far too much to risk angering them over executing their prince, even if he was caught spying.

Rharreth's tense muscles loosened, and he eased the

knife away from the spy's neck. A good sign, even if the heat did not entirely disappear from Rharreth's gaze.

"How is my brother? Farrendel? Have you had news of him while you were…visiting Kostaria?" Melantha wrapped her free arm over her stomach, hoping she sounded nonchalant.

The last time she had seen Farrendel, he had barely been holding himself upright and was so thin and wasted that his clothes had hung from him. It would be reassuring to hear that he had recovered after the torture and pain he had been put through.

"Due to the nature of my visit, all communications were kept vague." The corner of Prince Edmund's mouth quirked. That was as close as he would come to confirming that, yes, he was spying and most likely had been for the past three months since the war ended. "But I have been told that he is well and that his magic is stronger than ever."

Melantha was not sure if that last part was true or something that Prince Edmund added for Rharreth's benefit.

Rharreth huffed and sheathed his knife. "Fine. I suppose I might as well hear you out, spy, since I apparently don't have another choice."

"A wise decision. We can discuss how best Escarland and Tarenhiel can help without appearing to help. I have observed enough on my visit to know that you are still a much better alternative than your cousin for all kingdoms involved." If anything, Prince Edmund settled deeper in the chair. If he had not been bound, he seemed like he would have clasped his hands behind his head in total relaxation. "Now, I would appreciate it if you would untie me so that we can have this conversation as one member of royalty to another."

Rharreth yanked off the blindfold, but he did not remove the bindings tying Prince Edmund to the chair. Instead, Rharreth leaned against the mantel, his back to the fire, and crossed his arms. "That is the best you're going to get."

Prince Edmund blinked, his gaze darting around the room for a moment as if to take in his surroundings again. He gave a cursory tug on each arm to test the bindings before he settled back into the chair. "Was getting to your allies here at Gozat Stronghold your whole plan, or do you plan to go all the way to Tarenhiel?"

Rharreth just glared at Prince Edmund, a knot working at the corner of his mouth.

Melantha reached for Rharreth again, this time squeezing his shoulder. Odd that she had to be the calm and reasonable one right now. She drew on every scrap of the serenity she had learned to exude all those years in the Tarenhieli court. There was a time and place for anger and passion. But, perhaps, there was also a time for calm and thoughtfulness as well. "Rharreth, we need him."

Rharreth gave a growl in the back of his throat, but he focused on Prince Edmund. "We are on our way to Tarenhiel. We don't plan to ask for aid from either the Tarenhieli or Escarlish armies. We merely require the security of the border at our backs when I challenge Drurvas to take back my throne."

"I see." Prince Edmund nodded, his mouth pressed into a line. "I suppose you gave your supporters a place along the border to rendezvous. Is your cousin's army chasing you?"

"If they believed the false story that was fed them, then they are following the train tracks." Rharreth's gaze remained hard, as if it was internally killing him to share this much information with this Escarlish spy. "My army is to meet me elsewhere."

"Then it is a good thing I was able to alert King Weylind and King Averett of the coup so that they will mobilize at the border. I would hate for your cousin to take advantage of the situation to raid into Tarenhiel again while its defenses were down thanks to the assumption that the peace treaty was still in place." Prince Edmund glanced toward Melantha, his gaze searching.

Was he wondering if she had purposely caused this mess? It had been a risk, sending both armies to Weylind's doorstep without a chance to warn him. It would look bad, given her history as a traitor.

"We needed to draw the fighting away from the innocent citizens in Osmana. Drurvas was preparing to go door to door searching for us. We had to buy time for Rharreth's supporters to gather, especially since many of the warriors on our side are from the far-flung families." Melantha was not sure why she was desperately explaining herself to this Escarlish prince. Perhaps a part of her believed that, if she could make him believe her, maybe Weylind would as well. "This was our best option."

"I understand. I'm sure the coup was rather thorough. Most usurpers don't make a move unless they have a better-than-average chance of success." There was a grim set to Prince Edmund's jaw. Melantha had never heard of an attempted coup against the Escarlish King Averett, but perhaps such attempts had all been stopped before they had a chance to fully form.

Melantha glanced at Rharreth, once more seeing him gasping for his last breaths, his organs shutting down after they had been torn apart by bullets. "We only survived thanks to my healing magic. It seems Drurvas managed to retain at least one repeater gun that was not handed over to Escarland at the end of the war."

The line of Prince Edmund's mouth set even harder, grimmer. "Then this truly does make it Escarland's problem in more ways than one. Not only would we prefer Rharreth remain on the throne, but Drurvas has already broken the peace treaty with Escarland."

"Yes." Rharreth's posture had not relaxed, but he was at least glaring with less hostility at Prince Edmund. "He intends to start the war with Tarenhiel once again, and all the warrior families who were unhappy with peace have rallied behind him. He, and they, would rather continue to fight a losing war than ever admit defeat."

A bleak outcome. Once, Melantha might have been happy to know that the trolls were warring their kingdom into the dust, but no longer. Now, she desperately wanted to save this kingdom and make it flourish.

"If that is his intention, he might very well start the war again even before he has finished you off." When Prince Edmund rested his head against the chair this time, the gesture seemed more weary rather than feigned nonchalance. "Unfortunately, at the time I sent my message, I was not aware that the two of you survived. If Weylind and Averett have begun mustering at the border, it will be with the assumption that you are most likely dead and that Kostaria is likely to attack once again. They will see any troll army mobilizing as a sign of aggression. I don't think the Tarenhieli-Escarlish army will attack first, but if Drurvas raids across the border, they will strike back. Without information, they are just as likely to strike at your army as they are Drurvas's."

Melantha sank onto a chair, her stomach churning. Had she set up both sides for more bloodshed and pain? She had been trying to spare the citizens of Kostaria, but instead, she might have gotten more of them killed.

And their blood would be shed by Farrendel's hands. If Tarenhiel planned any counterstrikes and if Farrendel was as healed as Prince Edmund claimed, then he would lead the attack, as he always did.

She clenched her fists. "We have to stop this."

"If you let me go, I will see that another message is sent, alerting King Weylind of the presence of a friendly army on his border." Prince Edmund met Rharreth's gaze, unwavering even though he had to know such a request was unlikely to be granted.

"No. I would have to entrust you with the location of my gathering army, something I am loath to do." Rharreth shook his head, then glanced at Melantha. "The blizzard has lessened, and should clear up by morning. Now that you are awake, we will leave at first light. No spy's message will get to the border faster than we will, now that we have Ezrec's aid. And you, Prince Edmund"—Rharreth turned back to the Escarlish prince—"will be coming with us. You are our ticket across the border."

THE NEXT MORNING, Melantha found herself walking outside of Gozat Stronghold, bundled once again in her layers of warm clothing underneath her parka.

Around her, most of the troll warriors of Gozat were gathering. Many were strapping on skis or loading weapons and supplies onto sleds pulled by teams of dogs. The dogs varied from fluffy black and white to scruffy black-and-brown dogs to gray, rangy ones. All of them appeared to have some wolf in them, and Melantha made sure to steer clear rather than approach. The dogs sent up a constant howling bark until Melantha could barely hear anything over their noise.

Next to her, Rharreth pushed Prince Edmund in front of him. The prince was bundled in a parka and mittens as well. By the way he was holding his arms, wrists together, his hands must have been bound underneath the parka and mittens. Hopefully Rharreth had not made the bindings too tight. In this cold, it was especially important that Prince Edmund retain circulation in his hands.

Several of the troll warriors stopped and stared at Prince Edmund. Ezrec glared at the spy prince, as if he was personally affronted that a spy—a human spy, no less—had managed to infiltrate his town and stronghold.

Melantha was not entirely sure why Rharreth paraded his captured spy in front of everyone, but perhaps he was making sure that Prince Edmund's presence here was known. The human prince would be hard-pressed to return to spying in Kostaria, at least for a good long while.

Heading for one of the sled teams with ten dogs in harness, Rharreth shoved Prince Edmund onto the empty sled, then considered a moment, glaring at both the prince and the sled. "It seems he will have to ride with us. Since I have to steer on the back, that means he will need to sit either in front of you or behind."

That was the reason for the glare. Melantha crossed her arms and studied the sled as well. She was not sure which she would prefer.

Prince Edmund scooted forward, leaving space behind

412

him. "If I sit in front, I can block the wind for Queen Melantha."

Melantha quickly sat in the space before Rharreth could argue. She snuggled into the pile of furs at her back and tucked her knees up between her and Prince Edmund. It was less awkward than having him sit between her legs, and this way he could lean against her and keep her toes warm.

But she reached over his shoulder and tapped his cheek with a magic-laced finger, giving him enough magic that he should stay warm, even taking the brunt of the wind and cold. "You are oddly accommodating, for a spy."

Prince Edmund did not flinch from her magic or when Rharreth bent over, tying the prince's hands and feet to the sled. Instead, the Escarlish spy shot a grin over his shoulder. "I am a prince. My mother raised me to have some fine manners, after all."

Rharreth huffed, as if he wanted to argue with that statement but did not want to waste the breath. Instead, he tucked a few more furs around both Melantha and Prince Edmund before he took his spot standing on the back of the sled.

Melantha glanced over her shoulder at him. "I have always wanted to ride a dog sled. Some of the elves in the northern part of Tarenhiel have adopted it as a means of transportation, but I never had a chance to try it before."

"I wish I'd had a chance to take you out with our team of dogs back in Osmana." Rharreth's jaw tightened, his gloved hands flexing on the top of the sled. "I would have, if things had not been so tense."

What would it be like, if Kostaria found a way to live in peace both with its neighbors and with itself? Melantha could see herself enjoying time with Rharreth as they traveled to some of the outlying towns and warrior family strongholds. Travel would be pleasant if they were not fleeing for their lives through a blizzard.

Gozat warriors climbed onto their own sleds pulled by teams of dogs or gathered with skis in place to follow on foot with the sleds pulled by caribou.

Ezrec climbed onto the lead sled, then motioned and gave the order to move out. Each of the dog teams in line surged forward, leaving plenty of space between them and the previous team.

When it was their turn, Rharreth yelled, "Hike! Hike!"

The dogs in front of them lunged into motion, and the sled lurched before gliding in their wake.

Melantha gripped the edge of the sled as the breeze whipped past Prince Edmund to brush against her face, carrying competing scents of dog urine and crisp snow. All around them, scrub pine and spruces spread as far as she could see, their branches drooping under the weight of the crusting snow. In the morning sunlight, the snow glittered as if infused with magic, and the sky above had cleared into a glorious blue broken only by a few puffy clouds.

Now this was the way to travel. For the first time since leaving Osmana, Melantha let herself relax into the warmth provided by the bundled furs and enjoy their trip.

THIRTY-THREE

T he blanket was yanked off her, and Essie blearily blinked herself awake. She could still feel the rumble of the Escarlish royal train beneath her accompanied by the constant clacking of the wheels on the tracks. Their sleeping compartment was still cloaked in semi-darkness, the windows showing a gray, early dawn outside.

Beside her, Farrendel bolted upright, kicking the blanket farther to the end of the bed. For good measure, he yanked his shirt off over his head and hurled it across the sleeping compartment on the train. He hunched with his knees drawn up, breathing hard and trembling.

Through the heart bond, she could feel the tight sense of the room closing in around him. A nightmare and nightmare-fueled panic attack. A mild one, but the first one he'd had for a while. No doubt brought on by worries for Melantha and the thought of walking into battle once again.

Essie pushed into a sitting position as well and reached to touch his back. When he didn't flinch, she gently traced her fingers up and down over his tight muscles, her fingers catching on the puckered scars where the trolls' stone had pierced him. "Perhaps you should have taken the top bunk instead of squishing here with me. These bunks, after all, weren't designed for two people."

Farrendel didn't respond, his breathing going from ragged into a too steady rhythm that told her he was using one of the calming breathing techniques he'd been taught.

"Or, perhaps, we should look into renovating our sleeping compartment and figure out how to fit a bed big enough for two people into this space." Essie kept her voice soft and light, matching the movements of her fingers to the rhythm of his breathing. "After all, if we are going to be taking this trip from Escarland to Tarenhiel and back often as we split our time between our two homes, we might as well be comfortable."

Farrendel broke his steady breathing to huff a laugh, though he didn't yet raise his head or speak.

"Though at that point, it would be better to invest in our own train with a whole car all to ourselves. After all, if Averett or Julien or Edmund need this train, then they have first dibs because they technically outrank me." Essie traced her fingers along one of the scars over his ribs. "If your brother starts traveling more, we'll have to get our own train on that side of the border too. Or maybe we will design a train to run on both Escarlish metal tracks and Tarenhieli root tracks and have our brothers build a bridge over the Hydalla River. Then we could use the same train back and forth and never have to worry about the awkward transfer across the river each time."

Farrendel finally lifted his head, his breathing back to normal. In the heart bond, the tightness was fading, replaced

416

with warmth. He glanced at her, his silver-blue eyes bright in the faint light of dawn outside. "Perhaps, once I have my magical engineering degree, I could use my magic to power this train. Then we would never have to stop all the way from Estyra to Aldon."

"Now that's a great idea." Essie patted his shoulder, his skin warm beneath her hand. "Besides, I don't see your people allowing a coal-burning train into your kingdom, and it would be nice not to rely on anyone else's magic to power our train. After all, Averett has looked into upgrading the royal train to a magical power cell, but those can be tampered with a lot easier than a coal-powered engine and so far it has been deemed too risky. But I have a feeling your magic would be a lot more tamper-proof than a regular human magician's."

"Yes." Farrendel's muscles relaxed beneath her hand, and he sat straighter instead of hunching, resting his arms on his knees.

The growing light from outside shone against his back, highlighting the scars. Thin, white lines marked where the trolls had twisted stone beneath his skin fifteen years ago.

The scars from Farrendel's recent capture were deeper, more puckered, especially the ones on his back where the stone floor had stabbed him. Long, straight scars scored his collarbone and places along his ribs where the Escarlish surgeon had cut him when they had removed the stone after he was rescued.

Essie touched the puckered circle of a scar on his back. "This one must have hurt."

"It did." His tone was matter-of-fact. No blaming himself in some way. Just acceptance that what the trolls had done to him had been terrible. Instead of flinching from her touch, he

417

leaned into her hand, glancing over his shoulder at her. "I nearly died."

Essie had felt him nearly die, the heart bond straining to keep him alive until she had passed out from the strain of it. "I know."

"Melantha saved me. It was the first time she was allowed to heal me." His voice went quiet at the mention of his sister's name, his gaze straying from Essie to stare at the wall instead.

Essie wrapped both arms around his waist. "I know you're worried for her."

It was one of the things she loved about him. That he was so forgiving, even of the sister who betrayed him.

"If she has been killed..." Farrendel's fists clenched, his muscles going tense once again.

Essie could not let him dwell on the worst-case scenario. It would only make the nightmares and the anxiety worse. If Melantha was dead, Essie would be there as Farrendel worked through the grief. But there was no reason he should grieve until they knew for certain.

She tightened her arms around his waist and rested her chin on his shoulder. "You know Melantha. She's angry enough at the world that she will have survived out of sheer spite."

Farrendel's shoulders shook beneath Essie as he gave a hard laugh. "This is true."

Beneath her hands, she could feel the play of his muscles across his stomach. His shoulder muscles were strong beneath her cheek, and she appreciated the solid feel of him. Over the past few months, he had regained the strength the trolls had stolen from him.

When they faced whatever lay ahead, he would fight whole and strong.

The train gave a shudder and a squeal. Out the window, the shimmering expanse of the Hydalla River rushed closer. "Looks like we're almost there. We'd better get dressed and gather our things for the steamship ride across the river. You'll have to save your morning exercises for running across the elven train."

Farrendel shrugged, the corners of his mouth tipping up into a smile once again. "It is preferable anyway. The lack of tree branches passing over the train tracks makes running along the top of your Escarlish train too easy."

Too easy was not what Essie would call it. But this was Farrendel, after all. He did not get those muscles she admired so much by sitting and doing nothing.

THE ELVEN TRAIN pulled into the station at Estyra in the afternoon. The sun streamed through the massive tree trunks and turned the snow on the ground and on the bare branches into a glittering, soft yellow.

Essie stepped off the train and stared around at the grand trees, bare of their broad leaves. In the meandering streets and on the upper bridges of Estyra, elves strolled gracefully as they went about their business, long thick cloaks protecting them from the chill.

The thinner twigs were rimed with snow, but all the branches where the elves walked were free of any snow and ice.

Farrendel halted beside her, and she gestured toward Estyra. "How are the branches kept from being slippery?"

"Elves with plant magic place power on the walkways to melt any snow or ice before it becomes slippery." Farrendel gave her a soft smile, reaching out to clasp her first two fingers with his, pressing the backs of their hands together, in the elven style of holding hands. "Estyra is beautiful in the wintertime."

"Estyra is beautiful at all times of the year." Essie leaned against his shoulder, craning her neck to take in as much of Estyra's winter splendor as she could. "Once this is over, I look forward to spending time here."

"Yes." Farrendel's gaze strayed past her, and when she turned in that direction, she caught sight of a group of elves heading toward them. Farrendel's grandmother Leyleira led the way with Rheva, Weylind's wife, at her side. Jalissa followed, along with several of the elven generals and a few of Weylind's staff members trailing behind.

As Weylind, Averett, and Julien strode toward the generals, Leyleira, Jalissa, and Rheva headed for Essie and Farrendel. Essie gave them a smile, not letting go of her grip on Farrendel's hand even as he shifted, his gaze dropping to his feet as if he was nervous about seeing his family again.

Leyleira approached first, gripping Farrendel's shoulders and sweeping him from head to toe with a direct gaze. Her mouth tipped into a smile. "I see Escarland did you as much good as we hoped. You are looking well, sasonsheni."

"Yes." Farrendel lifted his gaze as his whole stance straightened. He smiled, first at Leyleira, then at Rheva and Jalissa. "I am well."

As Leyleira stepped back, Rheva gave each of them a smile. "I am glad. Weylind was unbearable while he worried over you."

"Of course he was. I'm sorry. That must have made life

interesting around here." Essie shared a grin with Rheva, glad she'd had a chance to bond with this sister-in-law. Then, she glanced past Rheva to where Jalissa had been hanging back. "And how have you been, Jalissa? Did you enjoy your time back in Estyra?"

"It has been quiet and peaceful." Jalissa glanced at Essie, but quickly looked away. Even in that brief glimpse, Essie had seen that her face was drawn, her eyes sad.

Was it worry for Melantha? Or was this still that same malaise that Jalissa had been suffering ever since their return from Kostaria? After all the bonding they'd done during the war, Essie had thought Jalissa would trust her enough to tell her what was going on.

Except...it might have something to do with Edmund, and maybe Jalissa didn't feel comfortable talking about it with Essie since he was her brother. Essie wasn't sure what Edmund possibly could have or would have done that would cause Jalissa to be this listless even three months later. Edmund was an honorable man and not the type to hurt Jalissa's feelings on purpose.

Farrendel, too, studied Jalissa, a furrow forming on his brow.

Before he could make any comments of his own, Weylind and Averett returned from consulting with the generals. Behind them, the generals moved off, and Julien went with them, still talking quietly.

Averett jabbed a thumb over his shoulder. "Julien is going to stay here to organize the Escarlish troops when they arrive on the next train and ride with them. The elven army units were already sent ahead of us as soon as they received word of the troll armies marshalling at the border."

Essie tightened her grip on Farrendel's fingers. This felt

all too much like the preparations for the war, and she needed the extra assurance that Farrendel was still at her side this time.

Farrendel turned to Weylind, his mouth in a tight line. "Any word on Melantha?"

"No." Weylind flicked a glance toward Averett before focusing on Farrendel. "And our scouts have lost contact with our Escarlish asset."

Now it was Essie's turn to glance at Averett. Lines dug into his forehead, and he wouldn't meet her gaze. Did they mean Edmund? He had been here, working with the elven scouts. Essie had assumed that meant he had been on this side of the border, but had he been in Kostaria this whole time? And what did it mean that the elven scouts had lost contact with him?

Just how many of her and Farrendel's siblings were in danger up there in Kostaria?

Averett and Weylind did not seem inclined to explain. At least, not in front of her. Annoying when they decided to go all protective and tight-lipped like that.

They boarded the elven train once again, and this time Leyleira, Rheva, and Jalissa joined them. Weylind opened his mouth, most likely to protest having nearly his whole family head to the border, but one look from Leyleira made him snap his mouth shut so fast Essie could hear the click of Weylind's teeth.

When they were all settled, the train pulled away from Estyra. Essie all but pressed her face to the window to gape at the winter-clad forest passing by outside.

Farrendel made a soft, throat-clearing noise beside her, and she turned around to sit properly in her seat again.

But he wasn't looking at her. His gaze flicked from his

family members to the floor before going to Essie with something like pleading.

Ah. He was trying to tell his family his big news but wasn't sure how.

Essie squeezed his hand between both of hers. *Don't be nervous,* she tried to tell him through the heart bond.

Farrendel drew in a deep breath, then faced Weylind. "Essie and I have decided to split our time between Tarenhiel and Escarland more evenly."

That wasn't the news Essie had expected him to share, but that was probably the best one to lead with. The rest of it would make more sense that way.

Weylind's face twisted, almost stricken, while Jalissa just blinked at the two of them. Rheva gave a small smile and patted Weylind's arm as if prepared to stop him from doing something foolish.

Leyleira gave a nod. "Sounds sensible. I would have suggested it, but I knew the two of you would come to this agreement all on your own without my interference."

Essie could have hugged Leyleira. This family needed more of her no-nonsense, sensible attitude.

Smiling, Essie leaned against Farrendel. "Tell them the rest. I know you wanted to wait until after you knew for sure, but I think now would be as good a time as any."

"Yes." Farrendel made another throat clearing noise as he stared at the floor. "A week ago, I...I..."

You can do it. Essie held his hand in both of hers. She smiled, hoping he'd understand what she was trying to tell him. *This is something to be excited about. You don't have to feel ashamed or like you are betraying your family.*

Farrendel braced his shoulders, though his gaze remained on the floor as if he couldn't concentrate on his words if he looked at anyone else. "I applied for enrollment at Hanford University in Aldon to study magical engineering."

Weylind made a choking sound, then coughed.

Rheva patted his back and looked like she wanted to roll her eyes but was too much of a dignified elf queen to do so.

"I have been working with an Escarlish friend who has a degree in magical engineering, and together we have been able to do things with my magic that I never thought were possible." Farrendel's words rushed out, as if he feared someone would argue with him if he stopped. "I would be able to take some of the courses via the mail while here in Tarenhiel, and the rest I would take while spending time in Escarland. Assuming I will be accepted."

"You will be." Averett's mouth quirked, and he leaned back on the bench as if to get more comfortable. "After you expressed interest, the professors counted down the days until they saw your application. Trust me. You will probably have an acceptance letter waiting for you when we return from solving this mess in Kostaria."

"Magical engineering sounds...interesting." Jalissa's face remained smooth, except for a twist to one corner of her mouth.

Leyleira just gave another nod, but the glint in her eyes seemed like approval.

Weylind swallowed back his coughing fit, and he lifted his head to meet Farrendel's gaze. "Will this make you happy?"

Leyleira gave a soft snort, and if she had been the kind to carry a cane, Essie was sure Leyleira would have thumped Weylind over the head with it. "Have I taught you nothing, Weylind Sasonsheni? That is not the right question to ask. It assumes that happiness is something fleeting to be chased and found in things or even in people. But true happiness, like true love, is far deeper than something so meaningless."

Weylind opened his mouth as if to protest, but Leyleira held up a hand, and Weylind sank back into his seat.

Essie struggled to keep her smirk off her face. Only Leyleira could put Weylind in his place like that.

"Happiness, like love, is the choice to dwell on the deeper joy, deeper contentment. Some, like our dear Elspetha, are born with the ability to do this without a second thought. Some have to learn to do this through a lot of struggle. It is, after all, what Farrendel went to Escarland to learn." Leyleira's eyebrow lifted as she glanced from Weylind to Farrendel, and even though the piercing gaze wasn't focused on her, Essie squirmed. "And did you learn it, sasonsheni?"

"Yes. At least, I am beginning to learn it." Farrendel shifted in his seat next to Essie, as if he, too, was unable to sit still under his grandmother's sharp gaze.

"Good." Leyleira's face lit with a smile. "Then the correct question to ask is if this degree will make you a better person. A better brother. A better warrior. A better prince. A better husband. And, someday, hopefully, a better father. If you believe that this will make you better able to fulfill whatever calling you are given in your life, and you obviously have thought through the logistics of your decision, then that is all I need to know."

"Thank you, Machasheni." Farrendel's smile was genuine, even if Essie could see the hints of strain in it.

It was time to take the focus of the conversation away from Farrendel so that he could have a minute to gather his bearings.

Since Essie had known they'd have a long trip on the train, she'd kept the bag with the mugs with her. On the Escarlish train, she had spent the few hours before she had gone to sleep putting the packets of hot chocolate in each mug and wrapping the whole parcel.

Now, she pulled out the bag and grinned. "Farrendel and I thought it would be nice to give all of you a little piece of Escarland."

Farrendel sank back against the bench, and through the heart bond, she could feel his relief. Yep, it was definitely time for her to take the attention onto herself.

While Averett crossed his arms and watched with a smirk on his face, Essie distributed the gifts. All the mugs had a large tree on the side, though each mug was a different color. They had a packet of cocoa mix and instructions in elvish on how to properly prepare a cup.

Leyleira inspected her dark purple mug with that approving gleam in her eyes again.

"This is lovely." Jalissa traced the tree design on her light purple mug, a smile twitching her mouth for the first time that trip.

"Yes, thank you for your thoughtfulness." Rheva gave Essie one of her soft smiles as she held her light blue mug in both hands.

"Oh, and, Weylind, you seem to have left this on the table in the parlor, so I brought it along for you." Essie didn't bother trying to hide her smirk as she pulled out the green and white elf ear mug that Weylind had, indeed, left on the coffee table as if hoping to conveniently lose it. She held it out to him. "Here you go."

Weylind gave the mug a sour glare and made no move to take it from her.

Rheva snorted softly and took the mug. "Thank you, Elspetha, for helping my forgetful husband."

Weylind's mouth worked, and he looked about ready to launch into another coughing fit. "Perhaps we can find some cupboard in our room in which to store this...thing."

Rheva met Essie's gaze over the rim of the hideous mug, her eyes twinkling even as her expression remained blank. "No, I was thinking a shelf in your study would show proper appreciation for the artisans of our esteemed Escarlish allies."

Now Weylind looked positively green.

Essie shared a grin with Rheva. "I think we would have been friends a long time ago if you'd let out your sense of humor more."

Rheva just grinned back.

Weylind glared at Essie. "You are corrupting my entire family."

"I know. I am such a bad influence." Essie plopped onto the seat next to Farrendel again.

Farrendel took her hand, sharing a smile.

Now if they would just find Melantha—and possibly Edmund—safe and sound, then perhaps she and Farrendel could finally relax and enjoy being blissfully happy.

THIRTY-FOUR

I t was later in the day than Farrendel usually exercised, but with all the busyness of transferring trains and greeting his family in Estyra, he had not had a chance earlier.

But he could feel the rising tension and jittery energy inside him. He needed the release to steady himself before they arrived at the border and faced the possible brewing war and news of Melantha.

None of the others questioned him when he quietly left the seating car and retreated to his personal sleeping car. Essie gave him a knowing glance but did not pause in her conversation with Rheva and her attempts to draw out Jalissa.

After tossing his shirt on the bed, Farrendel vaulted out the hatch set in the ceiling of the train car and landed on the sleek surface of the roof. He closed the hatch behind him and faced the oncoming branches.

A low-hanging branch was rushing toward his head. He flipped over it, then turned his landing into a spin to avoid another branch.

He threw himself into the exertion. Not feeling. Not thinking. Just pushing his muscles, his agility, and his reactions to their limits.

He was concentrating so deeply on flipping over branches that he did not notice that he was no longer alone on the top of the train until he heard the thump of feet behind him. He flipped, spun, and landed in a crouch.

Weylind crouched behind him, his black hair loose around his shoulders, missing his usual crown. He wore a shirt and trousers without a tunic over top, and it was the most relaxed Farrendel had seen him in a long while.

"Shashon? Is something wrong?" Farrendel swayed with the rhythm of the train.

The whistle of wind alerted Farrendel to a branch whipping toward him. He gave a backward flip over the branch and caught a glimpse of Weylind rolling over the branch with the graceful ease of someone who had also practiced dodging branches on the top of a train.

When they both landed, Farrendel raised his eyebrows. "You have done this before."

Weylind rolled his shoulders in a faint shrug. "You always needed the train's roof more. I usually waited until you were finished before venturing up here."

"I did not realize that." Farrendel spun to face the front again, just in time to duck underneath a thin branch. A branch as wide as his waist skimmed three feet above the train, and Farrendel used it to launch himself into the air, coming down on the train next to Weylind, who had merely jumped over the branch.

For several minutes, the two of them settled into an easy rhythm of ducking, rolling, jumping, and flipping. It felt strangely comfortable, being there with Weylind. Perhaps, if Farrendel had known, he would have enjoyed spending time with his brother like this.

Though, before, Farrendel had been so close to collapse that he would not have wanted Weylind to interrupt him.

"Are you truly well?" Weylind flicked a glance toward Farrendel before he focused forward once again. "Those Escarlish doctors were able to help you as hoped?"

"Yes." Farrendel tried to explain in a way Weylind would understand. "When a broken bone heals wrong, it has to be re-broken before it can be healed properly. It was like that, sort of. I would not have chosen to break again as I did, but it gave me the chance to heal as I was not able to before."

Not that he was fully or permanently healed. Perhaps, as Taranath had said months ago, Farrendel had learned how to better use the crutch he needed to live a normal life with his war wounds. He would have times he struggled more and times that he struggled less.

But he would have a life. And it would be a good life.

"You seem…well." Weylind was still giving him that cautious look as if he was not sure what to say or how to say it. "And this university degree. It is what you want?"

"Yes." Farrendel felt no hesitation in answering. He had been thinking this over for months now, and he was convinced it was the right course. But it would be best to present it in a way Weylind could appreciate. "Tarenhiel will also benefit. I will have access to Escarland's latest innovations and the people creating those inventions. I will better understand their way of thinking and how they go about crafting their magical mechanics. This is information that Tarenhiel will need so that we can adapt those inventions to our own magic and not be left behind by the humans."

"I understand, and I see why I should encourage more sharing of knowledge, as you have been suggesting in your letters." Weylind somersaulted over a branch in time with Farrendel, and they both landed on the roof in identical crouches. Only once they were steady did Weylind glance at Farrendel. "But I am asking not as your king but as your brother. Is this truly what you want?"

Perhaps Weylind understood more than Farrendel had realized. They had both changed, more than either of them had noticed, thanks to the influence of Essie and her brothers.

Farrendel focused on the branches whipping toward them, buying himself time to put his words into a proper order. "I was never taught how to use my magic. Not really. We were already at war with the trolls when I came into my power. Shortly afterwards, we found ourselves at war with Escarland as well. You and Dacha did your best to teach me what you could whenever you were home from the front, but you do not have my type of magic. No one else does."

Farrendel had been left without the guidance that normally would have been given to a young elf newly come into his magic. Melantha had apprenticed under Taranath, another healer, who could teach her the specifics of how to wield healing magic. Weylind learned growing magic from their father. Jalissa had also studied under their father and other elves with plant magic.

While Farrendel had been growing up, everyone had assumed he would inherit either healing or growing magic like the rest of his family. He had studied the basics of elven magic and learned about the parts of the plant and the parts of the human body in preparation for inheriting either type of magic.

Farrendel had even prepared himself for the reality that he might have a very weak magic, since no one knew what kind of magic his mother had, nor had anyone who had known her recalled her ever using magic. Some of the more snide nobles had dared tell him to his face that they believed a weak magic was all someone like him deserved.

No one had expected that he—the illegitimate son—out of all of his siblings would inherit the powerful magic of the ancient elven kings.

"Do you think the humans can teach you how to use your magic? They have no one who wields this magic either." Weylind's tone remained even, not accusatory as Farrendel would have expected. Simply stating the fact. His movements remained easy, not stiff or angry, as they both dodged a branch.

"I know. But, I have seen progress in working with the human inventor Lance Marion. He has ideas for how to push my magic in ways we elves have not considered, and I have gained more finesse." Most of Farrendel's practice in using his magic had come from battle, where brute force was all that was required. Farrendel swayed in time with the gliding train beneath him. "I cannot work with our inventions since they are powered by a living magic that my magic kills. But humans work with metal and machinery. I cannot kill what is not alive."

Instead of destruction, Farrendel would learn how to power trains and lights and anything else into which a magical power cell with his magic could be crammed.

How he clung to that hope. Not for the money Essie and Lance seemed to think it would earn. But for the satisfaction of building something useful instead of standing there spattered in blood, surveying a battlefield filled with charred corpses, and believing that death was all his magic could produce.

"I suppose what the humans do not know about your magic, they are curious enough to find out." Weylind's mouth twisted, as if he was no longer sure if he should grimace or smile at a statement like that.

"Yes." Farrendel flipped over another thin, whipping twig, not even knocking the snow from it as he whirled around it.

Professor Harrington had suggested that Farrendel should research past elves with his type of magic in the great library in Ellonahshinel. It was something Farrendel should have thought to do himself, years ago. But, between fighting in the war and fighting to recover mentally whenever he was home, he had never had the time nor energy for such a pursuit. Now that there was peace, he could finally devote himself to study.

Assuming Melantha was alive and that Rharreth would be able to take back his throne and quell this rising trouble at the border.

Farrendel threw himself into a more savage flip, then a tuck and roll, coming up with his hands gripped into fists as if he held his swords. Whatever the trolls attempted this time, it would be over quickly between Escarland's help and Farrendel's full magical power. There would be peace. For his own sanity, Farrendel had to believe the war had an ending.

And then, there was his future. Learning magic. Building a life with Essie both in Tarenhiel and in Escarland.

He risked a glance at Weylind as they ducked in unison under a branch that flew past at head height. "I need to do this, Weylind. Not just for me. But for any children Essie and

I might have. The odds are high that it is my magic they will inherit."

This time, the smirk cracked in full force across Weylind's face as he raised one, dark eyebrow. "Are you trying to tell me you and Essie will have yet another announcement to make before long?"

"I..." The tips of Farrendel's ears were on fire, and he could not meet Weylind's gaze. "No...we are not..." He had to draw in a deep breath. Words. He needed coherent words. "Maybe someday. But if or when that happens, I do not want my children to be as alone and lost with their magic as I was."

"I am sorry you ever thought you were alone." Weylind's shoulders sagged, his head bowing as his black hair whipped around him. "I failed you. I failed Melantha. Were all my siblings miserable, and I did not notice?"

How was he supposed to respond to that? Farrendel eyed the forest ahead of them. They were entering a stretch that was relatively clear of branches as the trees thinned the closer they came to the border with Kostaria.

Farrendel sat cross-legged on top of the train. The setting sun sent shafts of sunlight streaming between the tree trunks and shimmering across the snow. Now that he had stopped moving, the cold wind of the train's passing prickled against the bare skin of his back and chest.

Weylind also sat, staring off into the distance rather than looking at Farrendel.

Farrendel huffed out a long breath. "Perhaps you did not notice because you were miserable too."

"Perhaps." Weylind's answer gusted out on a sigh, as if he was finally admitting that to himself. After a moment, he leaned over and gripped Farrendel's shoulders. "No matter the cost, our family would not have been complete without you. Never doubt that, shashon."

Farrendel had to duck his head, unable to look at Weylind. Still, the words were a balm he had not known he needed. Weylind had said such things before, but never so bluntly and never when Farrendel was in a place to finally believe them.

After he released Farrendel's shoulders, Weylind leaned back against his hands, lounging on the top of the train. He seemed more at rest than Farrendel had seen him in years.

Maybe Farrendel was not the only one who had to be broken again in order to heal.

He could only hope that whatever breaking Melantha had faced in Kostaria had indeed made her a stronger, better person and had not killed her in the process.

THE TRAIN PULLED into the platform at the main northern army base that had been set up during the war and had yet to be fully dismantled. It was now in the process of being re-manned, with a large portion of the elven army settling into their treetop shelters, preparing space for the coming Escarlish army, and setting off for patrols along the border. A few Escarlish soldiers, the regiment that had been left to continue to guard the border, joined the patrols or worked near the large artillery guns.

Farrendel strolled through the camp from the train plat-form with his hand gripped in Essie's and tried to pretend that he had a clue where they were headed. Everyone else had just set off in one direction as if it were second nature, reminding him that they had spent some time here together while he had been suffering torture in Kostaria.

It was hard not to feel a little jealous, even though he knew the mental anguish they had gone through as they planned an entire war to rescue him. He had felt it through the heart bond with Essie, even if he had not been here himself.

They neared the cluster of large trees near the center of the camp. Several shelters had been grown out of the low-hanging branches.

Next to him, Essie waved to the shelter. "This is where the command center was during the war. Your brother and his generals had their shelters and command post in the trees while Averett and the rest of us slept in tents on the ground. I'm hoping your brother can be persuaded to make a few more shelters for us this time around. I got rather used to sleeping in one, and they are cozier than a tent in this kind of weather."

Essie gave an exaggerated shiver and tugged her dark green coat tighter around her shoulders. Her red hair swung in its braid across her shoulders and down her back. She was not wearing her gun or leather armor yet, but both sets of their armor and weapons had been packed on the train.

"Your Majesty!"

Ahead of Essie and Farrendel, both Weylind and Averett turned. "Yes?"

An elf raced through the bustle toward them. He gave a nod of his head first to Weylind, then to Averett. "Weylind Daresheni, we just received word from a patrol. Your sister Melantha Amirah and her husband Rharreth of the trolls have crossed the border and are requesting a parley."

The tightness in Farrendel's chest eased, and he took his

first decent breath since he had been informed of the coup in Kostaria.

Melantha was alive.

Not only was she alive, but she was here in Tarenhiel where she would be safe.

"Please instruct the patrol to escort them here." Weylind's shoulders relaxed as well.

The elf shifted, glancing at Weylind, then at Averett, before focusing on Weylind again. "That is the problem, Daresheni. The troll king is refusing to take another step into the kingdom, and he has a hostage."

CHAPTER
THIRTY-FIVE

Melantha stood next to Rharreth, her back straight, her head high, and tried to pretend her stomach was not churning. Her feet were planted on the soil of her homeland for the first time since she had betrayed her kingdom and her brother, and the only reason she and Rharreth had been allowed this far was the knife Rharreth held to Prince Edmund's throat.

Across from them, four members of the patrol squad— two humans and two elves—brandished rifles and swords in their direction as they waited for their fifth member to fetch Weylind. A thick stand of spruces and pines filled the land behind the squad, obscuring everything but their small clearing next to the gorge.

At Rharreth's and Melantha's backs, the Gulmorth River roared far below. Rharreth had collapsed the bridge he had created for the three of them to cross. If this went badly, they had nowhere to run.

But Rharreth had not wanted anyone from Kostaria to be tempted to interfere, and Melantha was thankful for that caution. Things would get tense, but they would get more tense if a gang of overzealous trolls came charging out of the forest and across a bridge into Tarenhiel at the wrong moment.

Instead, Rharreth had sent Ezrec and his men to meet the army gathering at Argar Point. Ezrec had not been happy, and by the way the back of Melantha's neck itched, it was likely a scout had been sent to keep an eye on the situation.

Prince Edmund gave a sigh and shifted. "Your claims of peace might be more believable if you didn't have your knife to my throat. Is this really the first impression you want to make?"

"Why should I listen to you, spy?" Rharreth growled. Every muscle along his back and arms was tense and had been ever since they had crossed the Gulmorth Gorge and entered Tarenhiel.

Prince Edmund huffed another sigh. "Unauthorized royal visitor."

Melantha was almost starting to like this human prince.

"Semantics doesn't change the truth that Escarland—and likely Tarenhiel—didn't exactly keep their claims of peace when they sent spies into my kingdom even after we signed a peace treaty." Rharreth's growl deepened, and his dark blue eyes flashed.

Melantha gripped his free arm and yanked hard. "Rharreth. Hush. Right now, we have bigger problems than one captured Escarlish spy."

Rharreth shook his head, but some of the heat in his eyes cooled. "I'm still not removing the knife from his neck. As this is the only punishment he and Escarland are likely to get for his spying, I am not in a hurry to end it."

That earned another eyeroll-huff from the Escarlish

prince. "Glad to know you aren't being petty. After all, you honorable trolls are above that."

"And you should hush as well." Melantha poked the Escarlish prince in the shoulder. "Do not provoke either of us. You also have bigger things to worry about than protesting your treatment after being caught on an 'unauthorized royal visit.'"

Prince Edmund snapped his mouth shut, though his eyes still held a twinkle as if he found the situation amusing.

Melantha felt heat building in her own chest, and she struggled to control it. Already she wanted to bash both Rharreth and Prince Edmund over the head, and her brother Weylind had not yet arrived to further add to the tension.

A rustle sounded in the trees behind the squad of elf and human soldiers, then more warriors poured from between the pines. Clicks sounded as human soldiers raised their muskets and cocked back the hammers. Movement higher in the trees showed where elves had climbed to the higher branches to get a better shot for their bows.

Melantha flexed her fingers and worked to keep her face blank. Her chest was so tight that she could not draw in a breath. It was the first time she would see her family again in three months, and last time things had been stiff and strained. Was Weylind here? What about Farrendel? Could she make things right?

The line of human soldiers and elf warriors parted, and Weylind stepped through the opening, his face hard, his mouth pressed in a tight line.

He was followed by King Averett of Escarland. King Averett's eyes flashed, and he clenched his fists, most likely at the sight of Prince Edmund with his hands bound and Rharreth's knife at his throat.

Melantha had known starting this conversation off like this was probably a bad idea. But Rharreth was not about to be budged, not even by her.

Two more people pushed forward to stand beside Weylind and King Averett. Melantha's breath hitched in her chest at the sight of Farrendel.

He looked well. Far, far healthier than the emaciated, tortured person he had been when she had last seen him. His hair had grown back to just brush the collar of his dark green tunic, and it was cut evenly. His shoulders relaxed, and he took a step forward as if he intended to run to her.

Weylind stopped him with an arm, saying something in a low voice.

Farrendel halted, his eyes darting from her to Rharreth and Prince Edmund. Next to him, Princess Elspetha gripped Farrendel's arm as if also intending to hold him back. Her eyes were fixed on Prince Edmund, the color draining from her face even as her jaw hardened.

Letting his knife fall to his side, Rharreth gripped the back of Prince Edmund's shirt and nearly picked him off his feet. "I believe *this* is yours."

King Averett's mouth twisted, as if torn between scowling and protesting.

Rharreth, still holding the knife between his fingers, reached forward and released the stone binding Prince Edmund's wrists. "I have no wish for war, King Averett. Please see that no more *unauthorized visits* occur in the future. We are at peace." As he finished, he shoved Prince Edmund toward the line of elves and soldiers.

Prince Edmund stumbled a few steps forward but did not fall. He glanced over his shoulder, and when Rharreth made no move to stop him, the Escarlish prince walked across the distance to join his brother.

King Averett swept a glance over Prince Edmund, as if to ascertain that he was all right, before he faced Rharreth. "I have no wish for war either, King Rharreth. We sent a *visitor* to Kostaria to keep an eye on the segments of your people still antagonistic to Tarenhiel and Escarland. Due to the recent coup, you cannot deny that those elements are still strong within your kingdom. When your kingdom no longer poses a threat to your southern neighbors, then I can assure you that my brother will make no more such visits to Kostaria."

Melantha felt all the sharp-edged jabs going back and forth between Rharreth and King Averett. In the glares and subtext, Rharreth had just told King Averett that he was not happy that Escarland had been spying on Kostaria. King Averett, in turn, told Rharreth that he was not pleased that Rharreth had not kept his people from violating the peace treaty and that Drurvas's rebellion proved that Escarland had good cause for spying.

Neither side mentioned that there were likely more spies —probably a number of Weylind's elves and maybe another human or two—as if both Rharreth and King Averett were willing to pretend Prince Edmund's presence was an isolated incident.

For several long moments, Rharreth and King Averett held each others' hard gazes. Then, they each gave a slight nod, coming to a silent understanding.

Melantha internally relaxed, though she kept her back straight and her expression neutral. Rharreth and King Averett had just agreed to let the matter of spying drop.

Rharreth clasped Melantha's hand, enveloping her

fingers in his large, calloused ones. His dark blue eyes searched her face. "Are you sure about this?"

That set Melantha's stomach to churning again. She knew this was the right thing to do. But that did not make it easy. "Yes. I need to do this to restore my honor before my family."

"I understand." He held out his knife. When she took it, he let go of her hand and reached up to trail his fingers through her hair before letting his arm fall back to his side.

It stiffened her spine that Rharreth truly understood. He was the one who taught her about honor, after all.

Gripping the knife, its hilt cold against her fingers, Melantha strode forward. She did not meet Weylind's or Farrendel's gazes, though she felt the prickling of their stares. When she stood only a few feet in front of Farrendel, she knelt on the ground and bowed. Her hand holding the knife trembled.

She drew in a deep breath. "Farrendel, shashon. I hurt you more than I will ever know. I was so very wrong about so many things. I am the one who brought shame to our family, not you. I am the one who is dishonored, not you."

Melantha gripped her hair with one hand and raised the knife.

"No. Melantha. Do not." Farrendel's voice was low, pained.

She finally dared to look at him. He was trembling, fighting against Weylind's restraining arm. Princess Elspetha gripped his other arm. A furrow bunched his forehead, his silver-blue eyes wide.

The vulnerable, open look to his face reminded her of why she had to do this. She had hurt him so very deeply.

And then, there in the dungeons of Gror Grar, she had tried to earn forgiveness.

But, in the end, trying to earn forgiveness was just another form of manipulation. She had been trying to manipulate Farrendel, Weylind, all of them, in order to benefit herself.

In contrast, true forgiveness was always unearned, undeserved, and given freely.

Still, they needed to know that she understood how wrong she had been and that she regretted it deeply. Her relationship with her family would likely never be the same. No matter how they reacted, she had to do this to prove to herself how much she had changed, if nothing else.

As she tensed her muscles and prepared to slice her hair, a part of her wanted to lower the knife to leave her hair a more appealing length. But, she could not give in to the impulse. It was a remnant of the selfish person she used to be.

Gritting her teeth, Melantha sawed at her hair, chopping it off close to her head much as Farrendel's hair had been shorn three and a half months ago.

In front of her, Farrendel made a strangled sound that might have been a *no* but she could not bring herself to look at him.

It took her far longer to slice her hair than it had King Charvod to slice Farrendel's since she could not get strength behind her movements, twisting around to reach the back of her head as she was.

But, within a few seconds, the long, thick strands of her hair came away in her hand. She dropped it onto the forest floor along with the knife, then bowed her face to the ground again. "I am truly sorry, Farrendel, for betraying you and betraying Tarenhiel. I am sorry for my failure as a sister. I am *sorry.*"

She had barely finished speaking when Farrendel crashed to his knees in front of her and hugged her. Not an elven hug, but one of those human hugs where he wrapped both arms around her and held her tight.

When he spoke, his voice was low, only for her. "I already told you I forgave you. You did not need to cut off your hair for me."

After a moment of stiffness, her arms awkwardly at her sides, Melantha relaxed into Farrendel's grip. Tentatively, she put her arms around him.

Something in her broke at his ready forgiveness. She had not known what to expect in coming here. Farrendel had said he forgave her when they last talked in Kostaria, but she was not sure if he would still feel the same way once he had time and distance to come to terms with what had happened to him.

Yet, here he was. Hugging her in the close, human way. Giving his forgiveness yet again without any hesitation.

She did not deserve it. Not in the least.

Her breaths came harder. Her chest ached. Her eyes burned, and tears spilled before she had any thought of trying to hold them back.

But once started, the release of tears felt too good to stop. Melantha held Farrendel and cried onto his shoulder, no longer caring that it was not something an elf princess should do.

Now, she was a troll queen, and troll queens were not afraid to show emotion before others.

In her arms, Farrendel stiffened, though he did not pull away as she might have expected. Instead, he patted her back as if trying to be comforting. After a moment, another set of arms wrapped around Melantha, and Princess Elspetha said something soothing.

Hearing Princess Elspetha's voice only made Melantha cry harder. The human princess—the sister Melantha had done everything to shun when she should have embraced her—had just as much reason to hate Melantha as Farrendel did. But here she was, hugging Melantha right alongside Farrendel.

It took several long minutes before Melantha could get hold of herself enough to lift her head from Farrendel's shoulder and pull back. Still sniffing, she gripped one of Farrendel's shoulders and searched his face. "You came. Even before I had a chance to ask for help."

"Of course, I came. You are my sister." Something in his eyes seemed brighter, without the lingering shadows that had weighed on him for so long.

Melantha found herself smiling, her cheeks crusted with her drying tears. "I am thankful to have you for a brother."

Farrendel's eyes widened, his shoulders giving a shake.

Before he had a chance to react more than that, Melantha turned to Princess Elspetha and placed her other hand on the princess's shoulder. "And, I am thankful that my brother has someone like you in his life. It seems a human was exactly whom he needed."

Princess Elspetha gaped, her eyes going wide. So wide, Melantha finally noticed they were green. She had never cared to pay enough attention to note that before.

"Yes. She is." Farrendel's face lit with a soft smile as he glanced at his wife. After a moment, he turned to Melantha, his smile widening and his eyes twinkling with a mischief that Melantha had not seen in him in nearly two decades. He touched the end of his hair. "If you would like, Essie has become adept at cutting hair over the past few months. You just need to hold still, otherwise she will cut your ears off."

Melantha started, her hands dropping from their shoulders.

Princess Elspetha rolled her eyes and lightly swatted Farrendel's arm. "Don't listen to a word this joker says. Yes, I have gotten good at trimming hair, but I won't chop your ears off."

"That is…reassuring." Melantha climbed to her feet, and Farrendel and Princess Elspetha did the same. When Melantha glanced over her shoulder, she found Rharreth only a few steps away, shifting in place like he was not sure what he should do. Melantha gave him a smile and a nod.

By the time she turned back around, Weylind was there, pushing past Farrendel and Princess Elspetha. Weylind gripped Melantha's shoulders, squeezing tightly. "Are you truly well, isciena? When we heard about the coup…" Weylind's voice broke, and it was his turn to look away.

Those tears were back, though this time Melantha swallowed them. This brother too had forgiven her. He still loved her and worried for her.

"Yes, I am." Melantha put all the warmth and contentment and determination into her gaze that she could. She was happy. She was safe. She loved Rharreth. She loved Kostaria. And saving Kostaria from Drurvas meant more to her than anything ever had before. "Is there somewhere we can go to talk? We would like to discuss how best to coordinate our efforts so that Rharreth can regain his throne with as little bloodshed as possible."

Weylind gave a sharp nod. "Yes. I can see how that would be a discussion we would not wish to have standing here in the open. Come. We can take you back to our encampment. Though, your troll husband may wish to wave to the watchers on the far side of the gorge to reassure them you are safe."

So Weylind had noticed them too. Good to know Melantha had not been imagining things.

Rharreth lifted a hand in something that looked like a signal, then he stepped closer to Melantha.

She pulled out of Weylind's embrace, picked up Rharreth's knife from where it lay on the pile of her hair, and held it out to him.

Rharreth took the knife, sheathed it, then wrapped an arm around her shoulders, holding her close.

She leaned into him, thankful for his solid warmth as she faced her family.

CHAPTER
THIRTY-SIX

Rharreth stood with his army at his back and his wife at his side, and faced his usurping cousin and his army across the narrow, rocky ground separating them.

The morning breeze brushed against his face and his hands, the only skin exposed by the leather armor Ezrec had provided. The snow crunched beneath his boots, the top layer sparkling and iced due to the frigid temperatures overnight. His breath puffed into a cloud in front of his face.

Beside him, Melantha stood straight, her chin held high. She was dressed in a leather tunic and skirt over her dark red, wool dress. Those were the only pieces Ezrec's men had been able to size down for her on short notice.

To Rharreth's left, the Gulmorth River roared deep in its gorge, the spray coating the walls of the canyon with a sheet of ice and icicles as long as Rharreth was tall.

Across the gorge, the elven and human army stretched in either direction as far as Rharreth could see. The Tarenhieli-

Escarlish army blocked Drurvas from trying to out-flank Rharreth's army by cutting through Tarenhiel, and they provided a silent, menacing witness to what Rharreth was about to attempt. Hopefully, their presence would convince Drurvas that a Dulraith was his only option.

At the front of the elven-human army, King Weylind stood in his dark green armor with Laesornysh in matching green, padded leather armor at his side. Interestingly enough, Princess Elspetha stood next to Laesornysh, her bright red hair standing out against the blue accents of her padded fighting leathers.

At her side stood King Averett, flanked by Princes Julien and Edmund. All of them wore plain, brown leather tunics embossed with a crown over an upright sword.

At least the Escarlish-Tarenhieli army looked impressive. Behind Rharreth, his makeshift army stretched into a semi-circle. The front row was formed of Ezrec's warriors and the warriors from a few of the other families that remained loyal to Rharreth.

But the rest of Rharreth's army was made of normal citizens carrying whatever weapon they could get their hands on. Rharreth recognized Mymrar, who had helped them in their escape from Osmana, along with a few of the other men and women whom he and Melantha had helped in Osmana. Others were common citizens from the scattered towns and villages and strongholds, even some from the strongholds under the control of warrior families supporting Drurvas.

Drurvas might have the support of many of the warrior families, but Rharreth had the loyalty of the common people.

Unfortunately, in a war, the support of the common

people would only get Rharreth so far before they were wiped out due to lack of training.

Rharreth drew his sword and laid it flat across his palms, the sign that he wanted to talk under truce.

With a smirk, Drurvas drew his ax from its sling across his shoulders and held it out flat as well. He sauntered forward into the empty space between the two armies, his stride sure and confident.

Why would he not be confident when he had the bulk of Kostaria's army at his back, all well-armed and well-trained?

If this came to a war, it would get bloody, and the only winner would be Tarenhiel, which would probably breathe a sigh of relief at the sight of a weakened and starving Kostaria.

Meeting Drurvas's gaze, Rharreth strode forward, still holding his sword flat. When he stood only a few feet from Drurvas, he halted. "Well, cousin, have you come to surrender to the true king of Kostaria? It seems all your attempts to kill me were unsuccessful, thanks to the power of my wife's healing magic."

Drurvas's smirk twisted for a moment, as if he wanted to scowl but did not want to give Rharreth the satisfaction of a reaction. "Yes. So I heard. A pity you did not take your opportunity to die quickly and quietly as befits a weakling like you. You have gone running to your Tarenhieli and Escarlish allies like a dog with your tail between your legs, showing that you are no true king of Kostaria."

Rharreth stuffed down the heat building in his chest. He could not let Drurvas get a rise out of him. "The armies of Tarenhiel and Escarland have gathered due to word of your actions and the instability you have caused in Kostaria. They are here merely to witness the outcome of our confrontation and will not interfere unless you decide to attack them."

"I would argue that you are the one who provoked Tarenhiel and Escarland by bringing our war to the border instead of keeping it in Osmana as befitting a fight between honorable warriors." Drurvas gave a light shake of his head, as if he could not believe the depths to which Rharreth had fallen. "And then you used deception to escape in the night. We are trolls, not the weak, tricky elves. Though, it seems you have become very cozy with them."

As he said that last word, Drurvas glanced past Rharreth toward Melantha with a twist to his mouth.

Rharreth curled his fingers over his sword, heat building inside his chest and begging for him to lash out. It would be so satisfying to take up the hilt of his sword and swipe that smirking head from Drurvas's shoulders.

But Drurvas would block the swing before it came to that, and Rharreth's actions in breaking the truce before all these witnesses would dishonor him and disqualify him from ever regaining the throne.

Instead, Rharreth glared back and did not say anything. He did not trust himself to speak, and it seemed wiser to let Drurvas get out his melodramatic mocking here and now before Rharreth challenged him.

If anything, Drurvas's smirk widened. "I see you have the Rindrin and Gruilveth family warriors at your back. I am sure they will be thankful to learn their sons survived their little mission to deceive my trackers, though I do not think they are enjoying my hospitality."

Still holding his ax flat with one hand, Drurvas gestured with the other, and the line of warriors behind him parted. Zavni and Eyvindur were shoved forward roughly and forced to kneel on the rocky ground. Their hands were bound behind their backs, and crusted blood marred their faces and clothes. Zavni had a large, dark bruise on his cheek and one eye was swollen shut. Eyvindur sported a large gash across his forehead. But both of them clenched tight jaws and flashed hard eyes.

Vriska was the warrior pinning Zavni down. She met Rharreth's gaze and gave a slow wink.

Rharreth could not let so much as a twitch betray his relief. She was still on his side, and she would know her mission. If Drurvas planned more treachery, she would escape to report it. If she could, she would help Zavni and Eyvindur escape.

Instead, Rharreth forced his face to harden, and he glared at Vriska with all the feigned hate that he could muster. "Vriska. I should have known you would have joined Drurvas in his treachery."

Vriska gave a smirk that mirrored Drurvas's, cocking one hand on her hip while she pinned Zavni on his knees with the other. "Of course. My loyalty lies with the strongest in the line of the kings."

Clever wording. She spoke the truth while deceiving Drurvas into believing that was him.

"There you have it, Rharreth. Even those among your shield band believe you are too weak to be king. Why should the rest of Kostaria follow you?" Drurvas raised his eyebrows, as if he truly wanted to know the answer.

It was the opening Rharreth had been looking for. He straightened and met Drurvas stare for stare. "If it is a test of strength that Kostaria wants, then I challenge you to a Dulraith. Let all of Kostaria see us pit our strength against each other and judge who is fit to be king and who will die."

Perhaps Drurvas, too, had known that this would come down to a Dulraith from the moment he had failed to kill Rharreth in Osmana. His smirk turned into something closer to a sneer. "I agree that only one of us can survive. We are the last of the Regdrir royal warrior family. Unless your elf bride already carries your whelp?"

Rharreth had to grit his teeth at another insult to Melantha. She would be safer if he denied that chance to Drurvas. "She does not. If I'm killed, she will be allowed to return to her people in peace. That is my only demand."

"I will only agree to this demand if you agree to mine." Drurvas's sneer showed his teeth, his eyes glinting. "You claim that peace with Tarenhiel and Escarland will strengthen Kostaria. If that is so, then let your *allies* prove it. I challenge your alliance to the Dulraith."

Rharreth's chest filled with ice. This was not the plan. Not at all. This Dulraith was supposed to be between just him and Drurvas.

Instead, Drurvas had brought Tarenhiel and Escarland even deeper into Kostaria's affairs without appearing to weaken his position at all.

Would the leaders of Tarenhiel and Escarland agree to this? They would not like it. Not one bit.

Rharreth tilted his chin, hating that even saying these words would make him appear weak in front of Drurvas and the rebelling warrior families. "I will have to consult with their leaders. I cannot speak for them."

"Of course you cannot." That sneer was back on Drurvas's face and in his voice, lashing at Rharreth. "You have until noon to talk to your allies, though I doubt they will have the stomach for this."

Rharreth was not sure he had the stomach for dealing with Drurvas's lies and treachery one moment longer.

But Drurvas had neatly maneuvered him into a corner. Either Rharreth talked representatives of Tarenhiel and Escarland into participating in the Dulraith, or he would have already lost his honor and his throne even before starting a duel where he would surely lose his life if forced to fight alone.

RHARRETH GRIPPED one of Melantha's hands as they strode across the bridge her brother King Weylind had grown early that morning out of sight of Drurvas's army for ease of communication.

But, like before, this was a conversation Rharreth had to have face-to-face with the elf king. There would be no entrusting this to a mere messenger.

King Weylind, Laesornysh, and all the Escarlish royalty were lined up at the tree line, waiting for Rharreth and Melantha. The shadowy figures of guards waited among the trees, but they did not intervene, just as Rharreth's guards waited by the far end of the bridge.

King Averett hurried forward as soon as Rharreth stepped from the bridge, his face more earnest and open than an elf or troll would ever allow. "Well, what is the word? Did your cousin agree to a...what did you call that fancy duel?"

King Weylind had his hands gripped behind his back, his jaw in a hard line. Beside him, Laesornysh stood, hale and strong, moving with that deadly, confident grace that spoke of the lethal warrior he was.

With a deep breath, Rharreth faced King Averett, keeping King Weylind in his peripheral vision. "The Dulraith is an ancient tradition in Kostaria. It is a test of physical strength that is fought to the death without mercy. No long-range weapons or magic are allowed. No one observing the Dulraith may interfere with the contestants whatsoever. If a rule is violated by either the combatants or those observing, the violator will be killed. It is a solemn, deadly affair, and a challenge of a Dulraith is only issued in matters of the gravest importance."

"Yes..." King Averett drew out the word, his forehead scrunched. The humans had never had many dealings with the trolls, with the buffer of Tarenhiel between them. He did not yet see what Rharreth was trying to tell him. "I believe you mentioned something last night about this Dulraith being a fight to the death."

Melantha's hand tightened in Rharreth's, her face pale. But she stood straight, her jaw tight. Until the night before, he had never told her that the Dulraith was to the death. There had been a lot of yelling once they had been alone. But she didn't voice her concerns now in front of the others.

Behind King Averett, King Weylind's shoulders had gone tense, and Laesornysh's eyes flared a harder, icier silver-blue. They sensed that if Rharreth was taking the time to reiterate the rules of the Dulraith, then he had a good reason —or a very bad one—for doing so.

Rharreth faced King Averett and King Weylind. "Yes, he agreed to the Dulraith. But, in return, he challenged the whole of our alliance to the duel."

Laesornysh stiffened, a hand reaching up to touch the hilt of one of his swords. King Weylind gave a slight shake to his head, though Rharreth could not be sure if he was expressing his disbelief or if he was already denying what Rharreth had to ask before he'd even asked it.

King Averett crossed his arms. "What does that mean, exactly? We already knew the alliance would end if he wins."

Rharreth shook his head. "Drurvas challenged the alliance, and, for the purposes of the duel, the fighters have to legally represent their kingdoms. They must be members of the royal families of Tarenhiel, Escarland, and Kostaria. You can't send in a champion to fight for you any more than Drurvas or I can, though Drurvas will be able to choose his best warriors for his other two combatants."

A tense silence fell over them. Rharreth could not bear to look at any of them. Not at Melantha, with the pain in her eyes. Not at her brother King Weylind with his hardening jaw and rising anger. Nor at the Escarlish king and his stricken, open-mouthed horror.

But especially not at Laesornysh, the enemy Rharreth had captured, treated dishonorably, and allowed to be tortured. Who was Rharreth, of all people, to ask this elf to fight at his side after what Rharreth had done to him?

"I know I cannot demand this of you. This is far more support than your kingdoms ever agreed to provide in the alliance. But if you do not agree to this, I will fight alone against three, and all of Kostaria will see it as proof of the weakness of alliances in general and of Tarenhiel and Escarland specifically." Rharreth grimaced and let go of Melantha's hand so that he could wrap an arm around her waist, tucking her closer. "Drurvas will use it as an excuse to resume the war as soon as I am dead."

Digging her fingers into his shirt, Melantha buried her face against his shoulder, murmuring low enough that only he could hear, "If you let Drurvas kill you in this duel, I will never forgive you."

He pressed his face into her hair, holding her close and not caring if her family was there to witness such an embrace. If they refused to fight at his side, then this was one of the last moments he would have with Melantha. He wished to savor every heartbeat he had left.

THIRTY-SEVEN

Farrendel was cold. So very cold. Not because of the snow crunching beneath his boots or the crisp air fogging his breath.

But he was cold from the ice in his veins and the stone in his heart.

He would have to fight. Either he fought now in this duel or he fought later in the war. He would shed blood either way.

When he glanced at Essie, she was gazing up at him, her eyes wide. Almost as if she wanted to plead with him to refuse but knew there was no other way forward than this. Through the elishina, he could sense the ache in her heart.

But there was nothing he could do to reassure her. Not at the moment.

Farrendel stepped forward, though he did not let go of Essie's hand. "I will fight for Tarenhiel at your side, King Rharreth."

"Farrendel…" Weylind reached for him, as if to hold him back.

Farrendel glanced over his shoulder, meeting Weylind's pained gaze. "I will bear the burden of battle regardless of whether I fight now or later."

Weylind sighed and let his hand drop to his side, his shoulders slumping. "Yes, of course."

"I will fight for Escarland." Julien pushed forward, a hand on the sword he had taken to wearing at his side since he and Farrendel had begun their early morning practices.

Some of the tension eased in Farrendel's chest, even as he felt Essie's fear spike. Julien was good. Perhaps, on his own, he could not stand up to a troll or elf warrior one-on-one, but together he and Farrendel routinely defeated Iyrinder, Captain Merrick, and several other human guards.

"No, I will." Edmund grasped Julien's arm. "Of the three of us, I'm the most expendable."

Julien shook his head and tugged out of Edmund's grip. "I know you can fight, but I have been practicing for the past three months with Farrendel and his guards, both elven and human. I have far more experience in this kind of combat, and Farrendel and I have developed a rhythm and team-work. That experience and practice could very well save both our lives in the duel."

Farrendel met Julien's gaze and gave him a slight nod. If this was a scouting mission or an assassination, Farrendel would probably pick Edmund to go with him. But in straightforward hand-to-hand combat, there was no other human he would rather have guarding his back than Julien.

Edmund opened his mouth, like he wanted to protest, before he snapped it shut, his gaze pained. "You're right. I don't like it, but you're right. Just, don't die." Edmund switched his gaze from Julien to Farrendel. "Any of you."

This time, Farrendel tipped his head to Edmund,

acknowledging the sentiment. With Essie's hand gripping his tightly, he knew exactly how much he had to live for.

"That's the plan." Julien shrugged, as if the thought of being locked in mortal combat with several trolls was not a problem.

Averett's jaw worked, as if he wanted to argue with his brothers but knew this was their only option. That usurping troll Drurvas had outmaneuvered them all, so far. Averett's gaze swung to King Rharreth. "How much of a chance do you have in defeating Drurvas?"

King Rharreth's shoulders fell, and his gaze dropped back to Melantha. Her face paling even further, Melantha's mouth worked, and she would not look at Weylind or Farrendel.

Cold settled in Farrendel's stomach. Based on Rharreth's and Melantha's reactions, Drurvas was either equally or more skilled than Rharreth, and they were not confident in Rharreth's eventual victory.

Yet, as Farrendel knew well, a fight to the death changed things over a practice bout. There was an added ruthless desperation when death was on the line.

After a moment, Rharreth's shoulders straightened, and he met Farrendel's gaze with a hard ice to his dark blue eyes. "Leave my cousin to me. It would be best if I were the one to kill him. But I will need you to take care of the other two."

Farrendel nodded. As he expected. "I can handle them."

Julien sidled up to his other side and nudged him. "Just like practice. You take care of the offense, and I provide the defense."

"Yes. Though this will be much harder than our practice." Farrendel resisted the urge to grimace.

Presumably, these trolls would be some of the best

warriors Kostaria had to offer. And Farrendel would be facing two of them without the help of his magic, which had always given him the edge over the troll warriors he faced.

Beside Rharreth, Melantha straightened, the steel returning to her spine. "As long as you are alive, I can heal you. All of you." She swept her gaze from Julien to Farrendel to Rharreth. "Just stay alive, understand?"

Essie stepped forward and leaned against Farrendel again. Her voice was too low for anyone else to hear as she mumbled, "For once, I agree with Melantha. Just don't die."

Even though they were surrounded by both of their families, Farrendel kissed her temple and murmured against her hair, "I am not planning on it. I still have to show you Estyra in the winter and help you get all of Tarenhiel addicted to hot chocolate."

That earned him a soft snort, but he could still feel her distress through the heart bond. He wanted her smile, not her fear right now.

He shoved his own lingering tension away. "Besides, I would hate to disappoint all those professors at Hanford University who are so eager to turn me into their experiment."

Essie tilted her head back and laughed. It was not as rich or as hearty as her normal laugh, but it was filled with her warmth and joy, reminding him of all the reasons he had to live.

WHILE THE NOONDAY sun beamed down from a bleached, winter-blue sky, Essie tried not to shift as she stood next to Farrendel, doing her best to look tough and warrior-like in her fighting leathers when all she really wanted to do was grip Farrendel's hand and prevent him from stepping into the cleared space between the two armies. She could barely breathe past the tension in her chest.

Next to her, Farrendel was hard and cold and all Laesornysh. The heart bond crackled with so much magic she could not feel much of his emotions. Hopefully that meant she wasn't distracting him with her own churning fear.

Weylind, Averett, and Julien stood with her and Farrendel in front of a small army of Escarlish soldiers and Tarenhieli warriors that Weylind and Averett had moved across the bridge once Farrendel and Julien had agreed to participate in the Dulraith. Since Drurvas had brought Tarenhiel and Escarland into this fight by challenging the alliance, they were no longer mere observers.

The Tarenhieli-Escarlish army filled the space near the gorge while the troll army loyal to Rharreth filled the other half of the clearing up to the tree line. Rharreth and Melantha stood at their head, both of them dressed in leather armor.

The bulk of the Tarenhieli-Escarlish army remained across the gorge in Tarenhiel, prepared to spring into action as quickly as possible. The Escarlish army even had hidden artillery currently trained on Drurvas and his army.

Jalissa, Rheva, Leyleira, and Edmund stood at the front of the army that remained on the Tarenhieli side of the border. Jalissa had wanted to cross the bridge to join the rest of them in Kostaria, but Weylind had argued that it would be better if the royalty of Tarenhiel and Escarland were not all on the Kostarian side of the border in case something happened. Averett had then ordered Edmund to stay behind as well. Edmund now stood off to the side, well away from Jalissa.

Essie's ability to use Farrendel's magic was the only reason Averett and Farrendel weren't arguing for her to retreat to a safer location as well.

Across the way, the rebelling trolls started up a howling chant as six troll warriors sauntered a few yards into the cleared ground between the two armies. The one in the lead was a tall, muscular figure with an easy smirk playing on his face. Rharreth had pointed him out as the usurper Drurvas.

As he stripped off his shirt, the sun played along the hard, bulging muscles along Drurvas's arms, shoulders, and chest. With one last smirk in their direction, Drurvas turned to his army and began shouting a highfaluting speech to get them all riled up.

Two of the other male troll warriors with him stripped off their shirts. The other three trolls carried bowls of black paint that they began to smear in ancient runes across the three warriors' chests, faces, and backs.

"It is time." Farrendel glanced at Essie, then held her hand in the elvish fashion as they both marched a few steps forward.

Julien, Averett, Rharreth, and Melantha also strode forward as the combined army of trolls, humans, and elves remained perfectly silent.

Turning his back on the enemy trolls, Farrendel grimaced as he unbuckled his swords and handed them to Essie. He then pulled his tunic and shirt over his head and handed those to Essie as well.

She didn't need the heart bond to know how uncomfortable he felt, standing there in front of so many people with his scars exposed for all to see. His shoulders hunched, his hands giving a tremble at his sides as he clenched them into fists.

Next to them, Julien and Rharreth also stripped to the waist.

Melantha held up a bowl of black paint, and Rharreth gestured to it. "Normally, it is customary to paint runes on the combatants. Ones that speak of past battles and victories. But..." Rharreth glanced at Farrendel, his gaze sweeping over the numerous scars. "Perhaps you, Laesornysh, need no runes to boast of your past battles. Your scars already do that for you."

Essie juggled Farrendel's swords and shirt to touch his cheek, brushing her thumb over the scar there. "You have no need for shame."

Julien cleared his throat and jabbed a thumb at Drurvas, who was still being painted while he worked himself and his followers into a frenzy. "Perhaps we should skip the paint as a contrast to that."

Melantha dipped her finger in the bowl, all traces of the fear she had shown earlier wiped from her face. Now, she looked as hard and icy as Farrendel did. "I think you all need just one rune."

She raised her voice as she painted a symbol on Rharreth's forehead. "Think honor."

For the first time, the trolls supporting Rharreth broke their silence and gave a howling war cry. Based on their reaction, Essie assumed this rune was from a time when elves and trolls were the same people.

"Speak honor." Melantha painted the same symbol on Rharreth's cheek, then on his chest. "Love honor."

Another war cry came from the trolls with a few smattering cheers from the human soldiers, who couldn't understand the elvish being spoken but seemed to think cheering along was what they were supposed to do.

Essie swayed closer to Farrendel. This was a mirror of an elven wedding ceremony. For that ceremony, the runes were more than a mere hope but were a blessing and a binding. Perhaps it was the same here, before this solemn battle.

Instead of stopping there, Melantha painted the symbol one last time on the backs of both of Rharreth's hands. "Fight with honor."

The cheer from the trolls was a roar, drowning out even the frenzy that Drurvas had churned up across the way.

Melantha handed the bowl of paint to Averett, then quietly talked him through painting the symbols on Julien. Where Melantha had shouted out each blessing in elvish that seemed to be taking on a troll accent, Averett shouted in Escarlish, earning loud cheers from the Escarlish soldiers. Most of the trolls continued their howling cheers as well, giving support to this human soldier fighting at the side of their king.

Then the bowl was in Essie's hand, and she was facing Farrendel. Unlike during their wedding, she understood what was happening and what was being said. This time, she was sending her husband off to a fight that he might not win.

Her finger trembled, much as it had during their wedding ceremony, as she dipped it into the paint and traced the symbol on Farrendel's forehead. She spoke in elvish, since Farrendel was the warrior representing the elves. "Think honor."

Now it was the elves' turn to cheer, a surprisingly loud sound given the normally reserved nature of the elves. But Farrendel was their beloved Laesornysh, the elf warrior who had single-handedly saved them time and again during the war with the trolls.

The volume increased as the Escarlish army joined in. They, too, had witnessed the strength of Farrendel's magic during the final battle at Gror Grar. And, thanks to Essie's marriage, they considered him one of their own as well.

The troll army, however, fell silent. Even with Farrendel fighting at the side of their king, they weren't ready yet to cheer for Laesornysh, the elf who had killed hundreds of their people.

Essie painted the symbol on Farrendel's cheek, the one that wasn't scarred. "Speak honor."

When she painted the symbol on his chest, there was no jolt of magic the way there had been at their wedding. But the heart bond crackled strongly inside her. "Love honor."

She painted the rune on the backs of Farrendel's hands. "Fight with honor."

The cheering reverberated from both sides of the gorge, and Farrendel shifted under the force of it.

Essie handed the bowl back to Averett after he finished a one-arm hug with Julien, murmuring something too low for Essie to hear. As Averett moved on to Farrendel, Essie launched herself at Julien, giving him a tight hug.

Julien gave her one of his bear hugs, and Essie didn't care that they were probably smearing the symbol Averett had painted on Julien's chest. A lump formed in Essie's throat. If this was her last moment with Julien, what should she say to him? What words would leave both of them with no regrets as he walked into such a dangerous fight? Finally, she squeaked out, "Don't die. I couldn't bear it if I lost either of you."

Julien chuckled, patted her back, then pulled out of her

grip. He gently tugged on her braid. "I'll be all right, Essie. All I'm going to do is hold a shield while that elf husband of yours does all the work."

"I know. Just…watch his back, all right?" Essie glanced at Farrendel. Weylind had joined their group and was currently gripping Farrendel's shoulders as if he had no intention of ever letting go. "He will go to great lengths to keep you safe with no thought of the cost to himself. Don't let him be reckless. And don't be reckless yourself."

"I already got this speech from Avie. And Edmund earlier this morning." Julien's tone was light, but his grin didn't reach his eyes. He was hiding whatever concerns he had going into this battle behind his cavalier words. "Now stop lingering with me."

She didn't need his slight push in Farrendel's direction. Both Averett and Weylind backed off, giving her and Farrendel space.

Essie wrapped her arms around Farrendel's waist and rested her face against his warm chest. His arms came around her, and he leaned his face against the top of her head.

She didn't want to let him go. She couldn't let him walk into that battle, knowing she would have to watch him fight and possibly die right in front of her.

But, she had wanted to be strong enough to guard his back during battle. And that meant letting him go, no matter how much it shredded everything inside her.

He cradled her face, his gaze searching hers. "I need you to promise me something."

"Anything." She leaned into his hands, staring up at his serious, silver-blue eyes.

"Promise that once the fight starts, you will not watch

me." His fingers tightened against her face, still gentle but enough to convey his urgency. His voice remained low so that only she could hear. "Instead, I need you to watch the trolls across the way. If I appear to be winning, the rebel trolls will not be happy, nor will they wish their defeat to be at my hands. Their hatred of me might be enough for them to be willing to violate the rules of the Dulraith."

This whole morning, she had been worried about the Dulraith itself. But Farrendel could be in just as much danger—perhaps even more—from the rebel troll warriors observing the fight.

If it meant a chance at killing the infamous Laesornysh, a troll warrior might be willing to shoot Farrendel in the back while he was distracted with the fight and bound by the rules of the Dulraith not to use his magic to defend himself. The rebel troll warrior might even consider the honor of killing Laesornysh worth the death penalty it would incur. The trolls might not even bother to follow their own rules for the killer of Laesornysh.

Farrendel's eyes searched her face. "If I were to use my magic to defend myself, I would violate the rules and my life would be forfeit. But, if you use my magic to stop another from interfering, it will technically not be against the rules. And it would be better if you did it than Weylind. Escarland is neutral enough—more neutral than Tarenhiel—that both sides are more likely to respect Escarland's position in this."

More than his earnest expression, more than the length of his explanation, what worried Essie was that Farrendel then dumped even more of his magic into the heart bond, as if he feared the oceans of magic already crackling between them would not be enough for what he was asking of her.

Essie straightened her shoulders and met Farrendel's gaze. "I promise. I will guard your back."

He held her closer, still cradling her face. Then, even though they stood before four armies, he leaned down and kissed her mouth.

She traced her fingers up his neck and into his hair. Even as she kissed him, a tear scalded down her cheek.

She was not brave enough for this. How could she let him go?

It didn't matter if she wasn't brave enough. She had no choice.

When he pulled away, she didn't cling to him. When he drew his swords from the sheaths she held, her hands didn't shake. And when he spun on his heels and walked toward the center of the cleared space, she didn't reach to hold him back.

Rharreth was a stride ahead of Farrendel, a large, square shield in one hand and his sword with its wide blade in the other. Julien marched after Farrendel, also carrying a shield, smaller than Rharreth's, and his slim sword.

Essie forced her feet to move as she retreated to join the other observers on her side of the clearing.

As she returned to a spot standing between Weylind and Averett, she caught Melantha's gaze where her elf sister-in-law stood alone in front of Rharreth's troll army. Melantha's face reflected the same pain Essie felt inside her own chest.

There was a strange kinship in that moment, an acknowledgment of what they both stood to lose if things went wrong. They both could lose a husband. They both could lose a brother.

For the first time, Essie saw the real Melantha, the person

who hurt and loved and lived beneath that cold mask she used to wear all the time.

And, finally, even more than in the moment when Melantha cut her hair while kneeling in front of Farrendel, Essie forgave her.

THIRTY-EIGHT

Farrendel gripped the hilts of his swords, their weight comfortable in his hands. A frigid breeze prickled against the bare skin of his chest and back. If it were up to him, he would not have chosen to go into battle in this state of undress yet again, but he had done worse. At least this time, he wore his boots.

Across the way, Drurvas and his two hand-picked troll warriors were also striding toward the center of the cleared space between the armies. All three were smeared liberally with the black paint, with dark circles smudged around their eyes. With their white hair and gray skin, the black paint made them look even more like wraiths intent on death.

Drurvas had his battle-ax resting on his shoulder, his stride such a confident swagger that Farrendel was almost jealous that Rharreth had already claimed him. Farrendel would have liked to wipe that smirk off his face.

Though, the other two trolls were also smirking, also sauntering. One hefted a large, single-edged sword much like Rharreth's and clutched a dagger in his other hand. The second troll carried one of the large, square shields on his arm and gripped the handle of a mace in the other. A short length of chain connected the handle to a large, metal ball with sharp spikes protruding from it. The mace swung in time with the troll's steps.

"Keep an eye on that mace." Farrendel flicked a glance toward Julien keeping pace beside him.

Julien hefted his shield higher, flexing his fingers on his sword, as his gaze remained fixed ahead of him. "I see it. I bet it packs a punch like a cannon shot."

Most likely. Farrendel eyed the length of the chain from ball to handle. Between that chain and the troll's arm, the troll would have a longer reach than Farrendel would. It would be a close thing, trying to get past that mace and shield to kill that troll, especially since the other troll with his sword and dagger would keep up a constant attack.

Rharreth tilted a tight nod toward Farrendel. "I never thought I would fight with you at my side, Laesornysh."

"Nor I with you." For all Rharreth had once been a part of so much misery, no anxiety tightened Farrendel's chest at that moment. Rharreth had done what he had out of loyalty to his people and his kingdom. Farrendel could not blame him for that.

Though, he was not yet ready to consider him a brother nor did he feel the same forgiveness for Rharreth as he did for Melantha. Some things took time.

Rharreth and Drurvas halted two yards away from each other, and Farrendel came to a stop facing the other two trolls, Julien at his side.

Farrendel dropped into a crouch, waiting for the signal. He drew in steady breaths, his heartbeat a normal rhythm.

Any tension faded into a cold iciness that strengthened his muscles. He was ready.

Drurvas swung the flat of his ax against his shield with a ringing clang. "So let it begin."

"So let it end." Rharreth clanged his sword against his shield in reply.

With a roar, the trolls charged toward Farrendel. Out of the corner of his eye, he saw Drurvas closing with Rharreth, swinging his large battle-ax.

Farrendel launched himself forward, ducking under the swing of the troll's large sword and blocking the troll's dagger with one of his smaller, elven swords. He stabbed with his other sword, aiming for the troll's chest.

Before he could connect, the other troll was there, his massive mace swinging at Farrendel's head.

Farrendel changed his stab to a swing that sliced a cut along the troll's sword arm. Then, Farrendel threw himself into a roll to avoid the hurtling mace. As he came up, Julien hunkered in front of him, taking one troll's sword across his shield and pounding the other troll's shield with his sword.

Julien had bought Farrendel the heartbeat he needed to hop safely to his feet. With a running start, Farrendel gripped Julien's shoulder, keeping his sword clear of Julien's neck, then launched himself off Julien's back to give himself enough height to clear both Julien's and the troll's shields.

With a flip, Farrendel kicked the troll's sword out of the way, then stabbed downward as he angled toward the troll's chest.

Once again, the other troll swung his mace. The metal ball came whistling toward Farrendel's side, and he was forced to change the direction of his momentum so that he kicked off the sword-wielding troll's face and flipped back to land safely behind Julien's shield.

Julien's shield shuddered under another strike of the troll's sword, even as he parried the dagger, then blocked the other shield. The mace had a longer reach, but it was slower to change course, and so far the troll had been saving it for fending off Farrendel.

Several yards away, Rharreth gave ground beneath Drurvas's furious attack with his massive battle-ax.

When Farrendel used Julien to launch himself into the air, he could feel the tension in Julien's muscles as he strained to hold back the troll's onslaught.

Farrendel kicked the sword aside as he came up and over the shield, hoping to give Julien a moment to recover.

This time, Farrendel aimed his attack toward the troll with the mace. He would not be able to take out the troll with the sword until he took care of that mace.

The mace started coming toward him. He kicked off from the troll's shoulder, gaining enough height that the weapon whistled just below his toes as he tucked his knees to his chest.

He came down on the mace's backswing and stabbed his sword into the troll's shoulder where his neck met the rest of his body.

The troll roared with pain and lurched backwards.

Farrendel threw himself off the troll's shoulder and landed in the dirt in front of him between his body and his shield. This troll did not have a weapon for such close quarters. Even Farrendel's swords were slightly too long, but he twisted, trying to get his swords up to stab the troll's chest and finish him.

The troll smashed the inside of his shield into Farrendel's

back. Farrendel stumbled forward, unable to get his swords up in such a confined space, especially with the shield and the troll's arm pinning him.

Before Farrendel could squirm free, the troll bashed his forehead into Farrendel's face. Stars burst across Farrendel's vision, and his knees buckled. The troll shoved Farrendel away from him, and Farrendel stumbled back, falling to his knees.

He blinked furiously, trying to clear his vision.

"Look out!" Julien's voice cut through the buzzing in his head.

Farrendel snapped his head up and scrambled to his feet, but he was not quick enough. The mace swung toward him and smashed into his side just above his hip, tearing the breath from his lungs. Pain burst through his middle as he was flung off his feet.

He struck the ground several feet away, the last gasp of breath leaving his lungs. Pain shredded his insides as he struggled to draw in a breath. Definitely several broken ribs. Probably other damage.

Farrendel gasped and coughed on a breath, tasting blood. He forced his eyes open, trying to gather the strength to breathe, to move, to push to his feet. Through the heart bond, he could feel Essie's fear, painful and raw.

Do not watch me. He silently pleaded with her as he drew in as deep a breath as he could manage.

Then Julien was there, raising his shield and crouching over Farrendel to protect both of them. "Are you all right? Can you get up? I can't hold off both of them by myself."

Farrendel coughed again and pushed himself onto an elbow. Even that much movement tore through him.

All he had to do was survive, and Melantha could heal

him later. But if he did not get up now, neither he nor Julien would survive.

Farrendel clenched a bloody hand around the hilt of one of his swords. He was not sure where the other one had gone.

"Farrendel?" Julien's shield shuddered, his whole body shaking as he absorbed another blow.

With something between a groan and a growl, Farrendel used Julien to pull himself into a crouch. Steeling himself, Farrendel launched onto Julien's back, then onto his shield.

As they had practiced so many times during their early mornings in Aldon, Julien stood in time with Farrendel's jump, launching him even higher than Farrendel could by himself.

Farrendel's feet barely left the shield before the mace came swinging in from the side, missing Farrendel but catching the edge of Julien's shield. Julien cried out as the shield was wrenched from his arm, the mace's spiked head still embedded in the wood.

The encumbrance gave Farrendel the opening he needed. He came down on the troll with the mace, who was struggling to lift his weapon with the extra weight and with his arm injured, pouring blood down his chest. Farrendel sliced the troll's throat, then stabbed his chest for good measure before landing on the ground by the dying troll.

Julien parried a blow from the other troll's sword, but Julien's shield arm hung at his side, probably pulled from its shoulder socket and possibly broken. The troll stabbed his dagger toward Julien, taking advantage of Julien's unprotected side.

Julien dodged, but the dagger laid open a gash along his chest.

Something tugged in the heart bond a moment before Farrendel caught a movement out of the corner of his eye. In the second row of the enemy troll army, a musket was lifting, its muzzle swinging to point at Farrendel.

But the weapon never fully rose. A bolt of blue magic lashed out, blasting the gun from the troll's hands.

"No one will interfere!" Essie shouted as more magic crackled through the air.

Farrendel spun, his breath hitching in his chest.

Essie stood in the center of a firestorm of his crackling blue magic. Bolts twined around her fingers as her braid floated behind her, wisps of her red hair standing out starkly against the fiery power. Her gaze was focused past Farrendel, her green eyes blazing.

She was *glorious*. In her hands, his magic was still deadly, still powerful. But it had an added beauty and grace. Something beat hard in Farrendel's chest as he fell in love with her all over again.

Time to end this. Farrendel whirled and charged toward the remaining troll. The distraction of Essie wielding Farrendel's magic had been enough for Julien to skip back a few paces to gain breathing room.

The troll surged forward, yelling as he swung his sword. He was so intent on Julien, that he did not seem to notice Farrendel until Farrendel was nearly upon the two of them. The troll tried to check his swing and turn to face Farrendel, but he was too late.

Farrendel grabbed the troll's shoulder and used his momentum to hook a leg over the troll's sword arm. As Julien blocked the troll's frantic stab, Farrendel gripped his sword in both hands and drove it into the troll's chest all the way to the hilt.

THIRTY-NINE

Rharreth threw himself backwards to avoid the swing of Drurvas's ax. The large, double-bladed head passed so close Rharreth could feel the chill breeze of its swing past his face. He countered with a sword thrust, even as he kept his shield in place.

Drurvas blocked Rharreth's strike, then hammered his ax into the side of Rharreth's shield, trying to knock it from his grip.

Gritting his teeth, Rharreth held on tightly. Against the battle-ax, he would be dead if he lost his shield.

Lips drawn back in a snarl, Drurvas hefted his battle-ax again. The impact against Rharreth's shield rattled him from his arm and shoulder all the way down to his toes.

Rharreth surged forward, trying to find a weak spot in Drurvas's defenses. But Drurvas blocked each strike and stab with his shield, and any time Rharreth tried to gain an advantage, that deadly battle-ax came whistling toward his head.

Somewhere in the distance, Rharreth registered shouting. A crackle of familiar magic filled the air, but he could not take his attention away from Drurvas long enough to look.

Drurvas lashed out with his foot, and Rharreth jumped back. Drurvas swung his ax again, and this time he hooked the edge of Rharreth's shield and yanked so hard that he sent Rharreth stumbling forward a moment before his shield was ripped from his arm.

Rharreth tried to throw himself backwards, but he was too late and too off balance.

Drurvas smashed his shield into Rharreth's face, and Rharreth stumbled, then fell. Another strike from Drurvas's shield flung Rharreth all the way to his back, the stone cold against his skin.

With that smirk on his face, Drurvas stalked to Rharreth and leered over him. "There is no yielding this time. I finally get to finish you."

Rharreth forced himself to remain calm. He no longer had his shield, but he still had his sword, though it was partially pinned beneath him. He was not about to give up, and he would have one chance to do the unexpected.

Dropping his shield to the side, Drurvas planted his foot on Rharreth's chest and raised his ax in both hands. "I never could have defeated Charvod. But you, Rharreth, are weak. Now die and show all of Kostaria that you were unworthy to be king."

The ax flashed down. Rharreth gripped Drurvas's leg with his free hand and used the leverage to roll off his sword. He thrust upward even as Drurvas put his whole body behind the downward chop. Drurvas's eyes widened, but he could not stop his momentum as he plowed forward into Rharreth's sword.

The ax chopped into Rharreth's right shoulder, slicing through bone and muscle with a shock of pain. Yelling, Rharreth rolled away from Drurvas and staggered to his feet. His sword dropped from his nerveless fingers, clanking onto the stone at his feet.

Drurvas sank to his knees, blood pouring from his stomach. But he still gripped his ax, that grin turning maniacal as he glared at Rharreth. He gasped wetly as he struggled to raise the ax. "I will kill you."

Black spots danced before Rharreth's vision as blood spurted from the deep wound in his shoulder. His right arm hung uselessly at his side, but his left still functioned, though it ached, and he was pretty sure some bones in his hand were broken when he'd lost his shield.

Gritting his teeth, he bent and scooped up his sword with his left hand. He stalked to Drurvas, forcing the last bit of strength into his legs and arm.

Drurvas tried to lift his ax, but it was far heavier than Rharreth's sword, and he only managed a half-hearted swing that ended when the ax thudded against the rock a few inches from Rharreth's foot.

Rharreth raised his sword. He did not have the energy for any fancy speech. Nor was he the type to gloat. He took no enjoyment in this moment, for all Drurvas had betrayed him and tried to kill him several times now. Laesornysh had saved Rharreth from having to kill his own father or brother. But it turned out, for the good of Kostaria, he could not avoid having the blood of family on his hands.

Putting all his remaining strength behind his swing, Rharreth sliced his sword across Drurvas's throat and stumbled backwards as his cousin's body slumped forward, falling in a heap on his ax.

Rharreth glanced around, taking in the two armies that were shouting at each other, weapons drawn. In front of the elf-human army, Princess Elspeth had crackling bolts of Laesornysh's magic twining around her.

A few yards away, Laesornysh dropped to the ground as a troll fell dead at his feet. The other troll warrior lay in a heap beyond that, also clearly dead.

Still gripping his sword, Rharreth pressed his hand to his shoulder, calling on his magic and filling the wound full of ice. It would temporarily stop the bleeding until he had a chance to have Melantha look at the gash.

But not yet. The trolls who had supported Drurvas were howling and a few had started charging forward, as if intending to start the war again right then and there. Rharreth's army closed around Melantha and brandished their weapons.

No, Rharreth couldn't allow a war to break out now. The Dulraith was supposed to prevent bloodshed, not escalate it.

Facing the trolls who had betrayed him, Rharreth strode forward as steadily as possible, trying to stave off the dizziness caused by pain and blood loss. He raised his sword in his left hand. "Warriors of Kostaria! The ancient test of the Dulraith has spoken! I have fought and bled and proved my worthiness as your king. I am Rharreth, the last of the royal warrior family of Regdrir, and by the right of blood and battle, I demand your loyalty."

The warriors facing him halted in their tracks, though they still gripped their weapons. A silence fell upon the armies once again.

To the side, Laesornysh still gripped one of his swords, crouched as if he wasn't sure if his skills would be called on yet. His human brother-in-law, Prince Julien, stood by him, also still hefting his sword.

One of the older troll warriors stepped forward, his gaze sweeping from Rharreth to Laesornysh, then the gathered troll, elf, and human army arrayed behind him. The warrior flexed his fingers on his sword. "You have won the Dulraith, but you still show your weakness as you need elves and humans to stand with you. You are no true troll."

Rharreth would have shaken his head, but the movement would make him too dizzy. Instead, he met the warrior's gaze and gestured toward Laesornysh. "We have all witnessed Laesornysh fight, both with and without magic. Time and again, he has single-handedly defeated the best that Kostaria has to offer. If he were a troll, he would be our most respected and revered warrior, as he is for the elves. It is strength, not weakness, to recognize the strength in others."

The warriors across from him did not relax, though they did not resume their charge either. Perhaps bringing up Laesornysh was not the best route to go. For all that he was an impressive warrior, it would take much to erase the hatred that the troll warriors held for him.

Instead, Rharreth waved behind him toward the combined army. "We trolls have always appreciated strength and honor. Together, Tarenhiel and Escarland defeated the best we could muster in a mere week, and that was while we held Laesornysh captive and used Escarlish weapons against them. If the last war was a Dulraith, then Escarland and Tarenhiel defeated us soundly. Honor now demands that we humble ourselves beneath the outcome. From here on, there will be no more war with Tarenhiel, but peace."

The troll warrior tightened his grip on his sword, taking a step forward. His jaw went hard, his eyes flashing. "You dare compare what they did to Kostaria to a sacred Dulraith? Perhaps it is time for a new royal warrior family, if this is what the family of Regdrir has come to after all these centuries."

Rharreth gripped his sword tighter, standing alone between the two halves of his people. He had fought the Dulraith and won. What else could he do to prove himself to his people? Would his kingdom always be torn in half?

FARRENDEL FACED the angry army of troll warriors. His side and stomach hurt, and stabbing pain shot through him each time he breathed.

Julien stood behind him, his left arm still dangling as uselessly as Rharreth's right, though, like Rharreth, Julien still brandished his sword in his good hand.

Farrendel gritted his teeth and felt a snarl working its way up his throat. This Dulraith was supposed to solve the problem. Rharreth had won, and still these trolls refused to recognize his strength to be king. What fools. Did they think they had something to gain out of continuing the war with Tarenhiel?

Heat built in Farrendel's chest and worked its way into his fingers as he drew on his magic, letting it build inside him. He had followed their rules. He had fought their Dulraith. And yet they had still attacked him.

There would be no more war. Farrendel was done fighting a never-ending, senseless war along this border because these trolls were too foolish to know when they were beaten. Farrendel had a life to build. He had classes to take at Hanford University. He had Essie and the children they might have someday.

This war ended today whether the trolls liked it or not.

"Enough!" Farrendel released the magic building inside him and sent it toward the rebel trolls. As much as it would be easiest to kill them all now, Rharreth and Melantha would never forgive him. Nor would he forgive himself.

Instead, he sent his magic racing along the ground, tossing all the trolls off their feet. He pinned them to the ground, coating them with a sizzling layer of power. A few cried out as his magic brushed their skin.

He steeled himself against the sound and pressed his magic tighter. They were helpless. With a mere twitch of his hand, a blaze of his magic, he could snuff out their lives in a second.

Fear. He could taste it. Sense it beating against the bolts of his magic.

Good.

These rebel trolls had to cower. They would never love him. Never forgive him for those he had killed in the wars. But they would fear him, and, perhaps, some would even respect him for his power. They had to see how utterly fool-hardy it would be to challenge him and his magic ever again.

The trolls loyal to Rharreth shifted, raising their weapons as if they intended to attack Farrendel as well. They might not like those who rebelled, but they still hated Farrendel more, even if he fought at Rharreth's side.

Through the elishina, Farrendel sensed Essie's questions, her readiness to protect him. She alone knew with certainty that he was fully in control of his magic this time.

Farrendel risked a glance at her, trying to communicate what he wanted.

After a moment, she pulled magic from the elishina and surged it into a shield around the elf and human army, putting out a hand to hold Averett back.

Behind Farrendel, Julien waited, crouched with his sword in his good hand.

Rharreth held up his hand, holding his army in place as he faced Farrendel. "What is the meaning of this, Laesornysh?"

Farrendel worked to keep his face hard, his eyes blazing as he met Rharreth's gaze, willing Rharreth to understand the calculation beneath the mask of wild anger. "You tried to end the war your way, Rharreth. Now I will end it my way."

Farrendel yanked the weapons and shields from the grips of the rebel trolls. He held the weapons before the trolls where all could see them before he squeezed tight with his magic, melting the swords, axes, and shields to nothing.

The army of trolls that Farrendel held captive flinched or groaned, eyes widening. If they had not believed they were about to die before, then they did now.

Rharreth held Farrendel's gaze, jaw hard. But then, his head tipped in the slightest of nods. He dropped into a crouch, his magic flaring around his fingers as if prepared to attack Farrendel. "Stand down, Laesornysh. If you kill them, it will destroy the treaty."

Farrendel tightened his grip on the magic, letting it brush against a few of the huddled troll warriors so that they cried out again. "They already destroyed the treaty. They will attack my kingdom yet again if given the chance. I might as well kill them now."

"Please, shashon." Melantha strode forward, the dark red

of her skirt flapping in the slight breeze kicked up by his magic. Her short black hair spiked around the troll queen's diadem, its emerald flashing in the sunlight. She held her head high as she joined Rharreth, meeting Farrendel's gaze. "Please do not kill them. For my sake."

These trolls would see their king and queen united. Hopefully, by seeing Farrendel stand down thanks to Melantha's request, they would believe their elf queen was all that stood between them and death at Farrendel's hands.

Farrendel held the magic pinning the trolls for a heartbeat more, letting the power course against their skin in a way that would be painful but would not do any permanent damage. Just enough to let them know just how close to death they all were.

Reaching deep inside his chest, Farrendel gripped his magic. He was an elf warrior, wielding the magic of the ancient kings. Like the last great elf warrior before him, he was capable of securing peace for Tarenhiel. Not just for today. Not just for tomorrow. But for hundreds of years to come.

He would just have to hope he did not kill himself in the process.

"Very well. I will not kill them for your sake, isciena. But I will protect Tarenhiel with all the strength of my magic." Releasing the rebel trolls, Farrendel held out his arms as he shoved his magic outward along the edge of the gorge.

A crackling wall of his magic rose into the sky until it loomed taller than the nearby trees. The troll warriors of both armies scrambled backwards, trying to put more distance between them and his fiery magic running along the gorge.

On his left, the human and elven army huddled inside

the barrier that Essie held surrounding them. He could feel her reaching in the heart bond, bracing herself for whatever he had in mind.

He closed his eyes, pouring more power into the wall as it traveled along the gorge. Farther and farther until his magic covered miles in either direction.

More, he needed more magic. If an elf warrior like himself had once created the Gulmorth Gorge, then surely Farrendel could coat its length in magic.

He dug deep inside himself until it felt like he was being torn in two with the force of magic surging from him. He fell to one knee and braced his shoulders under the strain of holding so much magic. The wound from the mace clawed at his side with each ragged breath he took.

His magic stretched for miles. Then hundreds of miles. Flowing along rock and beside trees. Following the contours of Kostaria's side of the gorge.

Sweat beaded on Farrendel's forehead and trickled between his shoulder blades to trail down his back. Somewhere deep in the heart bond, he could feel Essie as she gripped the roaring wall of magic alongside him, holding it steady even as he gave every drop of magic he could find within himself until he sensed his magic sizzle against the distant ocean to the east and into the far-off freshwater lakes from which the Gulmorth River flowed.

Magic joined the sweat pouring across his body. When he raised his head and snapped his eyes open, a crackling blue haze covered his vision until the cowering troll armies were nothing but a blur of shadows.

His voice came out raw in his throat, his body pulsing with heat and fire. "I am Farrendel Laesornysh, and I promise you now that no troll shall set foot in Tarenhiel with thoughts of war in his heart ever again."

Gathering the last of his strength, Farrendel shoved the great wall of magic down into the ground with all the force he could muster.

The ground shook, heaving with the explosion of Farrendel's magic. Farrendel had to press both hands to the now burning stone to keep himself in his crouch, gasping as he released the tide of magic, letting it dissipate into the earth.

When he managed the strength to lift his head, he found himself the center of attention. Some of the warriors were still picking themselves off the ground, but most had kept their feet. In the stunned silence, not one troll made a move toward Farrendel.

All along the gorge, the stone glittered faintly blue with Farrendel's magic seared into it. No troll besides Rharreth would be able to use magic anywhere along the gorge.

Rharreth turned, then strode toward Farrendel and went down onto one knee facing him. "And *that* is why I chose peace over more war. But I promise all of you now— humans, elves, and my own people—that I will use all of my strength to build bridges of peace between Kostaria and Tarenhiel so that we might again know a semblance of the ancient kinship that once existed between us."

With that, Rharreth pressed his hand to the ground. Icy white magic swirled from his fingers and flowed into the stone beneath Farrendel, turning it cold once again.

This close, Farrendel could see the way Rharreth's jaw worked, his mouth twisting with a grimace. With the rock so seared with Farrendel's magic, it was clearly an effort for

Rharreth to work with the stone, though he was the only troll who had the power to do so.

A rumble vibrated through the ground beneath Farrendel and filled the gorge. Farrendel glanced over his shoulder, gasping at the pain caused by the twisting motion.

A section of the rocky point was shifting, flowing, until it jutted farther and farther, reaching for the Tarenhieli side.

Then, Melantha was there, resting a hand on Rharreth's. Her green magic flowed into him, and green started to coat the icy magic. The grimace faded, and he met Farrendel's gaze. "Pour more magic into the stone."

Farrendel was not entirely sure what Rharreth hoped to accomplish, but he reached for the remnants of his magic anyway. When he pushed the crackling bolts into the stone, his fingers burned, but not as much as he had expected. Melantha's healing magic was coating Rharreth's so that his and Farrendel's power slid side by side into the stone without clashing.

The stone bridge reaching for Tarenhiel now glittered blue with Farrendel's magic along with the white of Rharreth's.

Weylind appeared beside Farrendel and pressed his hand to the stone. His darker green magic joined the roil of magics surging through the ground, and roots burst out of the side of the ledge. They coiled outward, forming a railing, wide girders, and decorative arches soaring above the arching stone of the bridge. Where Weylind's roots met Rharreth's stone, Melantha's magic curled around them so that they meshed together instead of burning each other.

Farrendel pushed his magic up and over Weylind's roots as well. Normally, his magic would have incinerated them, but Melantha's soothing magic kept his magic in check as it coated the beams and decorative features.

The stone stretched and grew, arching over the rushing Gulmorth River far below, until Rharreth's magically grown stone crashed and melded with the far bank. Weylind's roots anchored themselves in the far gorge wall as towering pines grew on either side of the end of the bridge.

On the Kostarian side, tall pillars of stone shot from the ground, guarding that end of the bridge the way the two pine trees guarded the other.

Rharreth pulled his hand from the ground, cutting off his magic. Weylind and Melantha followed suit, and all three of them stood.

Farrendel gratefully ceased the flow of his magic. It was getting harder and harder to crouch like that, putting pressure on the stabbing pain in his side. He shoved to his feet and tried not to grimace at the pain. His head buzzed with dizziness, and he was not sure if it was from blood loss or from expending so much magic.

None of the armies had moved, silently gaping at the new bridge that now spanned the Gulmorth Gorge.

Rharreth gestured with his good hand at the bridge behind him. "There stands the symbol of the peace established this day between Kostaria and Tarenhiel, a bridge that only I can dismantle and only Laesornysh can destroy."

Perhaps it was the show of Rharreth's power in working with stone laced with Farrendel's magic. Maybe the awe-inspiring sight of elf and troll magic working together finally convinced the trolls of the strength of this alliance.

As one, the troll warriors in the rebel army stomped their feet and shouted, "Rharreth, our king!"

The trolls who had supported Rharreth joined in the

howling cheer, raising their weapons toward the sky. They did not stop cheering even as Rharreth wrapped his working arm around Melantha and kissed her.

Shaking his head, Farrendel finally let himself relax. This was over. He stared down at his sword on the ground. He could not remember when he dropped it. Blood ran down his side and soaked his trousers from the wound in his stomach.

"Farrendel!"

He barely had time to glance up before Essie slammed into him, wrapping her arms around his neck and pressing kisses to his cheek and mouth.

Pain flared through his side as he awkwardly hugged her. "Gently, Essie. Gently."

"Oh, sorry." Essie stepped back, her forehead wrinkling as her gaze swept over him. "That mace probably jellied a few of your internal organs. Melantha?"

Melantha pushed away from Rharreth, her gaze dropping to Farrendel's side. "Right." She held up a hand, her fingertips glowing green. "Who would like to go first?"

Rharreth gestured toward Farrendel. "You should see to your brother. He fought valiantly to secure my throne."

Farrendel tried to hide how much he was leaning on Essie as he hunched over his wound. But, even a few feet away, he could see the way the blood was pooling beneath the ice Rharreth had coated over his wound. He clearly needed Melantha's help far more than Farrendel did. "No, help your husband first. He is about to lose that arm."

"Males." Melantha shook her head with a huff, pushing away from Rharreth so that she stood within arm's reach of both of them. Green magic glowed around both of her hands. She pressed a hand to each of their shoulders at nearly the same time.

Farrendel sucked in a breath as her magic flooded into him, easing the pain inside his middle.

Melantha pulled her hand away from him, though her other hand remained on Rharreth's shoulder. "That should hold until you can get another elf healer to finish healing you. You were right. Rharreth's arm needs more immediate attention." She turned her narrowed gaze on Rharreth. "Now hold still. I am going to do my best to heal this arm so that you can properly wield your sword again, but we will need to put it in a sling while my magic finishes the healing process."

As Rharreth and Melantha moved away, Farrendel leaned more onto Essie, holding her tightly. "I think it is time we left."

"Yes." Essie patted his chest as they started making their way back to the Tarenhieli-Escarlish army. "Let's get you cleaned up and see if Rheva can pump you full of more healing magic. You aren't fooling me. You're still wincing with each step."

He was not wincing. Maybe a tiny twitch to his muscles along his jaw. That was it.

Julien hurried to catch up with them, his dislocated and broken arm stiff at his side. "What about me? Who is going to heal me?"

"Rheva will heal you as well." Weylind fell into step with Julien. He was carrying both of Farrendel's swords.

As they joined the army, Averett reached them for a round of back-slapping and celebration. More would probably follow as soon as they crossed the bridge and met Edmund, Jalissa, Leyleira, and Rheva.

But that was all right.

Farrendel took a moment to hold Essie close and kiss her temple. Everything in him felt...calm. Far more relaxed and content than he usually felt after a battle.

His family was safe. His and Essie's kingdoms were safe. And he was truly free to build whatever future he wanted.

FORTY

E ssie sat at the long table in the command shelter in the largest tree in the Tarenhieli-Escarlish encampment. Somewhere outside, squads of elven warriors, human soldiers, and troll warriors protected their royal families. Essie could not help but feel sorry for them, having to patrol on such a chilly, snowy evening.

Inside, the shelter was cozy, lit with globes of elf magic and warmed by so many people packed inside. Leyleira sat at the head of the table with Rheva, Weylind, Averett, Rharreth, and Melantha along one side and Jalissa, Julien, Edmund, Farrendel, and Essie along the other.

It was strange, sitting across the table from Melantha. Stranger still was Melantha's smile as she leaned forward to join in the conversation as they ate their meal of venison, bread, and vegetables.

Next to her, Rharreth's mouth held a smile as well, though he spent more time watching Melantha than joining the discussion. His right arm rested in a sling to allow it to finish healing. Farther down the table, Julien wore a similar sling.

Still smiling, Melantha turned to Essie. "Did anyone ever tell you about the time Farrendel went through a climbing phase when he was a child?"

"Only a phase?" Essie patted Farrendel's arm, grinning.

He hunched slightly on his bench, but he was smiling and his wound no longer seemed to be paining him since Rheva had added her healing magic to Melantha's.

"True. But when he was a child, he would climb up the walls and cling to the ceiling. Then, when someone walked by, he would drop onto their heads like a shrieking, giant spider." Melantha curled her fingers and gave a screeching growl.

It must have been hilarious to see a tiny Farrendel drop from the ceiling, his silver-blond hair flying. Essie couldn't help the laugh that bubbled inside her chest as Farrendel shook his head and huffed, as if he could not believe Melantha was telling this story in front of everyone.

Melantha could barely talk through her own laughter. "Gave each of us a good scare. Once, Weylind even gave a rather high-pitched scream."

Weylind crossed his arms. "I did not scream." His tone dripped with his usual snootiness, though his mouth twitched at the corners as if he was trying hard not to smile.

Farrendel shook his head, though his mouth, too, was pressed into a line as if he was trying to hold back his grin. "I paid for that. Dacha grounded me."

"Grounded you?" Edmund nudged Farrendel with an elbow.

"Yes. I was not allowed to climb anything besides the stairs for two whole months." Farrendel's smile burst past his attempts to hide it. "At the time, I thought two months stuck on the ground was a horrible punishment."

"I know now where Leyleira got her gray hair. Seriously, your entire family should be commended for making sure you survived to adulthood." Essie clasped his hand beneath the table where no one else would see.

"Yes, he was such a mischievous terror." Melantha's dark brown eyes were twinkling in a way Essie had never seen before. "I thought you should be warned, considering your children could inherit his climbing tendencies."

Now the tips of Farrendel's ears were turning pink. Essie's own face was burning. Their poor future child would probably blush like a tomato from nose to ear tips.

Averett, Julien, and Edmund were all smirking. Rheva wore her soft smile, and even Leyleira had that knowing twitch to her lips.

Rharreth watched Melantha with a warmth to his eyes. Essie was not sure she was ready to embrace either of them as family, but it was good to see them happy. It was a glimmer of things that could come: a closer family for Farrendel and a healed kinship between Tarenhiel and Kostaria.

Only Jalissa still hunched miserably in her seat between Leyleira and Julien. Essie still hadn't managed to find a chance to talk to her about what was going on.

"Actually, Melantha, that reminds me. Farrendel had a gift for you." Weylind jumped to his feet, hurried to the edge of the shelter where all of their things had been shoved to make room for the table, then fished through his pack for a moment.

Essie glanced at Farrendel. As far as she knew, the only gift they had for Melantha was a mug and hot chocolate they had picked out in Aldon. Farrendel just shrugged, his forehead scrunched.

Weylind returned to the table, holding something behind his back. When he halted by the end of the table, he brought his hand around and flourished an object at Melantha. "A gift from the artisans of Aldon."

The green and white elf ear mug perched on Weylind's hand, just as hideously cute as it had been the day Essie had gifted it to Weylind.

Next to Essie, Farrendel went stiff. Farther down the table, Rheva was slowly shaking her head, giving a small huff of a laugh under her breath.

Melantha grinned and took the mug from Weylind. "This is perfect! Look at it, Rharreth. It looks like our magics are mixing together."

Essie blinked. Melantha…liked the mug? Who knew that she and Melantha would have the same weird taste in hot chocolate mugs?

As Rharreth whispered something to Melantha, Essie leaned closer to Farrendel. "I guess Weylind has now discovered the time-honored tradition of re-gifting."

That brought the smile back to Farrendel's face. "I do not blame him."

Melantha raised her head, glancing between Essie and Farrendel. "Thank you. A gift was unexpected."

"Well, that gift was meant to be a joke, more than anything. Here, let me grab your real gifts." Essie pushed away from the table, located her pack in the jumble, and found the last two mugs there, since she had left Brina's and Ryfon's on the elven royal train. Now that they had made peace, she was glad she had thought it best to buy one for Rharreth as well as Melantha.

She presented each of them with the gift, and even Rharreth smiled as he studied his gray mug with an embossed mountain on the side. Melantha's mug was a dark red with the same tree that all of Farrendel's family received.

"Thank you once again for the mugs and for the—what did you call it?" Melantha's smile slipped as she studied the packet of dark brown powder.

"Hot chocolate. The instructions for how to make it are folded inside." Essie waved toward the mugs Rharreth and Melantha held.

Melantha tilted her mug, then nodded. "Of course. A hot drink will be appreciated during the long winter nights in Kostaria." She glanced up at Rharreth, her eyes and smile going soft and warm once again.

Did Essie look that mushy every time she glanced at Farrendel?

Probably. Based on the way her family was always complaining, probably even mushier.

"If hot chocolate is something that you think would catch on, I would definitely be open to negotiating that into our next trade deal." Averett turned to Rharreth, ever the king to take advantage of an opening when it presented itself.

Essie could only shake her head and smile as Rharreth and Averett's discussion roped in Weylind, and the three of them moved from talking about trade to discussing the possibility of building another bridge like the one now spanning the Gulmorth Gorge, but this one across the Hydalla River. It would certainly make all this growing trade easier if goods could travel across bridges rather than having to be loaded on ships to cross the large river.

The noise level rose as everyone around the table laughed and talked.

Essie leaned against Farrendel as his fingers clasped hers beneath the table. It was good to see Farrendel's family so happy. Weylind was even smiling while Melantha was laughing out loud.

In all those quiet, sedate dinners with Farrendel's family, Essie never would have expected they could be capable of this much noise and laughter. Sure, Essie's brothers were still by far the loudest, though she suspected Rharreth could probably laugh with the best of them if he wasn't on his best behavior at the moment.

But there was genuine happiness around this table instead of the tense, quiet discussions she had experienced when she had first joined the family. At the time, she had assumed the tension was caused by her presence. But, perhaps, she had not been the only reason.

"Have you ever seen them like this before?" Essie whispered in Farrendel's ear.

"Yes, but not in a long, long time." Farrendel swept his gaze around the table. The smile that tilted his mouth seemed caught between happiness and a wistful kind of sadness. "This is what my family was like when I was growing up. Before Dacha was killed."

If she and Farrendel had children someday, she wanted them to grow up seeing this side of their elven heritage, not the stiff and formal version filled with all too much tension. Not to mention that it would make the half of the year that Essie and Farrendel spent in Estyra much more pleasant.

"I'm so glad we're going home to Estyra tomorrow. It will be nice to spend time with Illyna and everyone. We weren't there long before we left for Aldon." Essie leaned her head on Farrendel's shoulder and stifled a yawn.

"Yes. And I cannot wait to show you Estyra in the wintertime. You will love it." Farrendel released her hand so that he could instead tuck his arm around her. "There is a large hill north of Estyra where we elves go boarding. We should bring hot chocolate for everyone and start your mission to introduce it to all of Tarenhiel."

"Sounds perfect." Essie let her eyes fall closed, though she told herself to stay awake. She pictured her and Farrendel sitting on a sled, Farrendel's arms warm and strong around her. "What is boarding?"

"You stand on a large, flat board and slide down a hill. Is this not something you humans do?" Farrendel's voice rumbled beneath her ear, his breath brushing against her face.

"No, we go sledding, where you sit down on a wooden board with a curved front and go down the hill that way." Essie opened her eyes so that she could reach over and pat Farrendel's chest. The image in her mind shifted from being held inside Farrendel's arms to standing there in the cold while her thrill-seeking husband balanced on a board and whooshed down a hill. "Of course, you elves would show off your superior balance by standing on a board instead of sitting on it. I've seen my brothers try something like that, but they usually fall."

"Perhaps your sleds are designed differently than our boards." Farrendel tilted his head, his voice low so that only she could hear. "If you want to try, I will help you balance with me."

And, now she was picturing Farrendel holding her steady as wind whipped past them and she screamed in utter terror.

But, it probably would not be that bad. Farrendel would

keep them balanced, the way he had while they were ice-skating. How big could this hill be?

"Sounds perfect." Essie grinned and felt complete happiness seep into her muscles and bones.

As THE EVENING GREW LATE, Melantha and Rharreth climbed down the stairs from the shelter to where Zavni, Vriska, Eyvindur, and Brynjar waited along with the rest of the troll guards who had come along. While they all remained tense and alert, there did not seem to be any trouble between them and the Escarlish-Tarenhieli armies filling this encampment.

Still talking with members of the Escarlish royal family, her family lingered in groups on the forest floor or took their time walking down the stairs from the shelter.

"Melantha?" Farrendel's voice was quiet behind her.

She turned to see Farrendel approaching her with his wife Princess Elspetha still at his side. Melantha glanced to Rharreth as he rested his good hand on her shoulder, lending her a steady warmth with his presence. His other arm remained in a sling, still healing as her magic worked to repair all the damage from Drurvas's ax.

For a long moment, Farrendel and Rharreth regarded each other. Melantha glanced between them, seeing the new respect layered over the wariness. As much as she might wish it, her husband would probably never feel at home among her family. But as long as Rharreth no longer hated Farrendel, Melantha could be content with that.

Rharreth tilted his head in a nod to Farrendel. "I thank you once again, Laesornysh, for your assistance in the Dulraith today. It was an honor to fight beside you, and I…"

Rharreth paused for a moment, and when he spoke again, his voice had a rough edge. "I regret the part I played in your capture and torture."

"And I regret that I assassinated your father the way I did." Farrendel's shoulders hunched, and he glanced to Elspetha beside him as she tucked herself closer to his side.

Melantha patted Rharreth's hand still resting on her shoulder. This was more reconciliation between Rharreth and Farrendel than she had expected.

Rharreth gave Farrendel one last nod before he turned to Melantha. "Take all the time you need, my queen." He strode away, giving Melantha space as he talked in a low tone with Zavni.

At least he understood and was willing to give her this time. Soon, they would cross the new bridge and return to Kostaria, and Melantha was not sure when she would have another chance to see her family. It could be months. It could be years. When she left this time, she wanted to make sure she left nothing undone or unsaid.

When she turned back to Farrendel, he was studying her with those grave, silver-blue eyes of his. "You appear to be well."

"I am." Melantha smiled, and the gesture felt more natural on her face than it had in years. "I have found the freedom to be myself there."

"Good. And...I understand." Farrendel glanced over at Elspetha, sharing a smile with her as he squeezed her hand. But when he turned back to Melantha, his expression was solemn again. "Will you...will you write? To let us know you are all right?"

She would never deserve the level of forgiveness he was giving her. "Of course, I will." She swallowed, not sure if she dared ask. "Will you write in return? Though, I guess I should ask Elspetha to write, if I want to receive anything more than a sentence."

"Yes, I will write. But, you are correct that Elspetha would be more verbose." Farrendel's gaze was warm and gentle as he glanced down at his wife. The sight would have angered Melantha before, but now she was just grateful that Farrendel had found such love.

Elspetha held Melantha's gaze, her eyes and mouth tightening with a warning, as if she were telling Melantha that she would protect Farrendel from any emotional manipulation Melantha might try to slip into a letter.

Still holding Elspetha's gaze, Melantha tilted her head in a small nod to let her know she understood the unspoken message. Farrendel deserved to have someone protecting him, and Melantha fully agreed that she should be kept accountable, given her history.

As if satisfied, the smile returned to Elspetha's face, though her words held an edge, as if they were a test. "Did Farrendel mention that he has applied to get a magical engineering degree at Hanford University in Aldon?"

"Essie, it is not official yet. They could still say no." Farrendel ducked his head and shifted, as if embarrassed to find himself the center of attention. Or perhaps he was worried about Melantha's reaction.

Six months ago, she would have scorned such a choice. But now, all she could think was how good a fit this was for him. He had been such a curious child, incessantly asking *why* until it drove all of them to distraction. She smiled and reached out to squeeze his shoulder again. "Good for you. It is time you showed everyone just how brilliant you are."

When Farrendel peeked up at her again, he flashed his

smile, that same one he had worn as a child when he discovered something new and interesting. "I will write and let you know if I am accepted."

"I would like that." This was what Melantha should have been doing all along. Encouraging her siblings to pursue their talents and abilities and dreams in whatever place and calling they had been given.

Something in Elspetha's shoulders relaxed, and it gave Melantha hope that she had passed the test. Elspetha's voice was brighter, more genuine, as she said, "I hope you and Rharreth have a more enjoyable, less harrowing return trip to Osmana."

"So do I." The time alone with Rharreth had been pleasant, but nearly freezing to death had been far less so. "I would invite you to visit Osmana, but I fear it may be a long time before it will be safe for Farrendel to travel in Kostaria."

Farrendel gave something like a shiver. "I am sure it is beautiful, but I have no wish to spend more time in Kostaria. I think any visits might have to occur on the new bridge."

"Yes, that is probably for the best." A part of Melantha ached that she might never be able to share her new home with her family. But, that was all right. As long as she could still share her life through letters, it would be enough. And far more than she deserved.

"I can still give you that haircut, if you wish." Elspetha gestured first at Melantha, then at Farrendel as if to show off her skills.

Melantha touched the short spikes of her hair. It was ragged yet, but she had clipped it into some semblance of order. "Thanks for the offer, but I believe I am beginning to like my current style. Short hair will be more convenient while treating patients."

"Yes." Farrendel nodded, reaching up with his free hand to brush his own shorter hair. "I have to worry less about it tangling in a gear or catching on fire when I am welding."

Magical engineering sounded dangerous. But Melantha probably should have expected Farrendel would not pick a new pursuit that was entirely risk-free. She rested a hand on his shoulder for one last embrace. "Stay safe, shashon."

After Melantha and Farrendel exchanged arm-embraces, Farrendel and Elspetha strolled off, Elspetha leaning against him as she said something too soft for Melantha to hear. Farrendel gave a laugh under his breath in return.

He was happy. Knowing that, Melantha could be content to leave Tarenhiel behind.

"Isciena." Weylind and Rheva strode out of the darkness. Weylind halted in front of her and gripped her shoulders firmly. "Will you be all right, returning to Kostaria?"

Even now, after everything she had done, her protective brothers were looking out for her. Melantha embraced Weylind's shoulders and met his searching gaze. "Yes. It feels like where I am meant to be."

Weylind's mouth tipped into an expression that was almost sad. "I always knew you were too confined at Estyra. I am sorry there was not more I could do for you."

Rheva stepped in and replaced Weylind in hugging Melantha's shoulders. "And I am sorry I did not see how miserable you truly were."

Melantha gripped Rheva's shoulders, and she had to swallow several times before she could speak. While she was glad to return to Kostaria with Rharreth and her new life there, her heart still ached at leaving her family behind. "Do not blame yourselves. Everything I did is solely my fault. I have shifted the blame for my bitterness, my anger, and my actions onto others too long to allow you to do it for me."

"Still, I am your friend and sister. My magic should have given me an edge to sense your troubles. Of anyone, I should have seen more than I did." Rheva's dark brown eyes were soft and sad. "I will miss your support. And I will definitely miss all your help in organizing events. You know how I hate talking with large groups of people."

"I think our newest sister Elspetha will be more than happy to take on any duties you give her when she and Farrendel are in Estyra. She will be the breath of fresh air to the elven court that she has been to our family." Melantha glanced past Rheva to where Elspetha and Farrendel had disappeared into the darkness of the forest.

She was almost sad that she would not be there to see the chaos—the good kind of chaos that would shake the elven court from its stale ways—that Elspetha would unleash on Tarenhiel if given the chance. Hopefully Farrendel would think to include those details in his letters.

"Yes, she will do wonders for the court, I think." Rheva's smile had a tilt of mischief to it. "Weylind and I are also planning to give more duties to Ryfon and Brina, now that they are older."

"Could you tell them that I am disappointed that I missed seeing them?" Melantha wished she could have had more time to visit with her only niece and nephew. Did they still hate her, after all she had done?

"I will." Rheva's smile lingered as she gave Melantha's shoulders another squeeze before she stepped back. "Stay safe in Kostaria, and please feel free to write now that trade will likely strengthen between our kingdoms."

Weylind gave her a last embrace and a nod before he and Rheva turned to walk away.

Melantha reached out and caught his arm. "Oh, and Weylind?"

He half-turned to her, raising his eyebrows.

"Could you keep an eye on Jalissa? I think I may have given her bad advice months ago." Melantha searched the darkness under the shelter, spotting her sister lingering near a tree. Hopefully Melantha would have a chance to speak with her directly, but this time Melantha was not going to take any chances. She met Weylind's gaze. "Please make sure she does not make the same mistakes I did, all right?"

Weylind nodded, glanced over at Jalissa, then he and Rheva strolled away.

Rharreth and Zavni were still talking while the other trolls stood tall and unshifting. Hopefully none of them were too impatient yet.

Melantha strode toward Jalissa, hoping her sister would not run when she saw her coming.

Perhaps Jalissa also wanted to speak to Melantha for, instead of running away, she leaned against the tree and crossed her arms, scowling. "I still have not forgiven you."

"I know. I do not deserve your forgiveness, nor do I expect it." Melantha stared at her feet, trying to hide how much Jalissa's words stung anyway. She wanted her sister's forgiveness, even if she knew that she had no right to ask for it. Not after what she had done.

Melantha drew in a deep breath and forced herself to meet Jalissa's deep, burning eyes. While she had the chance, she had to try to undo some of the damage she had done. "Before you left Kostaria, I told you that the duty to marry into the elven nobility would now fall on you. I realize that I never should have said that."

"But you were right. It is my duty to Tarenhiel to marry one of the nobility, especially after you and Farrendel married non-elves." Jalissa straightened her shoulders, something in her eyes going hard and almost dead.

Melantha's stomach sank cold all the way to her toes. What had she done? Her warm, friendly sister now looked like she was on her way to execution in the forsaken grove. "Please listen, Jalissa. I know we have a duty to our kingdom, and both Farrendel and I have found love in our arranged marriages. But, if I had done what I thought was my duty and married someone like Hatharal earlier, I would have been miserable. Please, do not feel as though you have to choose a loveless marriage. Weylind will figure out a way to deal with the consequences if you fall in love with someone not from the nobility. Pleasing the court is not worth being miserable for the rest of your life."

"Yes, well, it seems I do not have a choice when it comes to that." Jalissa pushed off the tree and brushed past Melantha, stalking off into the night in the direction of the main part of the Tarenhieli encampment.

Melantha sighed and braced herself against the tree. If Jalissa continued like this, it would be another thing to weigh on Melantha's conscience.

"I see you have discovered the perils of giving advice." Her grandmother Leyleira's voice came from the forest behind her, as crisp as always. "Even with the best of intentions, advice can all too often turn out to be wrong."

"And yet you always give out plenty of it." Melantha turned to face Machasheni Leyleira, bracing herself for what she had to say. Melantha had not talked to Machasheni since her betrayal of Farrendel had been revealed, and she deserved whatever tongue-lashing she was about to receive, no matter how she dreaded it.

"Yes, but I am always right." Machasheni Leyleira's mouth twitched with her smile. "Perhaps you will be too, once you have lived eight hundred thirty-seven years."

"I doubt if even then I will be as wise as you are." Melantha leaned against the tree behind her, soaking up its living presence while she could before she returned to the stark coldness of Kostaria's mountains. "What advice do you have for me now?"

Machasheni tilted her head, her smile widening a fraction. "I would tell you to never pretend to be less than what you are, but it seems you have already discovered that for yourself."

"That would have been helpful advice years ago." Melantha huffed a sigh, trying to rein in the wisp of heat that threatened to grow inside her chest. She was done resenting people for the smallest thing, even if it was still far too easy to do.

"Yes, but you were not ready to hear it then." Machasheni gestured in the direction in which Jalissa had gone. "Nor is she ready to hear advice now. But I trust that she will be brought to learn a few lessons of her own soon, as you have learned yours."

Melantha winced as Machasheni Leyleira's gaze and voice turned sharp on those last few words. Her grandmother could pack so much rebuke into so few words. "I am sorry for what I did. If I could go back and undo it, I would. Not for my sake, but for Farrendel's. I was foolish and wrong."

"If I did not know that you were sincere, we would be

having a different conversation." After another moment of that sharp look as if to make sure Melantha was well and truly squirming, Machasheni's face softened, and she gestured in the other direction toward Rharreth and the troll warriors with him. "Now, I do believe that troll husband of yours is waiting. Go on and do not look back. Your life and heart no longer belong to Tarenhiel."

Melantha nodded and, as she pushed away from the tree, she released the last ties she had to the kingdom of her birth. Machasheni was right. Melantha's life lay ahead of her in Kostaria, and she had to give herself to it wholeheartedly. There was no room for regrets or longing for what she had left behind. There was only the future and the life she had ahead. "Thank you, Machasheni."

"Of course." Machasheni Leyleira patted Melantha's cheek. "Besides, I am ready to have a few more great-grand-children."

Before Melantha had a chance to answer, Machasheni strode away at a surprisingly fast clip for someone her age.

Melantha just shook her head. Machasheni should go pester Elspetha and Farrendel if she was so eager for more great-grandchildren. Melantha would like children with Rharreth someday. But, she had a feeling her brother would become a father sooner rather than later.

With one last glance at the massive trees of Tarenhiel, Melantha turned in the opposite direction, heading for Rharreth and their troll escort.

As she reached Rharreth, he put an arm around her, tucking her closer. The last of her lingering tension eased with his warmth and strength. They were not yet in Kostaria, but as long as she was at Rharreth's side and he was at hers, she was already home.

CHAPTER
FORTY-ONE

Rharreth leaned against the doorjamb of the set of
rooms that Melantha had turned into a hospital. The
front part of the large space had been filled with
comfortable, padded chairs and benches. A servant served
warm drinks and dried meat sticks to those waiting. The
Escarlish hot chocolate seemed to be a favorite.

In the corner, Vriska and Zavni kept a wary eye out in
case of trouble. Not that there had been any. In the two
weeks since Rharreth and Melantha had returned from the
war, the story of how she had saved Rharreth's life with her
magic, survived a hazardous trip through a blizzard, and
caused the fearsome Laesornysh to stand down had spread
first through those who had been loyal to Rharreth, then
through the ranks of those who had rebelled against him.

While resentments still simmered, more and more of both
the common people and the warrior families were coming to
respect Melantha and the worth she brought as their queen.

The door opened, and a patient stepped into the waiting
room. Melantha stood alone in the doorway, the dagger

Rharreth had given her at their wedding now once again belted at her waist.

Behind her, a wall of shelves held glass jars filled with various colored liquids. Bundles of herbs sent from Tarenhiel hung from pegs set into the top row of shelves. Cupboards below the shelves held everything else Melantha would need, from bandages to surgical instruments. An exam table stood in the center of the room.

Two skylights angled toward the south beamed weak, winter sunlight into the room, giving Melantha as much natural light as possible.

The white and green elf ear mug sat on the countertop, filled with peppermint sticks. Both the mug and the candy were a favorite among Melantha's child patients—and a few of the adults as well, though the warriors would never admit it.

The female patient turned back to Melantha and gave her a bow, then bowed again to Rharreth as she passed.

Rharreth strode into the room, giving nods to the two trolls left in the waiting room as he joined Melantha. "Are you almost done for the day?"

"Almost. Let me check on these two, and then I will be finished." Melantha gestured to the two trolls, a male with a gash on his arm and a female troll who stared down at her hands. "They have been waiting so patiently for me. I do not want to turn them away."

"Of course." Rharreth pressed a kiss to her forehead before he joined Zavni and Vriska leaning against the wall in the corner. He nodded to each of them. "Thank you for so diligently guarding her."

"It is my honor, Your Majesty, and the least that I owe

both of you." Vriska dropped her gaze, rubbing her hand against the hilt of her sword.

"You proved your loyalty in feeding us the information on Drurvas and keeping Zavni and Eyvindur alive when they were captured." Rharreth didn't want any lingering guilt to hold Vriska back. He had so few left of his shield band. He had to depend on those who remained.

"And I am eternally grateful." Zavni dropped an arm around Vriska's shoulders, grinning. "I rather like being alive, thank you very much. After all, I am eager to see the long overdue changes that Rharreth and his queen make to Kostaria."

"A little at a time." Rharreth shook his head, watching as the final patient entered the room.

The previous patient left, a smile on his face and his healed arm now swinging at his side.

The emphasis on war and conquest had started during Rharreth's grandfather's time over a hundred years ago. And their hatred of the elves went much deeper, ingrained over centuries of animosity ever since the elves and trolls had severed their kinship. Healing would not happen in an instant. Perhaps it might not even be fully accomplished in Rharreth's lifetime.

But as he watched the last patient exit the room with Melantha behind her, Rharreth had hope that with his elf queen at his side, together they could heal Kostaria and build it into a kingdom of worth and honor.

Melantha strode to Rharreth, her steps light. The bitter lines that had been dug so deep into her face had smoothed out, replaced with laughter and smiles. "I am all finished."

"Ready for some time in the arena?" Rharreth placed his

hand on her lower back, steering her toward the door. Zavni and Vriska fell into step behind him.

They navigated the passageways of Khagniorth until they reached the training arena. In the cavernous space, Eyvindur and Brynjar were already sparring with their swords, though they stopped as Rharreth, Melantha, Zavni, and Vriska entered.

Rharreth strolled down the steps of the tiered gallery until he and Melantha halted on the sand floor of the combat arena.

The four remaining members of his shield band gathered around them. Zavni turned to Melantha with a solemn expression rather than his normal grin. "Queen Melantha, we have been talking, and we have decided to make you an honorary member of our shield band."

Melantha started, glancing between them before her gaze latched on Rharreth. "Really? You can do that?"

Rharreth nodded, a grin tugging on his face, as the rightness of this settled into his chest. He rested a hand on the hilt of the elven dagger in his belt. "Yes. Husbands or wives of shield band warriors can be made honorary members if they don't have a shield band of their own and if the shield band agrees. Usually, it would have been done right away, and normally the shield band doesn't object. But our marriage was unusual."

"Yes, it was." Instead of looking offended, Melantha's mouth tipped in a wry smile. "And I suspect Drurvas probably stood in the way of adding me."

"Well..." Vriska shifted, as did Brynjar behind her. "Several of us stood in the way. I think Zavni was the only one wholeheartedly in agreement with Rharreth about adding you back then."

Zavni smirked. "You have to remember, Drurvas and I were the only two that Charvod allowed in to patch Rharreth up after that whipping he took. I knew then that you were no ordinary prisoner to him."

Melantha ducked her head, the tips of her ears turning slightly pink. Rharreth reached out to tuck her closer against him. He so rarely saw her uncomfortable that he could not help but savor the moment, even if the memories of that day were mostly painful and still filled him with fear. Both of them carried the scars.

"Well, are we going to do this or not?" Zavni drew his sword.

Vriska, Eyvindur, and Brynjar drew their swords and formed a loose circle around Melantha.

Rharreth stepped away from her to fill his spot in the circle and drew his sword as well.

As one, he and the others gripped their swords by the blades and held them out, the hilts toward Melantha in the center of their circle. "We pledge to you our steel, our loyalty, and our honor. For the shield band!"

Melantha hesitated, then after a moment she ran her fingers over each of the hilts facing her, flicking her gaze at Rharreth as if to check whether she was doing this right. He gave her a nod to reassure her, and she rested her hand on his sword last. "For the shield band."

Rharreth, Vriska, Zavni, Eyvindur, and Brynjar all sheathed their swords. Zavni was the first to thump Melantha on the back. "Welcome to the shield band, my queen. It is our honor to have you."

"You just want to be my first priority when it comes to healing battle wounds." Melantha grinned, and her grin widened when Vriska held out Melantha's hardwood staff.

Taking it, Melantha faced Rharreth, a feral grin on her face and a wild light in her eyes. "Time to spar?"

Rharreth took a second quarterstaff when Vriska held it out to him. As he swung it into position, Melantha gave a battle scream and swung her staff with the weight of her shoulders behind the move, just as Rharreth had taught her.

He blocked, the force of her blow vibrating the wooden staff in his hand. His own grin felt wide and dangerous as his blood thrilled with the release of the exercise and the rhythm of the fight.

If he had ever dreamed what marriage and love would be like, he could never have imagined this. Because this— what he had with Melantha—was far better than anything he could have pictured, given his own parents' strained relationship.

With Melantha, Rharreth's life would be good. They would still face challenges. They had a long road ahead of them to reform Kostaria and build it into something that could hold its own in this new era. But, together, they would change Kostaria's future and leave their children a legacy of true honor.

FORTY-TWO

S itting on the table in his and Essie's main room in Ellonahshinel, Farrendel tilted the heating device that Lance had helped him create. One of the wires seemed to have melted after several uses of being subjected to Farrendel's magic. Perhaps he and Lance needed more experiments to find something else that would stand up to the strain.

Or perhaps Farrendel could learn a way to tone down the power of his magic so that it put less strain on the mechanics. If Hanford University ever replied to him. It had been two weeks. Surely, he should have heard something by now, considering how Essie and her family kept insisting that there should not be any problems with his enrollment.

The door opened, and Essie breezed inside, accompanied by a gust of cold wind and a few flurries of snow. She shook off her cloak, then hung it up on the peg by the door, juggling what looked like a large bundle of paper.

Farrendel set the heating device aside and hopped off the table. "How is your planning coming along?"

"Rheva is putting together the invitations, and last I checked, the hot chocolate and mugs I ordered will arrive from Escarland in time." Essie swept across the room and set the stack of papers on the table next to his heating device. "Rheva seems confident that at least some of the nobility will be willing to come, and, of course, Illyna, Fingol, and the others will be there."

She wrapped her arms around Farrendel's waist and pressed a quick kiss on his cheek. Her eyes sparkled, her movements easy and quick, as if the time spent planning a fundraiser with Illyna and Rheva had rejuvenated her.

It sounded like a lot of work and far too much people time to Farrendel. But, planning events like this was to Essie what his morning exercises were to him.

Farrendel held her close, even though she was still slightly snow-covered and cold. The tip of her nose was red, and her fingers were icy as she buried them in the back of his shirt.

She grinned up at him. "It was a brilliant idea, setting up a boarding and sledding day as a fundraiser for wounded elf warriors. Not only will we hopefully gain more support among the nobility for those suffering long-term effects of the war, but we should raise enough money to pay for the Doctors Harwell to come here to help those who need counseling and hopefully start training any elves interested in learning their methods. And we'll introduce a whole bunch of elves in Estyra to the wonders of hot chocolate and further trade between our kingdoms. Not to mention we'll all have a fun day. It's a win all the way around."

"If I can get my heating device to work reliably." Farrendel glared over his shoulder at it. "One of the wires melted."

"Hopefully the replacement parts and stuff you'll need to make a few more will arrive soon. Otherwise, we can always heat the hot chocolate over cook fires. Though I was hoping to show off your magical engineering skills since you can use your devices here in Tarenhiel because you elves don't have the same regulations we have in Escarland." Essie pushed away. "Oh, well. I guess that will have to wait until after you get your degree."

Reaching behind him, she pulled an ivory-colored envelope out of her stack of papers and flourished it at him. "It came."

Farrendel eyed the paper, his chest constricting so tight he could not breathe. What if, after he had told her family and his, the university turned him away? How would he face everyone? What would he do then? He swallowed, yet his voice still came out scratchy. "Could you read it?"

Essie slid her finger under the seal and tore the envelope open. She pulled out several sheets of a thick stationary, unfolded them, and scanned the top sheet quickly. Her widening smile gave the answer away even before she began to read out loud in a pompous, official-sounding tone, "Prince Farrendel Laesornysh of Tarenhiel, it is our great pleasure to inform you that you have been accepted for enrollment at Hanford University."

Farrendel sagged against the table behind him, relieved and yet also still tense. He had done it. He had gotten in.

Now he would find out if he was up to this task that he had taken upon himself.

"The rest of the letter is more official gobbledygook. But the rest of this…" Essie flipped through the pages. "It looks like Professor Harrington sent along a letter himself, personally congratulating you and laying out a schedule of lessons for the rest of this school semester that he and the other professors think would be best, pending your approval, of course. It is too late for you to sign up for any classes until next fall, but he says here that you can use the time until then taking some of the correspondence courses specially tailored to you. Apparently, he sent along an assessment questionnaire…ah, that would explain the large packet of paper."

Tests? Assessments? Just what was he getting himself into? Farrendel stepped aside as Essie dug through the stack of paper she had set on the table and pulled out a large bundle wrapped in brown paper and tied with twine.

She held it out. "This must be what he was talking about."

Farrendel took the packet from her, feeling its heft. Just how long was this questionnaire?

He could not do this. This was too much. Too much. His chest hurt, his stomach churned. His head felt light as he struggled to draw in a breath.

Then Essie's soft hands rested on his cheeks. "Farrendel. Breathe. Deep breaths."

Farrendel squeezed his eyes shut, focused on the feel of her hands against his face, and counted in his head as he breathed in through his nose, then out through his mouth.

It took several long moments, but the tension in his chest eased. He opened his eyes and met Essie's gaze.

Her smile was soft, understanding, as she brushed her thumb over his cheekbone. "Take it small steps at a time. You don't have to tackle all of this at once. Perhaps it is best that you aren't able to sign up for classes until next fall. This way, you can get used to the rhythm of learning and taking tests and such before you tackle a class at Hanford University itself."

The tension threatened to grip his chest again. How would he ever face taking a class with a bunch of strangers?

"Maybe we can arrange for a couple of tours so you can see the layout first and get comfortable with it. Maybe when we announce a few of those scholarship funds we're going to sponsor." Essie traced her fingers along his jaw before brushing some of his hair behind the point of his ear. "Aren't you excited? This is still what you want, right? You can back out and no one will blame you. Well, you'll disappoint a few university professors, but anything can be smoothed over."

The utter conviction in Essie's voice and the warmth in her smile banished the last of his anxiety, at least for now. He would probably have to talk this over during his next counseling session with the Harwells and with Taranath. But, for now, Essie was able to ease his tension so that he could think straight.

He set the packet on the table behind him so that he could wrap both arms around her, holding her close. "It is a lot to take in, but, yes, this is what I want."

It might take him longer than most to settle into a new rhythm and new challenges, but he would adjust, eventually. He was beyond ready to stop merely surviving each day and, together with Essie, start truly thriving.

"Good. Then I will be with you every step of the way." Essie stood on her tiptoes as she linked her arms behind his neck, her face close to his.

"I could not do it without you, my shynafir." He brushed a kiss to her forehead, then the freckles on her nose. Then, finally, he drew her close and kissed her with all the hopes and dreams of their future bright inside his heart.

FREE BOOK!

Thanks so much for reading *Troll Queen*! I hope you enjoyed the healing found by both Farrendel and Essie as well as Rharreth and Melantha. If you loved the book, please consider leaving a review on Amazon or Goodreads. Reviews help your fellow readers find books that they will love.

A downloadable map and a downloadable list of characters and elvish are available on the Extras page of my website.

If you ever find typos in my books, feel free to message me on social media or send me an email through the Contact Me page of my website.

If you want to learn about all my upcoming releases, get great book recommendations, and see a behind-the-scenes glimpse into the writing process, follow my blog at www.taragrayce.com.

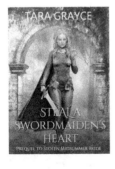

Did you know that if you sign up for my newsletter, you'll receive lots of free goodies? You will receive the free novella *Steal a Swordmaiden's Heart*, which is set in the same world as *Stolen Midsummer Bride* and *Bluebeard and the Outlaw*! This novella is a prequel to *Stolen Midsummer Bride*, and tells the story of how King Theseus of the Court of Knowledge won the hand of Hippolyta, Queen of the Swordmaidens.

You will also receive the free novellas *The Wild Fae Primrose* (prequel to *Forest of Scarlet*) and *Torn Curtains*, a fantasy Regency Beauty and the Beast retelling.

Sign up for my newsletter now

DON'T MISS THE NEXT ADVENTURE

PRETENSE

Essie and Farrendel are living their happily ever after...until Farrendel's greatest secret leaks to the Escarlish press.

With his reputation set to be forever ruined, they race to do damage control. Yet, an even greater danger lurks behind the leak, threatening more than just Farrendel's reputation.

To save his brother-in-law and rescue the alliance, Prince Edmund of Escarland proposes a fake courtship to Jalissa, the elf princess who has broken his heart not once, but twice, even if she doesn't know it.

Edmund and Jalissa struggle to unravel the conspiracy, save Farrendel, and attempt to keep their fake romance from becoming all too real. It might be more than this spy prince and elf princess can handle.

Find the book on Amazon today!

IN THE MOOD FOR FAE
FANTASY ROMANCE?

STOLEN MIDSUMMER BRIDE

Steal a bride. Save the library. Try not to die.

Basil, a rather scholarly fae, works as an assistant librarian at the Great Library of the Court of Knowledge. Lonely and unwilling to join the yearly Midsummer Revel to find a mate, Basil takes the advice of his talking horse companion and decides to steal a human bride instead.

But Basil never expected to find a human girl waiting for him, wanting to be snatched. Nor had he expected a girl like Meg, an illiterate farm girl who has no use for books.

With the barrier with the Realm of Monsters wearing thin and the chaos of Midsummer Night about to descend, will this unlikely pair put aside their differences long enough to save the Great Library from destruction? And maybe find a spark of love along the way?

From Tara Grayce, author of the bestselling *Elven Alliance* series, comes a new no spice fae fantasy romance inspired by Shakespeare's *A Midsummer Night's Dream* and perfect for fans of K.M. Shea and Sylvia Mercedes!

Find the book on Amazon today!

ALSO BY TARA GRAYCE

ELVEN ALLIANCE

Fierce Heart

War Bound

Death Wind

Troll Queen

Pretense

Shield Band

Elf Prince

Heart Bond

Elf King

COURT OF MIDSUMMER MAYHEM

Stolen Midsummer Bride

Forest of Scarlet

Night of Secrets

A VILLAIN'S EVER AFTER

Bluebeard and the Outlaw

PRINCESS BY NIGHT

Lost in Averell

ACKNOWLEDGMENTS

Thank you to everyone who made this release possible! To my writer friends, especially Molly, Morgan, Addy, Savannah, Sierra, and the entire Spinster Aunt gang for being so encouraging and helpful. I would not be where I am without you guys! A special thanks to H.S.J. Williams for the lovely, motivating fan art and inspiring chats about tortured elves.

To my dad and mom for always believing in me. To my sisters-in-law Alyssa and Abby for continuing to adore Essie and Farrendel. To my brothers who are not at all the inspiration behind Essie's brothers (*wink*). To my nephews who definitely are the basis for Essie's nephews. To my friends Bri, Paula, and Jill for always being excited about my books no matter what I write. To my proofreaders Tom, Mindy, Annie, and Deborah, thanks so much for helping to eradicate the typos as much as humanly possible.

A special thanks to those who participated in the Name that Character contest, especially the winners: Megan Elizabeth Astrós Jones for the names Harrington and Eyvindur; Kamila Brys for Vriska; Esther for Harwell; Winter Lark and Katelyn Repke for the name Merrick; Alexis Parchman for Eugene; Adare Elyse for Darvek; and Jenny Bjordal for

Brynjar. Honorable mention to Jolynn Jones, Jemima Sambu Kaleta, Ashlyn, Sue McKenzie, Laurie, and Jen Mulgrew.

Printed in the USA
CPSIA information can be obtained
at www.ICGtesting.com
JSHW012050110524
62882JS00010B/132